Time Skip Protocol

TIME SKIP
PROTOCOL

Robert Shawgo Jr.

**TOPLINE
FRONTIER**
FICTION

Copyright © 2023 Robert Shawgo Jr. All rights reserved.

Published by Topline Frontier, Eagle Mountain, UT

ISBN: 978-1-962040-01-3

Dedicated to Hannah, who always loves stories

Prologue

Sam Freeman had expected to find some petroglyphs or a food cache when his students, Kevin and Andre, told him they had a site he needed to see, but the site before him left him dumbfounded.

He pulled out his satellite phone and called the dean of anthropology at the university.

"Hi, this is Tracy," the voice on the line said.

"Tracy, this is Sam. I'm on a sat phone, so I'll keep it brief. I need a site registered at my GPS coordinates dated as of today. It was a long hike out here, and I want to get something we can use for carbon dating before we leave. Get as big a radius as you can."

"How big are we talking?" Tracy asked.

"It's big. I'll need a team to excavate. We'll probably find pit houses and adjacent settlements."

"So, it's a native site?"

"Yes, prehistoric. And see if we can get at least a jeep trail cut in closer to the site. It's a brutal hike. Keep a lid on it as much as you can until we get it protected."

"We have to write it up," Tracy said.

"I'm going to write it up, but the most important thing is that we protect it." Sam ended the call.

Kevin walked up next to Sam. "Pretty sick, huh," Kevin said.

"Pretty sick, Kevin."

Along with Kevin, Sam had brought three other students with him, Andre, Silvia, and Izzy.

In front of them sat an entire cliff village, seemingly untouched. Dozens of dwellings filled the space, both under an overhang and out in front of it. Erosion had deteriorated walls, and sand had filled much of the area.

"How did you find this again?" He asked Kevin.

"I was going through old prospector journals and one of them had a map sketched out and an X labeled 'pueblo' and nothing else. I checked it against maps of the area, and nothing showed a pueblo, so Andre and I came out to have a look. I didn't take any pictures with my phone because you know how phone pictures store location. And I didn't want it getting out until you saw it."

"Yeah, good thinking. Now that we have the cameras not connected to GPS, how about the four of you start grabbing pictures, before we disturb anything."

After surveying the immediate area and staking out an overall grid, they began moving through the village.

"Have any of you seen any visible artifacts?" Sam shouted across the site.

Four answers came back that no one had yet found anything lying on top.

"Pick a grid to layout a sub grid, and we'll dig some preliminary holes before the sun goes down."

Sam picked what looked to be the center of the village where a circular depression indicated a possible kiva. He hoped to find a few artifacts they might be able to carbon date. Since all they had to dig with were the spades and brushes they had packed in with them, the digging would be minimal.

As the sun set, Izzy shouted out from one of the structures not far from where Sam was digging.

"No way," Kevin said who had been digging closest to Izzy.

Sam arrived as Izzy was brushing sand away from what was clearly a carved spoon. The wood of the bowl had split from drying for who knows how long.

"I thought Anasazi used fired clay spoons," Kevin said.

"That's what's been found at other sites, but that doesn't mean that's all they used."

"I hope it's not something that old miner left behind," Silvia said.

"I hope it's older than that, though that's historically significant too," Sam said. "Let's log that and dig for another hour or so then move away a bit and set up camp. Widening out that spot might produce some other artifacts that can help solve whose spoon that is."

Silvia joined Izzy in widening the search in that sub grid. At the same depth, they found two halves of what appeared to be a fired clay bowl.

"Those designs don't look like something a miner would be carrying," Silvia said, pointing to the bowl.

"Now we know where the dish and the spoon ran away to," Sam said.

"What?" Andre asked.

"It's from a nursery rhyme," Izzy said. "I'm naming this grid Hey Diddle Diddle."

From the look on Andre's face, he didn't know that reference either.

Sam climbed up to the rocks above the village and took a few more pictures before they all headed a couple hundred yards back the way they had come and set up camp. It was a cold camp, with just a couple of backpacking stoves to cook on. They made every effort to minimize their impact. Sam knew that would all change when they got the dig up to full speed, but for now, they needed to be sure they didn't contaminate it.

It took about two months for the BLM to agree on a road to be cut into the site. Which Tracy said was amazingly fast, even though Sam felt like it took seven weeks longer than it should have. The surveyors, after looking at the terrain from every possible angle had ended up along nearly the exact track that Sam had suggested. Sam had gone out with the survey teams and the road crew to make sure they didn't infringe on any adjacent sites or relics.

Sam watched as Kevin piloted a drone over the area.

"Call it back in," Sam said as he looked over Kevin's shoulder at the feed coming back from the drone. "We can analyze the footage more closely and see if we missed anything. Something around here should indicate a progression from pit houses to cliff dwellings."

"Maybe they came from farther away."

"Yeah, maybe. But we can't search the whole desert for them – at least not at twenty-five minutes per flight."

"What if I layout some likely points based on terrain maps?" Kevin asked. "We can go to those areas and fly the drone over the next several days?"

"Try using satellite photos and see what stands out. We may also be able to get our hands on some 3D images like the forest service uses. I'm not sure what the forest service would want with pictures of this place, but it's worth a try. I'm going down to see what Izzy and our latest batch of diggers have found."

Sam made his way down into the village. He was particularly interested in what headway they had made on the kiva. It was mostly dug out now, and they had put up a canopy so the diggers could work in the shade.

"We hit stone in the middle," Izzy said, "and thought we hit bottom, but it turns out that it was a circular stone platform in the middle with the actual bottom all around it."

"Like a table in the middle?" Sam climbed down into the kiva. "I've never seen that before. Why go to all the trouble when they could just put a wooden table here?"

"And look at it," Izzy said. "The top is perfectly round. Structures in other cliff dwellings have been roughly built to the shape of the rocks used. These rocks have been worked to fit tightly and form an exact circle. I set a piece of tape there at the center point and measured it. The diameter is within a centimeter no matter where I measure."

"That's definitely out of character. Why would they go to the trouble of making it perfectly round?"

"And look at this," Izzy said, tapping the level app on her phone. She set the phone in the center of the table. The circles on the screen aligned, and the screen turned green. "It's perfectly level."

"How would they do that?" Sam asked. "Do you think they filled it with water then ground the stone down to the level of the water?"

"How they did it is less a mystery than why they did it," Izzy said.

Andre, who had been standing at the edge of the kiva tapping on his phone, said, "The ratio of the diameter of that table and the diameter of the kiva is 1.618, the golden ratio."

Izzy practically jumped out of the kiva to look at Andre's phone. "Show me what you calculated," she said.

Andre showed her the numbers on his notes, then calculated the ratio again.

"Professor Freeman," Izzy said. "You don't think Mayan's came up here, do you?"

"If they did, they came up pretty late. The artifacts we've tested are from 1400 to 1450. If Mayans came here, they were refugees of the decline of Chichen Itza – late-in-the-game Mayans. And besides the golden ratio, what do we have that points to Mayans, no symbols or script. Cultures all over the world have stumbled onto the golden ratio. It's ubiquitous in nature. I admit, we have a mystery. Let's keep gathering facts and get more data."

Chapter 1

Kira Waterborn ran her hand over the stone base she used to grind corn. Was the curve a segment of a circle or more of a parabola? If it was a circle, would the angle of force applied eventually turn it into a parabola. She thought about tilting it on its side, drawing graphing lines in the sand, and gathering measurements. But instead, she kept grinding corn.

She had ground corn until her hands were as rough as the stone cliffs that shaded her quiet village. Complaining did no good. Who could complain about preparing food for one's family? It was boring, but life was full of boring tasks. Later she would watch her mother turn the flour into cakes. That was boring, too. Even when she married, if she married, life would continue the cycle of grinding, cooking, washing, weaving – an endless path of boredom.

Close by, sitting in the doorway, Patala hummed a faint song as she wove a pair of shoes in the afternoon light. She could say it was more difficult to weave than to grind, but Kira knew it was the calluses her sister avoided. Men didn't sing to a girl with rough, callused hands. But men came to sing to Patala nearly every night – the four howlers Kira's friend Matusu called them. Two of them were his cousins, and he attributed their scrawny, coyote-like build to their tireless effort to avoid hard work.

"Keep grinding little squirrel," Patala said. "If you can't please a man's eye, at least you may feed him well."

Kira knew that she had nearly the same features as Patala, though the lavender in Patala's hair seemed to shimmer a bit more from all her combing. Patala derided Kira for tying her hair back, rather than preening herself each morning. "I'd throw this stone at any man who came singing for food or pretty hair," Kira said.

"And I suppose you will build your own house and grow your own crops? The sun has baked your little squirrel mind. Now finish grinding. Father will be home soon."

Kira covered the basket of grain and brushed the last of her grindings into a shallower basket.

"You are not done!" Patala insisted.

"That's enough for three meals," Kira said as she brushed the dust from her clothes and pulled her hood into place shading her face. "If you want more to feed your singers, you can grind it yourself."

Patala began to get up to block the doorway. But Kira knew the most important thing on Patala's mind. "Isn't that Yinus there?" Patala turned to look, and Kira jumped past her and ran across the village toward the field. She could hear Patala threaten her, but she ignored it. Patala would never yell so loud that anyone would notice, and the stars would fall the day she would let herself be seen chasing Kira.

Kira didn't care so much what people thought, especially singers. Girls her age already had singers courting them. That was true. Some Patala's age had even joined with men and had their own houses. Those girls spent too much time keeping their hair and hands smooth. Loose hair was just something to snag on branches, and smooth hands were no good for climbing rocks.

As Kira ran along the sandy path that led down to the fields, she heard footsteps fall in behind her. Without looking back, she knew it was Matusu.

"How can you run every day, yet still be so slow?" He said, not even out of breath.

He waited beside the trail for Kira most days, most days that his father didn't have him carrying stones or mixing mud. His father was the best builder in Hochonal, a reputation which allowed Matusu plenty of practice carrying rocks.

Kira hurried faster, mostly to aggravate Matusu. He was certainly faster than she was, but he rarely passed her. He seemed to prefer staying on her heals, taunting her. When she came to the boulders and leapt from one to the next as quickly as her feet would move, she heard Matusu's heavy steps land right where her feet had been. He never missed a step. Finally reaching the bottom of the wide canyon, Kira fell into the tall, cool grass to catch her breath. Matusu stood beside her, hardly breaking a sweat and breathing as though he had just woken from a deep sleep. Sometimes his breathing was so slow that Kira wondered if she would hear him take another breath.

"Sit down Matusu. I'll let you have a break before we go on. Running is a lot more work for a big man like you. Are you sure you aren't part tree or mountain? Maybe someday you will be as fast as me."

"With such speed, I'll be able to catch all the tortoise I can eat." Matusu smiled as he sat down in the tall grass.

Matusu rarely engaged in serious conversation. Kira wondered if he would ever sing to a girl. She also wondered what he would do if anyone ever started singing to her. He didn't seem to have many other friends. He was smarter than the other young men in the village, and being bigger made him stand out. By brains and brawn, he should be the natural leader, but he never stepped up to lead or fell in line to follow.

Kira began to stand to continue on, but the sound of her father talking stopped her. This would be a good place from which to launch a sneak attack when he approached.

"Dreamer or not," her father, Jornatha, said, "let her enjoy her youth, time will tell us soon enough."

"That's just it. She's not a child anymore. My own daughter is a year younger and already promised to a fine man." The man speaking with Kira's father was Kurmach, Kira's uncle on her mother's side. He seemed intent on helping to make a proper woman of Kira. "And as for time, you know as well as I – what once howled from the mountain, now nips at our heels."

Leaning to hear what was being said, Kira snapped a branch under her knee. Kurmach and Kira's father cut their conversation short. "It seems my escort has been lying in wait," Kira's father said as he pushed back the brush to reveal Kira and Matusu.

"Do you intend to be a bride or a hunter?" Kurmach shook his head as he turned to go up to the village. "I'll see you at council," he said over his shoulder to Kira's father.

They watched the slightly older, portlier man disappear up the trail. "I suppose you have come to walk an old man home," Kira's father said, looking down at Kira and Matusu. "Lead on."

Hiking back up the trail offered little excitement. Kira led on toward a more interesting route back to the village.

Kira led her father and Matusu along the base of the cliff back in the direction of the village. Soon the broken cliff they had descended became a sheer wall of red rock, stained with patches of black where water has run down them for thousands, maybe millions, of years. When they were well past the village, they came to a crack in the rock wide enough for three to stand across. Kira walked in. She smiled at the cool, wet feel of the air, where the sun only touched briefly each day at its peak. She looked up to glimpse the sky in the narrow crack far above her.

Following the narrowing crevice with all its twists and bends, Kira finally reached the place where the sand ended, and the fun began. She took off her shoes and tucked them into her sash, then looked back at her father and Matusu. "Who's first?" she asked. Her father merely smiled and gestured for her to begin the climb.

Locking a fist and a foot into the crack, Kira pulled herself up. Hand over hand and foot over foot, she continued up the well-worn route about thirty steps to where it began to widen a little and form a ledge. Hopping onto the ledge, she stretched her fingers out to a crack in the wall and looked down for the others. Matusu was right below her.

"Are you all right?" He asked as he stepped past her and leapt up to catch a handhold on the ledge above. Without so much as a grunt, he pulled himself onto the ledge and continued up.

Kira heard her father laugh as he stepped up on the ledge beside her. "It looks as if Matusu is out-running you at last."

"Not today," Kira said as she leapt to the hold on the next ledge and tried to pull herself up. A single arm lacked the strength for the pull.

"Your legs are what carry you," her father reminded.

Kira swung to the side and found a shallow depression with her foot. Pressing beneath her with the palm of her free hand, Kira shifted her weight to the foot hold and regained her momentum. She continued up the sloping, left face of the widening crack – feeling her muscles burn as she stretched out to pass Matusu.

She caught him as he slowed to move sideways along the wall to the next set of holds. Looking across to the opposite wall, she saw a broken shelf in the rock that would allow her to go straight up past Matusu while he worked sideways. Pressing one hand into a crack, she swung around to face the opposite wall, planted both heels into the narrow ledge beneath her, and leaped across the divide.

"Kira!" Her father's voice boomed through the canyon.

Only as she locked a hand and foot into the shelf did she realize the risk she just took. She looked down and gave her father a quick grin acknowledging his concern. Then she was off on a diagonal path past Matusu and up against an overhang. The overhang was too wide to reach around, and she realized she had to descend or risk another leap across the now wider canyon.

Not wanting to waste time and give up her lead, she fixed her eyes on her target back on the opposite wall. Glancing down, she saw that Matusu had secured three holds on which to rest and watch her magnificent leap. Her father had also stopped climbing, just below Matusu. Gathering her strength and breath, Kira squatted tight against the wall and lunged for the opposite wall. She made a half turn in the air and touched her hand against the wall a palm below her target. She fanned out her hands and feet searching to catch another hold – nothing. As her speed increased, she felt a scream coming up into her throat. She bit her teeth together and swallowed it down.

Her left leg jerked from under her and her whole world went upside-down. That scream jumped out as she swung by one foot through open air. A soft, yet certain thud brought her to a stop upside down against her father's chest, his arm wrapped tightly around her.

"Has your desire to be first outstretched your desire to live?" Her father asked, a touch of excitement still in his voice and his breathing heavy.

Kira could feel Matusu still holding her ankle, and she wasn't sure she was ready for him to let go. She drew another deep breath. "Thank you Matusu," she said, trying to sound less grateful than she felt.

Matusu released her ankle, and Kira reached up around her father's neck and swung right-side up to share his ledge. As hard as she tried to maintain her grace, she knew that she was visibly shaken.

After a long silence, with her father and Matusu watching her, Kira again began her climb.

Matusu moved aside to let her pass.

"Get climbing," she said. "Maybe I can catch you next time."

Matusu moved on ahead of her. The canyon began narrowing again toward the top. Another ledge and two more pitches brought them through a narrow crack and open sky. The crack was so narrow Matusu and Kira's father barely fit through.

Kira felt the sun touch a place on her leg where cloth had torn. Using a piece of her spare sash, she quickly wrapped it.

From the top of the canyon, they could see the village nestled against a half circle of boulders, which looked like small mountains themselves. Kira's father put an arm around her, "Perhaps we could go around behind the village and scramble over the boulders, or have you had enough falling for one day."

Kira shrugged away from her father and glared at Matusu hard enough to drive the grin from his lips.

As they returned to the house, Kira's sister stood waiting for her at the door. The smile on her face belied the vengeance in her eyes. Kira avoided her gaze, not wanting to give her the satisfaction of spilling out the horrible punishment mother had waiting for her.

Kira's mother didn't say a word – just shook her head and handed Kira the large water pot. Fetching water was a heavy task usually handled by Kira's father or older sister. Still weak from the climb, Kira could already feel her knees wobble as she anticipated carrying the heavy pot. She knew Matusu would offer to carry it for her, but she also knew she would not let him – not today.

Jornatha Waterborn slipped into the dwelling where his wife, Remelle, had already started a fire. She worked over a basket of sweet roots and peppers, peeling away the outer shells to add them to her cakes. He sometimes wondered if the work was too much for his family. Had he stayed in Thresdenal, manual labor would have been done for them. He would have worked in the tower, and Remelle would have managed a household, still work, but work without calluses. He enjoyed the work, eating his own harvest, ending each day with no thought but tomorrow's labor.

Kira entered and deposited the pot of fresh water beside the fire. Patala brought the cleaning water pot in. It was the same water she had soaked basket reeds in. Water should never be wasted. Remelle began making cakes and handing them to Patala and Kira who padded them flat and placed them on the hot stone in front of the fire.

"Liaton came by about mid-day," Patala said, glancing at her father.

Jornatha knew the boy – really a man now. He came from a good family.

"He asked about when you lived in Thresdenal, what it was like."

"And you told him?"

"What could I tell him? You've told us almost nothing. We hear more about your life in Thresdenal from other people. They tell us what they know and wait for us to tell them more. How big is the city? Did you have many adventures there? Did you ever see Ka'Te' what's-her-name?"

"Ka'Te'Losa," Jornatha grimaced. "She was only Te'Losa when I lived there."

Jornatha closed his eyes. Where to start? His daughters were curious. Their village, surrounded by vast deserts was like an island. Few visitors came with news of the outside world. He did not want to start at the beginning. Starting there could take all night. The founding of Thresdenal often took three or four nights to tell well. Something personal would be more suitable.

"My walk to Thresdenal," he said adopting the formal tone of a storyteller.

Both girls sat up quickly. Remelle gave him a subtle look of surprise.

"How young were you?" Kira asked.

"Not yet old enough to sing to a girl – about your age Patala. All I thought of was climbing and eating. My father took me to Thresdenal on the advice of a wandering teacher who had come through the village. I had not listened to his stories or even taken time to learn his name. Then one night I saw him in one of my dreams. He told me to follow him. I did. We walked up a long canyon not far from Hochonal to a waterfall. I knew the place but did not recall the clear flowing waterfall. He stepped through the waterfall, and I followed him. I found myself standing in a green valley full of wildflowers. He stood in the middle of the field waiting for me. I asked him where we were, and he told me I was in the dream. The waterfall was a gateway. He picked a yellow flower and asked me to turn it blue. He told me to concentrate. I focused on it for a long time. He just waited, not saying anything. Then for no apparent reason, the flower turned blue. I asked him how he did it. He said that I did it. A few days later, he convinced my father to take me to Thresdenal."

Jornatha continued his story as they ate. He recounted his journey from Hochonal to Thresdenal. Mostly he remembered walking on what seemed to him an endless path. His first impression of the city had been amazement that so many people could dwell together. He spent half a day just walking past the fields that were needed to feed the people of Thresdenal.

"Perhaps someday we shall walk the streets of Thresdenal together," he said. Then he stood, kissed Kira and Patala each on the head, and stepped past them into his sleeping chamber.

He sat on the edge of his mat looking at the stone and mud walls of his room. Remelle had already been in and lit a small wax lamp. He focused on the flame and called up an image of the lights in the great hall of Thresdenal. He wondered again why he had left. He told himself that this was a better life – an honest life. At the same time, he had denied his children the choice.

In Thresdenal, they would only grind grain and weave baskets if they wanted to. They would still attend school and meet hundreds of other children. They would, of course, also learn about politics, power, and deceit. Was it his right to shield them from those things? Was it his right to expose them to those things – all the things he had been exposed to? He was never sure it was his right to even be in Thresdenal. He only excelled because of a gift – a gift he was born with and never had to earn.

Remelle entered the room. "You are missing Thresdenal. Perhaps after the harvest you should take the girls to see it. Maybe some in the village would go with you – a delegation from Hochonal."

"Wouldn't you like to go?" Jornatha asked.

"What is there for me? Their corn is no sweeter, their sky no bluer. They may have forgotten about us – no teacher in eleven harvests."

"Te'Natha still teaches our children in the dream from Thresdenal. And she or another teacher will come soon to meet and teach the younger children. They still send guards with the regenerator every few months."

"Yet, they neither seek our council, nor acknowledge our leaders. We are also Thresden, are we not?"

"I will be taking a journey to Thresdenal. I wish I could wait until after the harvest." Jornatha blew out the lamp and laid down beside his wife. "Thresdenal may not have sent a teacher in a long time," he said, "but they have not forgotten Hochonal. They could no sooner forget Hochonal, than Hochonal could forget the harvest."

Kira lay awake wondering for a while, wondering why her father rarely talked of Thresdenal. He could have told her stories of Thresdenal her whole life. All she knew were little things she heard from friends who had never been there. She tried to picture the city filling up the center of a valley. Tried to see herself walking past fields for more than half a day. She could not imagine such great fields. How many would it take to harvest so much?

She had asked their teacher, Te'Natha, in the dream, but she always stuck to lessons. She said quenching a child's curiosity about unimportant things was not her purpose.

So many questions filled her mind. One question moved to the front, "Why had Father decided to tell them now?" The question that somehow seemed important slipped away, as she felt herself drifting to sleep. She was definitely going to ask her father some more questions tonight.

Kira felt herself falling. She hated when dreams started this way. It was hard to gain control. Putting out her hands she felt the rock wall of the narrow canyon. The rock came into view, and she could see a ledge coming up at her quickly. She caught the edge of it and came to an immediate halt. Finding a path, she climbed down the rest of the wall and ran down the slot to the larger canyon floor. The stars and a sliver of the moon lit the sand more than they should have. It was the half-light of the dream.

Just before reaching the fields, where the canyon became more of a walled valley, she came to a familiar wall of bristle tail that grew on the creek bank. The dew soaked bristletail was a gateway to her father's dream. She stepped through and was knocked sideways by a blast of wind. She stood on stone in a valley of red pillars. Thunder boomed in the valley. Lightning flashed along the rim of the cliffs that rose up far to her right.

She continued forward, trying to find her father through the darkness and the blowing sand. He would be at the center of the dream, and if she entered at the edge of his dream circle, he must be directly ahead. She just hoped the circle was not very large. A flash of lightning lit up a pillar of stone directly ahead. Her father was standing on top. He seemed to be talking.

A blur, like a shadow or smoke, hovered in front of him. Kira moved closer and the shadow seemed to look more like a person. She looked again at her father. What does he see? She concentrated. The shadow took on a more solid form. A person not as tall as Kira's father stood in front of him. The person wore a teacher's cloak with her hood dropped back, and though Kira couldn't tell clearly from where she stood, it looked to be a woman.

"Father," Kira yelled. Her father didn't acknowledge her. Another flash of lightning revealed her father and the woman talking – probably louder than normal to hear each other over the wind and thunder. Kira moved closer, and cupping her hands at the sides of her mouth, she yelled, "Father!"

This time, Jornatha turned and looked at her. The woman also turned, and a flash of lightning lit up her face for a moment. She was very old, older than anyone Kira could remember seeing in Hochonal. Her hair had gone completely gold with age. The woman stared at Kira for a moment then turned back to Jornatha, and pointing at Kira, said something Kira could not hear.

Jornatha turned and beckoned Kira to come up to him. She ran to the base of the pillar. But could find no holds to climb up. She circled round it, finding nothing but smooth rock. It wasn't that high – three or four good holds and she could be on top.

"Just be on top," her father's voice said in her ear.

She jumped and almost fell over. Her father was standing next her. Then he was gone in a blink. She looked up, and he was again looking down at her from the top of the pillar.

She felt a bit foolish at forgetting how he had taught her to move through a dream. She pictured herself standing up there on top of the pillar. Instantly she was beside her father facing the old woman. The air was calm here and no longer tugged at her.

The woman stared at Kira for a moment as if sizing her up then asked, "What do you see?"

Kira hesitated for a moment because the question seemed so obvious. "A woman," she replied.

The woman's eyes penetrated Kira, not in a fearful way but as though her very look had power in it. "Am I a young woman?"

Kira didn't know if she should laugh at the joke, but instead simply shook her head.

The woman smirked as if she did indeed see the jest, finally lifting her penetrating gaze from Kira. "Jornatha, did you create this link? Did you bring her here and open her sight to see me?"

"You know that is not a talent I possess."

"How old are you, child?"

Kira looked to her father, wondering about this stranger who took such an interest in her. At her father's nod she said, "twenty-one."

The woman looked back to Kira's father, a stern reproach in her gaze. "How long?"

"I think that..."

"How long?" Her voice rose.

"Just over a year," he said. "We will be coming once the peak of the harvest has turned."

"Sooner, if you please. Expect a teacher soon."

The woman looked back to Kira, and the stern look she had given Kira's father faded. Then, ever so gently, her face lifted in a smile. "May the stars guide you child," the woman said and faded away.

Kira's father put his arm around her and pulled her close. "This may not be a safe place for you," he said.

"Who was that woman?" Kira asked.

"An old friend from another time." From his tone, Kira knew he would tell her nothing more of the stranger.

"Why have you chosen such a stormy dream? Where are your grassy fields covered with flowers?"

"This dream chose me," her father said. "It reflects concerns that weigh on my mind."

"What concerns?"

"I do not know yet. I must have seen signs that brought this storm to my inner mind. Kurmach echoed them with his troubled tone today. Now I hear them from faraway places. Something momentous is happening, momentous and troubling."

Bits of rain spit down, and lightning flashed three times in close succession. Kira was certain that the lightning was moving closer as the thunder crashed with the flash of light.

Kira's father moved her behind him and turned to face the storm. As Kira looked down, she saw three deer dart past the pillar. Even the animals had sense enough to run from this storm.

As the wind hit the pillar, she peered around her father squinting her eyes to look into the blowing sand and rain. The clouds seemed to be rolling down on them, lightning crashing on other pillars all around them.

Her father stood against the storm as solid as the stone they were standing on. Raising his arms, he spoke so low Kira could barely hear him, "Here I am."

The wind that had been whipping Kira's hair and tearing at her clothes faded to a stillness again – just around her. She stepped sideways around her father and looked up at him. The wind and the rain were focusing on him. The storm was funneling into his open arms. Kira almost grabbed hold of him as lightning split the sky and danced across his arms and face. His composure never changed. A look of serenity and a slight smile belied the vicious battle Kira seemed to be witnessing. Soon the rolling clouds were being drawn into his embrace at a faster and faster pace. Then the storm was gone as if it had never been.

Slowly, Kira's father lowered his arms. After a moment, he turned to her with a kind smile.

She saw the lightning still flashing in his eyes. Dreams may mirror reality, but they could also be very unreal. "Do you feel the storm inside you?"

Her father nodded.

"Does it hurt?"

Her father laughed. "Accepting my own storms can be a little painful, but it gives me a power I can take back with me when I wake."

She felt the warmth of sunshine on her cheek. She reached for her hood out of habit, but realized she didn't need it here.

She looked around to see a brightly lit mountainside full of wildflowers. Three deer stood not far from her, grazing on the tall green grass. She could swear they were the same deer she had seen running from the storm.

She stepped away from her father to look at the refreshing vision he had created. "Now this is the kind of place I want to visit in my dreams," she said.

"Spend all the time you like. Learn it. Make it yours. For me, I just need some rest." Her father laid down on the grass with his hands behind his head. The lightning flashed again in his eyes before he closed them.

Kira knew he would keep the dream going a while longer. She picked a blue flower and held it up in front of her. Concentrating on it, she thought that it should be yellow, and it turned yellow. She laughed. Then blowing on it as she let go, she watched it spin off into the meadow.

She knew that she needed to rest too. Laying down on the grass, she closed her eyes and slept.

Kira woke to the sound of a gentle rain on the roof. Not the kind of rain that filled the canyons and cut them off from reaching some of their fields – this was the light, life-giving rain that urged their crops to grow, that left a sweet smell of green living things hanging in the air.

Kira rose and dressed quickly so she wouldn't miss a walk in the rain before she had to start her chores. Hochonal was busy with activity and full of smiles in the morning shower. She ran across the village to where Matusu stood outside his house rubbing sleep from his eyes.

"Matusu," Kira called. "Let's climb up on the rocks and watch the rain coat the village."

"You want me to climb up slippery rocks and sit in the rain to watch stuff get wet?" Matusu asked.

"Yes," Kira said, not holding back her smile.

"Sounds fun."

Kira knew he really wanted to go. They often climbed the rocks to see a glowing sunset or watch the activity below. Anything was better than standing around waiting to be told to strip logs or make rope or carry heavy pots of clay and water.

Going up on the rocks behind the village wasn't really climbing – it was more of an uphill walk over boulders that looked as though they'd been smashed together like great balls of red dough. The path was worn and polished by all the Hochonal children who had climbed and sat on these very stones.

The village was protected by two walls of stone. The one they were on and one on the south side of the village. The north and east sides of the village dropped off steeply into the wide canyon where they planted their crops and drew water.

On the southern wall stood the village calendar. A small round house with holes in the walls and markings carved in the floor. It told them when to plant and when to harvest. Village leaders also used it to count the years. It was now 97 years since the founding of Hochonal and 751 years since the founding of Thresdenal.

From where they sat, Kira and Matusu could see down the canyon to where men were already working in the fields despite the rain. The fields ran down the canyon filling it along both sides of the creek and continued around a bend in the canyon, out of Kira's view. Kira could just make out her father down near the bend working at planting a field. Her uncle worked beside him. They had left their shirts and hoods behind today, letting the rain cleanse them as they worked, while the heavy cloud cover blocked them from the sun.

Movement drew Kira's attention to the top of the far canyon wall. A person was standing there looking over the fields. Another person appeared, and they began moving down the narrow trail cut into the side of the canyon. Soon, more people appeared and one by one the line grew as dozens of people followed the narrow trail toward the men working in the field. The men in the field appeared not to have noticed the approaching visitors.

Chapter 2

Kira jumped up and started to run, hopping from boulder to boulder to get back down to the village. She had to reach someone – had to warn her father. She ran right past her house where Patala sat under the porch shade grinding grain on the stone.

"Kira! Come back here! I'm not doing all your work!"

If Kira heard her sister, it was only background noise behind her own breathing. She sped down the trail to the fields, jumping over every stone or bush that stood in her way. Twice she stumbled but didn't fall. She had to reach her father and warn him before the strangers reached the fields – or worse, went around to the village while most of the men were in the fields.

As she reached the canyon floor and started down toward the lower field, she noticed Matusu at her side. He must have been following her the entire time, and here where the trail was wider, they were able to run together. He didn't seem to be breathing nearly as hard as she was. She took the right fork to the lower fields, dropped down into the lower path of the stream, and splashed across it and up through a broken wall of bristle brush.

She emerged from the brush onto the lower field. Her father was on the far side with his planting and harvest basket slung over his shoulder. He and Kurmach were walking the newly turned rows of the field planting seeds. Before Kira could call out to him, the strangers emerged from the rush wood that grew at the base of the canyon on the far side of the field.

Kira began to run across the field. "Father!" She pointed to the men walking along the edge of the field toward her father.

Kira's father waved to her then turned to see what she was pointing at. On seeing the strangers, her father and Kurmach both set their baskets on the ground and walked to the edge of the field where the strangers now stood waiting for them. Her father embraced one of the men.

Kira stopped running. Her thoughts pulsed in rhythm with her breathing as she tried to understand. She had always been told that strangers were dangerous. That men would come hunting beasts, and the village must gather in for safety. These people didn't look like hunters. There were women and children with them. They looked worn and tired.

"Who are they?" Matusu asked. The fatigue of running was barely noticeable in his voice.

"Not strangers," Kira said, shaking her head.

Arriving back at the village, Kira's father announced the arrival of friends from the north. "Humans have driven them from their homes. They will stay with us until they are provisioned to continue on to Thresdenal." He put an arm around the man closest to him, who seemed to be the leader. "This is Lohonath. Some of you know him. He lived in Hochonal as a boy. His return is welcome."

Kurmach stepped forward. "Everyone please bring out grain," Kurmach said. "Build fires. We have food to prepare. Tarol and Matusu find the other young men and bring up as much water as our pots will carry."

Matusu went off with some other young men to carry water. Kira followed her mother and sister to get grain for their new guests. Both Patala and Kira helped their mother grind the grain to flour that could be used to make cakes and to thicken soup. Kira did not often see her mother grinding. She produced more than Patala and Kira combined. And her flour was much finer. Soon, they had three baskets full of meal to take back to the main fire at the center of the village. Kira and Patala carried baskets while their mother gathered up her herbs.

Women had already started frying cakes on the hot, flat stones at the edge of the village fire. Kira's mother sat down near the fire and began mixing flour and water with her herbs. She would make balls of dough and hand them to either Kira or Patala who were expected to flatten them and place them on the cooking stones.

Matusu's father was building wood shelters not far from the fire. They were simply two posts with a rail lashed between them near the top and smaller logs leaned against the rail. Thatching could be added to shed water when it rained. They were not as nice as the homes the people of Hochonal lived in, but they could be easily taken down and the logs reused after the visitors left.

Kira had about ten cakes cooking when she noticed that she didn't see any of the visitors about. Just then, she spotted her father approaching from the canyon trail. Followed by several of the people from the north. They had wet hair and looked much cleaner than when they arrived. Father must have taken them down to the bathing pools.

"Mother," Kira said, "I thought Hochonal was a small village. We have twice the people as their village."

"Their numbers have dwindled. That is why they left. Humans have taken their village."

"Why?"

"That is the human way. Their numbers grow faster than ours, and they are always spreading to build new villages. It is their land, their right. We are merely visiting. That is why we settled among the rocks and the sand, the least hospitable places. Even Thresdenal is surrounded by a vast desert."

"But Hochonal has been here for almost a hundred years," Kira said. "And Thresdenal for seven hundred. That's a long visit."

"Humans began living here over thirty thousand years ago. And earlier species go back two hundred thousand years. It is their home."

"The humans around here haven't been here that long. We learned that they came to this continent much later," Kira said.

"Well, this planet is their's. One day you will have all the stars to call home."

"I was born here, so were you and father. I think it's our home as much as theirs."

Kurmach had walked up just then. "We must share what we have Kira. They will be moving on to Thresdenal soon." He obviously thought she was complaining about the visitors.

She really didn't mind the visitors at all. She even thought she could make friends with some of them if they would stop huddling together and talk to anyone else.

Kira woke to a commotion in the village. The visitors had been there a few days, so it must be something new. She could hear others moving past her door toward the village center. Slipping past her sleeping sister, she opened the door to the coolness of the morning. Patala had been out late listening to another singer while father was at council. She would sleep late and then be angry at every little annoyance. Kira was sure that if the singer spent a morning with Patala, he would never come singing again.

As Kira stepped outside, Chisa, the potter's daughter, almost ran into her. Grabbing hold of the girl to keep her from falling, Kira asked, "What's happening? Why are you running?"

"To get Father. A teacher is here." The child ducked under Kira's arm and ran off toward her house.

Kira walked toward the center of the village, where this teacher must be. Half the village had already gathered around him at the mound in front of the council chamber. Kira worked her way through the crowd to get a glimpse. Teachers were said to have the ability to read thoughts. Some even said that teachers could disappear and reappear far away in a blink. It had been years since Kira had seen an actual teacher in the village.

Working her way through the crowd of people, Kira finally looked on this new teacher with a sense of disappointment. He looked just like anyone else. He was normal size. His hair was a common shade of bluish green. His eyes were as black as anyone else's – no fire shown in them. If not for his dusty teacher's cloak, he might as well have been a farmer as a teacher. Of course, no farmer also travelled with four guards. They stood back by the wall of the village.

In the dream, their teacher seemed grander. Te'Natha would change the setting of the dream and make lessons appear and demonstration charts move.

Kira watched this teacher for a time, thinking that maybe he would do something miraculous. But he just stood talking to Kira's uncle. Kira felt a hand rest on her shoulder. Her father had stepped up beside her.

"Has the teacher taught you anything?" Her father asked.

"Just that he is no different than anyone else."

As though he heard her whispered descent, the teacher turned and looked straight at her. She immediately dropped her eyes, hoping she had not shown disrespect.

The stranger came toward her. She risked a quick look at his face and realized he was not looking at her, but at her father.

"Te'Jornatha," he said with a bow of his head, "your presence is an honor."

"It is you that honors us with your visit. I am merely Jornatha here. You seem to know me. Have we met?"

"I am Te'Roan of Chosaetal. I was a child when you instructed teachers in Thresdenal. I remember seeing you."

It took a moment for this revelation to become clear in Kira's mind. Her father had always seemed to her the wisest farmer in the village, but this was because he was no farmer at all. Why hadn't he told her? What else was he hiding? Why hadn't he ever taught her any of her lessons? Mother had taught her the basic lessons and Te'Natha her advanced lessons, while dreams with father just seemed to be play – creating fanciful worlds.

"I have requested to address the council as soon as possible," said Te'Roan. "Kurmach has agreed to meet this morning, and I have agreed to assist with today's planting."

"Kurmach would ask Ka'Te'Losa herself to plant corn if she happened by."

"All who eat shall labor," quoted Te'Roan.

"And all who labor shall give to the wanderer as to themselves. Have you eaten?" Kira's father asked.

Te'Roan shook his head.

Kira's father smiled at her. He always smiled when he was going to ask her to do something, as if it were a wonderful treat. "Will you run and ask your mother to make extra cakes for the teacher?"

Kira turned and ran quickly back down the lane. Listening to her father talk with the teacher was just one step up from grinding corn. He may be just like anyone else, but he made her nervous all the same. Village children and travelers told stories about teachers punishing those who did not follow wisdom.

"A teacher...coming to eat...with father." Kira was still breathing hard.

"An old wanderer telling stories more likely," said Patala.

"He's not a wanderer, he's asked for council, and he knows father from Thresdenal."

Her mother looked up in surprise then turned back to padding her cakes.

"And he's not old. He's as young as your silly singers," Kira said to Patala.

Patala dropped the basket she had been working on and hurried into the room she shared with Kira. It wasn't really a room like father and mother had. It was just a space behind a thatched wall that father had put up to separate where they slept from where the family ate.

"If he's a teacher from Thresdenal, then he's probably older than he looks," Kira's mother said. She wasted no time mixing more flour and patting out more cakes.

Patala came from the room. She had changed into the clothes she wore for her singers.

Kira laughed out loud, but Patala ignored her and went back to her basket. Kira could tell from the look on her mother's face that she was trying hard not to laugh, too.

When her father and the teacher arrived, Kira was happy to give up her stool to the guest. She took her cake, kissed her mother's cheek, and left to find Matusu.

Across the village, she found Matusu standing in the shade of the cliff behind his dwelling stripping bark from a fire tree log. The bare logs were laid to one side and the strips of bark were piled in a basket at his feet. Kira had watched him twist the thin strips into rope that his father used to lash logs together or pull stones up when building food caches high on the cliffs around the village.

"How did you ever get so strong sitting around peeling bark off logs?"

"I also catch falling rabbits."

Kira knew she would be hearing about that for a long time. "I have a secret," she said.

"Is it that a teacher has arrived or that he is eating his morning meal with your father?" He didn't even bother looking up to see the nasty face she was making at him. "My father just left to go to council," he said. "The teacher no doubt followed the villagers from the north out of their village. They apparently wanted to stay, hoping to defend themselves against the humans."

"His name is Te'Roan. And why do you think he followed the villagers from the north?"

"Why else would he show up right now, right after they got here?"

"The old woman in my father's dream said she would send a teacher."

"How could you see someone in your father's dream? I thought you could only see those you already know."

"Apparently, my father is a very gifted teacher. He used to train teachers in Thresdenal."

"Did he teach your mother? Or what about Te'Natha? That woman knows her spacial mathematics."

"Don't remind me. Last week she had me doing time dilation calculations with ascending gravitational effects."

"You have to admit that her observatory is amazing though," Matusu said. "You don't think Te'Roan came to meet us so he can be our new teacher do you?"

"Could be, but I think he's here about something else. And the guards probably just came to bring the regenerator."

"They are early by half a month. How many guards?" Matusu stood up, dropping the log he had been working on.

"Just the usual four," Kira said.

"Let's go see them," Matusu said as he started walking toward the center of the village.

The guards stood near the regeneration chamber, a roof built over a circular hole. Through one of the windows, Kira could see the regenerator on the stone pillar in the middle and some of the elderly people of the village already sitting around it. The tradition was for the elderly to sit with the regenerator first and then younger members of the village, all the way down to children. They had discovered shortly after arriving on Earth that radiation here damaged their cells. The regenerator helped them maintain their normal lifespan of 180 to 200 earth years. Without it they might only live as long as the humans. Sometime later today, Kira would take her turn.

"They say there's another one always running in Thresdenal, a bigger one," Kira said.

When Matusu didn't answer, she saw that he was wandering off toward the guards. Kira quickly stepped toward him and took hold of his arm.

"Don't bother them," she said. "They are busy."

"They aren't busy," Matusu said.

"Then they're dangerous."

The guards were looking at them now.

Matusu looked at them and said, "My friend thinks you're busy and dangerous. Are you?"

The guards exchanged glances. One seemed to smile with his eyes, but not his mouth. "We aren't busy," he said.

Matusu turned back to Kira. "See, they aren't busy."

Matusu walked up closer to them. "I meant to ask last time you were here, well, not you, but the other guards. The clothes you wear…"

"Our uniforms?"

"Yes, your uniforms. How are they made? I mean, the way the material blends with the rocks and the sand, they would be great for hunting. And the weave of the cloth is so tight, it has to be tough right?"

"Would you like to get a uniform like this?" The guard asked.

"Uh, yes. Yes I would."

"Come to Thresdenal and join the guard. If you are excepted, you get the uniform. If you pass the tests and training, you get to keep it."

"Just some tests and training?"

The guards all laughed, then the one who seemed to be in charge said, "Yeah, kid. Just some tests and training."

After the morning council, Kurmach asked that no one go far from the village for the next few days. The teacher led a group of young men down the canyon and along the ridges to the north to hide any trails that had become too well worn.

Over the next few days, the visitors rested a little and began helping with the planting. They quickly moved to grinding and cooking for themselves. The whole village still came out to the village fire each night to eat the evening meal together. It was exciting to hear new stories. Lohonath was a master storyteller and told many of the children's favorite star stories in a way Kira had never heard before. He was so animated, giving each character in the story a voice and adding little details, that the stories seemed as though they might really have happened.

He told about Cor the Sailor who's ship shone brightly in the southern sky this time of year. Lohonath told how Cor sailed for a year without seeing land, a story Kira always dismissed as too fantastic to believe. He told such details of how Cor and his sailors ate and worked and survived that Kira started to see how it may have happened. She still couldn't imagine so much water that he could travel for a year without seeing land. But Lohonath's stories were so captivating that even the adults stopped conversing to listen.

After a day or two, most of the children began to play together. Some of the boys had their spinners with them and competed with the boys of Hochonal. Kira had played at spinners when she was younger, but found that the older and better she got, the less the boys wanted her in the game. Matusu was still one of the best at spinning, though he didn't play with the boys. He had carved his spinner out of the heart of a twisted stone tree, and it was perfectly balanced. She and Patala had helped him make the pull string so that there were no thick spots, just a perfectly smooth string from one end to the other.

If one of the younger boys seemed to be falling behind or was embarrassed about how he did, Matusu would let him use the stone tree spinner to give him an edge.

Although she enjoyed watching the boys play at spinning, Kira spent her time weaving sandals and baskets with the visiting girls and women. Kira's weaving was usually quick and coarse. She knew Patala would always be asked to do the finer work. Yet now with these visiting girls, Kira wanted to show that Hochonal girls were as good at weaving as anyone, anywhere.

Lohonath and Kira's father spent most of their time together planting the lower fields or sitting at the village fire talking about Hochonal when they were young. Lohonath seemed to like Hochonal, but he compared it to the northern village in ways Kira didn't appreciate.

"You can do so much more with a river," Lohonath said. "In the northern lowlands near our village, we were able to plant our rows wider apart and divert as much water as we liked from the river. Our stalks grew taller than anything I had experienced at Hochonal. And they were heavy with grain. We even planted extra for the deer."

Kira's father laughed with Lohonath, but Kira thought of how she had to climb up and load the grain stores to keep it away from the deer. "We must protect what we grow and let the deer find their own grass," her father had told her. This northern village sounded wasteful with their grain and their water.

"Perhaps when the humans have gone home," Lohonath said, "you and I can visit the village again." Lohonath held his smile, but his eyes were no longer laughing. His words sounded like a wish without hope.

"I would very much like to see these fields by the river," Kira's father said. "Perhaps from Thresdenal, you will be able to settle an equally fine canyon."

"A small village up some hidden canyon is probably best," Lohonath said and gave out a quiet sigh.

Kira wondered why her father didn't say something. A small village up a hidden canyon was worth more than a sigh. This small village saved his people from days of wandering without food. Staying small and hidden was wisdom. Kira glanced across the fire at the teacher who had been listening to all of this bragging. Shouldn't he be rebuking this talk of wasted grain and wasted water. Wasn't it his job to teach wisdom.

Kira rose and returned to her house. She knew her mother was cooking another cake for her, but she just wasn't hungry anymore.

That night, when Kira visited her father's dream, he was standing on a bluff overlooking a wide green valley with an enormous river winding along the bottom of it. It was a bigger river than Kira thought could ever exist.

"Father, where are we?" Kira asked as she walked up beside him on the bluff.

"This is the valley where Lohonath settled. Or at least this is how it looked before he settled here. I am certain it is now dotted with fields, and houses probably sit right where we are standing." One by one, fields began appearing in the low valley above the banks of the river. The fields spread out on both sides of the river. Channels of water spread from the upper part of the valley winding from field to field.

The valley was greener than any of the valley's around Hochonal. It looked like a perfect place for a village and for crops to grow. It was, however, not right for those who followed wisdom. This was a place to which the humans would come and not leave. "How do you know what this place looks like?" Kira asked.

"Lohonath and I came here when we were young. The season before I went to Thresdenal. We thought we had outgrown Hochonal and would find a new place to settle when we had families. Neither of us had even sung to a girl yet. We wanted the adventure of the journey. We wanted to be on the edge of what was known, as if there were anyplace unknown to the teachers. We passed up many fine canyons and streams, the kind of settlements wisdom suggests. We traveled further north than we thought anyone had ever traveled when we came to this valley. It is a fine place isn't it?"

"Green, yes. But building here does not follow wisdom."

Kira's father smiled down at her. He always approved her adherence to wisdom. "I have regretted our recklessness. Had I not gone to Thresdenal, perhaps I would have come back here with Lohonath and settled. This place could support many large villages. The river flows all year."

Villages of stone houses began to dot the low hills and bluffs across the valley. The ground under Kira's feet turned from grass to a hard-packed trail running down to the fields. Looking behind her, she saw that the village had grown onto this bluff as well.

"If it can support so many why didn't more people come here?"

"They did. Before he finally settled here, Lohonath went to other villages and found other young families. He even tried to convince Kurmach to come, but of course Kurmach had seen himself as the humble leader of Hochonal from almost the day he was born. Lohonath talks of the village, but this valley held enough for five villages, each one larger than Hochonal."

A dark shadow moved over the valley and fire rose up from the houses one by one. Black smoke rose from the roofs of the houses and crackled and crashed as they toppled in. The smoke began to fill the valley, and Kira could almost hear the cries of the children as they ran from their homes.

She realized she had a tear on her cheek and wiped it away before her father noticed.

The shadow and villages faded away. Grass and shrubs appeared in place of fields and irrigation ditches. The valley returned to what it had been.

"This place was not meant for us," Kira's father said. "Our dwellings should be built in dry places until we return home."

Silence hung for a long time as they looked out over the valley. What would it have been like to live in such a green place? They never worried if there would be enough rain – never going without bathing because all the water must be saved for drinking. Such a place would have been paradise. But it was not wisdom to follow such a path.

"How long until we go home?" The question hung in the air as if it had only been a thought. The line between thinking and speaking in a dream was thin.

Her father looked at her. She had spoken.

"The time is hastening. Things are changing. Humans are spreading faster. The teachers search for the most gifted to fulfill the plan." Her father paused. He seemed to know she was looking for a more immediate answer. "Ultimate patience brings immediate results," he quoted. "Wisdom keeps us safe if we are patient."

Her father began to fade from the dream. The valley began to fade. Kira suddenly found herself standing on the rocks overlooking Hochonal, the starting point of her own dream. She was alone.

Kira woke abruptly as her father pushed back the door to their dwelling and ran out. His footsteps pounded the earth as he ran toward the center of the village. Other people were also running. Kira started to follow her father.

Before Kira reached the door, her mother came out of the other room. "Don't leave the village," her mother said. "Stay close to the house."

Chapter 3

Kira waited by the door, not daring to go out at first. She heard people talking. She heard a woman crying. Looking back up and down the little alleyway leading from their house, Kira darted out and away from the village center.

"Kira! Come back!" Her mother shouted. "It's not safe!"

She didn't slow. She knew a place that was safe. She wove through houses on a well-worn path. She would stay away from the center of the village, but she would see for herself.

As she rounded the last boulder and laid down on her perch above the village, she saw the trouble. A large group of humans made their way down the other side of the canyon. From this far, they did not look ferocious. In fact, they didn't look much different than any other people Kira had seen. They carried sticks, some long, others short. They didn't cover their bodies from the sun the way her people did. They were naked to the waist, and their skin was more the color of the brown rock that was soft. Kira's mother said the human's skin protected them from the sun's radiation. Whatever the reason for their color, it was more earthy than her pale, almost blue skin and did not standout against the rock like that of her people. Human skin did not shine when the sun hit it, but looked as if it were covered in dust.

Most of Hochonal's adults stood below at the village center.

"Let them have the fields. Let them burn the fields." Kira heard Kurmach's voice above the others. "Stay here. Bring your families out. Let them see how many we have in the village. We are many. They will not come up."

Kira looked over the land from the cliff top. The land lay empty as far as she could see. The humans could leave them their village, a mere opening in the rock with a trickle of water running below it.

A movement in the rocks along the opposite rim of the canyon caught Kira's attention – another human perhaps, a straggler. She watched his shadow move across a rock face. He was moving slowly, not trying to catch up. He stayed back from the rim, out of sight from the village below. Kira rose to her knees to lean and maybe see this hidden human better. At that moment, the hidden figure moved from behind the boulder. Kira froze. He wore the robe of a teacher. Like the guard uniforms, it blended with the desert around him. Had he held still, she may not have noticed him. She glanced down at Te'Roan among the men of the village. He wore the same robe.

Was this man following the humans? Had he come to help? Or was he also a human, wearing the stolen robe of a teacher? Kira couldn't be sure. The robe covered his head and shadowed his face. He had his hands tucked away in the robe, and the rocks still hid him from about the knees down.

As if they grew from the rocks, two more human warriors stepped up next to the one in the teacher robe. There was no conflict. They stood close, like friends. Kira could see now that the one in the robe was taller than the humans, taller like one of her people. Then the one in the robe turned and pointed up toward Kira. At that moment, sun glinted off the shiny skin of his pale hand. He was no human.

Kira raised a hand to her mouth to hold back her startled cry.

The teacher must have caught the movement. He turned and moved behind another boulder. But the two humans started along the rim up the canyon. If Kira wanted to circle the village and get above it, that is the way she would go. She must warn them. A teacher was helping the humans.

Kira reached her house just as her father ran up from the opposite direction. He looked from her to the house. He looked as though he was about to get angry with her, but instead called her mother and sister from the house. "Come, all of you. Stand with the village," he said. "But stay behind me. No matter what happens, stay behind me." He turned to leave.

"Father," Kira said. She had to tell him.

At that moment, Te'Roan appeared from around a neighboring house. The flourish of his robe brought a sudden realization to her mind – a possibility she had not previously considered. Were Te'Roan and the other teacher in league? Could they be working together against her village? Was this some intrigue of Thresdenal? Perhaps Hochonal had lost favor.

"What is it Kira?" Her father looked at her.

Te'Roan also looked at her. A teacher may not be able to kill with a look, but she was certain he could kill. She couldn't tell her father in front of the teacher. Not here, where he could kill her whole family with no one to see.

"Be careful," she said. "That's all."

Kira followed her mother and her sister to the center of the village. Others were gathering. They gathered as they had when they had welcomed the people from the other villages. Only this time, no one smiled, no one wore finery or carried gifts. The people huddled together, children stayed close to parents and grandparents. All the people were looking out over the canyon, watching the human warriors descend the far side.

They had reached the bottom of the canyon and gathered together in one of the lower fields, drinking the water that flowed over a diversion. Two of them pried at a small diversion dam with their sticks until in broke loose, spilling its contents across the field. Two others, who seemed to be the leaders, pointed at the village. One then pointed to the rocks on the canyon wall to the south of the village, the wall where much of their grain was stored. Those two then called to the others, and they all started up the path from the fields toward Hochonal.

Some of the women from the other village, started weeping. Some fell to the ground as though they waited to die. Comments started to arise, "We should run, run now."

Kurmach's voice boomed above all the others. "We are twice their number. They will not hurt us. We will entreat them to move on and leave us in peace. We will offer them food to take with them. Stand together. Let them doubt and fear because of our number."

Te'Roan turned to Kira's father. In a hushed voice he said, "I must speak with you."

"Now?"

The teacher glanced back at the humans. "Yes. Right now."

"It cannot wait?"

"You know it cannot wait. We must leave now."

"And let Hochonal stand alone?"

"Hochonal is as good as fallen. I've seen these humans. Others are following them. They will try to win a victory first, and let the others carry away the spoils."

"Then we stop these and buy time for our people to escape."

"We cannot risk her in a battle."

Both men glanced at Kira, and a chill suddenly swept over Kira as she realized both men were talking about her.

At that moment, the humans came up over the rim at the entrance of the village. Kira's father stepped past Te'Roan and moved to meet the warriors ahead of the crowd of villagers. Kira wanted to run up next to him to be his strength, but her feet did not agree. They stayed planted, unable to move. It was at this moment, as her father approached the humans that Kira realized how big they were. They were not taller than Thresden but thicker, more muscular.

Kira's father put up a hand. "Peace," he said and then spoke words that Kira had never heard before. Was it the language of the humans? Did teachers truly know all things?

The leader stopped, and the others gathered behind him. Kira saw that they were all men – men wrapped in layers of thick muscles. They may be half our number, she thought, but they are warriors. The leader spoke, pointing his spear toward the south, toward the grain.

Her father responded, extending his hands in front of him and then motioning toward his mouth.

The human leader spoke again spreading his arms wide and pulling them toward himself.

Her father shook his head and gestured toward the people of Hochonal.

The human leader stepped back and turned his head slightly as he spoke to another human standing at his shoulder.

Te'Roan placed a hand on Kira's father's shoulder. "We must go now. I am under orders from Ka'Te'Losa herself."

"You don't think I know that? We will go. We will all go."

The human turned back toward him, spoke louder, and took a step forward, shaking his spear.

Kira's father also stepped forward, planted his feet, and held his hands open in front of him. He was clearly standing ground. They would barter now, find a bargain point. How much food would be given?

But the warrior did not accept the offer to barter. He lifted his spear, which Kira saw had a black pointed stone longer than her hand lashed to the end. In a quick and effortless movement, he threw the spear at her father. Some villagers gasped. A woman behind Kira let out a scream.

Her father leaned low to one side and plucked the spear from the air. He dropped the spear at his feet and again held his hands open in front of him, ready to bargain for the grain.

Two small stone axes came spinning end over end from behind the leader, then a third.

Kira's father caught the first ax and spun it to deflect the second.

Te'Roan stepped forward and caught the third ax. And the guards from Thresdenal moved into position to flank Kira's father and Te'Roan.

The human leader pulled his ax from his belt, took a spear from a man standing near him, and stepped forward toward Kira's father and Te'Roan. Her father stepped forward to meet the human. The big warrior made short jabs at him with the spear while holding the hammer higher, waiting for a moment to strike.

Kira's father didn't hesitate. As the human jabbed, he knocked the tip of the spear away with the ax he had caught. He spun inside the spear's reach and as he did, he reached up and locked his ax with the warrior's descending ax. Dropping to one knee as he let go of the first ax, her father took hold of the man's arm and threw him. The human landed hard on the ground losing his hold on his ax.

The warrior was up again in an instant, but as he turned and charged Kira's father, he was met by a foot to his chest. His wind blew out of him as he again fell to the hard packed ground. This time as he got up, he backed away, his spear held out in front of him with both hands. The confidence he had first shown faded. His resolve to fight seemed to remain.

Kira noticed that he glanced at the other men a couple of times. The human leader wasn't looking for their help, he was looking to see if he had lost respect. He was fighting now to remain the leader.

When they had attacked Lohonath's village, they had been like coyotes among rabbits. Now he was a coyote fighting a wolf.

Kira's father took a step back and dropped the ax spreading his hands apart again repeating what must be the human word for barter.

The warrior took this opening to attack.

Her father moved so fast Kira couldn't tell for sure what happened. He spun into the human in a blur, and the next thing she saw, the spear was in her father's hands with the tip hooked behind the warrior's knee. Her father lifted the spear pulling the man's leg out from under him. As the human leader dropped to the ground and rolled onto his stomach to get up, her father stepped over him and drove the butt of the spear into the fallen man's lower back. The warrior fell flat and lay still. He was conscious but seemed unable to move.

Kira wondered if anyone else noticed the pain and anger in her father's gentle eyes. He was a farmer, a dreamer, not a warrior.

The waiting humans seemed to realize their leader's challenge was over and attacked all at once. Te'Roan stepped forward grabbing a fallen ax to match the one he already carried. He charged into the first man dropping low and sweeping the man's legs from under him. He came up in time to grapple the outstretched arm of a second man and use the attacking man's momentum to throw him to the ground. The man cried out in pain and rolled to the side. Kira's father seemed to deflect and drop attackers with Te'Roan as quickly as the human warriors enveloped them.

The four guards engaged the attackers as well, using quick chops and thrusts to disable opponents with their spears.

Kira started to run forward to see what was happening to her father, but her mother's hand held tight to Kira's arm, keeping her away from the fight. Lohonath and Matusu's father joined the fight and were quickly cut down by the attacking humans. Other men awkwardly swung staffs and field hoes at the advancing humans to keep them from getting to the fleeing women and children. Matusu pulled his father's body away from the fighting. Blood flowing from the man's forehead showed that Matusu might be too late.

Kira and her mother hadn't gone far when the noise of the fight quieted. Looking back, Kira saw the humans retreating. Several fallen warriors lay on the ground near her father and Te'Roan. Her father stumbled sideways, and Te'Roan caught him. Kira jerked her arm free from her mother and ran down to them. She was at her father's side in an instant, supporting him, trying to hold him despite the blood that flowed from his side, staining her clothes. After they'd taken just a few steps from the fallen humans, her father stopped and lowered himself to the ground.

"Let me sit here," he said.

Kurmach and several of the men who had been guarding the path back to the houses came forward to help.

"Please, I'm fine," Kira's father protested. "Help our fallen and those of the humans. I must speak to Te'Roan."

Kira's mother knelt by them and laid a hand across her husband's brow. She ran her fingers through his hair before pulling his hood back up to shade him. "I will get my herbs," she said and hurried back toward the village.

"We must stop talking and leave now," Te'Roan said as he tore strips of cloth from the tail of his sash. He folded a strip and handed it to Kira. "Hold this firmly against his wound," he said. Sensing Kira's hesitation he added, "It won't hurt much yet. His body is still in shock from the blow. Te'Jornatha, with all respect, that was an advance party. The main group will be right behind them." Te'Roan wrapped a strip of cloth around Kira's father's chest covering the flowing gash.

"All the more reason for me to stay."

"Kira must not be harmed," Te'Roan insisted and tugged the knot tight in the strip of cloth.

He father winced.

"She must go to the protection of Thresdenal as soon as possible."

"Protection?" Kira's father laughed and grabbed his side from the pain. Blood was already seeping through the bandage. "Just new dangers. But you are right Teacher. She must go to Thresdenal. I am certain of it. And you will take her."

Kira began to protest, but her father raised a hand. He held a stern look. "I long for nothing more than to have you by my side, but Te'Roan is right. Go with him to Thresdenal. Your mother and sister will go with you. I will stay with the village to help them gather provisions and follow you. The guards too must go and return the regenerator to Thresdenal."

"Then we will wait and travel with you," Kira said. "We can help."

"No, it will take too long. You must go now."

His logic didn't make sense. Kira knew that more danger would shortly follow. But why did she have to leave? Why did the teacher have to take her, while leaving all the others here to face the humans?

"Two guards can return the regenerator. Two can stay and assist you," Te'Roan said.

Kira's mother returned and put herbs under the bandage on her husband's wound. He pulled her close and whispered in her ear. She shook her head, looked at him for a moment, and then nodded. She took Kira's hand and started up through the village.

With travel bags on their shoulders, Kira followed her mother, Patala, and the teacher up the rock path from the houses of Hochonal. Glancing back, she could clearly see her father still sitting at the head of the canyon trail. He was poised in meditation as he often was when entering a waking dream, as he called it. Kira was only able to just get to the edge of dreaming while she was awake. Her father's attention was fixed on the far side of the canyon. Looking across, Kira suddenly stopped and let out a startled cry.

At the rim of the canyon, more warriors began to appear. They slipped over the rim and held position in the sparse brush and fire trees on the slope. As she scanned the far slope, she realized that dozens of humans had already secreted themselves among the rocks, where they could watch the village.

"Kira," her mother said, "stay up."

"Look," Kira said pointing across the canyon.

The others stopped and looked back.

"There are too many. They will never be held back," Kira's mother said.

"Don't be so sure," said Te'Roan. "Your husband is in meditation. I can feel him drawing on the power of the village and the fear of the humans. The story of our brief victory has no doubt been passed among them. He will use that – amplify it."

"What do you mean?" Patala asked.

"We should leave, now. He is giving us time."

They had not gone more than ten more steps when Kira felt a low rumble. At first she thought it came from her father, but then it seemed to be coming from everywhere. She felt a pull toward him, so strong that she even took a step back toward the village. Te'Roan took a quick step toward her and grabbed her arm. The air around her father moved like heat waves flowing toward him. Children and babies in the village started to cry. Her father suddenly rose to his feet and stepped forward pushing forward with both hands together. A boom of thunder seemed to echo in Kira's ears. Many of the humans fell back as though they had been struck by a sudden blast of wind. The humans that didn't fall turned and tried to scramble away through the debris, dislodging rocks on those that had fallen. The panic that Kira had felt was suddenly gone, replaced by a quiet peace despite the panic ensuing across the canyon.

Her father's head dropped. He folded into his seated position, then slumped over onto his side.

Kira's mother started running back down toward the village. Kira tried to follow, but Te'Roan held her back.

"We must flee," he said. "What your father is doing is to allow you time to get clear from here."

Patala started to follow her mother, but stopped and looked back at Kira, obviously torn over what she should do.

Her decision was made for her. Their mother suddenly stopped and turned to her daughters. "Go with Te'Roan. Patala, take care of Kira. Take care of each other."

Kira paused only a moment watching her mother descend back down to the village, then Patala put an arm around her sister, forcing her up the trail with Te'Roan. As they reached the top of the village, they saw to the left, toward the tower and the main trail, two guards carrying away the regenerator as instructed. As they reached the base of the rocks, more than a dozen warriors came out of hiding and attacked them. For a moment, Te'Roan seemed torn between helping the guards protect the regenerator and protecting Kira and Patala.

Two of the humans broke off from the attack and started toward them at a run. Te'Roan stepped in front of Kira and Patala to protect them.

"Wait," Kira said. "There's another way." She quickly turned and started up a gradual rock incline. Patala and Te'Roan followed and so did the humans.

Kira cleared the top of the rock and ran across the flat red and yellow surface. She reached the narrow slot canyon, pulled off her shoes and tossed them into the opening.

The teacher looked into the crevice, shaking his head. "This is your other way?" he asked.

Kira stepped across the opening, leaned forward to place a hand on each side, and dropped into the narrow gap.

A handful of sand skidded over the edge and cascaded down the narrow shaft of light as Patala followed Kira into the crevice of rock.

Kira stopped when she heard a scuffle up above.

"Don't stop," Patala said almost in a cry.

The light from the opening above was suddenly covered by the body of a human warrior. The scuffle continued, then a cry of pain from what must have been the other human. The body covering the opening was pulled away and to Kira's surprise, Matusu looked over the edge.

"Are you both alright?" he asked.

"Matusu, what are you doing here?" Kira responded. Patala merely nodded.

Matusu just shrugged and began climbing down. Te'Roan was right behind him.

Kira was the first to the ground. Climbing down was less work, yet somehow more challenging, than climbing up. Patala seemed to slow things up a bit. She was trying to use the same holds Kira had used but obviously didn't know how to properly balance herself. She clung too closely to the wall which kept her from getting a good grip with her feet. She at least had the presence of mind to take off her shoes and drop them.

Matusu reached the bottom right behind Patala.

"I'm so glad you're here," Kira said, throwing her arms around Matusu. As she stepped back, she noticed the tear stains through the dust on his face. "Who's caring for your mother?" The look on Matusu's face told the story his mouth could not begin to shape. Kira felt ashamed. She suddenly realized that while she was worrying over her injured father and hastily packing to leave, her best friend had actually lost both his parents.

Te'Roan broke the silence in answer to Kira's first question. "Your friend is here saving you from the warriors. He came from behind and dropped one with a fist-sized stone to the head. He's got an accurate throwing arm. They will certainly give away our escape route."

When they had all reached the bottom, Te'Roan took the lead and headed down the narrow slot. "We need to get out of here before the others block off the end of this canyon."

"It will take them a day to find the right opening," Matusu said, seeming to focus on the task at hand. "We can head to the left, away from the village through canyons so twisted only a bird could see which route we take."

Kira was happy to have Matusu along. She wasn't sure she trusted the teacher as much as her father did. Three to one wasn't very good odds against a teacher, but it was better than just her and Patala being handed off to the humans without being able to fight back.

By sundown, they had followed more twisted breaks and turned up more narrow canyons than Kira had thought existed so close to her village. Twice they had to climb out of box canyons that suddenly ended. Once they had even had to backtrack and go up another fork in the canyon they were traveling. Always they moved quickly.

It was at sundown that they finally found water. All their water skins had been drained long before. It was just a catch of water in the hollow of a rock. Careful not to disturb the water and kick up any of the silt, they filled their bags. Kira wasn't sure if she was more interested in drinking or satisfying the gnawing hunger in her stomach. Te'Roan had instructed them not to eat until they found a supply of water.

"You can go a week or more without food, but only a couple days without water," he had said. "Eating causes your body to use more water, reducing how long you can go without it."

Now that they had water, Kira followed Te'Roan's silent lead and pulled a dry cake from her bag.

"Do we stay the night here?" Patala asked.

Kira truly hoped from the bottom of her feet that they were done for the day.

Of course, Te'Roan shook his head. "Night is our best time to travel. We need to get out of these canyons and get our bearing. Your escape route was well concealed, but I'm afraid all our travel today has taken us farther from Thresdenal. Get your fill of water and refill your skins. We still have a long way to go tonight."

The thought that they had gone farther from Thresdenal disturbed Kira. Thresdenal was the safe place. The place her father wanted her to be. Going farther from Thresdenal seemed to mean going closer to humans.

As the evening star reached its zenith, the plodding travelers reached the top of a mound that Te'Roan seemed to be aiming for. They had left the canyons behind, climbing out onto a sandy plateau. The fine dark sand of the plateau felt more like powder than the sand in the bottom of the canyons. It pushed away and to the side with every step, making walking more work and filling shoes with every step. At first, Kira and Patala would stop to shake out the sand every few steps, but after a while, they just let it stay. Kira felt as though she had a flat rock beneath the center of her foot and any attempt to dislodge it was so fleeting that it wasn't worth the effort. Matusu seemed unaffected by the sand.

Te'Roan finally halted and dropped to one knee over a flat rock. The others took this opportunity to drop their bags and water skins and simply sit down where they were.

"You should eat," Patala said to Kira. Without their mother here, Patala had apparently taken on the role. Even though Kira was hungry, she resisted getting food out just to push back at Patala's attempts to take charge. At home, she was able to do a few things her sister asked and then slip away. Out here, her sister would be on her constantly. Kira knew that if she didn't resist now, by day three, Patala would be telling her which rock to step on and which bush to go around. Kira looked over at Matusu, who gave her a knowing smile and proceeded to eat a cold cake.

Kira looked to see if Te'Roan was eating, but instead of a cold cake, he had pulled out a small bundle which he handled with great care. Kneeling next to a flat rock near the summit of the low hill, Te'Roan held what looked like a child's spinner. Only, it was smaller than the ones the boys in Hochonal played with.

Kira arose and shook the weariness from her legs. Quietly, she walked up to where Te'Roan knelt and wound a thin string around the little spinner. Matusu followed close behind her, walking around and squatting on the other side of Te'Roan. The teacher set a small shiny plate on the flat rock. Then, holding the spinner just above the plate, he pulled the string and dropped the whirling toy. As he did, he closed his eyes as if concentrating on something.

The spinner went faster than any Kira had ever seen. In fact, it seemed to speed up the longer it whirled. Soon it began to give off a quiet hum. A flat disk of light formed above the spinner. It was about at Kira's knees and an arm's length across.

Kira took a step back from the spinner and would have turned and run from it if Te'Roan and Matusu had shown any sign of fear. The strange display continued to transform before her. Patala let out a gasp at Kira's shoulder. They had never seen anything like this outside dream lessons with teachers.

Little lines of light shot from the spinner to the floating disk of light, changing the shape of the disk. It began rising in some places and falling in others. Parts of the disk even changed color. Most of the area was pale blue and green with occasional lines of red running across it. White dots appeared in places along the red lines. A golden dot appeared at the center of the glowing disk disconnected from the red lines. Words appeared floating just above the disk over the white dots and at places along the red lines. Te'Roan opened his eyes.

"What is it?" Kira asked.

"It's a map," Te'Roan and Matusu said almost in unison.

"It finds our location and then displays an image of surrounding terrain," Te'Roan continued.

"How does it know where we are?"

"It reads star positions to determine our location or relies on tracking movement when no stars are available. It then displays the geography it remembers."

"Remembers from where?" Kira looked at it, curious at how it could reveal all the hills and canyons. It was as if... "Did it fly over?" She asked.

"Sort of. Look, we're here at this yellow dot. These red lines are known paths, and the white dots are villages and sources of water. We're off trail now and need to get back on a trail. Here's the trail we were supposed to take. We've travelled a hidden, winding path to get away from the humans, but since it's taken us farther away from Thresdenal, we'll need to cross back toward the main trail as best we can. What we want to do is reach it as close to this river as we can. It only has a few places safe to cross. We'll probably find water along the way, but there's no guarantee."

"If we aim for this plateau," Matusu pointed to the map, "and go up this canyon here, we should be able to reach the nearest water crossing without traveling too much further out of our way."

Te'Roan seemed to consider it and nodded. Kira saw where he had pointed, but her mind was still caught up with how this thing knew where they were just from the stars.

"What I don't see," Te'Roan added running his finger along the map, "is a way off that plateau or across this river without going all the way up to the crossing at Spires Ford."

Te'Roan passed his hand through the light and held it over the spinner. The spinner slowed and wobbled to a stop.

"Toward the canyon it is," Te'Roan said as he placed the spinner in his bag.

As the teacher started down off the hill they had climbed, Patala and Kira hurriedly ran back and grabbed their bags and followed.

"Teachers truly are amazing," Patala said in a voice filled with reverence.

"It wasn't anything he did," Kira retorted. "It was that thing. Any boy who can spin a top could have made that map thing work."

"But who other than a teacher would be trusted with such an amazing device."

"Father was a teacher you know – long before Te'Roan."

"Is there something wrong with admiring the man who is saving our lives?"

"Do you really think Father would have let anyone hurt us if we had stayed at Hochonal?" Kira asked.

"I think Father wanted us away from Hochonal because he thought he might not be able to help us."

Kira knew that they had left because Te'Roan was under orders to take Kira to Thresdenal as quickly as possible. Father also knew that she needed to go. They left to get to Thresdenal quickly, not to save their lives. In all the day's travel, Kira's mind had been kept busy with trying to climb quickly and keep track of which canyon connected to which other canyon. She had been so busy looking behind her and looking up at ridges for humans that she hadn't allowed her mind to touch on what she really feared most.

"You don't think Father and Mother really sent us away because they thought the humans could... No. They would have come, but he was hurt. He'll catch up with us on the trail." Kira's feet had stopped their forward progress. She felt a tear rising in her eye and quickly wiped it away. She felt her sister's arm around her shoulders.

"Come on now. I'm sure everyone's fine," Patala said. "We need to get you to Thresdenal, and you need to help me climb up that canyon Matusu was pointing to."

That's what Mother would have said. There Patala went, trying to wield her authority again, yet somehow, this time, Kira didn't mind. She started walking again and jogged a few steps to catch up with Matusu.

If walking the sandy canyon bottoms had been difficult, crossing the open, boulder-strewn desert in near darkness aiming for the profile of some cleft in the side of a distant plateau seemed impossible. Every few hundred steps they would come to another canyon they would have to traverse. They would descend a sandy slope or hop down from boulder to boulder only to start climbing up an equally broken slope. As they broke the top of a particularly wide and deep canyon, they were met by a growing light in the east.

"We'll want to find shelter soon," Te'Roan said. "Out here in the open, we're too easy to spot."

The next ridge they traversed brought them to the shelter they sought. A thin stream of water trickled across, then descended along a low depression in the rock at the bottom of the shallow valley. Vegetation clung to is edges wherever there was enough soil to put down a root. The clear water filled little pots in the stone stream bed as it trickled along finally spilling over a cliff into a rock-rimmed bowl.

"Stay here," Te'Roan said as they looked over the edge of the cliff down to the inviting pool of water far below. Te'Roan headed down the canyon to where the slope tapered off to descend into the basin.

Kira could taste the mist rising from the water as it fell. Green, broad-leafed trees protected the down-stream end of the bowl, watching over the water as it flowed on its way. Smaller plants, with delicate vines clung to the walls of the misty bowl. The barren, sun-bleached hills surrounding it gave no sign of its existence. Had they reached the stream farther above or below it, they would have merely filled their water skins and missed this sight completely.

Te'Roan returned shortly. "No one appears to have been here recently. There are no tracks leading in or out."

Descending down a gentle slope Te'Roan had found, they moved through the trees and into the bowl. The truth was, there were dozens of tracks leading to and from the pool. Lizard, snake, rabbit, mouse, squirrel, and even deer tracks led to and from this life-giving pool.

"It's cooler down here," Patala said as she moved into the shade and pushed back her hood. "There's nothing like this near Hochonal. Have you ever seen anything like it Teacher?"

Te'Roan smiled. Kira could tell, he was trying to be modest.

Te'Roan looked over the pool and said, "It is a smaller version of Temple Summit Falls outside Thresdenal. Just above the falls, the river settles in a pool that overflows in three places sending cool clear water crashing together into one pool. The water at the bottom is so turbulent, it pounds through your chest until you feel that your heart is beating in rhythm with the cascading water."

"Is there really such a place? Will we be able to go there when we get to Thresdenal?" Patala asked in an excited tone that clearly prompted Te'Roan to tell more. Kira suddenly realized that she'd heard that tone in Patala's voice before. It was the tone her sister used when she talked to silly boys who came to sing to her. Kira wondered if the teacher would respond like a silly boy.

"Perhaps," was all Te'Roan said as he turned away. Laying his robe over a rock, he walked slowly out into the water. Patala gave a half pout then turned her attention back to washing her hands and arms. Kira may learn to like this teacher, so far he hadn't done anything that would make her not trust him.

Kira shook off her shoes and joined her sister at the water. They waded out until they were knee deep, then began to wash off the dust of the desert, as much as modesty would allow. Kira watched as Te'Roan waded closer to churning foam at the bottom of the falls, looking down into the water like he'd lost something. He suddenly turned and headed back toward the trees.

"Here you go," Matusu said, handing the teacher a forked stick, sharpened on each fork.

Kira hadn't even noticed Matusu get a stick or sharpen it. Yet there he was, knife still in hand.

"Do you always anticipate what someone will need?" Te'Roan asked.

Matusu shrugged and smiled. "My father is a stone mason. He's usually too out of breath fitting stones to ask for what he needs next. I figure it out."

"Keep anticipating. It's a long way yet to Thresdenal."

Te'Roan waded back into the water, stick in hand. He moved slowly with the stick held high above his head. Then in a quick motion he thrust the stick down into the water and pulled back a small fish. Its silver body glinted in the sunlight as it writhed back and forth to free itself. Te'Roan tossed it on the bank and raised his spear in search of another. Only a moment later, he had another fish on the end of the spear, a little bigger than the first. He laid the two out on the sand and quickly sliced them open and cleaned them.

They moved away from the water and the mist to a spot still shaded by canyon walls. The four of them gathered dry branches fallen from the nearby trees. Te'Roan inspected each stick as he laid them together for a fire. It only took him a moment to light a fire with the small bow and drill from his bag. He didn't use flint and ore like Kira and Patala carried. The smoke from the fire filtered up through the overhanging branches of the thumb leaf trees. As soon as the fish were cooked, Te'Roan piled sand on the fire to put it out.

"Let's eat these somewhere higher," Te'Roan said looking up.

Kira hadn't noticed until then, but a cloud cover had started rolling in. She'd been taught since she was a small child to stay out of canyon bottoms when the sky clouded over. Rainfall far away can turn even a dry canyon into a torrent. The canyon they were in showed evidence of high water from seasonal rains.

The four of them donned their travel bags and water skins and started down the canyon, back to the slope where they could climb out. With Te'Roan in the lead and Matusu at the tail with the fish, they circled back up above the waterfall, crossed the shallow little stream, and headed up the low ridge that bordered the stream. They found a secluded spot among some rocks near the top of the ridge. Patala used a bone knife to separate the fish into four sections.

"This has to be the best fish I've ever eaten," Patala said. "It may be that I've never been hungrier, but it is good."

Kira had to agree. The fish was delicious after eating dry cakes and nuts for nearly two days. Kira leaned against the rock at her back and watched the gray clouds slowly shift and merge.

Raindrops on Kira's face roused her from her sleep. Her blanket lay over her, keeping the rain from her body. The glow in the west told her that the sun had just disappeared over the horizon. She must have been exhausted, because she hadn't even dreamed. Patala lay beside Kira, also sleeping, also covered with a blanket. Matusu sat a few feet away, leaning back against a rock – relaxed but not sleeping. Te'Roan was nowhere to be seen.

As the absence of the teacher reached her conscious thought, Kira abruptly sat up. "Where is Te'Roan?" She asked.

"He went to the top of the ridge to get a bearing on that gap in the plateau before it got too dark. I guess he means for us to travel through the night again." Matusu rose, stepped over to where the bags were set together, and handed Kira her water skin.

"How long have we been asleep?" She asked and drank deeply from her water skin. Occasional drops of rain continued to land on her face and arms. She started folding her blanket to keep it from getting wet. Things dried fast enough after a rain, but a wet, heavy blanket would be no fun to carry.

"At least half the day." Matusu smiled. "It wasn't even noon when we ate that fish."

When she had her blanket safely stowed, Kira stepped back over to where she had slept and gently shook Patala's shoulder. "Wake up, dream girl. We have to get going, and I may need some mothering."

"You're beyond mothering," Patala said without opening her eyes. "But we have no village council to set you back on course." Patala took a deep slow breath and exhaled with a sigh. She sat up and brushed sand away from her clothes and blanket. Rising to her feet, she took a moment to adjust her hair and straighten her clothes before folding and packing away her blanket.

"Let's fill the skins and get moving before the rain really starts coming down," Te'Roan's voice preceded his appearance from around a boulder that blocked their view of the ridge.

"I'll take care of it," Matusu said as he gathered the bags and bounded down the slope they had come up.

"Is he always so chivalrous or is he just anxious to be moving again?" Te'Roan asked.

"Chivalrous," Patala said.

"Anxious," Kira said at the same moment.

Te'Roan laughed and knelt to make sure his bag was securely tied.

Over the ridge lay a shallow valley of crisscrossing gullies and washes gradually sloping up toward a plateau. The wall of the plateau stood like a border on the world, like they were traveling across a grand dish and had now reached the edge of it. As far as the eye could see to the left or right, only a single cut marred the otherwise unbroken wall.

A flash of lightning revealed the path ahead of them in sharp relief as the following thunder herded them down off the ridge. Kira had heard stories her entire life about avoiding ridges and gullies during storms. Now all her childhood training was tossed aside in their urgent escape. Though if humans were following, they surely would have been within sight from the ridge, especially after the long stop they had taken by the waterfall.

Kira hurried up next to Te'Roan. "I haven't seen anyone following us. Why are we cutting across all these canyons?" Kira asked. She tried to make it sound like an honest inquiry, but the challenge to Te'Roan's course was implicit.

"Kira," Patala said, "Te'Roan knows what's best. Do you think this is fun for anyone?"

"I just thought crossing all those gullies with rain coming…"

"I agree, Kira," Te'Roan interrupted. "This route makes me nervous. We'll try and cross them as quickly as possible, and we may be stuck out here should the rain get ahead of us."

"So you think someone is following us?" Matusu asked, bringing the conversation back to Kira's original statement.

"If a group of human warriors were tracking us, they would have found us by now. We put them behind us before we left the safety of the canyons. What I want to avoid now is meeting them on the other side of that mesa. They were moving southeast, just like us, and will probably follow the trails leading toward Thresdenal in search of more villages to raid. We need to stay ahead of them."

"How do we know we won't just meet up with them when we find the path on the other side?"

"Nothing about our journey is certain," Te'Roan said with a tone of finality.

Chapter 4

Kira held her breath as they descended each new gully, straining to hear even the slightest trickle of water, watching for the glint of moonlight on water. Once at the bottom, crossings were quick, almost frantic, as they raced to the opposite bank and up away from potential flash floods. They repeated the process throughout the night. The ragged sliver of night sky descending into the black wall ahead of them remained a constant guide as it grew higher and higher in the sky. They reached the base of the cleft as morning light added soft hues to the rock face.

"We can rest here a while," Te'Roan said as he led the way onto a ledge of rock a few steps above the floor of the narrow cut.

Kira dropped her bag against the wall of rock and leaned against the hard, sandy surface of stone. She closed her eyes and tried to relax her aching legs. She was finding, for the first time in her life, that her body had limits. She could only push it so far before it started pushing back. Of course, she was the youngest. Even Matusu was a few months older than her. Sitting down, she looked about for Matusu. He was so quiet. He sat at the far edge of the ledge, watching their back trail. Patala had followed Kira's lead and sat on the ledge inside the gap closer to Te'Roan.

Kira leaned back and closed her eyes again. She listened to the wind and tried to relax her mind, maybe reach a dream state. The throbbing of her legs and the ache of muscles kept tight for too long drew her back to the physical reality around her.

They heard the rain drops before they felt them. Big singular drops rattling the leaves of a tree that grew near the mouth of the cleft. First a few hit here and there, then increased rapidly. A flash and immediate clap of thunder directly overhead opened the sky and let loose a deluge. They tucked back against the rock face but dared not leave the ledge for fear of being caught on the canyon floor.

The sound of trickles from the gap overhead turned to the sound of flowing water. A small trickle ambled along the floor of the canyon toward them. As it flowed, it swelled until what moments before had been an ankle-deep trickle was a flood threatening to rise to the level of the ledge they sat on.

Te'Roan quickly grabbed each of their bags and threw them onto a higher ledge. He held out his hands as a step to lift Kira up onto the ledge. Matusu did the same for Patala, then let Te'Roan help him up as well. The rising water threatened to sweep the teacher's feet from under him by the time he jumped to grab the overhead ledge. Matusu and Kira managed to get him over the top, while Patala secured the bags away from the edge.

No sooner had they tucked tight against the wall for protection than a flow of water broke loose above them. Matusu lunged to grab two bags being washed away and was swept to the edge by the cascading flow. Kira grabbed Matusu's wrist, stopping his slide over the edge. She jammed her other fist into a crack in the wall and held on directly under the falling water.

Kira was in a secure position, albeit wet and muddy, but lacked the strength to pull Matusu against the flow of water. Te'Roan tossed a thin length of rope over the edge, but Matusu had to either let go of the bags or Kira to grab the rope. He chose to hang on.

In a few moments, the rain slowed and stopped, and the waterfall slowed to a drizzle. Kira was finally able to get some purchase with her feet and together with Te'Roan, pulled Matusu up onto the ledge. The flow along the sandy canyon floor was already fading away.

They turned their attention to getting on top of the mesa. Although it was longer than anything Kira had previously climbed, the trip up the cut in the wall proved to be less strenuous than she expected. Besides having sore feet from two days of walking, Kira found the only real discomfort was the empty feeling in her stomach. She was pretty sure they would not encounter any cheerful little streams bearing fish on the top of the mesa.

The fish they had eaten the day before no doubt made their way up from some larger river. Most desert streams didn't support fish because of the dry seasons and canyon falls that kept them from migrating from bigger waters. Her father had told her of the fish in the pools near Hochonal. They had been caught and carried in skins to the pools. Some had gone up and down stream, but the little population in their own pools seemed to thrive. Kira had helped chase fish into the deeper pools as the dry season approached, a favorite children's game in the village.

Thoughts of fish led to thoughts of grain and roots and spiced flat cakes. Kira didn't think she had ever been this hungry. Would their rations hold out until they reached Thresdenal? She didn't think so. Te'Roan would not have stopped to catch and cook fish had he thought they carried enough food. The real test was yet to come. Maybe that was why he kept moving them forward. Perhaps lack of food was like lack of water. When traveling without water, time was as big a factor as effort. Your body would continue to loose water at rest, so it was important to keep going. Kira knew a person could go longer without food than water, but maybe the principle was the same.

The sun was slipping down the sky by the time they topped out on the mesa. The route up had been more of a scramble than a climb. The gnarled fire trees along the edge of the mesa gave way to long needle trees that grew sparsely across its top. The reddish-brown trunks pushed straight up like each tree vied for a piece of the sky, determined to be the tallest.

The mesa, which from below seemed flat, inclined upward ahead of them and seemed to tilt off to the left.

Turning back, Kira stopped to look over the broken desert they had crossed. She couldn't begin to tell where Hochonal lay in the labyrinth of hills and winding canyons. The afternoon sun cut across the landscape, deepening valleys and highlighting ridges. This is what birds saw as they winged into the clouds. It was truly a land to get lost in, a land to hide in.

Patala stepped up next to Kira, "Kind of high, even for a squirrel. Come on. We still have work for you to try to get out of."

Kira drank in one last look, then turned and followed the others.

Te'Roan soon stopped by an outcropping of gray boulders. "We'll need to rest for tomorrow," he said.

The spot he'd chosen gathered the heat of the late afternoon sun into the rocks – probably one of the reasons he'd selected it. It would stay warm well into the night. They would wake in the shade. Every good thing had a tradeoff.

"Well, builder's son," Te'Roan said to Matusu, "can you build us a small wall to hide a fire? The cloudy dusk sky should hide the smoke, and we can get things burnt down to coals before dark. Patala and Kira, that leaves us to gather wood."

Kira didn't like the idea of being separated from Matusu, alone with Te'Roan. She still didn't know if he was with the other teacher, the one helping the humans. Of course, Patala was glowing at the mention of wandering among the trees with the teacher. Kira hadn't told her about the other teacher. She hadn't felt safe telling anyone.

Luckily, Kira didn't have to go far. Most of the needle trees had dead branches on their lower trunks that broke off easily and seemed fairly dry, even after the earlier rain. She kept Matusu in sight and more especially in earshot as she filled her arms.

Soon, all she had to do was wait for her sister who stood waiting for the teacher. Patala couldn't seem to stop adjusting her bundle of wood into a pleasing arrangement, straightening her clothes, and making sure her hair was pulled across her ear at just the right angle.

Te'Roan, oblivious to Patala's efforts, had thrown himself into the task of de-branching an entire fallen tree. He'd piled up a stack of branches twice the size of Kira's and Patala's put together, and he continued to add to it with vigor. When the pile was nearly to his waist, he stopped and, reaching down, grabbed the end of a small rope he must have set on the ground when he started. He then stepped around the pile and picked up the other end of the rope. Looping them together in a quick knot, he cinched the rope tight around the bundle and hefted it to his shoulder.

Patala took a step forward as if she were going to help him with his awkward load, but Te'Roan never gave her a glance as he started back toward the rock out-cropping.

Kira was grateful for the fire's warmth as she finished off a spiced flat cake. She'd lightly warmed it by the fire, which did nothing to make her only meal of the day more filling. The glowing coals reflected off Matusu's short wall of stones warming the boulders at Kira's back. The temperature had dropped quickly after the sun set.

Te'Roan sat a little further from the fire. His top spun and projected its faint blue glow that contrasted the red of the fire. Matusu sat with him looking over the route they intended to travel. Patala looked on, feigning interest.

"I don't see a gap anywhere near our route. The best we can do is this rim trail that follows breakoffs down the face of the rock to a debris pile about halfway down. We can descend along that onto the valley floor. We can use cracks and crevices or hollows where the slabs have fallen away to get to that debris.

"From there, we can travel east to reconnect with the main trail to Thresdenal. Hopefully, the humans who attacked Hochonal aren't going the same direction."

Kira had liked climbing a canyon to get onto this plateau. She did not relish the idea of descending a cliff face and an exposed pile of debris. Anyone watching from the valley would see them. Hopefully, the humans were searching far away. Or better yet, they had left Hochonal and gone back the way they had come.

Kira closed her eyes shutting out the sound and the continuing conversation between Te'Roan and Matusu. She focused on meditating to a dream state. She had nearly accomplished it on a few occasions. Perhaps her fatigue and the warmth of the fire would help bring on the dream.

She found herself overlooking Hochonal from her perch on the rocks. It was the twilight of a rising moon, yet she could see none. She quickly willed herself to the valley floor, to tall grasses and the water that served as a gateway to her father's dreams. As she pushed through the watery barrier, all she found was more grass, and more water. He was not there, or he was not dreaming. Kira wandered about the village, everything seemed to be in the same places she remembered. But of course, this was the dream. Everything would remain as she expected it.

She returned to the gateway to her father's dream and waited, hoping for some outward sign. She whispered his name, wondering if he could hear her. She continued to try to enter his dream but found the way wouldn't open.

After what seemed like forever, a form or shadow stood at the doorway.

"Who's there?" Kira asked. "Who are you?"

A woman in a teacher's robe stepped through the gateway. It was the same woman who stood talking to Kira's father the night of the dream storm. Only the woman looked different, like she was not all there. Like a reflection on water. Visible, but distorted and translucent. Her form almost seemed to be flowing.

"Who are you?" Kira repeated.

The woman's mouth moved, but Kira couldn't hear anything.

"Where's my father?"

Again, movement without sound.

"Has my father left Hochonal?"

The woman didn't respond.

Kira wasn't even sure she could hear her. "To Thresdenal. We are going to Thresdenal," Kira said.

The woman gestured forward with her hands as though saying, "Go." Then like a stone had been cast into her watery reflection, she rippled and faded away.

Kira woke with a start. The night had grown colder. Patala lay beside her. The others were a few steps away. A slight breeze rustled the needles of the towering trees. The pile of coals still glowed. A small stick lay burning atop it, recently added. Kira lay awake for a moment, trying to determine the time by how far Borthsis had moved through the sky. His nightly journey was half over. Kira closed her eyes, meditating. She did not seek a dream, but she listened, hoping her father might call her name.

Te'Roan Skyhaven woke to the cold darkness. The stick he had added to the fire was but an ember. He had sensed the need to listen and allowed himself to sleep.

Go quickly. The words still rang in his ears. Something must be wrong for her to send such a brief message. No explanation.

He rose and moved away from the dim coals. Wrapped in his cloak for warmth, he stood still by a lone tree and looked about. The scent of the fire had likely driven off any animals that would have normally come through here. He listened to the breeze, a breeze pushing a wisp of clouds. The clear sky they had briefly enjoyed would soon be gone, giving way to another rainstorm. They needed to be off the plateau and past the cliff face.

Why the urgency? Why had she told him to go quickly? Was something following them? Was something happening at Thresdenal that they needed him? Te'Roan couldn't make sense of it. He was not an exceptionally strong dreamer – trusted, resourceful perhaps, but not powerful. He wasn't able to easily build out a classroom or world the way some did. If someone was already dreaming, he could initiate a dream with them, but pulling in a group of students was difficult for him.

Maybe it was the girl they needed even more desperately. Te'Roan had accompanied other dreamer candidates to Thresdenal, but never with this urgency. Of course, the daughter of Te'Jornatha is no ordinary candidate. Every teacher knew of Te'Jornatha. It was said that he could maintain thirty-six students. Most masters reached the limit of their dreaming with twelve students. Te'Jornatha was said to be second only to Ka'Te'Losa.

As he wondered, Te'Roan looked about. The night seemed empty, a faint dawning in the east told him that the time to move had arrived. His three wards still slept soundly. He wished he could give them time to rest. A day of stories around the fire would do them some good, but they couldn't stop. He had to push them on.

Whatever the reason for the attack at Hochonal, Te'Roan couldn't help but see more than coincidence in it. He had been urgently sent to Hochonal, the hidden sanctuary of dreamers and strict followers of wisdom. Then the humans attacked, arriving right on his heels. The rising political strife in Thresdenal made every unusual event seem part of a conspiracy. Ka'Te'Losa still held to the protocol, but that rule was being challenged.

Te'Roan walked back to the fire and pushed sand onto what remained of the fading coals.

"Time to move," he said.

Kira wedged herself tightly in the rock chimney lowering herself in tiny steps. Matusu was below her. He had gone first and stopped every so often to wait for her. Kira supposed that if she slipped, they could plummet to their deaths together. Patala, though she tried to put on a brave front, was terrified as they started their descent down the stone chimney. Te'Roan, who had wanted to tie a rope to Kira, using the excuse that she was youngest, finally tied his rope to Patala. He would hold it secure while she moved, then catch up with her and let her descend again.

When Matusu finally reached the bottom of the chimney, he positioned himself to help Kira and then Patala transition onto a narrow curving ledge. The ledge looked to be the bottom edge of a massive breakaway. Looking down, Kira could see where the slab of rock had broken away and shattered on the boulders below. The bottom lip of the cavity descended to just above the debris pile. When Te'Roan caught up with the rest of the group, he was able to lower them one at a time onto the debris.

Kira stood on the top of the debris where it met the rock face and looked out over the valley. The light that filtered through the gathering clouds added mystery to the texture of the land, lending it perhaps more shadow than it would have in bright sunlight. It looked much like the broken desert on the other side of the plateau, except for a green strip snaking its way along the bottom of the valley. Water. It had been almost two days since Kira had seen flowing water. It was still some distance away, but it was along their direction of travel. Water to drink, perhaps enough to bathe.

Patala interrupted Kira's aquatic reverie. "How is Te'Roan going to lower himself down?"

Kira looked up as the rope dropped and bunched at her feet. Te'Roan had dropped a bit using the lip of the ledge as a handhold. He swung himself to the right, hooking his right hand and toe on holds that Kira could barely see. Letting go of the lip, he dropped catching another hold with his left foot and balancing with his left palm against the rock. He continued to move one limb at a time down the rock face to barely visible holds until he dropped beside the others. Gathering his rope, he smiled and started descending the debris.

Kira was glad to see that the valley was empty. She had feared they might arrive at the bottom only to be captured by some roving band of humans.

They didn't turn left at the bottom of the debris. Rather, they took the shortest route toward that belt of green, where there was bound to be at least a trickle of water.

As they approached the water, the brush got closer together and the land descended. The main course of the water lay at the low center of a much larger wash. As Matusu, pushed his way through the brush, Kira was suddenly aware of movement from both sides.

"Run!" Matusu shouted as he shoved back the first human, sending the warrior toppling down the sloped ground. Kira turned to run and saw two more warriors running at Te'Roan from behind.

Te'Roan responded immediately, turning to face the attackers.

As Kira started to scream, Patala grabbed her by the wrist and plunged into the brush. Dry brush tore at her legs and arms. She kept one hand up to protect her face, while Patala dragged her forward by the other. They emerged on the river side of the brush downstream from the crossing. Three humans charged along the steep bank to intercept them.

Patala pulled Kira ahead of her, placing herself between Kira and the pursuers. Kira ran with Patala right behind her. The steep, soft bank between the brush and the river was hard to run on. Looking back, Kira could see the humans gaining ground. The bank grew steeper with the occasional rock to jump from. Kira could hear the churning of the water below as the channel narrowed and the current increased.

All they needed was clear running room to escape. In this soft, sloped sand, the stout warriors would soon be on them. Suddenly, Patala screamed and fell.

Kira stopped and looked back to see Patala holding her shoulder, blood seeping through her fingers. A warrior's stone ax lay in the sand beside her.

"Run!" Patala stole only a glance at Kira, then grabbing the ax with her blood-stained hand, spun to her feet and threw it at the closest human.

It would have been an impressive attack had the warrior not caught the weapon out of the air. Patala had barely turned to run when the warrior let go of the weapon and grabbed her around the waist, lifting her off the ground. The second warrior grabbed her legs to keep her kicks from injuring his companion.

As Kira turned to help Patala, the third human, the biggest of them, moved into her path. She tried to dodge above him on the slope to get to her sister. The warrior grabbed her by her hood, pulling her to him. As Kira screamed and clawed at his hand, his other hand found her throat. She immediately felt the pressure of his grip cut her blood flow. She could no longer tell what was happening to Patala. She only knew that mere moments remained until she fell unconscious.

Pushing against the muscular warrior with her arms was useless. She didn't have his strength. She dropped to the ground, her legs folding beneath her. As darkness began to crowd the edges of her vision, Kira closed her eyes. Beneath the panic, her father's words echoed through her fading thoughts, "Your legs are what carry you."

Suddenly, her whole conscious thought shifted to her legs. Her feet pressed into the sand, ready to spring. She couldn't spring away from the human's grip, so she did the thing he would not expect.

The warrior was already pulling Kira toward him, so when she sprang, he increased her force. She felt her head connect with the warrior's face, felt the cracking impact against his mouth and nose. Then they fell. His hand came free from her throat as they tumbled over one another down the slope. Sand filled her eyes and mouth, the warrior clung tight to her hood. Then as water enveloped them, he released his hold.

Kira instinctively came up for air as the swift, deep water carried her away from the bank. It also carried the human warrior. He reached out and grabbed hold of her wrist. Bringing up her feet to his shoulder and face, she pushed away, slipping her wet arm from his grip.

Patala and the other warriors were out of sight. Kira watched the warrior flounder in the water a moment then she turned and swam toward the opposite bank. Kira had been swimming since she was a small child, but never in a swift current. The sandy spot on the bank she was swimming for quickly slipped away. In fact, the sandy slopes disappeared, replaced on either side by rock cliffs. The muddy flow plunged through a stone gap.

Without warning, Kira's hip collided with a boulder just below the surface. She spun, now swimming headfirst downstream. She saw a fork in the current ahead and rolled at the last moment, avoiding another boulder.

How would getting closer to the other bank help her if she smashed her head from not watching where the river was taking her? What good would her escape be? How could she go back and get Patala if she let the river kill her? The water where they had intended to cross was slower and wider. Maybe the river would flatten out again if she just kept herself afloat through this part – if she just stayed alert.

She swung both arms forward, tucked her legs under her and pushed them out in front of her. This is how mother taught her to float – arms paddling to keep her balance. She could stay on top of the water like this for a long time.

Looking downstream, Kira tried to see the tell-tale bumps and splits in the current that indicated rocks. Using her arms and kicking against the current to the left or right, she would move over enough to slip past the obstacle and quickly search out the next one.

Twice, she faced a series of boulders so close together that she couldn't shift in the current fast enough to avoid them all. For the most part, she was able to push off them with her feet when she came too close. Although, her hips and back continued to be slammed and bruised as the current carried her relentlessly down the canyon.

The cold water was also beginning to take its toll. What started as refreshing was becoming increasingly uncomfortable. Her breathing had become shallower, and she felt an uncontrollable quiver in her chin. The cold of the water seemed to be intensified by the shadow of the canyon. She needed to find a way out. A way into warmth, before the day was gone. How much of the day had passed? She couldn't tell.

She worked toward the bank. The current was still swift, but definitely slowing. As she used her feet to push off a rock, something bumped her head from behind, pushing her sideways around the rock. She paddled to the side and turned, expecting to see a log. What she saw didn't register immediately. The brownish mass floated silently next to her. As the realization of what it was hit her, so did panic.

Forgetting about rocks or currents or cliffs, she turned and swam as fast as she could away from the warrior. She reached the sheer rock face at the edge of the river but could find no way to climb out. She clawed at the surface, the current continuing to pull at her. Finally, she found a narrow crack in the rock. Jamming first a fist, then a foot into it, she pulled herself up out of the water.

She looked over her shoulder in time to see the lifeless body of the human warrior roll against a boulder then get carried away from her downstream. She watched until the body was out of sight. Only then did she look up to see what could be made of climbing this crack.

Like other crevices she had seen, a few feet above her it closed up and disappeared. She did notice that the current near the rock face was slower, at least where it ran parallel to the current. She had seen though, that where the rock face turned into the current, the water seemed to speed up and slam into the canyon wall. She just hung there looking about, knowing she would have to continue.

Across the river, she could see a break in the canyon wall, not so much a side canyon as a large split in the rock. She could imagine the rest of the humans waiting for her just inside the opening. As it was, she would never be able to swim across before the current carried her beyond the opening. But what if the break in the rock goes all the way across the canyon. She had grown up in canyons like this one. A large cleft in the rock could easily extend across even a large canyon. From where she hung on the wall, she couldn't really see the near side of the canyon.

As quickly as the idea occurred to her, Kira let go of the wall and plunged back into the current. As the current grabbed hold of her, she tried to stay close to the wall while avoiding boulders that seemed to dot this side of the river just below the surface. She kept a watch on the opening on the other bank, trying to determine the angle at which it intersected the river. If it did cross all the way, it would most likely be in a straight line.

When she was directly across from it, she could see that it angled downstream. Chances were, if an opening existed on this side, she hadn't missed it.

A large boulder loomed ahead. Kira could hear the sound of the water rushing past it on either side. In fact, as she looked ahead, the river seemed to drop off beyond the boulder. The sound of falling water filled her ears. A new fear filled her as she quickly swam to put herself directly behind the boulder. It rose gradually out of the water, sloping away from her. She was able to land on it, get purchase, and climb up onto the dry, rounded top of the immense rock.

She had been right about the break in the canyon wall. It was right ahead of her, just past a churning waterfall.

An eddy had formed at the mouth of the opening. Kira could make such a jump. But the water wasn't clear enough to see how deep it was. From the shadows on the cliff tops, the sun would soon set. The desert cold would come, and Kira would not survive the night sitting soaking wet on this rock. Her skin was ice cold, and she could feel her joints growing stiff.

Moving away from the edge, she stretched out trying to work blood into her muscles. Taking two steps forward, she launched from the boulder, over the fall toward the eddy. She prepared herself to hit ground just a few inches under the water. As her feet and legs hit the water, she tried to leave them loose enough to fold, yet tense enough to absorb the impact.

She plunged into the water past her knees and her waist before her feet connected with the ground. Only, it wasn't a flat surface, rather the sloped side of a submerged boulder. Her feet scraped along the boulder, pushing to the right, then her hip connected. The rock surface tore at her clothing, scraping her leg until she was finally able to bring her arm down and push away from the rock. Her feet finally hit a sandy bottom and she pushed off, trying to push forward into the gap and away from the current.

Breaking the surface, it only took a few strokes to reach the shore. The gap in the canyon wall ascended steeply away from the river. That was all Kira cared about at the moment.

She moved as quickly as her bruised, scraped, frozen legs would carry her. She needed to reach the top, to reach rocks that had been warmed by the sun before the warmth was gone. The ascent was mostly boulder scrambling. Places she would have normally hopped across, she crossed with careful steps, steadying herself with her hands. The cold and exhaustion had sapped her of her balance and to some extent her judgment. Distances weren't quite as they seemed. She caught herself more than once not stepping high enough to clear a rock, stepping down only to find the step longer than expected.

Reaching the top brought the expected warmth of the sun. She was on a boulder strewn plateau of red rock. The irregular surface flowed away from her rising and falling like a sea of red sand frozen in the midst of a great storm.

Kira found a rock slab slanted toward the afternoon sun. Pressing water out of her damp clothes, she laid out on the warm rock face to dry. She tried to pull torn spots together as best she could to protect her skin. She hoped the cloth would dry quickly.

She checked the contents of the small bag that still hung around her neck and shoulder. She still had her flint and ore, though she'd never been very good with them. Te'Roan was faster with his bow and drill. Her dry tinder would have to be replaced. The water had disintegrated the charred fibers. Nothing was left but wet, black ash.

Kira lay back on the warm rock, wishing to have her blanket and one more spice cake. Her shivering subsided as her body soaked up the heat. For now that was enough.

She hoped Patala had gotten away. Even as she thought it, she knew it wasn't the case. Patala was a fighter, but those two warriors knew what they were doing. No, Patala would not have escaped. Kira just hoped she lived.

Maybe Te'Roan and Matusu had somehow escaped. The teacher was a strong fighter. He would have been able to match three or four warriors. If that other teacher was with them, Te'Roan's abilities might not help him. The other teacher certainly would have been trained. Matusu had no skill in fighting, but he was strong, at least as strong as a human.

A breeze picked up, a chilling reminder of the night to come. The sun was nearly touching the horizon, taking with it the heat of the day. Kira pulled her shirt tight around her. Her shoulder rebelled at the movement, followed by sharp pains from her ribs. She didn't yet attempt pulling the cloth away from the burning scrape on her hip. Everything was still damp, but not so wet. Her renewed body heat, she hoped, would help dry it. A shiver ran through her. Apparently, her body had not warmed up as much as she'd presumed.

Leaving the warmth of the rock, she stood to make her way to a fire tree. Stripping dry bark from its lower limbs would be a start toward constructing a nest to catch a spark. Every step from the rock to the tree brought an audible whimper. Thank the stars no one was around to hear it. Matusu would tease her. Oh, he'd offer to carry her, but burn him if he wouldn't mock her with every step.

And Patala would try to mother Kira. Not the kind of mothering that's tender and helpful – rather the kind that asserts itself as superior, more capable. What would Te'Roan do? He would probably pretend not to notice yet stop more often to make the trek bearable. And Father, he probably had some herb remedy that would take the string from her wounds. That's exactly what he would do, and she thought, what Te'Roan might also do. Maybe that's what made her want to trust him. He always seemed to focus on doing the right thing, just like Father. But he wasn't Father. And Kira had reason not to trust him.

Right now, whether she trusted him or not, she needed him to get to Thresdenal. And if she couldn't trust him, she more desperately needed Matusu and Patala. Tomorrow, Kira would go back. She would find them and somehow, some way rescue them.

Kira carefully pulled strips of bark from the tree and twisted them into a nest. She was careful not to knock loose the thin fibers that clung to the bark. As the little nest took shape in her hands, she rubbed the sides of the nest together, allowing the smaller fibers to gather loosely in the bottom. Setting it on the ground, she began working to get a spark from her flint and ore.

Kira's hands shook from cold and ached from holding the small stone. She could barely see through the gathering dark, when her first spark shot into the nest. It flared against the dry fibers and went out.

She had been at the point of giving up, but now resumed with more vigor. A few tries later, she got another spark, this one brighter and stronger. The little fibers in the nest held the spark and glowed with it. Kira could smell smoke, then it went out.

She continued aiming at the same spot. Charred material was more likely to hold the spark. Her downward strikes were losing their exactness. Twice she struck her thumb with the flint, tearing yet another wound to afflict her. The shaking in her hands spread. She hunched her shoulders against the cold, and setting down her flint, she cupped her hands to her mouth to warm them. She could still feel some afternoon warmth in the rock. If she could just stop the shaking, she could get the fire going. Laying down on the rock, she closed her eyes and in her mind recounted the things she needed to do to survive the night and find her sister tomorrow. Build the fire, keep feeding it with wood, only sleep when it was blazing, feed it with wood, walk back upriver, find Patala, fight the humans, feed the fire.

Kira could feel the warmth of the fire. She was so glad she had fed it well. It was so hard to start. She pulled her blanket tighter around her. It felt coarse. She stopped. Stopped moving, stopped breathing. She hadn't started the fire. This wasn't her blanket.

She opened her eyes just a bit. She saw the flames of the fire. It took her a second to focus. She looked beyond the flames. As the figure across the fire became clear, Kira woke completely. A cry let loose from her throat as she recoiled away from the fire against the rock face. The human sitting across the fire from her did not move.

Chapter 5

Away from the fire, the night was completely black, Kira couldn't see a way to get clear of the human. She started to her left, to escape into the night. He made no move to stop her.

She hadn't gone a dozen steps when the pain in her hip and knee became too great, and she stumbled to the ground. She looked back. The human still sat by the fire. His head turned toward her, watching her. Other than that, he made no move to stop her.

Kira felt the cold surround her. All her joints and muscles had stiffened during the night. If it were day, she could get moving, let the sun warm her and set a course back to the others. But now, stiff and cold, she would not get far. If this human was taking her prisoner, he only needed to wait until she fell unconscious again. Next time, he could bind her. Why hadn't he bound her? Did he believe she was too weak to escape? He may be right.

After watching her for a long moment, the human rose. Kira tried to rise thinking that he was coming for her. But he simple stepped around the fire and picked up the blanket that had covered Kira. He shook the dust from it and folded it. He walked toward Kira.

Kira rose again to get away. Dizzy with pain, she managed a few steps back. He stopped and held the blanket out to her. If this was his trap to lure her back for the warmth of a blanket, she wasn't falling for it. The human took a few steps closer, set the blanket on the ground, and walked back to the fire.

When the human was again seated in front of the fire, Kira stumbled forward and took the blanket. She walked away from the fire and around a boulder until she was out of sight of the human. Then she lowered herself to the ground against the boulder, wrapping the blanket around her shoulders and over her legs. She lifted a hand to clear a tear from her eye.

How stupid was that? I have to be strong, to rescue my sister, to find Matusu, and all I can do is cry like a stupid girl. Crying over a few bruises and a stupid blanket.

Kira woke as sunlight reflected off the tops of the rocks to the west of her. The place she sat was still shaded. She sat for a moment remembering the night. She flexed the muscles in her leg and hip. They hurt as much now as the night before. She would have to put some serious effort into standing. Next to her lay a flat stone with a small cake and some dried meat.

Kira tasted the cake. The grain was coarsely ground, but she couldn't detect any poisons. Most poisonous herbs that she knew of had a bitter taste. She also doubted that this human really needed to go to the trouble of poisoning her. She ate the small cake and then inspected the meat. It seemed to have been thoroughly dried and didn't smell odd. She ate it. After all, she thought, bad food really was the least of her problems.

No sooner had Kira finished the meat than the human appeared at a distance from behind the rock. Kira didn't jump up this time. She wasn't even certain she could. She just froze, watching him. He pointed back toward his little camp.

"Fire," he said and turned to walk away.

"Wait," Kira called. "Did you say 'fire'?"

He turned back. "Fire." He pointed again.

"Fire? You speak my language?"

"Teacher words," he nodded. "Yes. Fire." He turned and walked away.

Kira sat for a moment wondering what to do. Maybe she could talk with this human – figure out where she was, find the trail where her sister was taken. After all, he was a human. He could probably track them. But would he help her? To share some food and a blanket was not the same as risking his life. Besides, the morning was still cold, and although the blanket helped, a fire would help more.

Pushing against the boulder, Kira lifted herself to her feet. For the first couple of steps, she thought she would collapse. As she got her muscles and joints moving, the stiffness subsided. She still felt the burning in her hip each time she put weight on it, but walking with a bit of a limp made it bearable. She reached the fire and sat down across from the human. She kept the blanket wrapped tightly around her.

For the first time, she took a good look at this man who had, apparently, rescued her. He wasn't exactly old, though wrinkles had formed at the corners of his eyes and mouth. Unlike the long-haired humans who had attacked Kira's village, his hair was cut at his shoulder and held out of his face with a simple head band. He also wore a shirt and trousers. Kira could see a knife in his belt and a bow and quiver lying a few steps away from him.

He suddenly smiled.

Kira realized she must have been staring and looked away.

"Fire good." He crossed his arms around himself and rubbed his shoulders as if warming himself.

Kira nodded. "How do you know Keslin, my language, my words?" She asked.

"I know words from Te'Salanin. Te'Salanin and father friends."

"Your father was friends with a teacher? That's forbidden."

"Te'Salanin grow corn." He held up a small cake.

"He taught you to farm? Wow. Wisdom states that no…" Kira stopped. A discussion about her people's laws wasn't really going to get them anywhere. "Excuse me. That doesn't matter. I'm glad you speak Keslin. I am Kira." She pointed to herself.

"Iactah," he said pointing to himself

"How did you find me? Are you a tracker?"

Iactah laughed. "Good tracker. No find tracks. See you in sleep."

"You found me when I was sleeping?"

Iactah thought for a moment then shook his head. "No, I sleep. Many suns ago. I see you."

"A dream. You saw me in a dream while you slept?"

"A dream. Yes. See you. See river. See here."

"Did you see my sister? My friends?"

"Sister? No. I see you."

"Did you see how I got here? Can you help me find my sister?"

Iactah shook his head again. "I find you here now."

"Do you live near here?"

"Live?" He gave Kira a confused look. "I live. You live. Here, yes?"

"No. Is your village, your home, near here?"

"Home far walk. Many suns walk."

"Why? Why come all the way here?"

"Dream show I find you. I help you. You lost, no more. Now you go Thresdenal."

"You know where Thresdenal is? Have you been there?"

"I know Thresdenal path. I show you path."

Kira hadn't expected this. Going to Thresdenal was her plan, but not without the others. She needed to get to them first. "I can't go to Thresdenal," she said. "Not without my sister."

"You walk Thresdenal. Thresdenal your path to help the people"

"My sister was taken by humans at the river crossing. We have to go upriver and find her." She pointed upriver.

Iactah shook his head. It seemed that his only intention was to take her to Thresdenal. They sat in silence.

Every so often, Kira rose and walked slowly about the little hollow. They were close enough to still hear the river, but she didn't go near it. She feared that the other humans might have followed it downstream. She hoped they bypassed the little cut in the canyon where she had climbed out. Even better, she hoped they stayed to the other side of the river and that Patala had somehow been rescued by Matusu and Te'Roan. She could still hear Patala screaming at her to run.

Kira asked Iactah about his village and his family. From what little he said, she gathered that he was some kind of chief or councilor. Apparently, dreams among the elders of his people were not uncommon. A dream had told his father that a teacher was coming. So, they were not afraid when he showed up. Kira still thought it was odd that any teacher would share knowledge with a human. That was strictly forbidden. Wisdom taught them to avoid humans.

That night as Kira laid down, she found that naps during the day had left her less weary than the previous night when she had slipped unconscious. Where that night had been dreamless, as far as she could remember, this time she readied her mind to dream. She closed her eyes and meditated on her dream place. As she slipped from consciousness, a new consciousness came to life.

She stood on the rocks overlooking an empty Hochonal. She concentrated on the place by the stream where the reeds grew tall and suddenly stood before them. Pushing through them, she found no doorway, no hidden path to her father's dream world. Turning back, she looked around to see if anyone had entered her dream. The woman she had met was nowhere about. She knew Te'Roan could receive a dream, but she didn't know how to find him. She didn't even know if he was sleeping. If he and the others got free, they were probably traveling at night.

Kira returned to her starting place above the village. It looked peaceful, yet empty. Suddenly, a coyote wandered into the village, turned to look at her, and headed down the canyon. That was a first. Kira had seen animals before, but not one that paid any attention to her. Kira willed herself down to the canyon trail and followed the coyote. She followed the animal along dozens of turns and forks. At every point she thought she might lose sight of it, the coyote would stop and look back, as if assuring itself that she was looking.

The canyon eventually opened into a big rocky bowl where it converged with several other canyons and larger streams. There, on a sandy rise above one of the streams, stood a wood and mud hut. The coyote ran up the hill and laid down next to the hut. Kira walked up to it. She was a bit wary of the coyote, but it just sat there like a tame pet, tongue hanging from its mouth as it panted. Kira peered inside the hut. She could see blankets laid out on a mat of grass. It appeared to be empty. She stepped inside. And just as quickly as she stepped in, she was stepping out into the middle of a village.

Dozens of thatched huts were built around a central stone building. From where Kira stood, she could see into the open door of the stone building. Through the doorway, directly across from a small fire sat Iactah.

The coyote brushed by Kira's leg as it passed through the doorway. It trotted across to the stone building and entered through the door. It circled around behind Iactah, then came up to the man's shoulder and looked across the fire at Kira. Without warning the coyote leapt into the flames, a smoky shadow of the coyote rose from the fire and pranced in circles around the flames then up and out the smoke hole.

Kira walked to the low building, "Iactah, are you really here?"

The kindly human looked at her through the smoke. He smiled. "You speak the words of the People. You learn quickly."

"This is a dream, Iactah. We aren't really speaking. You hear my thoughts."

"Your thoughts sound like the words of the People. You have never spoken to me in the dream before. You slept where I found you. Then you walked with me to Thresdenal."

"That's because I wasn't really there in those dreams," Kira said. "This time I'm really here."

"I saw you then as I see you now. How were you not here then, but are here now?"

"Before, in your vision, that was a projection of me. Now my consciousness is actually here."

"All dreams are visions. All I see in dreams are visions that the spirits show me."

"But this is different because I am a dreamer. I can visit dreams and talk to people. I'd always been taught that I could only talk to others of my own people, but I guess no one ever met a human dreamer. Humans mostly just attack us."

"We are not the same as those who attacked you. We are separate. We would only fight to defend."

"I'm sorry. What are your people called?"

"The People."

"Well, that's pretty generic. We'll have to talk about this tomorrow when we're not just sharing thoughts.

"My people call themselves Thresden," Kira continued. "It refers to the place we originally come from. I'm not sure where it is, just that someday we'll return. My father says it's a place where water flows all around, and plants and moss grow on every patch of soil. This place, this desert, belongs to the humans, and I guess the People. My people stay hidden until it's time to return home."

"I do not think you need to hide. Te'Salanin helped us. He gave us corn, then showed us how to grow the corn. Many winters we had gone hungry. The children would cry for food. The old would die from hunger. We always moved. Sometimes others fought us and chased us away from their hunting grounds. Now we live safely and grow corn."

"Iactah, I am glad a teacher was able to help you. According to our laws, he was not supposed to."

"What law would stop a man from helping another? How can such a law be good?"

"I don't know." Kira looked into the fire and up at the smoke hole. "Iactah, did you see the coyote that was here earlier?"

"Yes, a spirit guide. Spirit guides often lead us to places in dreams."

"Did you see him jump into the fire?"

"He is spirit. Coyote, smoke, or wind, he is the same. My spirit guide led me to you and showed me the way to the path to Thresdenal."

"I know your vision said you would take me to Thresdenal, but can't you help me find my sister and my friends first?"

"I have been asking the spirits if that is right, if it is a part of my vision, but they have not shown that to me."

"What about what you want to do?"

"I want to follow the vision. That will best help the People."

"It seems that awake or asleep you are determined to take me to Thresdenal. Perhaps I'm actually here in your vision to ask you to help me find my sister and friends before going to Thresdenal."

Iactah smiled, "If that were so, you would be the spirit guide. The spirit guide led you here to test my resolve to follow my vision."

Smoke began to pour from the fire obscuring Kira's vision. She waved it from in front of her face. When the smoke dissipated, Kira found herself sitting in front of a small fire on the rock ledge overlooking Hochonal. Iactah and the stone building were gone.

Waking in the early morning light, Kira looked around for Iactah, but couldn't see him anywhere. The fire was still burning, so he must have added wood to it recently. She sat up and pulled the blanket around her.

She pulled her leg up toward her and stretched it out. The stiffness was still there, but it was definitely better than the day before. She knew she would have a long way to go. She wondered how to tell Iactah that she was going back for her sister. She knew he wouldn't help her, but she hoped he would wait for her.

The more she thought about going back, the more she realized she had no idea what to do once she found Patala. She would have surprise on her side. She doubted the humans expected her to come back. They probably thought she was dead. Patala probably thought she was dead. The last time Patala saw Kira, she was floating into a canyon fighting off a human warrior. But what good would surprise really do her. Even a surprised human warrior was enough to overpower her with very little trouble. If she ever got out of this mess, she would learn to fight like Te'Roan and her father.

But now, fighting was not an option. She would have to find them and sneak her sister and any others away unseen.

She limped about the little hollow collecting wood and feeding the fire as she waited for Iactah. A few dozen steps loosened up her hip and knee. She could almost walk without a limp. She wouldn't be doing any rock climbing for a while.

The day was half over when Iactah arrived. He was breathing heavy. Sweat beaded on his forehead and stained his shirt. Kira stood and snatched up her bag and the blanket, ready to flee from whatever might be chasing him.

Iactah simply dropped to his usual spot by the fire and breathed deeply as though trying to catch his breath.

"Where did you go?" Kira asked. "Why are you running?"

"I run river crossing. Many tracks. Three dead men...all human. Find woman track. Woman follow man. Other man follow woman. All teacher together."

"Which way, where did they go?"

"Follow river. Other side."

Kira rose to go toward the river. Iactah raised a warning hand. "Men watch river. One walk river this side. Pass in night. Before I find you. Other watches crossing. I watch. He not see."

Kira suddenly realized how close she came to getting caught again. Had she started her fire earlier that night, it would have led them right to her. If her sister was walking on her own with two men, all teachers, that had to be Te'Roan and Matusu. They must have rescued her from the humans. The warriors were probably trying to head them off at another crossing down river.

Following the river along those broken cliffs must be a hard journey. Kira didn't envy the climbing they would have to do. If she was back with them, if she'd gotten out on the other side of the river, she would be slowing them down. Maybe now that they wouldn't be looking for her, her slower pace wouldn't put anyone in danger.

She suddenly realized what Iactah wanted was her best option. "We need to move away from the river. If they double back looking for a crossing, they may find us. You were right, we need to go to Thresdenal."

Iactah started to rise, then sat again. "We go when I breathe... less."

After breathing a few moments, he said, "Oanit."

"What?" Kira asked.

"Oanit means the People."

Kira smiled. She had wondered if he remembered the dream.

When Iactah had sufficiently caught his breath, they started out. If Kira had thought following Te'Roan was difficult, following Iactah pushed toward the edge of impossible. He moved like no one Kira had ever seen. He seemed to skim smoothly over the roughest terrain, never slowing to work out his next step. Which was doubly amazing since he never looked down. His feet just seemed to sense the ground before him.

From the start it became evident that Kira would not be able to maintain his pace, even injury free. Iactah began scouting ahead, then coming back to check on Kira. Kira would just walk to the place she had last seen him, then look ahead to where he showed himself at the next rise. Kira trudged on.

After coming over a rise about mid-day, Kira saw Iactah sitting under a tree, eating. She walked to the tree and sat next to him in the shade. A moment's respite from the sun and the pain in her hip and leg allowed her time to think and to examine her clothing. She had used cloth from the tail of her shirt and her sash to wrap the torn openings over her legs, and to her surprise, her hood had stayed intact. Her shoes were holding together, but wearing quickly.

If Te'Roan led the others downstream on the other side of the river and Thresdenal was on this side of the river, they would have to cross eventually. The humans who followed the river must know this. They would find likely places to cross and set more traps. They were down to fewer men, but what if they had reinforcements. Te'Roan seemed to think the humans would come around the lower end of the plateau along the main road to Thresdenal. If more had come, the warriors on this side simply had to keep Te'Roan from crossing until the reinforcements arrived.

Matusu sat guard over their little camp while Te'Roan scouted ahead. They had hidden for most of the day and intended to travel in the late afternoon and evening. Patala was still asleep, though once in a while she would partly wake, sob, and fall back to sleep. She seemed as horrified by the bodies left behind as she was by the loss of Kira.

When Te'Roan and Jornatha had fought at the village, they gave many chances for their attackers to retreat. This time had been different. After incapacitating the man who had attacked him, the teacher had made an offensive attack on Patala's captors as they tried to drag her to the river crossing. He left them no quarter. Matusu had been right behind him as they rushed the men from the brush. The teacher attacked both men simultaneously. As his knife slit the throat of one, his foot crushed the chest of the other. Before the second man could rise to his feet, Te'Roan grappled the warrior's head and let his limp body drop to the ground. Two of their party standing on the other side of the river saw the quick demise of their companions and retreated into the brush.

When Patala told them of Kira's fate, Matusu wanted to swim after her. Te'Roan convinced them they had a better chance of intercepting her by land. The way had been rough and rocky, often taking them far from the water as the river plunged into an ever-deepening gorge. Each time they found a place to overlook the river, they would watch and wait. Hoping they had somehow gotten ahead of her or that she had managed to climb onto a rock or ledge.

The longer they followed the river, the rougher it became until they realized that their worst fear was the most likely. Patala had finally accepted that conclusion as the sun rose that morning. That's when Te'Roan left the two of them there with his water and bag.

Te'Roan sat in the shade of a twisted fire tree overlooking the river. The water rumbled far below him. His main concern now was the activity he'd detected on the other side of the river. The humans didn't leave. One seemed to shadow Te'Roan and his two remaining wards. He wasn't heavily armed but looked lean and fast – a scout perhaps. The other no doubt remained to watch the crossing. Didn't they know they had already stolen the prize? His single order had been to deliver Kira to Thresdenal. Although he had probably saved Patala and Matusu from a horrible fate, his mission had failed. His thoughts now had to turn to surviving – surviving to face dishonor in the council chamber at Thresdenal.

This had turned into a disaster. He had a simple mission to convince Jornatha to bring his youngest daughter to Thresdenal. Two teachers and four guards accompanying one girl on the well-beaten path. What could go wrong?

Watching the humans, he could see that the men had chosen a spot where they could see movement downstream between the river and mesa. These men who attacked them were no ordinary humans. They weren't a simple raiding party. They had targeted Hochonal, and now they targeted Te'Roan's group. In fact, they seemed to target Patala and Kira specifically. What was driving them?

When they reached the end of the mesa, the river would cross the road between Hochonal and Thresdenal – the trail they had hoped to intercept by cutting across the desert. Below that, Te'Roan knew of no other place to cross. If these humans were part of the group that attacked Hochonal, a larger force may be waiting in ambush where the river met the trail.

Once again, Te'Roan closed his eyes and meditated. He sought the dream state where he could hear Ka'Te'Losa. "By the stars, speak to me." Time slipped by as he waited, open to the touch of a dreamer. Any dreamer from Thresdenal reaching out to him. "I have failed, but lives still hang upon my actions."

The sun was low when Te'Roan opened his eyes. The humans still held vigil on the other side of the river. When it was dark enough, he would go back and lead Patala and Matusu downriver. What else could he do?

Kira was ready to quit walking for the day and hoped Iactah came back for her. She had stopped three times to find shade from the afternoon heat, and he hadn't come back. Every time she started moving again, he showed himself ahead, guiding the way. The sun had dropped behind the hills, and the terrain was getting difficult to navigate. As she cleared a rise, she saw firelight reflecting from a covey of rocks at the bottom of a little hollow.

She would have run to it if she thought she could do it without injuring herself further. Iactah sat beside the fire roasting something on a stick. On closer inspection, Kira could see it was a large lizard. She'd heard that some humans ate crickets, so sharing a reptile with an Oanit wasn't a bad option.

"Is there enough for two, or do I need to catch my own?"

Iactah lifted a leafy branch next to him, and there lay another lizard waiting to be cooked. He handed Kira a sharpened stick.

After several awkward attempts to imitate the way Iactah had lanced his kill, Kira opted for down the throat. "May the stars take you," she whispered as she rammed the stick through.

The next morning's trudge felt easier than the day before. The terrain stayed pretty much the same, though Kira felt like the washes were shallower as they approached the mountains. Iactah stayed ahead showing himself now and then as if he instinctively knew when Kira was losing his path. They followed a fairly direct line across the desert toward the distant hills. A couple of times, they had veered off of their line, walking up a wash or following a rock outcropping. These side excursions brought them to water, usually in a natural rock pool. Once, Iactah dug into the sand at the base of a box canyon and within a few moments, water filled the hole.

The stiffness in Kira's hip seemed to fade the more she walked. If they stopped too long, she would stiffen again. Her shoes were still holding up, though she knew they wouldn't last more than a few days at this rate.

On the morning of the fifth day from the river, Iactah gave Kira the skins from two rabbits he had caught a couple days earlier. He had cut strips from the edges of the skins. He showed Kira how to wrap them over her woven shoes to keep sand out.

"Rabbit wear fast," he said. "Deer better."

"How many more days to Thresdenal?" Kira asked as she finished tying the second skin over her foot.

"Thresdenal over." Iactah gestured to the mountain. "We walk path. You walk Thresdenal."

"Why can't you take me all the way? Are you not allowed in Thresdenal?"

"Dream only show to path." Iactah slung his small bag over his head and shoulder and began walking.

Kira hurried to catch up with him. "How can a dream tell you what you're supposed to do?" She asked.

"Spirit guide show what is."

"I don't understand. How can you see something that hasn't happened?"

"Close eyes." Iactah stopped and pointed to her eyes. "Close eyes."

Kira closed her eyes.

"See place walked yesterday. Yes?"

"Yes. You mean a memory. You see the future like a memory?"

"Like memory. Yes."

Kira opened her eyes. "Can you see what's going to happen when I get to Thresdenal? Will my sister and Matusu be there?"

Iactah shook his head. "No. See my path. Like see my memories. Your memories, your path. I not see."

"How far ahead can you see?" Kira was nearly jogging now to keep up with the Oanit's pace.

"I see where spirit guide show."

Kira drifted back to her normal pace, thinking on how his vision was possible. Part of her would say it was superstition, but Iactah had known when and where to find her, like he said. He followed the dream with exactness because he believed it was what must be. But if the dream showed what must be, was the dream necessary at all. Without the dream, he would not have traveled so far to find her and then the dream would not be a prediction of the future as much as instruction for the future.

Kira ran the idea around and around in her mind as she trudged. It made time pass more quickly. About mid-day they reached the edge of sand dunes. They rested in the shade of what looked to be the last tree they would see before reaching the mountains. The dunes stretched out ahead of them, void of the smallest bushes.

"We wait and walk in the shadows," Iactah said.

Kira could understand waiting if it was summer. The heat on that sand would be unbearable. But this time of year, it wasn't overly warm. "It's not too hot to keep going," she said.

"Here in rock and tree, hard see. On sand, easy see."

"You think the other humans are still following us?"

Iactah nodded.

"Have you seen them?"

Iactah shook his head. "Later, run from them."

"Maybe we should start running now."

Iactah smiled. "You run in sand. I watch and laugh."

Kira sipped water from her bag. Whenever they found water Iactah drank more than she thought a man could hold. Yet he took very little from his bag. She wandered if maybe his body stored water somehow.

As the sun neared the horizon, they started across the dunes. The wind built up and got strongest at sundown. Iactah's pace slowed in the deep sand, but Kira's slowed even more. They seemed to stay on ridges most of the time. Kira found that if they walked a little to the upwind side, the sand was more compact. Although the wind never let up completely, the cool of evening seemed to take it down to a mild breeze. It was late in the night when they finally stopped to rest. They descended the leeward side of a dune, out of the wind, and settled into the soft sand. Iactah handed Kira his blanket and said, "You sleep. I watch. No fire."

Kira laid back in the cold sand and looked up at the stars. She went through the stories in her head, remembering how her father and uncle would act out the Battle of Rounsoom for the children of Hochonal. Her father had told her that the stars themselves played out the story as their galactic motion brought Trothril's Needle closer to the Eye of Rounsoom. She knew that the dim Needle was really much farther away than the bright Eye. Their close proximity in the sky was just an illusion. The light from the Needle's tip, her father once told her, had traveled over a thousand years longer than the light from the Eye.

Kira woke to Iactah's hand on her shoulder. It was still dark. The moon had risen.

"We walk in shadow and rest in light," he said.

The trudge resumed. The moon created a faint outline of the distant hills that were their destination. Near sunrise, they reached a rocky outcropping in the middle of the dunes. They found no vegetation or water, but the rocks provided some protection from the increasing wind and would shade them after the sun crossed its peak.

Kira climbed to the top of the rounded red stones to see across the dunes. It looked to her like they had come more than half way across the dunes. They had crossed at what appeared to be a narrow section of the vast, sandy waste. If they followed the same schedule as the previous night, they would easily make it across by morning.

They started out as the shadows lengthened. The afternoon wind picked up as before. Only this time, it didn't abate with the cooling evening. Instead, it rose higher, pulling up the sand as it blew.

Iactah had tied a cloth up around his face to cover his nose and mouth. Kira had her face guard up over her nose and mouth and her hood pulled down close to protect from the stinging blasts. Iactah began taking lower paths on the lee side of the dunes. The sand was softer and harder to walk through but gave them a little reprieve from the direct force of the wind.

They hadn't traveled nearly as long as the night before when Iactah halted at the base of a dune. Kira sat in the soft sand, between the cold wind and the suffocating sand, she was already exhausted. No stars shown. Even when the moon rose, she knew it would only add a faint, imperceptible glow to the darkness they travelled in. Kira leaned back on the sand. Within moments, she felt the drifts settling around her. How long would it take to cover her if she didn't move? She imagined the dune settling down upon her, hiding her in its trackless expanse.

Kira woke beneath a dark canopy a few inches from her face. Light filtered through the cloth, alleviating her fear that she was buried under a dune. Turning her head, she saw an arrow pushed into the ground, serving as a post for the makeshift blanket shelter. Another arrow served as a post on the other side of her head. Kira reached to edge of the blanket and pulled it away.

Iactah sat nearby. Kira looked at him and shook sand from her hair. He smiled. Sand pooled about him as though he had remained in the same position through most of the storm. Of course, he must have moved about a bit to put the shelter over Kira. He walked over to Kira, picked up the blanket and shook the sand from it. He pulled the arrows from the ground and returned them to his quiver. Throwing the blanket over his shoulder, he started walking.

"Wait," Kira said. "Shouldn't we eat first?"

"Wind return."

Kira didn't need any more encouragement than that. Her appetite retreated at the thought of spending another night in a blinding sandstorm.

She ran to catch up with Iactah. "Do you have any water left?"

Iactah shook his head. He pointed to the hills ahead of them. "Water there."

Unlike the previous two days where they stopped during the brightest part of the day, this time, they continued on. Kira knew that the situation grew desperate. By mid-afternoon the wind had picked up again. Again, the fierce blasts tugged at her clothes and blinded her view. She had to turn her head away glancing up only occasionally to make sure she still followed Iactah.

Near sundown, they reached a rock outcropping. The first in a series of rising formations that sloped up, away from the sandy basin. Iactah led the way upward through the twisting labyrinth of stone. Vegetation formed in pockets of trapped soil. Soon they came to a small pool sheltered by overhanging rocks. Both Kira and Iactah knelt by the water and drank deeply. Kira lost count of how many times she brought her cupped hands to her mouth. The water had a stale brackish taste, but it was wet. Like so much standing water in the desert, it was not so old as it seemed. Such small tanks lasted no more than a few days. This one probably filled during the rains that passed before Kira was separated from Patala and the others.

Iactah filled his water bag and started out in a new direction. He veered left off their previous path and began traveling parallel to the hills. He was heading for the path he had told Kira about, the path that led to Thresdenal. There he would leave her to find her way alone. Entering Thresdenal alone had never been part of Kira's plan. Her father had meant to take her there himself, to show her the city where he had lived and studied many years before. Then he had handed the task over to another, a teacher he trusted.

Now she must enter the city alone. She knew no one there. How would she know where to go, what to do? Iactah seemed to know she would go there, but beyond his own escort to the pass, he offered no help or additional information. She would enter in worn out shoes and wind sheered rags, no more than a lost orphan. She would enter a city filled with people, her people, and yet she felt more alone than ever.

That night, Kira tried to dream. Every time she saw her dream place, the rocks above Hochonal, the dream would fade to her imagined fears. She saw a deep valley with cliffs rising high around her. The cliffs were filled with dwellings. Dark eyes from the windows, looked down on her. Children pointed, she looked down at the dirty rags that hung from her, shoes no more than strands of twisted grass, clinging about her ankles. Children scoffed from the windows. Mothers just shook their heads. Cliffs rose in every direction. There seemed to be no end to the dwellings. All the populace of Thresdenal looked down on her with scorn.

Kira woke in a sweat, calmed herself, and tried to dream again. She must find someone. Her sister, her father, even the strange woman from her father's dream. Again, her dreaming was replaced with visions of her fears. By morning, Kira was as tired as though she had not slept at all.

Iactah arrived at their camp carrying a hare that must have been caught in one of the traps he set the night before. As he skinned it out, Kira went to work getting the fire going.

"How much longer until we reach the path to Thresdenal?" She asked.

"Soon. Today. End of today."

Kira knew she should be happy to return, to maybe find her sister, but some part of her no longer believed that was a possibility. She knew that an army of humans led by a teacher, a traitor, stood against Patala, Matusu, and Te'Roan. They were not likely to make it. And

Hochonal had probably been destroyed soon after they had left. Just like in her dreams, she was alone – except for Iactah.

"Maybe I shouldn't go to Thresdenal," she said. "Maybe I should go with you to your village. I saw it in the dream. I could go with you there. I could cook and work – be part of your people."

Iactah paused from skinning the hare and seemed to think for a moment. "No. You walk Thresdenal. I walk home."

"But what am I to do in Thresdenal? I don't know anyone. How will I eat? Will I beg in the street? All I know is my little village. I will have no place there."

"Thresdenal important. Spirit guide show."

"Why? Why does it matter to you?"

"Save the People."

"Whatever I do in Thresdenal isn't going to help the Oanit. That teacher, the one who taught your father to grow corn, he was never even supposed to talk to your father. We have laws against it. In Thresdenal, they train teachers to teach our people. They teach us to stay away from humans."

"Maybe Te'Salanin follow vision. Maybe he teach father then I save you."

"My people don't have visions."

"You dream. I see you."

"Yes, we dream. We visit each other's dreams while they happen. We don't see the future. The teacher who you knew was rebelling against the law. He was a traitor to wisdom."

Iactah looked at Kira. "Friend. He teach grow, share, work, help."

"I'm sure he meant well, he just…" Kira wasn't sure what to say. The teacher who taught Iactah's people had done good things. And yet wisdom taught them not to do those things. "He just didn't do what he was taught." The words sounded hollow to her. Her father and mother had taught her wisdom. They would know what to say. There was much they still had to teach her that she didn't understand.

"Some human learn kill people different than him. When I meet him, I hope he does not kill." The kindly Oanit positioned the hare to roast over the fire.

After eating and burying the fire, they were back to crossing a long series of low ridges and gullies as they travelled along the base of the hills. Iactah stayed farther ahead than usual. At one point, Kira spied him lying at the crest of ridge cautiously peering over. She froze and waited as he made his way over the top. They must be nearing the place where they must run from the humans.

As Kira traversed the ridge, in the distance, she could make out a trail on the valley floor. It wound toward the hills they skirted. She was certain they intersected. This must be the main trail to Thresdenal, the one they would have taken had humans not been pursuing them. The trail wound along among hills and through shallow arroyos. It must be fairly wide to be seen from this distance. If this was the path to Thresdenal, it would not be hard to follow. It would also not be long until Iactah sent her on her way alone.

At every rise, Kira scanned the trail, hoping that she might see Patala and Matusu and, at the same time, fearing she might see the pursuing warriors. It didn't take long for Iactah and Kira's route to intersect the trail. The Oanit waited for Kira near a large boulder that hid him from the trail.

"Wait," he said. "six men hide up path. They wait for us walk path."

"Can't we go around them?"

Iactah shook his head. "They watch hill and valley. We wait for shadows. I lead them away, you follow path." He pointed up between two hills.

"What if they catch you?"

Iactah smiled. "They not catch."

"Right. You dreamed it. Handy knowing the future." Kira sat down next to Iactah, back against the sandstone boulder. The slope above them was mostly a blend of red and white sandstone with black volcanic rocks scattered across its surface. The slanting light cast long shadows across the slope. Kira could feel a gentle afternoon breeze on her cheek, hear it rustling the branches on the sparse brush that grew in the bottom of the valley. Darkness was coming again.

A few days ago, Kira would avoid going out in the dark. She hated seeing the sun go down, hated waiting for the long evening to pass. Now she looked forward to the darkness. The cover it would bring. She was no longer afraid of what might be around her in the dark. Rather she feared what might see her in the light.

After Iactah slipped away into the night, Kira pulled her blanket around her and tried to disappear in the shadow of the boulder. He had told her to wait until the moon reached its peak, then follow the trail into the hills. Where the trail ended, he had said to follow the way of the rock.

The moon shadows were now as small as they would get. She hoped Iactah's plan had worked, that the warriors had followed him away from her. How had they known she would come this way? How had they found her again and again? The thought of the teacher who had been with the humans continued to nag at her. Why would he help them? What did he want with travelers from Hochonal?

Knowing that the night would get no darker, she moved out toward the path to Thresdenal.

Chapter 6

As Kira started down toward the trail, she felt like that teacher was still waiting for her somewhere. What if he was a step ahead of her still? What if he allowed Iactah to think he had led away the only humans?

Kira didn't walk directly on the trail. Rather, she stayed above it, moving from rock to rock. She kept the trail in sight and followed it toward the looming hills. She knew she could make better time on the trail, but it didn't feel safe. The humans were numerous, and the traitor teacher would know the best spots to ambush her.

The eastern sky showed a faint glow as Kira approached the point where the trail led up a narrow canyon into the mountains. The ground around the trail was becoming too steep to traverse. She would be forced to walk the main trail. Creeping close enough to hear a foot fall, she waited in the shadow of a fire tree. The way seemed clear, but how to know for certain? The darkness that protected her would not last. She realized that moving now would at least give her a good chance to escape back into the dark if someone was waiting for her.

As she crept out onto the trail, the brush on the far side of the canyon rustled. Kira froze, hoping that enough shadow still enveloped her that she would be hidden from the watcher. A rabbit hopped from the brush and darted down the trail. Kira slowly let out her breath and quietly jogged up the trail into the canyon.

The walls of the canyon rose on each side. If someone waited to capture her, she would have no escape but back the way she had come. A single follower could quickly cut off her retreat.

The light of day began to filter into the canyon at an almost imperceptible rate. Soon, the rim of the canyon glowed with golden light from the rising sun. The canyon continued to rise on a winding route into the mountain. At a bend in the trail, Kira saw something that was both comforting and disquieting. High on the rock, figures had been etched, figures that humans would not understand, but Kira's people would know at a glance.

The figures were of two men and a bird. The small man was Corinad the Brave. The tall man was Ariste Destroyer with his rod in his right hand. The bird was called Ren'Cravest, the eyes of heaven. The story was a long tale, but the meaning of the drawing was clear. It said, The way is watched that the brave may pass, but the destroyer may not. Kira wondered whose eyes were upon her. Were they the eyes of a friend. Kira stayed to the side of the trail that offered the most cover.

Soon she started to encounter small pools of water in the bottom of the canyon. A little further on, a small trickle of water worked its way along the canyon floor. She stopped and drank. This was the kind of water she preferred, a gentle trickle moving from pool to pool. She never wanted to see another river. In a couple of spots, the canyon widened out a bit. Sand shelves pushed up by seasonal water offered a path above the little stream. Then the canyon abruptly ended. Walls of rock encircled a little pool, fed by a trickle coming from a cleft at the base of the wall.

Kira stood for a moment, looking around. The stained walls revealed the seasonal floods that cascaded spring runoff along their faces. Small patches of moss and grass clung to clefts in the rock. Kira could see no way up. The walls on either side continued straight up for hundreds of spans and the wall before her at least half that. As skilled as she was at climbing, she could see nothing on which to gain purchase to begin a climb. As she turned in circles studying the rock, she notice that high up on the right wall, figures were etched in the rock. Again, they weren't anything a human would recognize. No arrow pointed the way out. Instead, the etching displayed a solitary figure holding a thick staff with a circle at the end. A star was positioned above one shoulder. Below his right foot was a mound and under his left foot a wave. This was Cor in the story of the star guide.

Kira looked down the canyon, wondering if the warriors had followed her. Perhaps the rock etchings scared them away. She didn't like the idea of walking all the way back down this canyon. She moved down the canyon a little ways and secluded herself in some tall grass. She had a clear view for a little way down the canyon – not that it would do her much good.

Why would somebody dangle from a rope on a sheer cliff face to etch the figure of Cor in the rock? And why that figure of Cor? It wasn't even the most heroic story. He didn't fight any battles. In fact, most of the story is dull repetition, as Cor sails up and down the same waterway searching for the passage to paradise. His crew nearly mutinies because he won't stop looking. Then one night, he has a dream about a red star. He wakes in the night and sees the star that guides him to a narrow, hidden passage. The narrow waterway leads deeper into the mountain to the shore of paradise.

Maybe it's a message. Maybe a traveler is supposed to wait until dark and follow a red star. Perhaps it's the star that the storyteller always points out when telling that particular story. Of course, the star lies close to the horizon, so said traveler would also have to be here on the right day at the right time of night for that star to be a useful guide. What are the odds? Maybe the artist also etched some clues about the date to look for the star. Kira had always liked watching the stars. She had most of their positions memorized. It wouldn't be hard to figure out the position the star should in be if she knew the date. Returning to the pool at the end of the canyon, Kira began scanning the walls for more markings.

Finally, sitting in the sand leaning back on her outstretched arms, neck aching, Kira concluded that nothing on that wall indicated a date. She stared up at the figure of Cor. He had been etched at a slight angle. The way he showed in the winter sky – the star over his shoulder. As she stared, it suddenly dawned on her, a passing thought she had when she first saw the etching. The star was over the wrong shoulder. In the night sky, the star shown above Cor's left shoulder. This figure showed the star over his right.

Kira jumped up. That was the clue. It wasn't the right date or right story she needed to know. It was the piece of the story – in this case the star that was wrong.

Kira hurried down the canyon to where the trickle of water flowed into the sand. Instead of looking up the trail, following the water as she had the first time, she returned holding to the right side of the canyon. She soon found a diagonal break in the rock. A shelf, the width of her foot, ascended at a gradual slope up the canyon wall. It blended in so well that she never would have noticed it had she not been holding so close to the right side of the wall.

Within a few steps, the shelf widened to an easily walkable trail. In no time, Kira was a hundred spans above the canyon. Looking down on the little stream, she neared the height of the rock face that had boxed her in. She could see the stream continue in the upper canyon. She focused her attention back on the climb ahead of her.

After days of walking, she had stopped noticing the injuries from the river. Now the added strain of climbing and the added stretching and flexing brought back the sharp pain in her bruised hip. The shelf continued higher, presenting no other way back down into the canyon, until it ended just below a ridge. Looking up the ridge to the head of the canyon, she saw a well-worn path heading toward what looked to be a low pass through the mountains.

The way to the pass was clear. More trees added shade to the path. Kira stopped briefly to rub out the stiffness from her leg. She hoped to clear the pass and find shelter before dark. Late in the afternoon, she reached the summit of the pass. Looking down, she first gasped, then wept, then laughed. Had she not been so exhausted, she would have run the rest of the way.

Matusu sat the watch motionless, nestled in the shadow of an overhanging ledge, behind the cover of a fire tree, far up on the bluff that overlooked the river crossing. This was the place where the main trail from Hochonal swung around the southern edge of the mesa to meet a wide ford in the river. On their arrival nearly two days ago, Te'Roan had pointed out the positions of humans who waited in ambush at the ford.

From what the teacher said, this was the only safe point of crossing south of their first attempt and the quickest way to Thresdenal. He seemed to think this was part of the same group who attacked Hochonal. Perhaps they were trying to cut off any who would try to escape to Thresdenal. They went way beyond what any of them had expected to ambush Matusu and his friends.

During the attack at the upper ford, their main focus seemed to be Kira and Patala. Why them? There were many more girls in the village that could be taken without traveling for days across the desert. It was obvious from the beginning that getting the girls to Thresdenal – or should he say getting Kira to Thresdenal – had been Te'Roan's main mission, one he would have undertaken alone. Now they were down to escorting Patala, and everything about Te'Roan's demeanor had changed. He had shifted from speedy flight to cautious reconnaissance. He would disappear He would disappear, forcing them to hold position all day and travel at night.

Where he used to take every opportunity to teach Matusu about travel, the stars, and what might await him at Thresdenal. Now the solemn teacher only let slip occasional clues as to what was on his mind. "They're too organized," he had said after returning from the river. "This is no human raid," he muttered as he slipped out of camp that morning. If not a human raid, what was it?

Matusu's eyes were drawn to motion below. Four humans charged across the river, splashing with high step lunges until the depth of the water slowed their progress. On the other side, six more came out of hiding from exactly the spots Te'Roan had pointed out. After watching those positions all day, Matusu had started to doubt the teacher. The ten men conversed beside the river, then one of them ran off to the south. The others moved into the shade and waited, apparently no longer interested in hiding their presence.

Matusu waited. He would hurry back to camp in a moment, but he wanted to see what became of the one that had run off. The answer to that question didn't take long to answer. Another group emerged from the brush below the ford. Matusu counted seventeen additional warriors.

Now Matusu had something to report. He slowly rose to a crouched position not taking his eyes off the group of humans. He was too far away for them to hear his movements, but he didn't want to take any chances. Quick movements catch the eye, yet the movement of stars goes unnoticed. Matusu was about to turn and retreat below the ledge, when motion below froze him in place. The teacher, his cloak draped about him, walked out of the brush right up to the group of humans. Matusu held his breath waiting for the attack. But no attack came. Two of them faced the teacher and bowed their heads. They were two of the humans who had just crossed the river. The teacher clapped one on the shoulder as though he were a friend.

Matusu couldn't move, couldn't breathe. His stomach knotted as he thought of Te'Roan betraying them. Was this all to deliver them to the humans? Was the fight a rouse to get them to trust him? But Te'Roan had fought and even killed humans.

The teacher reached up and lowered his hood. Golden hair streaked with green waved about his shoulders in the evening breeze. It wasn't Te'Roan. He was certainly no human either. One of their own had betrayed them. Matusu drew a breath of relief that it wasn't Te'Roan, to whom he'd trusted his life and the life of his friends.

Matusu slipped quietly below the ledge and up through a small split of rock out of sight from below. He quickly made his way back to camp along a route that took advantage of the cover offered by the broken hillside. Te'Roan was at camp when Matusu arrived. By the sweat on the man's face, he hadn't been back long.

"Te'Roan, the humans have come out of hiding and gathered by the ford. They are about thirty strong. And they have…" Matusu didn't quite know how to put it.

"They have what?" Te'Roan asked.

"They have a teacher with them."

Patala gasped.

"Or at least a Thresden who wears a teacher's cloak," Matusu added.

"Show me," Te'Roan said and started toward the overlook.

Patala followed.

As they approached the crack that led below the ledge and the hidden overlook, Patala waited as Te'Roan and Matusu crept into position. The humans were crossing the river in a single line, the teacher trailed behind them, his robe bundled under his arm.

"Te'Tregalt," Te'Roan said in almost a whisper. "I knew this was no human raid. They never would have followed us this far. Nor would they have brought such a force against Hochonal."

"Who is he?"

"A fool. A clever, dangerous, old fool."

Under the cover of darkness, Te'Roan led Patala and Matusu down to the river crossing. Patala had expressed concern about following such a large group of humans, but Te'Roan had ignored her and pressed forward. He wished he could safely leave the two of them. Alone, he could quickly skirt the human force, get to Thresdenal and return to capture the traitor before he regrouped with the rest of the humans. Te'Roan was fairly certain that the main body was still making its way from Hochonal by the main trail, which put Te'Roan and his two remaining wards directly between enemy forces. That would soon change, just not as quickly as Te'Roan preferred.

He wished he had time to converse with Ka'Te'Losa by dream. She had been reaching out to him each day as he meditated. She would want to know about this, but he didn't dare waste time. His urgent need to get back to Thresdenal had suddenly returned in the form of a new mission. A traitor was responsible for the loss of Kira and all that she represented to their people. Te'Roan would see personally that the traitor paid.

After they crossed the river, Te'Roan led them up river into broken country then proceeded away from the river parallel to the trail. It was rough going, but he had been right to be wary of the human force. Tregalt would no doubt set sentinels a good distance from his camp. He was surprised that no watchmen had ventured up to the overlook. They had seemed confident that holding the ford would accomplish their purpose.

Te'Roan made a cold camp. Patala and Matusu wrapped in blankets to await the dawn. They had only been risking fires in the morning light, when the glow was least likely to be seen. And even then, the fires were kept small and fueled by only the driest wood. Enough fire to cook a few small cakes or roots for the day.

Te'Roan didn't bother to check his map anymore. This close to the main trail, he knew the way. He would cut across country parallel to the trail. Matusu was getting better at looking about and noticing routes, but a meeting with the humans would still be more than he and Patala could handle. Te'Roan would have to stay with them. He would shepherd them to Thresdenal, and he would have to push them to travel quickly. He had considered setting them on the direction of travel and dropping back to deal with the traitor, but Ka'Te'Losa would not approve. She was very strict about not administering justice one on one. Teachers were to engage the might of the council and guards to bring in rogue citizens, especially rogue teachers.

The route they followed was not as straight as Te'Roan would have liked. He often had to take a less direct path to avoid being seen from the main trail. If Tregalt were truly aware of Te'Roan's destination, he would send a force ahead to guard the path up to the pass. Te'Roan's path would have to converge on that path to get back to Thresdenal. Tregalt was obviously unaware they had lost Kira.

Each day of silent travel brought them closer to the point where Te'Roan would have to make a critical move to get Matusu and Patala past the human forces.

"Why would a teacher choose to fight against us," Matusu asked. "They teach wisdom and work to protect the people."

"It's complicated." Te'Roan seemed to struggle to find the right way to explain. "The purpose of wisdom is to protect the people until the gathering. But there are some who have lost hope in the gathering. They are pushing to change wisdom and gain leadership over humans before they grow too numerous and powerful to resist."

"Like building up dikes before the flood comes." Matusu looked thoughtful. "That may not be a bad thing."

"Except that humans are not water to be channeled. And we don't have the right to use our knowledge to subjugate them."

"Shouldn't those with knowledge lead those without?"

"Setting ourselves up as their superiors would ultimately destroy us and likely them. Giving them what we know all at once would drown them. Humans need time to gain the knowledge for themselves and adapt their culture as the knowledge evolves. Separation and patience – that is wisdom."

"And what of the gathering? When is that supposed to start?"

"There are things that need to happen. A mystic might view them as signs. They are really prerequisites. We have to get certain things done before we can begin the gathering. The hidden villages, like Hochonal need to stay hidden until we are prepared."

"What things?"

"Things that would sound crazy to you."

"Crazier than a top that shows a map?"

"Sleep a bit, we will move on before it's light."

Kira looked out over a valley filled with fields and dotted with dwellings. The valley was rimmed with mountains like the one on which she stood. At the center, past more fields and villages than she could count at a glance, stood a lone mesa. It wasn't a broad tree-topped mesa like the one they had climbed, but a singular stone tower. Broad lanes flowed from the farms and villages toward the mesa.

Below her near the pass lay the first group of houses – low buildings dug into the hillsides, with paths leading down to rows of trees. In Hochonal, they had three fruit trees that they tended on a patch of soil above the stream. Here there must have been a hundred trees. No fields were seen near these houses, just the trees. Was that the way at Thresdenal? Each group of homes was so near that they could grow just one type of food and then trade for others. She saw people tending the trees. People walking in the lanes. Some pulled empty carts back from Thresdenal. Others loaded carts with fruit – perhaps for another journey tomorrow. Kira had spent most of the day traversing the hidden path. She knew it would be dark before she reached the main city.

Stopping at the homes would be best. She hoped the customs of hospitality were the same here as in her village. If they turned her away, she could move on until she reached the city. She would certainly find someone there who knew her father. Someone there could lead her to the old woman she had seen in the dream.

As she entered the open space among the houses, no one seemed to pay her much notice. Perhaps having others so close meant visitors were more common. Children played with spinners along the edge of the main path. A few women and girls were grinding grain outside their dwellings, talking among each other.

Finally, one boy looked up from his play and said, "What's on your feet?"

Kira looked down in surprise before remembering that she still wore the rabbit skins Iactah had wrapped around her shoes.

Other people looked at her now. Her tattered appearance was clearly out of place in the village. The worn skins on her feet, dirty abrasions on her arms and legs. Her clothes were dirty and worn. She hadn't rinsed her hair since being swept down the river, and it hadn't been touched by a comb since her last morning with Patala.

An elderly woman stood from her grinding. "Come here child," she said. "How long since you've eaten?"

Kira walked over to the woman. "Yesterday, near sundown."

"Then it is time for you to eat. Will you be my guest? I am Sillice. What is your name?"

"I am Kira. I would be grateful."

The woman squinted as though she were trying to puzzle something out. "Where are you from?"

"Hochonal."

The woman nodded knowingly then turned to the boys spinning tops. "Dree, go fetch me some water for our guest."

The boy gave a huff then grabbed the pot by the door and ran down a path.

"My grandson resists but obeys – like his father. Come sit in the shade while you wait for water. Then you can wash, and we can eat."

Kira was grateful and suddenly very hungry. She had worried that she would have to embarrass herself by begging for shelter. She should have known that of all places, wisdom would be followed by the people of Thresdenal.

As soon as the water arrived, the woman poured out some for cooking then gave the rest to Kira, along with a dish and a comb. Kira offered to help with the meal, but the woman refused. Soon, the woman's son and daughter-in-law returned from the orchard, and they began helping. The man, Drenree, was tall and not much older than the men who came singing to Kira's sister, and the woman, Tessa, reminded Kira a lot of Patala. She had beautiful hair and seemed to smile all the time, but more when Drenree looked at her.

Dree had run off after his mother arrived, and he came back carrying a bundle, which he gave to his mother.

Tessa handed the bundle to Kira. "My sister is about your size, and recently got new clothes and a hood. I asked if she could give me some of her spare clothes and a pair of shoes. She is always weaving shoes and baskets to avoid grinding grain."

"Thank you," she said as she accepted the gifts. "I will certainly fit in better in Thresdenal. I was starting to feel like an orphan in these worn-out clothes." Suddenly, Kira started to choke up. The kind woman could see it and gave her a hug. Kira realized that she might be an orphan. She didn't know what happened in Hochonal after she left. Her father was badly wounded, and her mother refused to leave his side. Her sister was still somewhere in the desert, likely being pursued. Maybe she was an orphan.

"So, you are going to Thresdenal?" Sillice asked. "Do you have family there?"

"My father used to live there. I am going to visit some people he knew at the School of the Teachers." Kira didn't like lying, but she didn't want to seem like a pathetic, lost child. She would find the old woman, that was all she could do for now. Eat, sleep, and find the old woman.

Kira rose at first light and put on the gifted clothes and shoes. She found Sillice already awake preparing food, while Tessa prepared herbs for the next meal.

"I will send some cakes with you dear. It is a long walk to the Hall of Teachers. You will find it at the center of Thresdenal within the tower. Who is it you are looking for?" Sillice smiled as she wrapped several cakes in a cloth for travel.

"Thank you. An older woman with long golden hair. She knew my father when he was a teacher there."

"Do you know her name?"

"I know her face."

Sillice's smile faded. She suddenly looked very grave. "Child you can't be more than eighteen."

Kira didn't answer, not realizing she looked so young. The sudden change in the woman's demeanor worried her.

Sillice lowered her voice. "How long have you been able to dream?"

Kira didn't know what to say. Was this a secret? Her father never talked about it in the village, so Kira never had.

Sillice smiled more warmly. "You don't need to tell me child. I think though that you shouldn't travel alone. Drenree and I will travel with you."

"Travel where? With whom?" Drenree asked, stepping in from the yard where he had been preparing some farm tools.

"I was just telling young Kira that I have been planning to make a trip into Thresdenal. You, of course, should accompany us and negotiate for the first harvest."

"Mother, I need to be here. And besides, Tessa's sister always gets the best prices, which is why we send her to negotiate."

"Drenree Windcast," Sillice said in a voice that only mothers seemed to be able to produce. "It would mean a lot to me. Besides, if I decide to buy some things, you wouldn't want a frail old woman carrying her own burdens all the way back here."

"Go dear," Tessa said. "Take Dree with you so he sees how to obey his mother."

"I suppose I will have no peace if I don't go," he said.

The road to Thresdenal descended quickly into the valley, then leveled out. Kira had tried to imagine what this place was like. She hadn't imagined anything so vast. They passed field after field. Some fields just grew plants used to make cloth. Sillice pointed out different fields and communities along the way. Any time Drenree asked Kira questions about her family or the reason she was going to Thresdenal, Sillice would interrupt and change the subject.

Dree ran ahead collecting every rock that he thought looked unique. By the time they stopped to rest, the pouch he wore around his neck was so full of rocks that he couldn't pull the draw strings closed. His father had him empty the bag on the ground and pick his three favorite.

As the boy ran ahead again, Drenree said, "He will have that pouch full again before we reach the gates. Then he will beg for me to carry the ones that he can't bear to leave behind."

"I remember a whole corner of your room filled with special rocks and unusual sticks. I guess it could have been worse. At least you didn't collect bugs."

"I just knew better than to bring those into the house."

The wide road they followed was nothing like the narrow paths of Hochonal. These were well-travelled and lined with rocks. Ruts showed where carts of produce and other loads had been hauled along the road. All across the valley people worked fields and built structures. They worked timbers and made tools and carts. Some children played. While others gathered for lessons under shade canopies.

In the center of the valley, the mesa rose and cast its long shadow. The fields and villages ended at a high wall made of logs. A gate stood open before them. Beyond were more buildings on the rocky ground that rose up to meet the foot of the red monolith.

"Is Thresdenal on top of that mesa?" She asked.

Sillice smiled. "That mesa is the heart of Thresdenal. The original city within a mountain. The area within the wall is Outer Thresdenal, the sanctuary we come to if humans were ever to invade our valley."

That mesa must be where the teachers were – where she would find the woman who appeared in her dream. This is where she would find answers.

As they wound their way past the buildings and the rocks along one of the many paths leading up from the wall, Kira found more and more things to draw her attention. Artists had carved figures in poses that reminded Kira of the star stories. On the face of a large flat rock was displayed a carving of the battle of Tosis, complete with the wave of water about to envelope the invaders. Kira could almost hear the telling of it as she looked at the intricate details.

They moved past these to an opening in the mesa, adorned with two large gates swung open to either side. Passing through the large opening, like a canyon that closed up above them, Kira moved into a world she couldn't have imagined. Large passages flowed off in different directions. Kira followed Sillice into a cavernous space busy with people. The mesa was hollow and opened to the sky through twisting slots that bent and softened the light as it flowed down. Vast hollowed out areas below the stone served as stalls for different kinds of wares.

Craftsmen displayed tools or cooking implements. And little Dree quickly found a woman who had the most exquisite spinners Kira had ever seen, aside from Te'Roan's device, which wasn't really a spinner. The surfaces of the spinners were smooth as water.

"Well, I can see that we won't be pulling Dree away from the toys without difficulty," Sillice said. "Kira, what do you say we leave our escorts here and go on ahead?"

Kira quickly agreed. As fascinated as she was to see new sights, she was more interested in reaching her destination and recovering some measure of security.

"I'm not sure how I will find the woman among all these people," she said. "I don't suppose we could gain an audience with Ka'Te'Losa. She may know the woman and might send more teachers or guards back to help the people in Hochonal."

"I know someone who may be able to help us find your mystery woman. And maybe even help us speak with Ka'Te'Losa."

They wound their way through the shops, past exquisite smelling foods and artisan weavers. Kira had never seen such a maze of passages. As the passages grew taller, she noticed openings higher up along the walls. Occasionally, she would see people up there looking down or passing by. Some of the openings were several levels above where she was.

"How high does it go?" Kira asked.

"Oh, I imagine it goes all the way to the top. There are passages behind the shops with stairs and ladders leading to the upper levels where people have their living spaces. The highest levels house guards and teachers who watch over the valley. Guards are also housed near the entrances to defend the tower."

"And the teachers?" Kira asked.

"Excuse me dear?"

"Aren't the teachers part of the security...because of how they can fight?" Kira asked.

"I don't know that I've seen teachers fighting," Sillice said. "Of course, Thresdenal is a peaceful place. Where did you witness such a thing?"

"In my village, humans attacked us, and Te'Roan and my father fought them. I had never seen anyone move like that."

"I know guards are trained in combat, I suppose training the teachers is prudent, with all that traveling about to distant villages."

As they reached the other side of the vast market, Sillice led Kira to an arched passage through which stairs led up and away on the left and right. Benches cut from the rock adorned each side of the archway.

"Now my dear, you wait here while I find the right person to talk to and get you where you need to go."

Kira thanked her and sat on the bench. The little mid-day breeze that had started up outside wound through the openings above to keep the heat at bay and the air fresh.

People came and went through the archway. Kira could hear children playing. Windows dotted the upper levels. They looked a lot like the windows on the star tower in Hochonal.

Sillice returned with a golden-haired man who carried a staff of white wood. He seemed to use the staff as more of an ornament than to keep himself from falling over. He reminded Kira of the elderly in her village who leaned on sticks and talked of all the work they had done in building the village.

He didn't wait for introductions but walked right up to Kira. "So who might you be, girl?"

"Kira Waterborn, sir. Daughter of Jornatha Waterborn." Kira stood.

"Ah, and how is Jornatha? I have not seen him in ages."

"Not well I imagine. He was injured defending our village on the day I left."

"I am sorry to hear that. You are a brave and resourceful girl to have made it all the way here."

Sillice stepped forward. "Pardon my interruption," she said. "I must be off."

The old man just turned and looked at her.

"Our agreement?" She said.

"Of course." He turned back to Kira. "Come along then. It seems your escort is to be rewarded for her kindness."

Kira followed the old man and Sillice up the stairs and through a maze of hallways until they came to a small room with a table and assorted sheets of hide, scraped and tanned so they were thin and stiff. The man scribbled something onto a small square of hide and handed it to Sillice.

"That should get you a good price at market," he said.

Without a word to Kira, Sillice turned and left.

"Don't mind her," the man said. "She is all about business."

Kira stood watching as Sillice turned a corner and left her feeling as alone as ever.

"Now, let's find a safe place for you while we inquire about your father or some other relative of yours. Leave your bag and belongings here for now."

Kira set down her bag and water skin and followed the man. He led her down the corridor in a different direction then they had come. Soon they came to another set of stairs going down. A lamp sitting on a shelf about shoulder height lit the way. Kira could see another at the bottom of the stairs.

"Tell me, Kira Waterborn, have you any relatives or friends in Thresdenal?"

"There is an elderly woman, a friend of my father."

"Do you know her name?"

"I'm afraid not, but I would know her if I saw her."

When they reached the bottom of the stairs, they were in some sort of storeroom. Several more lamps lit the room. The man took a lamp from a lower shelf, lit it on the one by the bottom of the stairs and continued to another set of stairs. Kira could see no lantern at the bottom of those stairs, but as the man led the way down, they looked very much like the first.

At the bottom of the stairs, they turned and walked along a corridor, lined on both sides with rooms. They were mostly empty.

"Our lower rooms are not yet filled – not like they are after the harvest." He continued on turning several corners. "Awe, here we are," he said stopping in front of a small room with a woven mat on the floor.

Without warning, he grabbed Kira at the base of her hood and shoved her into the room. She barely got her arms up as she collided with the far wall. The door slammed closed behind her, and a bar thudded into place. Kira was in darkness.

Chapter 7

Matusu watched as large groups of human warriors headed north and south. Te'Roan had been edging toward a gap in the mountain. The humans were setting up a line to guard that pass. They stretched far enough each direction that flanking them would be difficult if not impossible. As their forces stretch out, they seemed to blend into the landscape and disappear. They weren't trying to defend the gap. They were trying to catch anyone who approached the gap.

Matusu reported back to Te'Roan, who himself had just come from checking a flanking route up a small canyon. Te'Roan agreed that nothing could be done without confronting the humans at some point. If they tried to penetrate the trap too far from the canyon, they would be overwhelmed by the forces placed closer to the gap. Sneaking through at night was a possibility, by this wasn't like sneaking across the river ford. Tregalt had left that lightly guarded because he couldn't be sure if Te'Roan had already crossed the river. This however was a clear choke point that would have to be crossed. Flanking it would require going days out of the way through a sandy waste land that Te'Roan would not hazard.

"Aren't there other ways into Thresdenal?" Matusu asked.

"Yes but reaching them from here would take days of travel and require frequent stops for provisions."

"And how are we to know those aren't also watched?" Patala added.

It was full day now. The guarded trail offered no cover. They had made camp below a shadowed hill where they could remain concealed, but still watch the gap in the distance. Suddenly a human stepped out into the main path just below the gap. He seemed to come out from behind the line of warriors. His arrival caused a commotion.

Though Matusu couldn't hear from this distance, it seemed that the human wasn't part of the group guarding the way. All around him, the humans came out of hiding and started running toward him. He quickly ran off opposite the way he had come, and the bulk of the human force followed him.

"I don't know who that was," Te'Roan said, "but we go now."

After so many days on the trail, moving out was quick and quiet.

By the time they had covered the ground to where humans had guarded the way, the way was empty. Even though everything seemed clear, Te'Roan still held to the rocks and brush that ran along the side of the trail.

They had to leave their cover as the canyon narrowed and wound up into the mountain. Te'Roan scouted ahead warning Matusu to watch for anyone following. Soon they came to a trickle of water, then three figures drawn on the canyon wall. Matusu recognized the story.

"Does this mean that this canyon is guarded? I've seen no one."

"That is by design. You see no one, but they see you. Humans cannot follow us here. The traitor, however, would not be stopped unless the leaders in Thresdenal know to stop him."

"Do you think he would follow us alone?"

"I'm not sure what to think of him. If anything violent were to happen here, the guards should intervene."

The canyon came to an end where the stream fell from the rocks.

"We'll stay here tonight. It will take most of tomorrow to reach Thresdenal."

Kira sat alone in the dark. Her hands hurt from pounding on the door. No one seemed to be able to hear her. She needed to get out of here. She needed to find the teachers. Thresdenal was meant to be a safe place. Te'Roan said he was bringing her here to learn.

Why had they locked her in like this? Was this some sort of test? Maybe that was it. They wanted her to get herself out. Kira remembered how her father had drawn in energy from around him and sent that energy out in a wave. Maybe that was what she needed.

She sat in the middle of the room and closed her eyes. She wasn't sure how closing her eyes helped, since she couldn't see anything with them open. But she closed her eyes and tried to feel energy around her. Where had the energy come from? In the dream world, her father had drawn energy from a storm. Was the energy just in the air? If it was, Kira couldn't feel it.

She started to focus on the things she could feel. The earth beneath her was cold. The air smelled of earth, like the canyon walls drying after a rain. The air moved smoothly in and out of her lungs as she breathed. She could feel her heart beating. The air about her swirled, she opened her eyes and found that she sat at the base of a canyon. It was the narrow canyon she liked to climb with her father. She recognized the bent tree standing guard at the entrance.

She knew that this was the dream – that she still sat in the little black room in Thresdenal. But that didn't matter. She was doing something, and somehow she might be able to use this to free herself. She hurried down the canyon toward the gateway to her father's dream. It was still shut. She stopped and drank from the small stream in the bottom of the canyon. Even though it was a dream, it felt good and seemed to quench her thirst.

As she climbed up to the village, she looked for any sign of her father visiting her dream. The village seemed the same as the last time she visited it. She walked in and out of dwellings seeing what or who might be about. She was alone. Her own house looked the way it had, everything exactly where she remembered it. Most of the houses had less things than they ought to, though when she thought on what was missing, it would appear. Matusu's house was like she remembered it. In fact, she began to notice that things were mostly like she remembered them, but things she had not seen, like the inside of some houses had nothing in them. Was this because she didn't remember seeing anything in them? Her father had shown her things he had not seen – like the villages burning. How had he done that?

Kira walked into a house and began imagining what should be there. Things began fading into view – baskets by the door, a pot beside the oven, beds in the second room, then a curtain in the doorway. Soon a fire began to burn beneath the oven.

Leaving the house, Kira walked back to the center of the village. She imagined the baskets and pots that were there when the village ate together – like when the refugees had arrived. The village fire blazed up. She tried to hear the sounds. The fire was easy. Birds from a nearby tree warbled as they went about tending their nests. Looking to the trees, she could see the birds. She looked down toward the water and saw a rabbit come out from the brush to drink.

She tried to imagine people. This was more difficult. People began to appear around the fire, but they were not recognizable. It's like their faces were in shadows. She could figure out who they were, but having faceless people all around seemed more unsettling than being alone. She stopped trying to see them, and they disappeared.

Kira sat by the fire. She could feel its warmth, but at the same time, she knew it wasn't really warming her. How could she help herself? What could she do from here?

She stood and walked down toward the water to the gate to her father's dream. She hopped across the stream on rocks that she knew well. As she looked up from the rocks, she froze. The old woman stood in the grassy rushes that were the gateway to Kira's father's dream, just like before.

She wasn't like the people Kira had imagined into being. Her face was clear to Kira. Like before, Kira could see through her. It's like she was there, but not there. Like a woman of smoke.

As before, the old woman's mouth moved like she was talking to Kira, but Kira couldn't hear any words.

"I can't hear you," Kira said. "Can you help me? I need help."

Again, the woman's mouth moved.

This was frustrating. Kira moved closer to a sandy spot beside the stream. She bent down and wrote Thresdenal in the sand. The woman nodded and pointed to the word. She could see it.

"I'm in Thresdenal." Kira said and pointed to the word.

The woman knelt and wrote in the sand, but nothing showed. She couldn't affect Kira's dream. She must have realized nothing was happening. She raised her hands as if asking a question. Her mouth moved as if speaking, but Kira still couldn't understand.

The woman began to fade. "Don't go," Kira said. She moved closer, but the woman was gone.

This made no sense. The woman was obviously a dreamer, like Kira and Kira's father. Why couldn't she just be real the way Kira's father was? There must be a way. The coyote and Iactah had been real enough in the dream. What was different here?

Kira woke from the dream. She was back in her little dark room. Nothing had changed.

Matusu wasn't giving the massive settlement the awe it deserved. It was just another place Kira was not. Te'Roan's typically brisk pace had increased as they descended past groves and farms toward the large mesa at the center of the valley. Matusu took disinterested notice of the growing number of buildings stacked up on each other. He momentarily considered the timbers needed to be both ceiling and floor, but the thought quickly fell from his mind. Kira would be the only one who would have been interested.

Matusu followed on Patala's heels. He had told himself through their silent travels that he would at least see Kira's sister safely to Thresdenal. He also wanted to find out what could be done to rescue Hochonal and punish the humans that pursued them. Part of him wanted to avenge what they had lost. Another part of him just wanted to wander off into the desert and forget about everything and everyone.

As they reached the more populated part of the valley, Te'Roan stopped in front of a man with a cart of orange and yellow fruit. He exchanged something with the man, then turned and handed Patala and Matusu each a piece of fruit.

"A late breakfast," he said and walked on.

They had left that morning without stopping to eat. Even though Matusu didn't feel like eating since losing Kira, his stomach eventually told him otherwise. He followed Te'Roan's example and tore away the peal. He consumed the inner fruit in three bites, juice running down his chin. Patala ate the fruit with more reserve and less sticky juice. He watched her occasionally pull seeds from the fruit and place them in a pocket of her bag. Matusu didn't recall any seeds in his.

Soon they arrived at the mesa they had seen from the ridge. They followed Te'Roan through a maze of wide corridors and rooms within the hollowed-out mesa. Matusu could tell that wind and water had done much of the work here, but builders had carved it out further to meet their needs.

Matusu couldn't help but experience a little awe at the craftsmanship that formed the mesa's interior. Te'Roan led them directly to a hallway on the side of the main corridor. The broad entrance was wide enough for all of them to walk through side by side. They descended several stairs into a large room, lit by openings high on the wall on the other side of the room. Around the room rows of high stone steps served as benches. People sat in small groups talking with one another. Across the room the tiered benches ascended four high. On the top step sat an elderly woman in a white dress. Two women stood by her, as a man in the clothes of a farmer stood below talking to her. Two guards also stood nearby, alert but seemingly unconcerned about the man.

As they reached the bottom of the stairs, Te'Roan said, "Wait here." He proceeded forward across the room. As he proceeded, the room got noticeably quieter, people stopping to watch him.

It was only then that Matusu noticed how dusty and trail worn the teacher was. They must all look like that.

The woman on the top step noticed Te'Roan and stood. Holding the arm of one of the women near her, she descended the stairs to meet Te'Roan. He gave a formal bow and said something Matusu couldn't clearly hear. As Te'Roan stood upright, the woman stepped up and hugged him.

The woman looked past Te'Roan to Matusu and Patala. She left Te'Roan and began walking toward them. Te'Roan followed.

The woman took Patala by the hand. "You look older than I expected."

"This is Patala. She's Kira's sister," Te'Roan said.

"Where is Kira?"

Te'Roan's look said everything he needed to say.

"Where is Kira? Why isn't she with you?"

"We were attacked and…"

"Well, find her!"

"Ka'Te'Losa, she was swept away down the river. There was nothing…"

"Are you telling me you think she's dead? Preposterous. She is very much alive but lacks the ability to tell me where she is."

"How?"

"I have a fragile connection with her through her father – who, by the way I haven't been able to contact."

Patala let out a sob and held onto Matusu's shoulder. "Is my father…"

"I don't know if your father is alive or not. I just know that I haven't been able to reach him. What I do know is that I saw your sister last night, but she doesn't know how to reach anyone. You need to find her."

Matusu knew that Te'Roan and those he took with him had abilities Matusu didn't. As much as he told himself he could keep up, he felt that he would slow them down in their efforts to find Kira.

Te'Roan was leaving with a couple dozen men and women – some of them teachers. They stood beneath a group of trees just north of the mesa. They had their spears, bows, and provisions. All of them seemed to be experienced and trail hardened. Those not wearing the earthen-toned cloaks of a teacher wore guard uniforms that would blend into the desert.

"I want to come with you. I want to help," Matusu said.

"We have enough people. You can help more here. I've asked Ka'Te'Losa to consider you becoming a guard if that interests you," Te'Roan said.

Matusu had only the things he had arrived with – a blanket and a water skin. He had packed away the food he had been given by the serving women in the mesa.

"We will be back in a week. The teachers going with us are dreamers. Ka'Te'Losa or one of her aids will know when we find Kira." Te'Roan turned back to those with him.

A man sitting near the edge of the group stood. He was one of those wearing a guard uniform. He was older than Te'Roan. His hair had begun to turn gold along the front. "Is that the boy that crossed with you from Hochonal?"

"He is," Te'Roan said.

"I will take him," the man said. "He can be my recruit."

"That was his first journey," Te'Roan said. "We will be moving fast. Are you sure you want him tagging along?"

"He looks strong enough." The man looked at Matusu. "I am Ariste. What have you apprenticed at?"

"Building. My father was a builder. Mostly stone."

"See Te'Roan, he can carry heavy things." The man turned back to Matusu. "Do you want to be my recruit and go on this journey?"

"Really? Yes, of course."

The man tossed Matusu a chip of wood with some writing on it. "Show this to the senior guard standing just inside the mesa, the woman. Tell her you are Ariste's recruit, and she will give you things you need. We are about to leave, so don't delay."

"Thank you," Matusu said. He ran back toward the mesa. Even though he had gone in and out several times, Matusu was still amazed at the stone entryway as he entered it. He couldn't pass by without glancing up at the details of how the natural stone was perfectly cut.

Beyond the guards at the gate, a uniformed woman stood just inside the entrance. Matusu handed her the chip of wood and told her he was Ariste's recruit. She gave a quick glance down and up, no doubt taking in his tattered appearance. She then told him to wait and called another woman over. After receiving some instructions, the woman walked quickly away down one of the corridors.

Matusu waited by the guard. She didn't even look at him but resumed her post.

When the other woman returned, she was carrying a bundle and was followed by a man with a second bundle. They handed Matusu the bundles, which included a uniform, boots, a large water flask, a leather satchel, and a staff.

"You can change in there," the guard said, pointing to a small room off to the side of the entrance.

Matusu hurried into the room. The clothing wasn't exactly what he would call new. It was as though it had been made to look slightly worn, yet not to be worn out. Finely-woven under-layers, dyed to a brownish color, went on first. The over-shirt had animal skin patches sewn inside under the forearms and elbows and over the shoulders and upper back. The rest was the tightly woven cloth he remembered commenting on to the guards at Hochonal. The front part of the shirt doubled over so it had inner and outer layers. From what he had seen, the layer with the hood and face covering was the outer layer. The breeches also had patches of skins in the seat and the knees. Both the shirt and the breeches were a color that blended between the white, brown, and red stone of the area. The clothing fit loosely so that he could move easily without being constrained by it. The shirt hung past the top of the pants, but tied tight at the waste with a sash so it wouldn't be in his way.

The boots were different from the shoes Matusu was used to wearing. They fully covered his feet and had wrappings up almost to his knees.

Matusu stuffed his food stores into the satchel. The satchel contained several items he would have to look closer at when he had time. He slung the satchel and water skin across his chest. He slung his old water skin and blanket over his shoulder and, staff and old clothes in hand, left the small room.

When he returned to the grove where Te'Roan's party was preparing to leave, they were all standing, checking their pouches in preparation. Patala was talking to Te'Roan. She seemed surprised to see Matusu there in a uniform and carrying a staff.

"Are you going, too?" She asked.

"I've been accepted as a guard apprentice," he said.

"Recruit," Te'Roan corrected.

"Be safe," she said. "I would come, but I don't think..."

"I know," Matusu said. "I thought I would slow them down, but one of the men offered to take me as his recruit, so..."

"Not just anyone," Te'Roan said. "You have been chosen by Ariste. Half the guard captains in Thresdenal were his recruits. It's an honor."

"I guess that means he's going to make sure I keep up. Can you take my old clothes and shoes?" Matusu asked Patala. "Maybe someone can use them."

"Leave that blanket too. You won't need it," Te'Roan said.

Matusu hadn't noticed until then that none of the guards were carrying blankets. The teachers had those cloaks, but the guards just had the same things that Matusu had been given. He handed his old clothes, blanket, and old water skin to Patala. She hugged him, turned, and walked away. He knew that her anxiety about Kira had only increased as she thought about her out there alone in the desert. Matusu made a promise to himself that he would find Kira and bring her safely back.

Kira felt the cold of the wall at her back. Everything seemed colder here than under the stars out on the desert. She held her breath hoping to be able to hear even the smallest sound – any indication that she wasn't alone. The smell of dust and moisture filled the air. It wasn't like the clean, renewing smell of the desert after a rain. It was the smell of darkness and cold.

She heard footsteps in the hall. A light shone through the cracks in the door. Kira moved to the farthest corner, unsure what this meant. Had they discovered their error and come to get her? A small door within the door opened. She had not noticed this before. She hadn't really felt around the room.

"Hello," she called. "Who's there?"

No one answered. In the dim light, Kira saw a hand pass a basket through the little opening and set it on the floor. The door closed, and the light receded.

Kira went to the basket. She felt a jar with liquid in it – likely water – and two small cakes. The smell of the cakes reminded Kira how hungry she was. She quickly dismissed any thought that they might be poisoned, as her captors could have killed her at any time. She ate the cakes and drank the water. At least they didn't intend to starve her to death.

She placed the basket and jar near her mat where she could find them in the dark. Maybe she would find a use for them. If she knew where she was and where she might go if she got free, she might better understand what to do next. Even if she got free, what could she do? Who could she trust in this place? She couldn't just run about asking to meet with Ka'Te'Losa could she?

Kira remembered the words of her father – "The dream is wisdom, without the dream, wisdom will fail."

"Father," she had asked, "what can I do with the dream?"

"That is almost the right question. What can you do for others with the dream?"

Kira knew that the dream let her reach her father. She also knew she could see the old woman in the dream, but not clearly. She had more to learn, but her guide was gone. Perhaps it was time to use the dream to find a new guide. That's it, she thought, my guide.

Kira closed her eyes and meditated. She focused on her heartbeat – on her breathing. She sought the dream. She focused on the coyote – on Iactah.

She was back in her village of Hɔchonal. She needed to be somewhere else. She imagined the hut where the coyote had led her. She stood before the place. Smoke rose from the hut, but no one was around. Perhaps Iactah wasn't sleeping. Kira didn't even know if it was day or night. All she could do was wait. She sat beside the hut. Not daring to go in unless asked. She had become good at waiting. It was better to wait here than in the dark room where she had been imprisoned.

She caught a movement out of the corner of her eye. It was a coyote slinking through the brush weaving among the bushes on no apparent path. As it came closer, it seemed to notice Kira, then stood looking at her for a moment. Kira didn't know if it was going to attack – though she thought such behavior would be odd for the coyote. It swung around and trotted off in another direction. Kira followed.

Before long, the coyote had circled back to the same hut, and there sat Iactah. Kira tried to suppress her excitement.

"I didn't know if I would find you," she said.

"It seems that Coyote has brought us together. It must be important."

"I am locked in a room in Thresdenal. I was tricked and locked away. I need help."

"I cannot go there. The way is guarded."

"Are the men who chased me still there?"

"They are not the ones who guard the way. That place is always guarded from within. I thought you would be safe there."

"Maybe you can find my friends – my sister and the men with her. If they are alive, they will be able to help me."

"I believe they are at Thresdenal. My spirit guide told me to wait by the path and lead away other humans so your friends could also pass."

"So you stayed near the path?"

"I am far from that place. I will consult the spirit guide." Iactah faded away.

Kira felt herself waking. She fought to hold herself in the dream, but suddenly she was in the dark again, but not total dark. A light shone through the crack of the door.

Kira waited. She didn't move. The door opened a crack. Light poured in. A heavy man with a dull expression looked down on her. He set two small pots just inside the door and closed it. The light faded away with the sound of his footsteps.

Kira moved toward the pots and reached out carefully feeling for them, not wanting to knock them over. She could smell the food. It was as if being in the darkness was heightening her other senses. She just made out the sound of creaking from some other far away door. Perhaps it was the man leaving.

One pot contained water. Smelling it, it seemed fresh. How clean it was she could not know without tasting it. The food was a small amount of spiced meal. It was slightly warm but not hot. Kira lifted it out on her fingers tasting it. She realized how hungry she still was as she quickly cleared the entire pot in four scoops.

She tasted the water. It seemed fine, like it was recently dipped from a stream. She drank until it was gone – careful not to drip any, not knowing when she might get more.

How long had it been since she had eaten? How long had she been in the dream? She was never good at determining these things. She felt anger welling up inside her. She was angry at herself for being tricked, for following a stranger into this place. She was angry at the stranger and the woman for tricking her and locking her away.

She lifted the pot to throw and then thought better. What if they denied me food or water without the pots? What if I need them? She set them carefully in the corner with the basket and jar and returned to where she had slept.

She kept feeling the dream was her way out, that somehow she could use the dream to reach someone to help her – Iactah, the old woman, her father.

Matusu had no trouble keeping up with Ariste, though the older man moved with greater deft and speed than Matusu would have expected. Matusu was grateful that Te'Roan had pushed them to move across the desert, otherwise he doubted he would have the stamina to keep up with the man. They moved in a party with another guard and a teacher. The group that left Thresdenal broke into four smaller groups. Te'Roan went with one of the other groups toward the road where they had encountered the humans.

Matusu followed Ariste over a plateau to a path that dropped down into the desert and headed north of the road. They were cutting straight across to where they had first been separated from Kira. Perhaps this was the path they would have followed if they had crossed at the ford as they had originally intended.

"Do you think we could find her trail if she came this way?" Matusu asked over the wind.

"Whatever trail her feet made is likely getting old, and chances of finding it venturing out like this are slim. We will go to the ford and follow the river to see where she left. But look for signs as we travel. We may get lucky."

The men traveled long stretches without stopping, and when they did stop, it was for a very short time. Matusu got used to not getting settled.

The men walked in a single line following the teacher – a man named Te'Horace. He was a tall, slender man with a long stride. The group seemed to have settled on their direction before Matusu joined them. They didn't stop to consult a map device. Matusu wasn't even sure anyone had brought one along.

Matusu followed Ariste who seemed to never drift more than a few steps behind Te'Horace. Behind Matusu, the other guard, Jantorn, stayed close but occasionally stopped to check behind them.

At first, Matusu thought they would be better off spreading out to maybe see Kira's trail, if she came this way. After moving into the broken hills and gullies in the valley, he realized that they moved faster by following Te'Horace's lead.

As darkness began to fall, the group pressed on in the fading light of dusk. Not until full dark surrounded them did they halt to eat. Each man seemed to find a niche to settle into. Te'Horace wrapped in his teacher's cloak. The two guards removed their long shirts and used them as makeshift blankets. Matusu just did what Ariste did. The tunic, as Ariste called the outer shirt, had been doubled over and when unfolded made a decent, though narrow, blanket.

He wasn't convinced that it would stand up to really cold weather, but it was a comfort to have something to lay over him.

Time in the dark made it easy for Kira to drift into the dream when she wanted to. At first, she had stared into the darkness trying to see her small room. Soon she learned that if she cleared her mind and imagined Hochonal, she would be able to feel the dream and slip into it. Soon the village was around her with its familiar light and color. It was empty of people but still had the sound of the breeze in the trees and the stream below the village.

The village held no more clues than Kira had seen before. The old woman was nowhere to be seen. Kira sat by the village fire thinking about how she might reach the woman, how she might reach someone in a dream the way she reached Iactah.

She had reached Iactah by imagining the hut where they had talked. Perhaps she could go to Thresdenal the same way. Of course, the world in her dream might not have any relation to the real world. She was still unclear about that.

She imagined a place in Thresdenal, the shade under a tree outside the mesa. The village faded away around her and was replaced with the shady spot she imagined. She walked into the tower and tried to remember the path she had taken following the man who had imprisoned her. She noticed that the places she had been before had details pulled from her memory – a chair, a pot. When she turned down a hallway she hadn't been in before, the details weren't present. She saw just empty walls. This made it easy to follow the turns and stairs down to the room she was locked in.

She looked at the door to her room. She had only glanced at it when she was put in the room. Now in the dream, she recalled more detail. She could see the door had a bar on the outside. If she could get a thin stick she might be able to slip it through the crack in the door and move the bar. All she had was straw from her mat. She imagined the door open, letting in light to see details of her small room – her mat, the basket, the jar, and the two small pots.

The walls of her room looked as smooth as they felt. The ceiling was stone. Not a twig visible, let alone a thin stick. She pictured herself back outside the tower and was there standing by the tree. She imagined the world at night. The light faded until only the moon and stars cast shadows over the world. Is this what it looked like now? Was it night? Kira caught a movement to the side. It was the old woman the one that she could barely see in her dreams. Her mouth was moving like she was saying something, but Kira couldn't tell what it was. The woman looked around and then faded as quickly as she had arrived.

Matusu was on watch just before morning when the teacher sat up.

"We need to move," he said. "Ka'Te'Losa says she has seen Kira in the dream standing outside the tower in Thresdenal."

"You mean she's at the tower?" Matusu asked.

"It means the girl has been to the tower."

"How does Ka'Te'Losa tell you things in the dream, but Kira can't tell her where she is?"

"The girl hasn't learned how yet – or she doesn't have a strong enough connection with Ka'Te'Losa. She can enter our dreams because she knows us – has spent time with us."

"Kira knows me. She knows Patala. Why doesn't Kira reach out to one of us?"

"Like I said, she probably doesn't know how."

"She better figure it out," Matusu said as he finished tying off his sash.

Matusu felt a hand on his shoulder. "We will find her," Ariste said.

Te'Horace led out across the desert back the way they had come.

Ka'Te'Losa Starsight woke and hurried from her chamber, still in her sleeping clothes. Spotting a guard in the hall, she said, "Find Te'Rochrael and ask her to please come to my chamber."

Ka'Te'Losa returned through her outer chamber to her personal chamber and prepared herself more properly. *You must be slowing down,* she thought to herself. *You should have made this connection days ago.*

By the time Te'Rochrael arrived, Ka'Te'Losa sat at her table in her outer chamber properly attired and waiting for her.

"Who is the teacher for the advanced classes at Hochonal?" Ka'Te'Losa asked.

"I will find out," Te'Rochrael said. "Is there anything else?"

"When you find him or her, please bring them to me directly."

Ka'Te'Losa sat trying to be calm on the outside even though she was storming on the inside. She wanted to drop into the dream and try to reconnect with Kira but knew that would likely cause her more frustration.

Te'Rochrael entered the chamber followed by Te'Natha.

"Te'Natha," Ka'Te'Losa said. "Thank you for coming to me at this late hour. We need your help."

Kira paced back and forth along the ledge above Hochonal. She noticed that the sky had grown dark. Clouds had rolled in to match her mood. She could visit Hochonal, but still knew she was trapped in that room. The coyote hadn't returned. She hadn't been able to find Iactah during her last three trips to his shelter. Her trips to Hochonal weren't the settling escape they had been at first.

A woman appeared in the middle of Hochonal. As the woman lowered the hood of her teacher's cloak, Kira realized it was Te'Natha. Kira moved herself down next to her.

Te'Natha turned to face her. She was aware of Kira. They were sharing the dream.

"Are you really here?" Kira asked.

"Yes, Kira, I am. Ka'Te'Losa said you are lost and need help."

Kira hugged her. Something she had never done during any of their lessons. "Ka'Te'Losa is looking for me? How did she know?"

"She has tried to reach you several times but could not fully connect."

"The old woman from my father's dream is Ka'Te'Losa?"

Te'Natha laughed. "I won't tell her you called her an old woman. Do you know where you are?"

"I'm in Thresdenal. I'm locked in a room underground."

"You know how in your lessons I bring you to different observatories and laboratories to learn? You have the ability to change your dream to wherever you can imagine and to bring me with you."

Te'Natha took hold of Kira's hand. "Can you show me where in Thresdenal you are?"

"Yes, yes! I can do that. I've been practicing, tracing the route they followed to lead me here."

The world shifted, and they stood outside the entrance to Thresdenal. No one was there but Te'Natha and Kira.

"Follow me," Kira said and led her through the route she had followed. They passed through the market to the arch, up the stairs, then through corridors, and down stairs and more stairs to the door of her room. Kira kept looking back to make sure Te'Natha was with her. The teacher was right behind her the whole time.

"This is where I am," she said, pointing to the door."

Kira wasn't sure why, but the teacher hugged her again. Maybe she looked like she still needed a hug.

"I have to go now, but I will see you in the real world as quickly as I can."

Te'Natha faded from view.

Kira waited in the dark. Had she really done it? Was her teacher coming for her? All she had to do now was wait.

She jumped to her feet at the sound of the door opening. A lamp cast a soft light in her room. A man stood there, one Kira had never seen before. He was large and muscular.

"Come girl – we must go," he said in a low voice.

"Did Te'Natha send you?" Kira asked.

He paused for just a moment. "Of course. Do you want to stay down here? Let's go."

As she stepped through the doorway, the man grabbed tightly onto her arm and started toward the stairs. At the top of the stairs, they were met by two men in guard uniforms. As soon as he saw them, the man kicked one hard in the stomach, pushing him away.

He threw the lamp at the other and dashed past them, dragging Kira along with him.

Why was he fighting the guards?

They reached a fork in the passageway, and Kira started to go to the right, just as she remembered. He jerked her to the left. They were going the wrong way.

Kira suddenly realized that this might not be her rescuer, but another of her abductors. She pulled back at his hand trying to pull away.

The man's grip tightened down. He jerked her forward, almost off her feet.

Kira could hear the guards pursuing them. "I'm here. This way," she yelled.

Kira didn't even have time to think as the man swung around and blasted a fist across her cheek. This time she did fall.

Without a word, the man jerked her back to her feet and over his shoulder. His breathing was getting more labored, but the extra weight didn't seem to slow him down. If anything, Kira felt like they were going faster.

Kira kicked her feet about to throw him off balance. She hammered her fists against his back. He moved faster still. She could hear the guards coming. They were gaining. Kira had to slow her abductor.

She realized they were in a narrow passage. She had been focusing on him when she needed to focus on the walls. With all the strength she could pull together, she twisted and threw he legs out to one side. As soon as her feet connected with the wall, she shoved hard, knocking both the man and herself against the opposite wall. She tucked her arms around her head to protect it. The man, busy trying to hold onto her, had no such protection. She both heard and felt a solid crack as the weight of her body drove his head into the wall. They fell in a heap.

Kira scrambled to get up. The man grabbed at her feet, pulling her back to the ground. He rolled onto he knees with a groan, trying to gain control of her. He grabbed her around the waist like he was going to put her back on his shoulder. Then he suddenly let go and dropped to the ground.

Kira turned and in the low light of the lamps saw the two guards. One had the butt end of his spear extended. He had given the abductor another solid blow to his head.

He stepped forward and extended a hand to Kira. "Can I help you up?"

Kira moved back. "How do I know I can believe you anymore than him?"

A voice called from the corridor behind them. "Did you get her? Is she alright?"

"Te'Natha?" Kira asked, looking past the guards.

"Who else?" The teacher pushed past the guards and hugged Kira. "Let's get you to Ka'Te'Losa."

"This man tried to take me away."

"I know. He must have been a lookout and seen us coming. He'll be dealt with."

Kira entered a large, terraced room. Ka'Te'Losa stood in the center, hands folded in front of her, almost smiling. She wore a robe similar to a teacher's robe, except that it was nearly white and fell to the ground. Guards stood at each entrance to the room.

Ka'Te'Losa didn't speak but simply held out her arms. Kira could see the kindness in her eyes, like a parent adoring a child. As soon as Kira reached her, Ka'Te'Losa pulled her into an embrace and held her. Kira fought to be strong, to hold back tears.

"Child, you are safe now. You are safe."

"My father and sister and Matusu – our village."

"I know. Your sister is here. I've sent guards to get her. She is safe too."

"And Matusu and Te'Roan?"

"They are safe as well. They are out searching for you with groups of guards and other teachers."

"But how?"

"I'm sure you have many questions, but first, I must teach you a simple and important skill. Right here, right now."

"What is that?"

"How to connect in the dream. Learn that, and you can bring an army to your aid."

Chapter 8

Matusu was the first up each morning. Whenever they stopped to rest, he stood, always ready to keep moving. Ariste cautioned Matusu to pace himself. It still took days to make the return journey.

The second night, he dreamed of Kira. It was like she had found the hollow they were camped in and sat talking with him by a fire. She kept adding sticks to the fire as she asked him about what he had done after she left. He told her about the warriors along the river and how they had to slip past them. He asked her how she had gotten away from them and where she had gone.

"That is something of a long story, and you need to rest," Kira said. "I will see you soon."

The next morning as they hiked, Matusu told Ariste of his dream.

"So, you think Kira visited me in the dream because she now knows how?"

"Perhaps."

They continued in silence for a while until Ariste stopped at the top of a rise. "This talk of Kira's talents has reminded me that I need to teach you a few things. From here to the next rise, we will walk without leaving footprints."

As Ariste explained to Matusu how to travel across a place without leaving a path, Matusu realized he had seen Te'Roan doing just that, as he scouted out areas near the river.

He followed Ariste as they moved across the terrain in a broken gait, moving quickly, but not always in a direct line. They stayed to durable surfaces as much as possible and moved with carefully placed steps across softer places. Though he couldn't see any trace of Ariste ahead of him, looking back at his own trail left him wondering how such a thing was possible.

At the top of the rise, Ariste stopped and looked back over the path. "Hmm. We'll practice more when we have more time." With that he turned and continued at their usual vigorous pace toward Thresdenal.

Kira hurried along the passageways through the teacher's hall. Kira still couldn't believe how easy it was to connect in the dream. She felt the connections she had with the people she knew and especially the ones she was close to. They had been there all the time. Kira just hadn't noticed them. She could will herself to connect with their consciousness. The first person she connected with after Ka'Te'Losa was Patala. It seemed a little silly since Patala was sleeping across from her in their room in the tower. It was also exciting watching the surprise on Patala's face as Kira explained to her that she was really in her dream.

Patala said that Father had visited her dreams occasionally, as their teacher Te'Natha did. Now Kira knew that her talent was what Father was searching for. He had spent time with Kira because he was helping her learn to dream. He hadn't taught her all that she needed to know. He had planned to bring her to Ka'Te'Losa himself and continue her training in Thresdenal. Ka'Te'Losa was now picking up where Kira's father left off.

Kira tried to reach out to people from Hochonal but found no one. She didn't know if that was because they were so far away, they weren't sleeping, or they had died. Her connection with Matusu didn't seem to be affected by distance, so she was left to believe the worst.

Kira had met with several of the people who trained teachers. They seemed most interested in how Ka'Te'Losa had gotten into her dream. The fact that she could even see a person she had never met excited them.

They still hadn't captured the man who had locked Kira away in that basement room. When Kira had described him to Ka'Te'Losa and the guards, they seemed to know who he was, but he had apparently fled. Kira was starting to see that even though Ka'Te'Losa was the leader, multiple factions were at work in Thresdenal and things weren't as simple as they seemed. Just as her father and uncle had debated issues to come to an agreement, the people in Thresdenal often divided into groups to support or oppose actions. And they didn't always use just words to disagree, which is why Ka'Te'Losa was always surrounded by guards.

Kira arrived at the training room before the instructor. She loved the way light filled the room through windows high on the wall. Her first several days had been spent listening to explanations about dreaming and how connections with people worked. That had opened her understanding enough to make some easy connections. Today, they would start meditation dreaming to connect to others without having to sleep. She felt she got pretty good at that during her time locked in the room. Of course, being in a completely dark room with no distractions, it was often hard to tell the difference between being awake and asleep.

Kira's instructor shuffled into the room. Te'Marile was a small, thin woman who made a habit of asking questions only to answer them before Kira had a chance. Regardless of her methods, the woman was brimming with information. She had tackled the science of dreaming from a purely theoretical perspective. Her study of trends in families had led her to conclusions about dreaming being passed down from parents to children. The first dwellers had apparently come up with ways to increase the odds of producing dreamers. They worked on creating genetic probabilities, that Kira vaguely remembered hearing in her lessons. Since it dealt with things that could not be grown or climbed, Kira hadn't paid much attention. Now, all that had changed.

"What is the dream?"

Kira had the answer on the tip of her tongue.

"The place where consciousness connects outside of place." The woman answered her own question.

Kira was starting to wrap her head around the idea of consciousness being separate from place as well as person. While she, that is her body, remained in one place, her consciousness was able to move through connections to another consciousness through the dream.

"In the middle of the dream," Kira said, "I never really felt disconnected from my body. I felt as though I was still in my body – well, except for the ability to bounce from place to place. I could walk and move, even see my own hands and feet. I could feel a hug. I never felt like a disembodied consciousness."

Te'Marile explained, "You have framed a picture of your consciousness. The people you visited in the dream appeared to have a physical form based on your image of them in your mind."

But this didn't explain how Kira saw Ka'Te'Losa. This seemed to really interest Te'Marile. It defied all her in-depth theories about the science of dreaming. It also didn't explain Kira's dreams of the coyote and Iactah's hut, which she kept to herself, knowing how teachers felt about contact with humans. She was certain dreaming was more than the projection of her memories to create an illusion of the world of their consciousness. And what about the time her father had shown her the village by the river? Those weren't her memories. Much of what a person saw in the dream was created by the person they were with – like a shared consciousness. In her father's dreams, he always seemed in control, yet she was also able to do things. In her dreams, she hadn't really thought about who was in control or how to take control of a dream.

It seemed to Kira that the teachers were hurrying her training – focusing on her in individual training. She was occasionally placed with groups of trainees a little older than her, who were being taught all together about things like Thresden history and Earth cultures, at least what the teacher's data stores had of it. They were permitted to use tables with metal inserts that displayed information in a panel of light and were controlled simply by telling them what you wanted to see. These other students didn't interact much with Kira. From what she had heard, they spent months working up to the level of training that the teachers were providing Kira.

"How does the training usually start?" Kira asked Te'Marile.

"What do you mean by 'usually'?"

"When dreamers come in with a group, what do you teach them first?"

"We start by introducing them to a teacher skilled in dreaming, and the teacher spends time with them in their dreams. Eventually, the teacher shifts the dreamer to the teacher's dream."

"That's what my father did."

"Your father was especially gifted, as was your grandmother on your mother's side. I'm surprised your mother wasn't a more gifted dreamer, though genetics show that the trait doesn't diminish with a skipped generation."

"So my father and my mother were together for genetics?"

"Not completely. He did go back to Hochonal to marry your mother. Though he could have just as easily brought her here. Hochonal was founded by a concentration of dreamer descendants."

"You would have thought that dreamers would be better off here, where they could be better taught."

"The founders knew that if they tried to force marriages here – in a place as big as Thresdenal – they would eventually have a rebellion on their hands. It's easier to concentrate genetics in a small village. Also, people are…how do I put it…less promiscuous in a tightly knit village than in a larger city where they can maintain some anonymity."

"So I was born in Hochonal as part of the founder's breeding program."

"Left to natural selection, the traits required for a dreamer might have been watered down to mere reception. Then where would we be?"

"What do you mean by that?"

"I just mean that without dreamers, how would we maintain our culture, our science, and knowledge."

"We would be almost where we are now. Farming and raising families. Dreaming doesn't add anything to our daily lives, yet you make it sound like it's somehow vital to our survival."

Te'Marile sighed. "Such a smart girl. Wisdom is about more than just surviving here – wisdom is a means to an end and dreaming is part of making that end come about in a way that preserves our families and culture."

Te'Marile looked at Kira as if to say enough questions.

Kira knew there was more to wisdom and dreaming than she had at first considered. The idea that an entire world could be at risk, however, seemed way beyond anything she had considered. She suddenly had a hundred more questions, but didn't dare ask, for fear of angering the teacher. Ka'Te'Losa had warned her not to delve into things, but learn the lessons as they come. "Swim on the surface before you dive in the deep," she had said.

Why did the world or anything they did depend on dreaming?

Matusu didn't mind Kira visiting his dreams. She always asked about Matusu's training, especially defense and attack training. Tonight Kira wanted to see the fighting moves he had learned. He could only imagine what she had been through. As he studied with his teachers, he would ask Ariste to teach him the best ways to fight against a larger, stronger opponent. Ariste seemed to think this strange since Matusu was taller than Ariste and outweighed most of the other guards. He would rarely, if ever have to fight someone bigger than himself. He didn't tell Ariste that he was asking for a friend.

"Let's say you were going to fight me," Matusu said, as he showed Kira how to keep out of reach until the opponent was forced off balance. He then showed her a series of quick strikes to force the opponent more off balance and limit his ability to fight back. "Now you try," he said.

Matusu allowed Kira to force him off balance and even took the hits, which didn't really damage him here in the dream. He had worried about that at first. He had wondered if something that happened in the dream could cause him pain in the real world. Kira had explained something about consciousness being separate from body. Essentially, he could jump off a cliff in the dream and not affect his body at all.

Damaging the consciousness in other ways was a different topic. Kira said she hadn't learned much about that as the teachers seemed to consider it a forbidden area of practice.

Kira managed to throw Matusu twenty times. Ten throws would have worn her out in the real world.

"Knowing the technique is one thing," he said. "Having the physical strength to do it is going to take some work in the real world."

"Then teach me in the real world."

"I need to get better at it first. Ariste is good at pulling his strike before he does any real damage, and no matter what I do, he seems to be able to deflect or absorb my strikes without getting hurt."

"The teachers training me said defensive training comes after I've finished dream training. I'm told that takes years. The way things are around here, I don't want to be at someone else's mercy for years."

"You have the guards to protect you. You have me."

"I had you and Te'Roan in the desert when I ended up fighting for my life against a human. If he had been a better swimmer…"

"That was out there. Do you think Ka'Te'Losa would allow…"

"Ka'Te'Losa doesn't have as much power as people think. I've listened in on some of the councils and heard the older teachers talking. Everyone is broken into factions. Some are tired of groveling in a primitive existence. Others worry about encroaching humans. But wisdom says we stay and hide – hide ourselves and our technology until the gathering."

"Gathering? I've heard that before."

"Our teachers kind of glossed over it when talking about the first time skip. The gathering happens just before we get rescued."

"When will that be? I don't think we can hide much longer. Human numbers are growing."

"Plus, the factions are getting bolder and pulling in more people to pick sides. They're doing things like locking up young people, so they won't learn to dream."

"For all their trying to stop you, those guys seemed to make you a better dreamer."

"Yeah, well I hope you can make me a better fighter. If I ever see that woman or that old man again…"

"Ariste says they haven't been sighted in the city, though he seemed to know who the old man was and wasn't surprised he disappeared."

"Where did they go. I mean the place is big, but not so big that anyone can stay hidden when someone is looking for them," Kira said as she resumed her fighting stance.

This time she attacked. Matusu blocked twice. Kira retreated inviting Matusu to step in with his superior height and reach. Kira pulled him off balance simultaneously striking a disabling kick to his knee. She followed with a rib strike to impair breathing and a strike under the shoulder to disable his arm.

Matusu winced with each strike but kept his mind focused on the truth that Kira wasn't doing any real damage. She had taught him to focus on maintaining his own reality in his mind regardless of what his senses told him.

Kira dragged into class, tired from her extra-curricular dreaming. Even though she was meditating and sometimes sleeping during her dreams, it wasn't the same as truly sleeping and recovering from her day. Her body needed more than superficial rest. She needed to let her brain sleep.

Three teachers awaited her. Te'Juna was the oldest of the three and the keeper of the way finder, meaning that she tracked star movements and used them to calculate time and the current position of their star system. Te'Rochrael seemed to be the next in seniority, though as the first attendant to Ka'Te'Losa, she may have also been the most politically connected, if such a thing mattered to these master teachers. Te'Unoalie was, by all accounts, the most gifted dreamer among the master teachers. He took a keen scientific interest in dreaming and technology, though he seemed aloof on matters of politics.

Today was test day. Kira was supposed to meditate and engage the three master teachers in a single dream. She had met all three of them previously, so this wasn't a test of her ability to connect with someone she hadn't met. She wondered if they even had a test for that. She knew she was on a fast track. They wanted to get to that, but Ka'Te'Losa insisted they take her through the standard training to make sure her skills were honed completely. What they needed to be honed for was still a mystery. Every teacher in the city must have stopped by to talk to Kira by now.

The three master teachers didn't even speak, they just seated themselves on mats across from Kira and began meditating. She knew from her previous tests that the teachers wouldn't help her. They would wait for her to enter their dreams and create a doorway for them to join her dream.

She created her world of Hochonal as usual. She then focused her attention on the consciousness of the first teacher. She found herself in front of Te'Juna in the very room where they were holding the test. The only differences were that the woman was standing and she was the only other person in the room. Kira realized that she had planned on creating a doorway through some natural cover like her father did through the grass by the water at Hochonal.

She saw nothing resembling a covered doorway here. She considered the dilemma for a moment and realized that even a shadowed corner would work if she could force her reality onto it.

"Would you please follow me out the door?" Kira led the way out the passage from the room and through the darkness of the hallway she passed from the teacher's dream into a house in Hochonal. It was her uncle's house and had passageways between rooms. Looking back, she was pleased to see the teacher following her. She led the teacher out of the house and into the center of the village. She invited her to sit by the fire while she gathered the others. The second teacher was in what appeared to be her quarters at Thresdenal. The presence of a door made it easier to lead her out of her dream as they stepped out the door of another house in Hochonal.

The man, Te'Unoalie, was sitting on the top of a pinnacle of rock not far from Thresdenal. This was more difficult than the other two. She supposed this sort of thing would happen from time to time. She remembered being out on a pinnacle of rock like this with her father. He had moved up there with his mind and invited her to do the same. She needed the teacher to move himself to a place where she could find a doorway.

"Where are we?"

"A favorite spot of mine outside the city. It has a great view of the valley below. Though, I've never been up here in real life."

"Where can you see it from?"

The teacher faded away.

Kira searched out his consciousness. He stood at the base of a slot canyon. All Kira had to do was lead him through the shadows of the canyon and out a similar passage between the rocks above Hochonal.

If they added more people to this kind of test, Kira would have to find a more expedient way to gather the participants.

The man seated himself beside the others at the village fire. The first woman, Te'Juna, said "Now that you have gathered three of us together in the dream, we can begin the full history of wisdom. Have you ever wondered about it?"

Kira nodded.

"Protocols are in place for many events that might occur including being marooned on a planet," Te'Juna said. "Wisdom is a name we use for Protocol Three. As you might suspect from the name, we do have other protocols. Marooned protocol one is invoked when we land on a planet where inhabitants are sufficiently advanced. There we can establish relations as a fellow star traveling species. This happens from time to time.

"Protocol two involves arrival on a world with no sentient life. In such a case, we would go about the business of establishing a colony in line with our technology. This would include industrial power works, mining, agriculture, advanced cities, and space ports.

"Protocol three is for planets like this one, already inhabited by beings who are not advanced enough to live with us on parity in an advanced civilization but need time to get there. This is where we found ourselves when we became marooned here. We had only the pods we landed in – provisioned with basic survival supplies and some small defensive weapons."

Te'Juna looked to Te'Unoalie, who asked, "Would you allow me to adjust the dream?"

They had taught Kira that a world fashioned by one dreamer could be augmented by another dreamer but should be done with that dreamer's cooperation. They should be open to the change. Kira nodded.

The three of them were suddenly sitting in an enclosed space that was clean and white. Light came from panels in the ceiling and the walls. Kira, who was still facing the teachers, saw beyond them windows that looked out into the stars. Below the windows, were panels of lights and words that changed. Shadows of people sat in seats before the controls, hands moving about the panels. Through the windows, Kira saw a large blue sphere come into view.

The space around them changed again to an empty valley in which several vessels sat on the ground nearby and in the distance. They were shaped like fat fish, but as big as a house. As Kira looked around the valley, she immediately recognized the mesa of Thresdenal. This is Thresdenal at the time of the arrival.

"Upon our landing here," Te'Unoalie said, "we began the work of setting up a primitive settlement and preparing for the first time skip. Within a few months, we were able to hollow out the mesa in a fashion that would seem to have taken years for a primitive society."

As Te'Unoalie spoke, the scene around them shifted. Shadows of people moved about. Kira could see openings from inside the mesa. Houses began to be built, and irrigation ditches dug.

"We established farms and began harvesting crops. I was a young engineering officer at the time and along with other scientists broke down our pods for raw materials to build a gate for a time skip. We had to send out groups to gather a few bits of ore that weren't found in our pods. We mined only what we needed, trying to leave no evidence. Completely tearing down our pods and building the time skip took fifty-one years. We could only take what technology we could carry, such as the regenerators, the map devices, and the data store and readers. Our technology and location limited us to jumping just under six hundred years. But in that time, we didn't know what might happen at Thresdenal, so we had to leave only minimal trace of our advanced technology."

"By barest trace," Te'Juna said, "he means the time skip device, hidden deep within Thresdenal."

"We put it in a large hollowed out chamber that could easily be opened from within, but not so easily from without."

Te'Rochrael spoke up and said, "To our delight, upon arriving back at Thresdenal, we found that humans had not settled in this valley, and we were able to recommence the work of operating our settlement. We also realized that to build a gate for the next time skip bridge, we no longer had our ships to rely on and would require natural resources. Materials from the original bridge could not be used because they had become entangled at a quantum level in a fixed time and space connection. Luckily, this area has deep erosion cuts that allowed us to identify pockets of ore. That is why we have the outer settlements, like Hochonal. Hochonal is about a day's journey from a rich pocket of minerals that were needed for the time skip device."

"I've never seen any mines near Hochonal," Kira said, suddenly embarrassed that she had interrupted the teacher.

"We finished extracting what we needed, over 60 years ago," Te'Rochrael said, apparently unflustered by the interruption. "We did not abandon the outer villages as they had other uses."

"You mean like breeding dreamers?" Kira asked.

"That's a rather crass way of putting it," Te'Rochrael said. "We created concentrated genetic environments. No marriages or breeding were forced on anyone. And your gifts seem to have proven out our endeavor."

"We may have drifted off topic," Te'Juna said. "As a teacher, it is important that you understand the third protocol is the basis for wisdom, as we teach it to children, but the basis is to leave as little trace as possible while sustaining our family lines. We, as a species, have existed and maintained a historical record for hundreds of thousands of years. We maintain our species and culture by maintaining family lines. This leads to our highest ideal, the survival and education of our children. Upon our next time skip, our children will be reintroduced into a society that travels among the stars. Our duty is to see that they have the mathematical, scientific, and cultural knowledge to reenter that society and thrive. Do you understand?"

"At the beginning of my explanation," Te'Unoalie said, "I showed you the inside of an escape pod. Can you now recreate it from memory?"

Kira concentrated on being in that place and the dream shifted. They were back in the pod. As she looked about, she felt that many of the details were lacking. She concentrated just as she had done when recreating her walk through Thresdenal. Items began to appear filling in many of the details. She concentrated on the panel, and words began to change. The only things lacking were the shadows of the people. She concentrated, and the shadows of the people appeared, even their strange clothing. But they weren't moving about the way they had been.

"The people moved in my version, because I drew on an actual memory of people piloting the pod," Te'Unoalie said.

How old was he? Kira wondered to herself. How old were any of them, that they spoke with firsthand knowledge of the first landing?

"Kira," Te'Juna said, "over your next course of training, we will be showing you a completely new world of spaceships, laboratories, engineering centers, and other worlds our people have visited. Your job will be to master them as you have this one, that you may have the context for teaching the rising generation."

"In addition," Te'Unoalie said, "you will be taught in depth about the time skip gate and its workings in preparation for the next time skip."

There it was, the thing Kira wanted to know. "When will the next time skip be?"

Te'Unoalie and Te'Rochrael both looked to Te'Juna. "That will depend a great deal on your training, Kira. The time skip device is ready, and we are within range of the time for our rescue. Your training will involve using the gate to form the bridge."

"I'm supposed to form the bridge?"

Te'Unoalie leaned forward. "Yes, gather the people to the gate and open it. The time skip gate, like our long-distance starships, relies on a quantum interface that is too complex for manual operation. It requires the direct mental connection of a dreamer. An ordinary dreamer can pilot a starship, but only a gatherer can make the many connections necessary to open a bridge."

"A gatherer?"

"Someone like you, who can connect to people not yet met through their connection with another."

"That ability for me is unpredictable. Are you going to train me on how to make it consistent?"

"The records are vague on how it is done differently from normal dreaming."

"Someone must have opened the time skip device the first time."

"Sadly," Te'Juna said. "The former gatherers are no longer with us. We trust that your skills will grow. That is all for now."

Each of the teacher's faded from Kira's dream. Kira let go of the dream and felt surprised to see them sitting before her in the room in Thresdenal.

"Tomorrow," Te'Juna said, "you will start the next phase of your training." She gestured toward the door.

Kira rose and left.

Kira had just finished a dream meditation, where she practiced fighting with a staff as Matusu had taught her.

Ryrie, one of the initiates several years older than Kira stuck her head in the door. "You've been called to the council chamber," she said.

Kira stood and straightened her robe. This was not part of the daily routine, which she had to say, was becoming pretty routine. Going down two stairways and a shortcut down a ladder brought her to the main floor just a couple corridors away from the council chamber.

She had started to figure out the layout of the place. At first it seemed completely organic and random – which Te'Marile would call a contradiction of an unobservant mind. Soon, Kira realized that the corridors were a set of meandering but clearly defined concentric rings. The upper corridors clung mostly to open areas where living spaces received light from windows cut through to the many slots and open areas that rose to the surface. Kira's room had a window that allowed her to catch a sliver of blue sky if she stood on a chair, leaned into it a bit, and looked up.

As she entered the council chamber, she was startled to see the old man who had locked her away. He stood in the middle of the room – his hands bound in front of him. He was dirty and tired looking as though he himself had been subjected to time in subterranean confinement.

"Kira," Ka'Te'Losa said from her council seat, "is this the man that locked you in a room below the tower?"

A few weeks ago, Kira would have cried at the site of the man. Now, she had somehow changed. Here, surrounded by the teachers, Kira felt stronger. "That's him." She was suddenly angry. "Why did you lock me up?"

He didn't answer. He just stood with his head down.

"We know why he did it," Ka'Te'Losa said. "You can go now. We will deal with him."

"I want to know why!"

"You will know why in time. Right now, we must deal with this man." Ka'Te'Losa had a look that Kira recognized. It essentially said, Don't test me.

Kira bowed, turned, and left. She walked all the way to the end of the corridor before she notice the pain in her hands. She had clenched her fists so tightly that her nails dug into her palms leaving marks. She told herself she was over her time in the darkness – that it was just one more step in her trip toward Thresdenal, like falling in the river or surviving a night in a sandstorm. This was somehow different though. This included betrayal of trust. Rivers and storms were what they were. But her people were supposed to take care of each other.

She marched through the halls until she came to the training center where Matusu was supposed to be. The other guards said he had just left on a desert run and would be back soon. Kira didn't really want to talk to him. She didn't know why she had even come. She watched the guards train. They grappled and threw one another.

Most of their moves subdued an opponent without any injury. She thought about the fighting that Matusu had been showing her in the dream. This was the style – disarm and subdue without harming the other. Right now, she wanted to hurt someone.

She left the training center and headed back toward the teacher apartments. Her feet led her to her own door, where she was certain Patala would be home by now. Rather than turning and going in, she continued past. She went up to the next level to where she knew the older teachers sometimes met and talked.

The large room had low chairs where several teachers sat conversing or looking out the low inward-facing windows into the open area below. Two of Kira's instructors were here, but they paid her little attention. This was where they came to get away from students' questions, and this is where students could come and find relief from the incessant tests and challenges of the teachers.

Several windows spanned one wall at different heights letting in light. In dimmer parts of the room, lamps burned with a warm glow. Te'Roan sat in a corner near a lamp looking as though he was meditating.

"You need to teach me," she said.

"And what is wrong with the teachers assigned to you?"

"Nothing. You need to teach me to fight the way you fight."

"I see." Te'Roan did that long staring teacher thing, like he was assessing the worth of her soul. "And what would you do with such skills?"

"I'd make sure I never get locked up in a hole or pulled into a river or chased out of my home." Kira could feel tears starting to well up. She swallowed back the lump building in her throat. "I'd make sure that whoever tried to hurt me would regret it."

"You would have vengeance?"

"They caught the old man who locked me up."

"Yes, I know. He didn't really want to hurt you – you know."

"He certainly had a strange way of being my friend."

"He wanted to hurt Ka'Te'Losa."

"How do you know?"

"He knows that Ka'Te'Losa seeks dreamers to aid in fulfilling the third protocol."

"You mean gatherers," she said.

"Yes, a gatherer. If he could keep you – a possible gatherer – from reaching her, he would have more arguments to abandon the protocol."

"Why? What do you mean abandon the protocol? It's our way home, a way to preserve our families."

"A growing faction want to stop hiding in the desert. Some have traveled and seen too much of what is beyond the sands."

"Like the village by the river that the humans destroyed?"

"Far beyond that. This world has lush lands with great human cities. With our knowledge, we could rule those cities. But that is not the third protocol. That is not any of the protocols."

"So I was being used as leverage to get Ka'Te'Losa outvoted?"

"It appears so. Someone found out that you had made an indirect connection, and that was enough to make you the most valuable dreamer in a century."

"I'm not anyone's leverage. I won't be. You need to teach me to fight like you and my father fought in Hochonal."

"You aren't ready. You are just learning to use your gifts and learning what they are for. Focus on that."

"So you won't help me?"

"When you are ready, you will be taught. And when you are taught, it will be to preserve the people and wisdom."

Kira stormed out. He didn't understand. He was big and a teacher. No one probably ever tried to lock him up. She could see him in her mind fighting the human warriors. She also remembered how her father had fought with the same speed and force. It was something teachers did – a way of protecting themselves – but apparently they kept it secret from even the guards. It was like each group kept secrets to stay in power. The people were subject to the guards, and the guards were subject to the teachers. Kira wondered what secret Ka'Te'Losa knew that kept the teachers subject to her. No wonder a faction had risen up to seize power. Anyone who wanted to defend herself or himself should have the right to learn how.

Kira returned to her own room. Sure enough, Patala was waiting for her. Patala would have probably had to live on a lower level or outside the mesa if it weren't for Kira. She was there to offer some stability to their new home. A weaver in the market had taken Patala on as an apprentice. The woman created amazing blankets – many too beautiful, Kira thought, to be used as blankets. And though Patala said she was grateful, Kira could tell that she missed the life they had in Hochonal.

"Any word?" Patala asked. That was her standard question about mother and father and the rest of the village.

Kira shook her head – the standard response.

"Terrice sold two of my blankets today. She gave me sweet bread to say…" Patala's voice trailed off. "What's the matter?"

"They caught him – the man who locked me up. They caught him and called me in to confirm he was the one."

"That's good, right?"

"I just want to hurt him. I want to punch him and kick him and…stars!"

Patala had crossed the room to put her arm around Kira. She held her the way their mother had, holding her head on her shoulder.

"I just want to be what Father wanted – to finish learning what he started teaching me."

"I know. I just want to punch and kick and scream at everyone who attacked us, chased us, or locked up my little sister. Maybe Matusu will let us punch him," Patala said.

"He probably would, and it wouldn't even really hurt him."

"I think he hurts as much as anyone. He just doesn't show it. He's put all his energy into building a new life here, but I know he misses his parents and Hochonal."

Kira sat silently trying not to get lost in missing her parents – a path that always beckoned at the edge her thoughts. As she tried to come back to here and now, something Patala had said came back to her. "You have sweet bread?" she asked.

They shared the bread by the fading light of their window. They had a lamp that they didn't like to light too early. Everything here cost something. As an apprentice, Patala got whatever share of trade goods that Terrice was willing to give her. Kira on the other hand got just a little more food than she needed, so that she could trade for things like lamp oil.

Kira remembered the woman who tricked her and handed her off to her captors. She realized now that the woman had done such a horrible thing for assurances on the price for her crop. Kira thought that if getting more of something meant betraying another, it wasn't worth the price. She would enjoy the sweet bread when it was given, but she wouldn't get to the point that she would do anything to anyone for it. That was probably a good thing, because as far as she could tell, teachers were destined to live off the kindness and generosity of the people they taught.

After eating, Kira just wanted to lay down and go to sleep. But she also knew that the mental discipline to succeed as a teacher and a dreamer only came a little at a time. She sat on her bed and began her evening meditation. Missing a day would leave out drops of mental toughness she would need. Each day's lessons were tougher than the day before, and Kira could not afford to let up.

She slipped into the dream as if beckoned. She sat in a chair beneath a tree across from Ka'Te'Losa. Glancing around, she realized they were near the tower, but all the other buildings of Thresdenal were gone.

"It is good that you do your meditations," Ka'Te'Losa said.

"I'm honored," Kira said.

"I wanted to talk to you away from distractions."

Kira thought she knew what this was about.

"Your outburst at the trial – is that how teachers conduct themselves?"

"No Teacher."

"Then I assure you it is not the way a leader conducts herself."

"I am sorry. I was overcome with…"

"You were overcome by fear. That is natural, but that does not help our people."

"I just want to see justice done."

"Walk with me," Ka'Te'Losa said. She stood and began walking among the boulders around the base of the mesa they called the tower. "When I became a teacher, this is all there was of Thresdenal. We were preparing for the first time skip. Do you know why we built so much more?"

"We needed to feed the people with farms and gather minerals from the places that are now the outer villages."

"And why did that matter?"

"Because caring for the people mattered," Kira said.

"Your path cannot lead to personal retribution or personal comforts. That man who locked you away is an enemy to wisdom and therefore an enemy to us all. Your greatest response to such attacks is to press forward and continue to follow wisdom. Then you will have won."

"Has the man been punished?" Kira asked.

"Not fully. His full punishment will come when you have done all that your talent allows in caring for the people."

"Will he even know?"

Ka'Te'Losa stopped walking and turned to look directly at Kira. "Does that change what you have to do?" Ka'Te'Losa took Kira by both hands. She seemed to know the doubt Kira was feeling. "You'll figure it out."

The dream faded.

Chapter 9

Matusu thought he was prepared for the heat. After all, he had grown up in it. This was different. He jogged on – following the other guards across a black lava flow as wide as any he had ever seen. Unlike the canyons of his home that created shadows protecting one from the sun most of the day, this place offered only heat. He felt the fire through his boots and ached to step on the occasional patches of white sand among the dark stones. But that would leave a print. The stones offered a way to cross this expanse without leaving a trail.

Matusu had used most of his water on the way out, he longed to stop and drink more now, but did not want to fall behind. A lizard darted between the rocks – small enough to make use of the scant shade they offered. The little reptile seemed to taunt Matusu with its ability to find respite from the sun.

The training team Matusu was a part of travelled the third leg of their journey scouting a known crossing along a small river to the south. They were learning to search for humans without being seen by them. Matusu was learning to blend with the desert like the coyote, while listening, looking, and smelling, like the rabbit that kept its distance. Their instructors pointed out signs of humans passing through the area, and Matusu soon became adept at finding the signs for himself.

Now their job was to return without leaving any signs for humans to follow.

Matusu wished he had been trained like this before the journey from Hochonal. He may have been better able to detect the warriors by the river and avoid getting separated from Kira.

Each night, their training team camped in some rocky nook where they were out of site and leaving no trace. They would perform their exercises to maintain mental and physical discipline. And each night as Matusu fell asleep, Kira would visit him.

She plied him with questions about his training. He was amazed at how real the dream world could seem when she was there. He began showing her the advanced defensive moves he had learned. Nothing as impressive as the fighting they had seen Te'Roan and Jornatha do, but it was the same foundation. The same balance and movement. He also showed her how the guards moved across the desert.

"Hold."

The words – nearly a whisper – snapped Matusu out of his mind back to reality. He held absolutely still. His balanced gait allowed him to hold right where he was without any motion. Ever so slowly, he lowered himself to crouch on the rock – reducing his profile.

"Drink," the leader said. "We'll be back in the valley soon."

Matusu didn't hesitate to finish off the rest of his water. His stamina had increased, and he was able to do more with less, but it did not change the sense of peace he felt from the moisture – warm as it was. Limited water was something he was getting used to on these desert treks. Hochonal, with its year-round water flow, had spoiled him. Now he understood why his father had told him to get used to being thirsty once in a while. He also remembered why he avoided being thirsty.

He suddenly felt a buzzing in his mind, a voice almost too soft to hear. He closed his eyes. He shut out the sounds of the slight breeze and the heat. He put all of it outside and focused on that voice. It was clearly Kira, though he could barely hear her. And how was she reaching him outside of a dream? Was he getting better at hearing, or was Kira getting better at reaching out?

"We're moving," the leader said – breaking Matusu's concentration.

Matusu moved on. He didn't have the ability to concentrate on the voice and also move the way he was trained. Glancing back, he was pleased to see that his passing left no trail. Now he would need to learn to split his attention and make this automatic so he could think of other things as he travelled. He was learning how to transform himself into more than he had been. The most important thing to focus on was the here and now. That was something else he had changed. He no longer dreamed of the ways his life would change or of the places he would someday go. That life had begun.

Kira broke off trying to reach Matusu. He had been gone for a couple of days now. Reaching him at a distance was a good test of her skills. She felt like she had gotten through, could sense his presence, but couldn't hear him consciously respond to her. The teachers had taught her to consciously reach out to those she had strong connections with. It had worked perfectly with her teachers, but with Matusu, it wasn't quite there. She continued to reach out to others she had reached before. Patala was easy. Of course, she had told her sister what to expect.

"I'm guessing by the smile on your face you have succeeded," Ka'Te'Losa said.

Kira was startled by the woman's sudden presence. She was usually announced by someone before she arrived in the training rooms.

"I was able to reach my sister outside of the dream," Kira said.

"That is good. Your progress is nothing short of amazing. What of others besides myself who you have not shared a dream with?"

"Not yet."

"You will need to." Ka'Te'Losa turned to one of Kira's teachers. "Let me know when she achieves that." Then she paused, looking at no one as though distracted by some thought.

"Ka'Te'Losa, how do I find people I haven't already found in the dream?" Kira asked. She had read the accounts of the gatherer process, but as the master teachers had said, the accounts were vague.

"How did you find them the first time in the dream?"

"I focused on them and searched for them, but they were already in the dream."

"Kira, we are all in the dream."

That was rather unspecific. It seemed that the further Kira went in her training the less specific the instruction became. It was as though they were blind guides coaxing her forward based on rumors of some unseen trail.

As abruptly as she'd arrived, Ka'Te'Losa left the training room.

Kira resumed her meditation – this time reaching out to make a waking connection with someone she knew but had never contacted in the dream. She groped in the dark looking for any beacon of light. She could feel the presence of those she had shared the dream with. They glowed brightly. But others…

"There are no others," she said to no one in particular. "What am I looking for?"

"Perhaps," one of the teachers started tentatively, "you need to focus on something else for a while. You've made great progress today. Tonight, when others will be dreaming, focus on finding a dream of someone you have not met. Someone close to someone that is close to you."

"Share a stranger's dream?"

"Ka'Te'Losa had not met you, and yet the two of you found each other in the dream."

"But we had seen each other in my father's dream. We had a connection."

"Then start there. Find someone who knows someone whose dreams you have visited."

Kira imagined she would run into the same problem of not knowing what to look for. She would try.

People seemed to be bustling more than usual as Kira returned from training.

"Did you hear?" Patala asked, stopping Kira in the hallway outside their quarters. "The guard patrol that just got back found more signs of humans than usual. They think a large group of them have been traveling by night looking for other passages into the valley. Passages that aren't watched."

"That sounds like they know where the city is, and they also know the canyon entrances are watched."

"Te'Roan told me that they could get into the valley by scaling cliffs to the south, but it's unlikely."

"Are you spending a lot of time talking with Te'Roan?" Kira asked.

Patala blushed and rolled her eyes. "He stopped by the weaver's shop today."

"I'm sure he stops by every day," Kira said, grinning.

"Now stop. This is serious. Everyone is preparing in case the humans do make it into the valley."

"There would have to be a lot of them to take on all the guards and teachers in Thresdenal. A guard is worth five human warriors in a fight, and a teacher is worth ten."

"Kira, you know that's not our way. We only fight when cornered. Apparently, we would have to leave. Guards can delay them, but we would have to disperse to the outer villages."

"I'm not running anymore. I've been studying how we lived before we came here and how we can live when we leave. This way of life isn't meant to be ours generation after generation. It was a stop gap – a temporary way to cope and survive until…"

"Until what? What do you know?"

"Patala, I think we came here to do more than escape Hochonal. I think they…we…everyone have been waiting for some way to escape the humans…to escape this world."

"What do you mean escape this world?"

"Some of the older teacher's dream of things…things they've studied or things they remember about where we came from."

"We know this Kira. We are visitors and humans belong, but we can't just dream our way back into the stars."

"We don't have to. Wisdom was meant to give us time to create our final escape. It won't be long before we time skip again, but this time it will be to our rescue. We can leave this world."

Patala, the one with her feet firmly planted in the needs of here and now, looked at her sister for a moment and gave a sigh. "They were right when they called you a dreamer. You'll have to figure out how to time skip us later. Right now, you need to make sure you have a bag ready for travel. We've all been asked to have one ready in case we need to flee."

Kira wondered how two sisters could be so different. After preparing her bag and eating dinner, no one had called for them to flee, so Kira went to bed.

She set out first to find those teachers she had shared dreams with, but she didn't enter their dreams. She sort of hung around on the fringes looking for any sign of someone she didn't know. Then she had an idea. From her own dream, which she still saw as Hochonal, she entered the dream of Ka'Te'Losa but rather than searching out the woman, she began looking around the edges of the dream for anything that looked like a doorway to another dream. It didn't take long, though it was kind of tricky because Ka'Te'Losa's dream was a rocky hollow just outside Thresdenal. She imagined that Ka'Te'Losa must be connected to dozens of other dreams. She found that shadowed folds of sandstone were actually gateways.

The dream she entered looked familiar, and she quickly realized it was one of her teacher's dreams. She returned to Ka'Te'Losa's dream and began looking for another passage.

The next passage she entered led to a place she hadn't been before though it reminded her of the tunnels she had passed through during her captivity. Occasionally, she could see lights shining from the walls. The stone was different. It was lighter and seemed to be a combination of sandstone with larger rocks and stones embedded in it. She soon found the dream's main occupant. A man dressed in a very old and worn teacher's robe. She had never met him before. He seemed startled to see her. He stood at a table that contained several map devices like the one Te'Roan had used. Several other odd looking devices sat on the table as well. No sooner had Kira glanced at them than the items all disappeared. He apparently wasn't interested in sharing.

"Have we met," he asked. His eyes carried more than a hint of suspicion.

"I don't think so. I'm new here. I'm…"

"Kira Waterborn," he said – the suspicion replaced by astonishment.

"Can you read my thoughts?"

"No, no." He smiled. "It's just that Losa had mentioned...but I never thought. Do you know how you found me?"

"I came through Ka'Te'Losa's dream."

"Amazing. We've tried that. We've tried so many things." He reminded her of a child at the harvest feast talking about the foods he tried – a very old child at the harvest feast.

"So many things to what?"

"To get to dreams beyond those we know. We started to doubt if it could be done again. Most started saying that the talent had been lost, but Ka'Te'Losa wouldn't give up. Without it the gate would... well, still there's more isn't there – like getting to those none of us know. Some say we're all connected...the reason the teachers go out, but the teachers can't go everywhere all at once. And once the gathering starts it will have to be just at the right time, no time for searching around."

He had completely lost Kira. His ramblings turned to muttering. Items started appearing back on the table, and he turned his attention to them as he talked. "I wanted to send communication devices out to everyone, but Ka'Te'Losa wouldn't risk it. Wisdom. She's right." He paused and looked at Kira – completely focused again. "And look, here you are."

Kira thought that this lucid moment was her chance to learn something. She started with a simple question. "Who are you?"

"Oh, me. I'm Rory. I keep...well...this." He gestured toward the items on the table.

"What is the gathering?" Kira asked.

"Well, it's when everybody comes in when they get ready to leave. Only we can't gather until we open the gate...well not that we open the gate...the gate forms the bridge. And that's what I've spent my life working to do. If you're the gatherer, we better meet so you can open the gate." Suddenly, they were no longer in the room by the table, they were in a large room cut into the rock, similar to the one they had just been in, but much larger.

"What is this?" she asked.

Rory turned, almost startled she was still near him. "You are an accomplished dreamer aren't you? And so young."

"I'm not sure age has anything to do with talent."

Rory shrugged and walked closer to an intricately designed metal circle on the floor. "This is the gate that forms the bridge that everything else is meant to get us to."

"You mean the circle in the rock?" Many different metals formed patterns in it.

"Well, yes. Though it's not really in the rock. That's just where we set it. It won't turn on until a dreamer of sufficient power connects with it. The power works, everything works, it's just hasn't been opened yet."

"Te'Rory, how does the dreamer operate the circle or gate?"

"It's about making multiple connections that then connect to other connections – the specifics for doing that only a gatherer can tell you. Though they seemed to figure it out last time. But then, the last person had also piloted a starship – very different, but the same. And just call me Rory. I haven't been a teacher for years."

"Hmm," Rory grunted, like he had an idea, and they were back in the room by the table. He picked up a small rod, not much longer than his hand. Running his finger across it caused it to light up and display in front of him. Not as big as the map Te'Roan had displayed, but big enough that Kira could see a picture in the light with figures displaying around it.

"Well this doesn't help me here since I can only see what I already know or what you already know. You need to know the target date. Are humans really coming?"

The question carried so much worry with it, Kira didn't know how to answer. "Not enough to worry about," she said.

"Well, thank you for your visit. Tell Losa I'm ready."

"Where are you in the real world?"

"To the west...." Rory and the devices faded from view. A moment later the table faded.

Kira exited back through to Ka'Te'Losa's dream.

"That is the way to Rory," Ka'Te'Losa said.

Kira jumped, thinking she was alone.

"Did you visit with him?" Ka'Te'Losa asked.

"I did," Kira said.

Ka'Te'Losa smiled. "I knew you could do it, Kira. I knew the moment you saw me in your father's dream."

Ka'Te'Losa faded from the dream, and Kira found herself in her own dream in Hochonal. She'd solved the mystery of reaching someone she didn't know, but she had uncovered a basket full of questions that she never even thought about asking. And she still hadn't figured out what to do about someone that no one knew.

Kira knew that battling in a dream was easier because you didn't actually get hurt, but she forgot to account for feeling pain. She could tell Matusu held back, but that didn't make the ground any softer when he swept her feet out from under her. The lessons were the same ones Matusu had been learning in guard training. They were meant to deflect an opponent's blow and limit his opportunity to immediately strike again. Kira found this very effective as she had yet to land a single blow on Matusu.

"Again," she said and rolled back to her feet. She came at him as hard as she could.

Again, Matusu deflected her blow and left her in the sand. He had not as yet used a single offensive attack on her. He had told her to learn defense first, but Kira had opted for attack. If she were captured again, she would not wait for her captors to attack her.

She could feel the anger welling up inside her. Matusu was making it look too easy. He was holding back on the attacks he had taught her. He hadn't shown her everything. Or was she really just too weak. That was a thought she would not except. She dug deep, looking for untapped strength and let loose. She felt a surge of energy, and Matusu stepped back missing the first deflection.

Kira caught him hard in the shoulder, paralyzing his arm for a moment. She stepped through her attack hooking her leg behind his knee and dropping him to the ground.

"What was that?" Matusu asked, startled.

Kira stepped back half shocked half smiling. She had done it.

"What was that?" Matusu repeated as he got up from the ground.

"It was the attack you taught me."

"No. Before the attack when you pushed me back. How did you do that?"

"You just stepped back. I didn't do anything."

"You definitely did something."

Kira thought back to the day her father fought the humans making them fall back in fear. She remembered him drawing the storm in the dream world. Was that what she did? Did she use some kind of mental surge on Matusu? She didn't even know how.

"What did you feel?" Kira asked.

Matusu looked down for a moment as though thinking about what he had felt. "I felt fear. Like a wave of fear passing through me. I know that sounds strange."

"It's what my father did in Hochonol. It has to be. I just don't know how it happened."

"So you can't do it again?"

"I don't know. I don't think I want to do it again. It might hurt you."

"It startled me, but I don't think it hurt me. It was like I felt fear or weakness for a moment."

Kira concentrated on how she did it the first time and tried to push the wave again. Nothing happened.

"I'm not sure what I did. Maybe I can't do it repeatedly. I kind of felt it building up and then it was gone."

"Even if you can only do it once, it can really set your opponent back. It completely surprised me and gave you an advantage."

"I'll keep working on it."

"While your brain is working on that, can we work on your defensive moves? I worry more about someone attacking you then about you being the aggressor. No matter how angry you feel, it just isn't you."

"I'm not sure I know what or who I am these days."

"Come on Kira, you're just learning more about what you can do. That doesn't change who you are."

"It seems to change who others think I am. I met a man named Rory in the dream. He knew about my abilities. He said he'd been working to get things ready for when I arrive, and he seemed to get fairly anxious."

"Arrive where?"

"He said that we needed to get ready to go, and he had a time skip device, a gate, he was working on, but I had to make it work. I think I'm supposed to bring all the people of Thresdenal and the outer villages to go through the gate. That's why Ka'Te'Losa wants me to visit the dreams of people I haven't met."

"You can do that?"

"I have done that – though I haven't yet figured out how to reach someone with no connection."

"You wouldn't have to."

"Why not?"

"Because the teachers travel around to every village?"

"I thought that was to teach people."

"That's one of the things they do, but the real reason may be so there is a connection to every village. If you can connect to all the teachers, you can connect to all the villages."

"Well, they know I can do that now. What are we waiting for?"

"Maybe it's that gate that Rory was working on. I mean, all the people from Thresdenal and all the villages can't just go there and hang out. There isn't enough food. Each village – including Thresdenal – grows just enough food for itself and a person can only carry a few days' worth of food with them. I mean what if you gathered everyone, and it took another year for you to learn to open the gate?"

"We'd all starve," Kira thought about it. "So they want to make sure I'm strong enough to open the gate before they gather people."

"That makes sense," Matusu said.

General assemblies of the teachers had been called several times since Kira arrived in Thresdenal, but this was the first time she had been directly invited. And to make it even more uncomfortable, she had been asked to sit on the dais near Ka'Te'Losa. The chairs were mostly the same, except that Ka'Te'Losa's chair had cushions on the seat and back, where the others had ornately woven patterns. As Kira took her seat, she noticed Rory sitting in the front row. This was the first time she had actually seen him in person. He was covered in dust as though he had just made a long journey and hadn't had time to wash and change.

People milled around the room. Every teacher Kira had ever seen was here, along with most of the senior guards. She didn't see Matusu, but then, someone had to be actually out guarding. The low noise of dozens of quiet discussions filled the room. People seemed to look at Kira or gesture toward her frequently. She felt that she was a main topic of conversation.

The room quieted as Ka'Te'Losa entered from the side of the dais. She wore her formal white teacher's robe that just skimmed the floor. She walked to the center of the dais and stood in front of her chair. When the room had fallen silent, Ka'Te'Losa took a step forward and spoke. "I see we have finally been able to gather a quorum among our teachers." Ka'Te'Losa looked to the left and right to the teachers sitting on the dais – several of them as old as Ka'Te'Losa, all of them older than Kira by many years. She recognized those who had instructed her.

Gesturing toward the audience, Ka'Te'Losa said, "Many of you have come in from your travels to be here. Thank you. It is a momentous occasion. After nearly a hundred years, we have reached a turning point. Many of you who have visited the outer villages have noted that humans press in on us in greater numbers. They are poised to fill the land that has been our refuge. In this, our time of need, wisdom has given us a gatherer."

Ka'Te'Losa didn't point to Kira or even say that it was Kira, but everyone's eyes were on her. Kira couldn't help but feel the weight of the room – the hope, the doubt, the fear of change all resting in the hands of a girl that had arrived mere months ago.

"Our gatherer is the daughter of Te'Jornatha Waterborn and Remelle Starward. Te'Jornatha, who many of you knew, could very well be standing here now had he not chosen to follow the urging of wisdom and return to our place of hope in Hochonal."

In all of that, Kira was struck by one word. Ka'Te'Losa had said knew…many of you knew. It hit Kira with force – her greatest fear, one she had been denying for months. The thought consumed her mind. Her father was gone – he had died. Ka'Te'Losa knew it. She hadn't said anything to Kira, because as a dreamer, Kira herself should have known it. She had known it, and now Ka'Te'Losa confirmed it.

"Kira, please stand," Ka'Te'Losa said.

Kira suddenly realized that Ka'Te'Losa had said it twice. She rose to her feet trying to shake off the anguish that filled her mind. She must focus on the now. She must push away her own grieving for another time. Just like when she was carried away by the river, she couldn't think about her loss, she must focus on surviving now. She looked into Ka'Te'Losa's eyes – focused her thoughts there. She was not alone.

Around the room, whispers and low spoken comments broke the silence. Ka'Te'Losa raised a hand to regain the room's attention. "As those of you who have studied the turnings of wisdom know, the arrival of the gatherer heralds the beginning of the gathering. And authority is turned over to the gatherer, who will guide our steps in this endeavor. I would do that today if it were not for a concern that stands in the way of the gathering. I wanted this brought out before the full council and teacher body that you all would understand and work to assist us. Rory Whitecrest has come to tell us of his concern."

Rory stood and made his way up the three steps onto the dais. He looked out over the audience and back at Ka'Te'Losa and Kira. He smiled and nodded at Kira as though they shared a secret.

"As Ka'Te'Losa and Kira are aware and many of you who know the turnings, the gathering is to be immediately followed by a departure through a gate – a point of quantum connection through time. The gate, completed a decade or so ago, has not yet been tested. We need the young gatherer here to test it, as none of the rest of us have the means to make the connections. The thing is that once she tests it, the clock starts…" Rory fumbled through a bag at his side and pulled out two hourglasses. Kira knew what they were from her lessons, though she had never actually seen one. "You see, once we start even a micro test on our end, even if we shut it off…" He turned over one hourglass. "Time connects on the other end." He turned over the other hourglass. "And they will run in parallel from then on. That is until the gatherer fully opens the gate, then it can run for approximately one day before shutting down, never to be used again."

"Thank you Rory," Ka'Te'Losa said. "We don't need to know all the details now. Perhaps you can explain what it is we need to do."

"Well, we need to get the gatherer," he gestured to Kira, "to the gate to test it, and once she does that, people need to get moving toward the gate. Now this didn't seem to be a point we needed to hurry on, but with the humans…"

Ka'Te'Losa raised a hand to silence Rory. "With the humans growing in number and making inroads closer and closer to Thresdenal, we don't have the time we once thought we did. I ask that Kira's lessons be given priority over all else and that each of you meet with her and give her access to your dreams, especially those of you who have traveled to the outer villages."

Te'Marile spoke from her seat on the dais. "Forming a bridge with the gate is complex. If she can't open it, what then?"

"We keep trying until she can open it," Ka'Te'Losa said.

"So wisdom may fail us," said a teacher from the audience that Kira didn't know. She would not soon forget him though. He had a scar running down his face from the outside corner of his eye to the corner of his mouth.

"We would not be lost, merely delayed," Ka'Te'Losa said.

"What if this girl performs the test, but cannot fully open the gate," Te'Marile said, adding another argument to the descent. "We could not then let the years tick by and still hold to protocol three," Te'Marile pointed out.

"True," Rory said with a sigh. "Once we test, time isn't working in our favor, when you consider the window for doing this will only be open a few years. The gate was built to reach out as far as we know how, that's why it wasn't used right when it was built. That and not having a gatherer. If we don't arrive within the timeframe that our rescuers are watching, we will be trapped here…well…trapped here in the future."

The noise in the room grew as dozens of discussions broke out.

Kira finally realized that the teachers were divided because they lacked hope. Some may have started thinking they could just live and wait for the ship, but her ancestors knew the humans would fill the land, and they believed that was the right of the humans.

"I can do this – wisdom guide me – I can do this," Kira said. The room quieted.

The man with the scar laughed. "And how do we know that?" He asked.

The noise in the room grew louder.

"Should we not prepare a contingency?" Te'Marile asked. "Another refuge in a more hidden place would be wise to establish."

"Wisdom relied on a gatherer," Ka'Te'Losa said, "which we knew we could expect. There have been others who some of you knew. Kira found me while still untrained. She has found many of you and connected with others you know. She is the most powerful dreamer among us by far."

"I am ready," Kira said.

"I put it to a vote. Will we accept Kira as Gatherer to open our way home?"

A counting of the votes fell in favor of Kira attempting to open the gate.

"We shall provide her with an additional month of lessons here, and then she shall depart to open a test bridge at the gate."

Kira noticed looks between Te'Marile and the man with the scar. The man nodded slightly and then looked away.

Chapter 10

"How long does more training need to take?" Kira asked, pacing the length of the room she shared with her sister.

"Kira, it's only been two weeks. Are you really that anxious to go out across the desert again?" Patala asked.

"Te'Marile somehow worked her way into controlling my schedule and keeps forcing me to review mundane abilities that have nothing to do with gathering or operating the gate."

"Te'Marile seems to have the best of intentions just like you. What if you can't even do it?"

"I suppose you're right about Te'Marile, but I have doubts about that other teacher – Te'Srin. He seems too hostile to the plan – maybe his hostility came with the scar."

"As long as he sticks to wisdom…well, even father didn't stick completely to wisdom, did he?"

"Father did what he did against the human warriors so we could escape. And now he's…"

Patala stood and put an arm around Kira. "We've known since we left Hochonal. Now we live up to the things he taught us. We finish the task he set us on...the task he set you on."

Kira heard footsteps approaching just before Te'Roan appeared at the open door.

He had a grim look on his face. He stood for a long moment. "I have no easy way to say this. Ka'Te'Losa has passed away," he said, leaning back against the wall. Patala guided him to a chair.

Matusu stood next to Kira's seat among a group of teachers and guards as Te'Marile addressed the group.

"It is with great regret we mourn the passing of Ka'Te'Losa. At this crucial time in our history, we have lost a great leader. With that, as Ka'Te'Losa herself taught, leadership changes, but we still follow wisdom. Before her passing, she believed that we had found the gatherer. We will continue her training to verify Kira's ability."

At the word "verify," Matusu looked across the room at Te'Roan. He shook his head slightly. Just days ago, Kira was regarded as the long-sought-after gatherer. Something wasn't right, and Kira was in the middle of it. Matusu looked around the room and noticed something else. The guards had changed. The guards who had always watched over Ka'Te'Losa – the most senior and trusted guards – weren't in the room. In fact, Matusu barely recognized most of the current guards. He thought he had seen a few of them on occasion coming in from the outer guard stations. Why would Te'Marile have changed the guards?

"Before we press forward in this exercise of trusting everything to this initiate, I invite Kira to join me here."

Matusu noticed that a small table had been brought in and set to one side of the open space on the floor of the hall. Te'Marile walked toward it, inviting Kira to join her. A teacher walked up and handed Te'Marile a small, wrapped bundle. Te'Marile opened it revealing a map device and small metal plate. She set the plate on the table, held the top over the plate, and spun it. The top spun and as Te'Marile focused on it, a map of light formed above it, showing the topography around Thresdenal. No one seemed impressed, as many teachers in the room had used this device. The map blinked away, and the top began to wobble. Te'Marile took hold of it and handed it to Kira. "You try," she said.

Matusu wanted to jump forward and yell at the teacher that this was not fair. A quick look from Te'Roan warned him that he should not interfere.

Kira wrapped the string around the top, held it over the plate, and spun it. It began to whirl. A flat plane of light materialized above it. The light never resolved into a map. After a moment, the top began to wobble and tipped over on the plate.

"This is the simplest of our dreamer controlled devices. If the gatherer cannot control this, what hope should we put in her controlling the gate, our most complex device, and dare I say our most treasured device? Kira you may return to your place."

Matusu wondered who else noticed Kira's balled up fists as she returned to her seat.

He put a hand on Kira's shoulder, then leaned down and whispered, "I need to leave."

He slipped out of the hall and headed toward the south guard barracks. The place was emptier than it should have been. Several squads were missing, including Ariste's squad. Would his mentor have gone out on the desert without telling him?

Matusu knew a good way to check. He grabbed his pack and headed for the city exit closest to the guard barracks, one primarily used by guards. As he expected, he found more prints than he could track, but as he circled away from the city, the prints spread out and separated, leaving distinct, readable impressions.

Matusu focused on the prints that left the least noticeable trace, then headed that direction. He moved as swiftly as he could across the desert. He found no more sign of prints, not because they were trying to hide, but because that was how they moved. Their skills had become instinct.

Just beyond the last farm, Matusu caught a faint smell of smoke, though he saw none as he looked around. He moved up the rise on his left to get a better vantage point. From there, he scanned the area. Not far ahead was a small grove of trees up next to a cleft in the rock. If he were going to start a fire, that's where he would do it, where the trees would dissipate whatever smoke came up. Had they really been hiding, they wouldn't have made a fire at all, but instead, they stopped to eat where it would be least noticed. Had Matusu not been searching for them, he may have passed by without a second look.

He found Ariste and three other guards roasting a rather large snake over the fire. Snake was good meat when you could get it. A rattle lay on a rock by the fire telling Matusu what kind of snake they were eating.

"We've been hearing you for a while," Ariste said. "It's about time you arrived. Though I'm afraid, if you want to eat, you'll have to get your own snake."

Ariste was with Shallan, another captain of the guard and two senior guards, Orr and Krethfel. One had commanded the watchers, but Matusu wasn't sure which one. Along with Ariste, they represented the four most senior members of the guard.

"I came to find you," Matusu said. "Te'Marile has taken over the council and, by default, the city. In the absence of Ka'Te'Losa, she has assumed what should be Kira's, and no one is doing anything to stop her."

"And what is it you think we can do?"

"Not leaving would be a good start."

"Would you have civil war? She has changed the guard leadership and given us a choice to follow or leave. Those who would follow us were sent away. A large group left to wipe away Thresden footprints in Hochonal. We thought it a good time for a hunting trip."

Matusu was silenced for a moment by the mention of Hochonal. He knew what Ariste meant by wiping away footprints. He, Kira, and Patala were all that were left of his village. He was glad he hadn't been sent there. But he also didn't want his mentor to disappear into the desert. "You don't really need to go on a trip to catch a snake," he said.

"That's just traveling food. You should come with us. Up in the mountains are some amazing herds," Orr said.

"You sound like humans."

"We'll have to avoid them," Krethfel said. "But that's pretty much what we do."

The other men laughed.

"We also protect wisdom," Matusu said.

"No," Shallan said. "We protect the teachers at their bidding. And when they stop asking, we stop protecting."

"Kira still needs to be guarded," Matusu said. "Rightfully, she's the single most important teacher that needs to be guarded."

"Is her life in immediate danger?" Shallan asked.

"Well…"

"Is she asking to assume her place as leader?"

"She doesn't…"

"If we went in and set her up as Ka'Te'Kira, would she have the respect of the council and the teachers, or would they see it as a coup?"

"That's only because Te'Marile…"

"Yes, Matusu, Te'Marile has sown the seeds needed to swing support to her cause. She has spent years positioning herself to replace

Ka'Te'Losa, and that is all the more reason for us to stay out of it." Shallan turned his attention back to cooking the snake.

"If you won't protect Kira, I will."

"Now you're speaking like a guard," Ariste said. "That's exactly what you should do. Your junior rank poses no threat to Te'Marile and her new captains. Stay close and protect the gatherer. Things will change. Things always change. Now catch something to eat and join us. We will provide you with a little more training before we leave for the mountains."

Kira sat in the room of mourning where Ka'Te'Losa's body lay covered by a shroud. She would be cremated after five and one days of mourning. Why five and one? Why not six? Kira sometimes found it hard to believe that her people were advanced enough to travel the stars, but still clung to such meaningless ideas and phrases.

The herbs and flowers piled around the body didn't completely mask the smell. Perhaps the one day after the five was a way of saying one day too long. Many people came and left while Kira sat there. She pondered her visits with Ka'Te'Losa, especially her dreams. She still looked for the woman in the dream. The place they had met near Hochonal seemed lonelier.

A presence next to Kira brought her back to the present with a start. Patala sat down next to her.

"Sorry to disturb you," Patala said. "I thought you would like to know that I saw Te'Marile and a group of teachers heading toward the council chambers. I think they mean to resume the council without you."

"More likely, they mean to resume council about me. Te'Marile has to see me as a threat to her power. She claims to be working for the good of the people, but she is more interested in making sure she stays in power. She might even believe I'm right, but saying so gives her no advantage to sway others against me."

"Do you think she will try to have you physically removed?"

"I think she already has, but I don't have any proof. She hid her tracks too well."

"What are we going to do?" Patala asked.

"How would you like to take another journey into the desert?"

Patala didn't answer, but the look on her face spoke of her dislike for the idea.

"We could probably get Te'Roan to go with us. That is, you could get Te'Roan to go with us," Kira said.

"How do you know he won't just force us to stay here?"

"Do you remember how deeply respectful he was of Father? And how close he was to Ka'Te'Losa? I've seen Te'Roan here more than any other teacher. I believe he supports their vision of things, and that includes trusting me to lead out."

"Do you think other teachers will go with us?" Kira sensed that Patala was considering that a caravan would be far less vulnerable than a small group, like the small group they had leaving Hochonal.

"I'm not looking to create a split and lead a mass exodus from the city. We need to slip away quietly for our plan to work. Keeping teachers in place that support Ka'Te'Losa's vision will help keep Te'Marile in check until we return. The smaller the group, the better."

Kira stood in the dream next to a rock formation. She first pulled Te'Roan into the dream, then Matusu and Patala.

"Practicing again Kira?" Te'Roan asked.

"I'm not sure why I try to sleep anymore," Matusu said.

"Practice is over," she said. "We are in danger and need to leave. Do you know this place?"

Te'Roan and Matusu both looked about.

"It's just north of the city," Te'Roan said. "I know it."

"Yes, I know it too," Matusu said. "We did some guard training near here."

"I need you to wake, gather what you need for a long journey in the desert, and meet me here."

"Just like that," Te'Roan said.

"Please," Patala said. "Who knows how long until Te'Marile makes a move against us. She's already been holding council."

"I wasn't called to any council," Te'Roan said.

"Exactly," Kira said. "She has decided who stands with her and will make everyone else look like the aggressors trying to divide the city. We only have a short time before dawn and need to be well clear of here."

"And where are we going," Te'Roan asked.

"First, we will travel to the gate. That's the easy part. After that, we shall see."

"Is it just the four of us again?" Matusu asked.

"Unless you know a couple of guards we can trust to go with us."

"Wait for me as long as you can. If you feel you have to leave, I will catch up," Matusu said.

"And Te'Roan, will you bring your map device?" Kira asked.

"I wouldn't go into the desert without it."

Kira released the dream.

Matusu waited in the dark as Ariste and the other guard leaders discussed his proposal. He knew it was a long shot. Luckily, they hadn't travelled far from the city in case they needed to make a swift return.

Ariste finally broke away from the group and approached Matusu. "You know we all swore to protect the teachers and wisdom. So, your proposal merits splitting our forces. You said Te'Roan would be going with you?"

"Yes," Matusu said.

"And Kira Waterborn."

Matusu nodded.

"In that case, Orr and I will accompany you. We can help you avoid humans and scout ahead. And Orr knows exactly where the gate is."

Orr walked up. "Why does Kira want to go to the gate?"

"She needs to go there. She visited it in a dream and needs to get to its actual location."

"It's well hidden. Wisdom calls for it to stay locked away and hidden as centuries pass during the skip."

"That's something I hadn't thought about," Matusu said.

"Hang around teachers long enough, you hear a lot about wisdom and protocols most people don't know."

Within moments, Orr and Ariste had gathered their gear and were following Matusu to the meeting place.

Kira and Patala arrived first. The moon was low in the west casting long shadows that obscured the area. Staying near the rocks kept them hidden from any who might pass this way. They weren't expecting anyone to be out at this time, but Te'Marile might have guards roaming about in case of trouble. Kira wasn't certain how far the woman would go to silence any resistance.

After a short while, Te'Roan arrived, somewhat out of breath. He carried a bundle with him.

"We can't stay here," he said as he unrolled his bundle and handed each of them a teacher's cloak. "You were spotted by three of the new guards. I took out the one who turned back to report, then caught up with the other two not far from here."

"You killed them?" Patala asked.

"They are not dead, which is why we need to be away from here. When they wake and untie themselves, they will certainly report your departure."

"We have to wait for Matusu," Kira said.

"He wouldn't want us to," Te'Roan said.

"But he won't know the way."

"You don't even know the way."

"It's west," Kira said. Which she knew was a weak answer, but it's all the gate keeper had told her. She would know more as they travelled, and she reached out to him in the dream.

Te'Roan looked back toward the city, as if checking the trail. Kira could see he was mulling over some decision. It was the face her father got when he had to make a decision he didn't like. "Do you remember how we traveled only on rocks when we first left Hochonal? I need you to climb up and follow this outcropping of rock as far as it runs to the west. You'll see two fingers of rock rising up before a sand dune. I will find you there."

Matusu followed the older guards as they made a wide arch around the city. He knew this was slower than cutting across the city, but would probably save them time in the long run. Had he been by himself, no one would have looked twice at him. Ariste and Orr, on the other hand, were well known, and the guards were on alert to watch for them.

They reached the meeting place just before dawn. They found footprints, but not Kira and Patala.

"Well, Matusu, which way do you think they went?" Ariste asked.

That would have been good information to get, Matusu thought to himself.

Orr had stepped up the rock face a bit to have a look around. "If they had any idea where the gate was located, they would head west from here." He turned his attention back toward the city. "And we better get moving that way ourselves before those guards get here."

Matusu and Ariste climbed up next to him. A group of at least ten guards had just come out of the city heading toward their meeting place.

"I really thought it would take them longer," a voice said from above them.

"Te'Roan, how long have you been up there," Ariste asked.

"I just got here. I've been laying a false trail which the guards should reach anytime now."

They watched as the whole party suddenly turned to the east.

"If we hurry, we can get to Kira and Patala about the time they get to the spot I told them to wait for us. I really don't like them being on their own," Te'Roan said.

"Although you have to admit, Kira is very good at taking care of herself," Matusu said.

"Ever since I've met her, chance has watched over her. Most people would have died in that river. She not only lived, but somehow found the only human in that desert who didn't want to kill her."

Just below the top of the rock outcropping, they turned to travel below the ridge. They didn't want to be silhouetted against the dawn sky. They moved swiftly until they spotted Kira and Patala approaching the two fingers of rock that marked the end of the outcropping.

Matusu let out a sigh of relief on seeing them. After all, the whole point of their coming was to keep those two safe. Matusu thought that Patala might have been better off to stay in the city and had said as much to Kira. Te'Roan had made it clear that if they left Patala behind, Te'Marile would find some way to use her as leverage.

Ariste was the first to reach the shade of the stone pillars with Matusu at his heals. "Gatherer, you move quickly across the desert. Are you certain you haven't trained as a guard?" Ariste said.

"I'm just motivated."

"I've tracked rabbits that moved slower. I hope you also make good time across the sand. It will be the most dangerous part of the journey. We will leave a trail that can be seen from great distances, by both city guards and humans."

Te'Roan and Orr arrived. They had been watching their back trail for followers.

"Do you think the city guards will follow us this far?" Kira asked.

"If not the city guards then some of Te'Marile's loyal teachers."

Kira didn't seem phased by that, maybe the presence of three guards and a teacher gave her more confidence. "Let's get on with it then. If we hurry across the sand, an afternoon wind might follow us and clear away our tracks."

"How well do you know the way?" Ariste asked Kira.

"I know we go west, and then tonight, I will find Rory and learn more."

"I can help you there," Orr said. "And you can let old Rory get his sleep."

"You know Rory?" Kira asked.

"Our paths have crossed," he said. "So Ariste, if you would do the honor of watching our back trail, I'll lead out."

By the time they stopped, the sun had set and Kira was exhausted. Earlier in the day she had been thinking they should push on through the night, but now all she wanted to do was sleep. They had left the dunes behind and moved upward into a hillside of fire trees. A breeze had kicked up in the afternoon, but nothing strong enough to cover their tracks.

"Please tell me we won't be crossing anymore sand like that," Patala said.

"Oh no," Orr said. "From here the travel gets much more difficult. I hope you know how to climb."

"That is my sister's specialty."

"Patala could weave us a lovely basket to carry her up a cliff in," Kira said.

"Patala can scramble up a rock face with the right motivation," Matusu said. "I don't seem to remember her slowing us down when human warriors were chasing us."

"Thank you, Matusu," Patala said.

"Or when Te'Roan was watching," Matusu added. Patala shot Matusu a warning glare, while Te'Roan acted like he didn't hear.

"At least we have a decent amount of food with us this trip," Kira said. "Do you think it's safe to build a fire?"

"Maybe tomorrow," Orr said. "We'll pass into broken lands where we can find hidden places to build a fire that won't be noticed."

As much as Kira wanted to sleep, she knew she wouldn't be able to until she did one other thing.

"Te'Roan," she said. "Will you teach me to use the map device?"

"Now?" Te'Roan asked.

"I don't want to go another day without knowing the thing Te'Marile used against me."

Te'Roan opened his map bundle and put the small plate and map device on a flat rock. "Now pick it up and sense its signature."

"Its what?" Kira asked.

"You know, its quantum signature, just like the quantum signature you use to connect to people. It's the first thing they teach you when they explain connections."

"Te'Marile must have left that part out," Kira said.

"This whole time, you've just been working by native feel?"

"I guess so."

"That's actually impressive," Te'Roan said. "You have a natural sense of differentiating quantum signatures."

Kira fumed a little at how much further along she could have been if Te'Marile hadn't been withholding information from her.

"With people, we believe you are recognizing intention, a key to sentience in living things. With a device, you are looking for reception, a point to which your intention can connect. This is what guides the device. You give the device intention. Without intention, it just makes a pretty blue light."

Kira picked up the device and held it, focusing on finding it or seeing it. She sat down and slipped into her dream meditation. In the dream, she sat by the village circle in Hochonal, she concentrated on the connections at the doorways all around her and on the one in her hands. She left the dream and looked down at the device.

"It's not like a person in the dream, it's more like an object in the dream that you can interact with."

Kira slipped into the dream again and pictured a yellow flower in her hand. She concentrated on turning it blue. It turned blue. She slipped out of the dream.

"What did you do?" Patala asked. "A blue light just shot out the top of the device, just for a moment, without it even spinning."

Kira stood and put the device on the metal plate. She closed her eyes and sensed the people around her. She could sense each of them and even their positions in relation to her. Then she imagined the flower. It was there on the rock in front of her, only it was no longer the flower. It was the device.

Kira opened her eyes, held the device above the plate, and as she pulled the string, dropped the device. It spun as it should. She connected to it. She could sense its attributes and abilities. She imagined a map, not a specific map, just the idea of a map of the place they were. The layer of light resolved into a topography. The device showed no signs of slowing down. She asked the map to show her more, as if she were higher above it. The map changed scale showing her a larger section of terrain. She asked the map to show less, to show closer detail. It was like they dropped from the sky until they were looking at the terrain just around them.

"You were right," Kira told Te'Roan. "This isn't very hard at all. It's similar to imagining a space and objects into being in the dream, only without all the infinite possibilities."

"In the dream, I only see what I imagine. But this device shows me things I don't even know."

"It stores the terrain information and waits for you to ask it to display what you want too see."

She turned the map, slid it to the north so their position was on the southern edge of the map, then slid it to the south. "I'm wondering why you didn't show this to me a long time ago."

"I was certain it would be covered in your formal training."

"Just imagine Te'Marile's face, if I had done this in the teacher hall that day."

Orr hadn't been wrong about the lands being broken. Over the next three days they seemed to go up and down as much as they went forward. They passed through valleys of stone pillars and giant mesas as they worked their way farther west and veered north a bit.

On the third night, Kira was getting used to the travel enough that she didn't drift into deep sleep and was able to step into the dream. As she entered her dreamworld in Hochonal, she looked for the doorway to Rory. It had opened after meeting him in the dream. As she stepped into it, she found him sitting on the ledge by the gate, looking down at the river.

"Kira, you are a talented young woman. I left Thresdenal as soon as I heard about Ka'Te'Losa. I didn't want to be around. There's always too much commotion as teachers debate and compete to lead. I prefer being alone, working out other problems…bigger problems, really."

"There wasn't much debating. Te'Marile swooped in and took over, just like that."

"Oh? That's odd. There are factions among the teachers that… let's say things may not be as simple as they seem. Is anyone calling her Ka'Te'Marile yet?"

"Not when I left."

"You left…but you are the rightful…I see. You worry she'll do something to get you out of the way."

"She did stand me up to embarrass me in front of the teachers. Though, I don't think she would have me killed. After all, I am the gatherer."

"I wouldn't trust that to keep you safe from Te'Marile. Some say she secretly sides with those who would forget wisdom and rule the humans. To those people, you are a huge threat. They were getting close to having their way until you showed up."

"What about you, Rory? What do you think?"

"I think you have more supporters than you know. And to get their way, the group that favors ruling will need to separate."

"Separate?"

"Yes, send a group off to form another colony somewhere hidden for a while until they take over a large enough population of humans that they are beyond reach."

"Perhaps they already have." Kira told Rory about the teacher who travelled with the humans who attacked her village. "They even stole the regenerator that had been brought to Hochonal."

"Well, they would need that. A lot of damage could be done in the time it would take them to construct their own. Forget about Te'Marile. Our tests should begin as soon as you can get here. If they establish a colony that they can claim is safe, they can draw away a lot of people. Breaking the protocol will not end well for humans."

Kira saw that Rory was fading. She should let him sleep. "Rory, we are coming to you. Orr is bringing us to the gate."

"Safe travels," Rory said as he faded away.

Kira found herself standing back in the half-light of her dream in Hochonal. She slept.

The day started like the days before it – leaving before light, stopping to eat at sunrise, not stopping again until midday. Only this time, rather than continuing west, Orr led them down a cut to the south that opened to a stone path showing some wear. Like the paths around Hochonal, people had walked this path for a long time. They must be getting close to Rory.

Within a few hundred yards, the path dropped down into a wide hollow with a small stream running through it. Stone houses were built up against the rock face on one side of the hollow.

"A village," Patala said and seemed to quicken her pace.

"Sonal," Orr said. "Home of the gatekeepers."

People were working in gardens near the stream. Children played on rocks above the water. Further up by the houses, Kira could see a group of children gathered around an adult for lessons. It wasn't as big as Hochonal. Kira doubted if more than thirty people lived here.

"Trassa," Orr called out to a woman in the garden.

She looked up and ran over to them, brushing the soil from her hands. "Orr, have they run out of food in Thresdenal that you come to eat ours?"

"It's good to see you too sister." He hugged her and introduced her to the others. "Is Rory about?"

"He was here this morning, but I think he has gone to the gate."

"Can you take us to it?" Kira asked.

"First eat and rest," Trassa said. "When Rory gets back, he will decide if he wants to take you to the gate."

Kira was about to explain the urgency.

"Patience," Te'Roan said. "It won't interrupt your plan to accept some hospitality."

Patala nodded her agreement. Patala seemed to become the dignified, caretaking big sister whenever they reached civilization.

Kira thought of a few things to say, then swallowed them down and followed Trassa and Orr up into the village.

Before they reached the houses, they had a small entourage of children following them. The other children had broken off their lesson to come and greet the visitors. Kira remembered the day, that seemed so long ago, when Te'Roan had arrived in their village. The village buzzed with excitement that a teacher had come. I think they would have been excited that anyone had come. She had longed for any kind of excitement, and now she longed for that quiet village again. That place of innocence where even the meanest people were actually kind and could be trusted to watch over you.

As they reached the center circle in the village, people were already getting a fire going and bringing out meal to make cakes. A girl brought Kira some sweet roots that had been freshly rinsed in cold water. She and Patala had always loved the way the roots snapped, giving off a fragrant flowery scent. Kira chewed the fibrous root which seemed to quench her thirst.

Trassa passed water around in small jars. Kira had started to forget that all water didn't taste like animal hide. The heavy jars seemed to hold in the coolness of the water.

When Trassa had settled down with them, she asked Orr, "What news from Thresdenal? Rory said that Ka'Te'Losa had passed, but nothing else."

Orr looked at the others as though he was unsure how to answer. "You know Thresdenal – lots of teachers and lots of talking. They are debating things, and…well…it could go on for months. Ariste and I were looking to get away from things for a while, and young Matusu mentioned his friends were off to visit Rory. So, here we are."

Trassa addressed Te'Roan. "And what is it you need of Rory?"

"It's more the gate," Te'Roan said. "We need to see it."

"Certainly, knowledge of the gate is among records at Thresdenal," Trassa said.

Te'Roan glanced at Kira. Was he trying to keep some secrets?

"I need to see it in person, to understand the path to reach it and how it works," Kira said.

Trassa seemed confused. "Couldn't Orr explain how to get here without coming all this way?"

"Well, it's more of showing others how to get here. I need to build out the details to this location in the dream."

Trassa looked at her brother. "What's going on, Orr?"

Orr looked at Kira, then at his sister.

Stars, Kira thought, if I'm going to be in charge, I'd best start acting like it.

"I'm the gatherer," Kira said.

The people around her looked at each other and started to whisper. It felt strange, as she said it. She hadn't been sure of it herself, but now that it was out there, she could feel the truth of it. Something that came naturally to her was something extraordinary – something her people had been waiting for a long time.

They all seemed to be waiting to hear what she had to say next. "I need to clearly fix in my mind where the gate is so that I can guide others to it. And I need to test the gate. And for that, I need to be at the gate with Rory."

She thought about the things she must learn before calling the gathering and fully opening the gate and decided to keep that to herself. She wasn't sure who Rory had talked to. Kira didn't want to be the cause of people losing faith in wisdom.

"Then the gathering has begun?" Trassa asked.

"Not yet," Kira said. "Hopefully soon. Of course, you will know better than anyone. Everybody will come here to go through the gate."

Trassa smiled, "Well, they better bring their own food, for Orr will have certainly eaten all of ours."

A young man ran up, who actually wasn't much younger than Kira. When did she get so grown up? He ran up to Trassa and said, "Rory is coming."

The older man appeared through a cleft in the rock above the houses. Kira and her group stood as he made his way down between the buildings to the circle. A little girl ran up and jumped into his arms hugging him. "We have visitors, Grandfather," the little girl said.

"Yes," he said. He settled down in the circle with the girl on his lap. "Te'Kira Waterborn and a fine looking entourage. Orr it is good to see you. Thank you for taking care of our young teacher."

Rory no longer wore the robe of a teacher. He looked more like a village craftsman.

"I'm just Kira. I haven't yet..."

"It should be Ka'Te'Kira," Rory said. "Your abilities have given you your title, not that squabbling bunch in Thresdenal. Don't you agree Te'Roan?"

Te'Roan nodded.

"Ariste I know. And who are these other young people you've brought with you?"

"This is my sister Patala and my friend Matusu. He is a guard."

"My apprentice," Ariste said.

"Then he is in good hands."

"How far is it to the gate?" Kira asked.

"See there," Rory said. "You're taking to leadership just fine – focusing on the task – full thrusters. If you'll allow an old man his supper and a night's sleep, I will take you there at first light. It isn't far, but not someplace you want to stumble around in the dark."

Kira wasn't sure what "full thrusters" meant or that she was taking to leadership well at all. The task at hand seemed to be her only focus, where a real leader would also focus on the needs of the people helping her with that task.

"Patala," Rory said. "Tell us about Hochonal. I have always wanted to visit it."

Patala began to describe their village and its people.

Kira could almost see their faces. As Patala spoke, Kira stared into the fire and imagined herself there.

The fire seemed to shift or was it the light around her that shifted. She found herself sitting by a fire in Hochonal. She no longer heard Patala's voice. She had slipped into the dream.

Perhaps her mind was still focused on the task at hand. She had reached Rory and would soon see the gate. She thought of Iactah and his people. Would the coyote continue to lead them away from danger? After opening and passing through the gate, would he be beyond her reach?

Last time she had tried to get to him, she had tried to follow him. This time she focused on the place she ended up instead. Like when her father was on the rock pinnacle and told her to just see herself there. She focused on the sand hill and the hut. She could see them in her mind, the dream wasn't shifting. She focused on seeing Iactah. She tried to pick out a detail from her previous dream. She remembered the coyote, the way its eyes noticed her. She focused on those eyes, concentrating on those eyes. The light shifted again, and she was looking into the eyes of the coyote, sitting inside the hut on the sand hill.

"Kira," a voice said. She turned and looked into the eyes of her friend Iactah.

"I found you," Kira said.

Iactah smiled. "I was not aware I was lost."

"I need you to know something." Kira stopped. Again, she was putting the task before the people. She started again. "How are you? Are you home safe with your people?"

"Yes. I am well. And you? Do you walk a safe path?"

"I suppose. I am with my friends and my sister – safe for now. Though someone may be trying to change that."

"You said I need to know something," Iactah said.

"Yes, my people need to leave this place, this world. When we do, I fear that we will no longer be the focus of the other humans, and they will come for your people."

"My people have little to offer the others. I believe they may come and then go on their way. Besides, we learned to provide from the teacher who taught us wisdom. If the others are too much trouble, we will move on."

Kira asked about his family and this year's crop. It was so strange the way they talked in the dream, yet had had such brief, stilted conversations in the real world. After talking a while, Kira could tell that Iactah was growing tired.

The light shifted gently. She was back in Hochonal before the fire. She felt the warmth of the fire, the warmth of a blanket around her, someone sitting close.

The dream faded, and she was sitting in the real world in front of fading embers. It was night. Patala was next to her holding a blanket around the two of them.

"Where did everyone go?" Kira asked.

"They've all gone off to sleep. Except Matusu, Te'Roan, and the guards. They're hiding out keeping watch somewhere."

"How long was I …"

"Long enough. You created a sense of awe among the children. The gatherer slipping into a dream trance right there in their village. They are pretty sure you were calling everyone to the gate."

"I wish it were that simple," Kira said. "And this could all be over. I visited Iactah. I don't know how many more visits I will have with him before we leave."

"You can just pull him into a dream like one of us?"

"It usually involves finding a spirit guide."

"A spirit guide?"

"It's a human thing. It guides them in the dream. Iactah has a coyote that guides him. We don't dream that way, we just control the dream ourselves."

"What are you going to do?"

"I'm going to see that gate."
"Full thrusters," Patala said smiling.
"What does that mean?"
"I don't know. Come on. Trassa has a room for us."

Matusu woke Kira and Patala at sunrise. They ate with Tressa and a few little kids that were early risers.

"Are we ready?" Rory asked as he walked up beside them.

Orr stayed in the village while the rest of their group followed Rory up and out of the village through a cleft in the rock. They traveled across a broad plateau of sandstone that descended slightly toward a canyon rim. Moving over the rim, a fairly broad trail led them down into the canyon. Rocks seemed to have been moved in a few areas and parts of the trail built up to make it easy to follow. Far below them they could hear and occasionally see a river. The river had cut the canyon they were descending, leaving exposed cliff faces hundreds of spans tall.

They had descended well over halfway down the canyon when they came to an opening in the rock face. At some ancient time, the river had been at this level and gouged out a section of the cliff leaving a large overhang. The path led under the overhang and among a pile of boulders that had fallen from above. The boulders concealed a passageway leading down toward the back wall under the overhang.

They reached an entrance to a cave. Rory stopped and touched a spot on the wall – it illuminated. Moving forward, he lit up several more stones along the wall. Soon they came to a fork in the passageway.

"That way is my workshop," Rory said pointing to the right. "This way to the gate."

He travelled down the passage on the left. The passage, also lit by panels, descended and curved around opening into a large cavern with the metallic circle with intricate patterns. The circle was about three paces across and sat at the center of a much larger room.

"This is it," Kira said to Matusu.

They all avoided walking on the gate.

Matusu bent down for a closer look. "Can I touch it?" He asked Rory.

"Oh yes. It's inert for the moment."

Matusu inspected the stonework along the edge of the device. "Is the gate part of the stone?" He asked.

"No. The gate simply sits in a hollowed out cavity we made in the stone. It's a segment or slice of a sphere," Rory said. "About the bottom sixth, set in a hole perfectly carved to receive it."

Kira closed her eyes and retraced in her mind the path they had followed. She noted the position of landmarks in her mind.

"Rory, are there any landmarks, like rock spires or domes or unusual clefts in the rock directly above us or where the trail begins?"

"We are below the eastern edge of the opening we came in through, but I don't recall what is at the top of the canyon wall right here."

"Perhaps I can help," Te'Roan offered reaching in his bag. He pulled out his map device and handed it to Kira. She had been practicing with it every time they stopped on their journey from Thresdenal. As before, it projected a miniature of terrain around them. Kira expanded the map showing their position in the canyon and the surrounding cliffs.

"There," Kira pointed to a tall spire of rock and a shorter spire of rock near where they were. "What direction are those from where we are now?"

"Nearly due north," Te'Roan said.

"We should find that when we get back up to the top. That could be the key to finding the gate."

"Or you can send people to the village, and we'll show them the way," Rory said.

"That would be my first choice," she said. "As long as they aren't under human threat at the time."

"Are we ready to test it," Rory said.

Kira thought about how Rory had said the times linked when she tested it. What if she couldn't really control it? What if she jumped in with both feet, and it went to full before they were ready?

"What about the power source?" Te'Roan asked. "How does it stay powered until it's opened?"

"The power is internal," Rory explained. "Once this end is powered up, it is powered in both times through the connection. It will slowly regenerate power over time, drawing on energy from things around it. You really have to think of it as one gate, existing in two points in time and space."

"Why couldn't our ancestors have just built a gate to take them home?" Patala asked.

"You have the right idea. But two limitations prevented that. The same gate would need to be here and there, and to go that distance, it would take the energy of Earth's Sun collected for about a year to cover the distance."

"A year doesn't seem that long compared to how long our people have waited," Patala said.

"All the energy that star produces for a year," Rory said. Rory started walking out of the gate room and the others followed.

"How would you...oh," Patala said. "That seems less possible."

"It's the same reason dreamers here don't visit others of our kind in space or on our home worlds. Dreaming is limited in its range. We've never been able to successfully do it beyond the confines of a single star system. Even getting across a star system is difficult. Planetary dreaming, though, that's doable by most dreamers. What were we talking about? Oh yes. Finding the signature of the gate is like finding the signature of a map device," Rory said. "Except a gate has many quantum signatures to connect with." Rory turned down another hallway.

"How many?"

"Well, that's hard to say. Exponentially more than navigating a starship, but that's to be expected when factoring in position, velocity, and time." Rory led them into another large room, not as big at the gate room. Carved into the walls were shelves holding different gadgets. Kira noticed at least two map devices.

"Those comparisons would be useful if I had ever piloted a starship," Kira said.

"Okay, I've got it. Like most dreamers, you work by feel, like sensing the personality of a connection, and you're visually goal oriented."

"I'm what?"

"Here." He picked up a metal rod from a shelf, the one Kira had seen in the dream. "Let's go back to the gate." As they walked, Rory tapped the rod to bring up a display. Kira could see now that the display rod wasn't actually round, but a rounded off rectangle.

Kira wondered why she never saw anything like that in Thresdenal. Did the teachers at Thresdenal even know he had that?

"Look," Rory held up the display rod. "I want you to connect with the gate and focus your intentions on this date." He had displayed a star date.

Kira studied it and made sure she had it clearly in mind.

"I have already entered this date into the gate, but it will wait for you to make quantum connections and direct it to connect to the date. Think of it like a password for your intention."

"Wait," Kira said. "What if I accidentally turn it all the way on. You said we have about a day to get through."

"You won't," Rory said, "I have power restraints set. Locks restrict the power flow so that only a momentary micro-bridge forms."

"So, I can't mess it up?" Kira asked.

"I really don't think all these pieces would have come into place for you to mess it up," Patala said. "You are the gatherer. You are learning just as gatherers before you."

"The previous gatherer who did this was also a starship pilot," Kira said. "So don't get overly confident on my behalf."

Kira closed her eyes and focused on the gate like she had on the map device. She found an object, a distinct connection. It was a small sphere of light more solid and real than an object in the dream. It lay at the center of the circle. She expanded it in her mind and looked for connections. Rays of light began to appear going to other objects, which appeared as additional spheres of light. The objects rose upward as Kira found and connected more and more points. It was like she was finding thousands of map devices and connecting them together. This was taking longer than she had imagined it would. She carefully sat down on the stone floor not wanting to open her eyes and lose the connections she had made.

She lost count as more dots of light formed into a sphere with a latticework of crisscrossing lines. When it seemed that no more connections were joining the sphere, she focused on the date that Rory had shown her willing the gate to connect to itself in the future. The sphere quivered but didn't seem to do anything. She opened her eyes to see what the sphere looked like. Nothing was there. She had expected to see a projection like the map device made. She closed her eyes and found it was still there in her mind. Again, she willed it to move forward in space and time. It refused to move.

What else could it be? Should she rest and come back? What if she keeps resting and coming back until the humans have destroyed Thresdenal and hunted her people across the desert. She worked to hold onto the thousands of dots connected in the sphere as images of warriors attacking Hochonal flashed across her mind. What if ten times that number attack Thresdenal? Her imagination conjured up scenes of ruthless attacks on the farms and the buildings and the tower of Thresdenal – homes burning, people driven and struck down. The fury of the thought built inside her. She could feel it like a storm. Then she knew.

"That's it," she said. "The gatherer provides the spark." She concentrated on the date and the place. She could see the world she was on floating in space in orbit around the sun in some far off location. She pushed her fury into the sphere. The sphere seemed to split in two and the new sphere shot off into infinity, lines of light stretching out between the points in both spheres.

Kira opened her eyes in time to see a dot of light appear at about chest height above the center of the circle. It hung there for a moment – this tiny glowing orb. Then the light flashed and went out, and a tiny drop of water fell and splashed on the center of the gate.

They all stared at the water – leaning in to see if that's really what it was.

"That shouldn't happen," Rory said.

"What does it mean?" Kira asked, standing to look closer.

"Best case, the gate in the future has somehow been moved outside and, we just timed it perfectly to catch a rain drop. Or…"

"Or what?" Te'Roan asked.

"Or the gate is under water."

Chapter 11

"Under water?" Kira, Matusu, and Patala all repeated at the same time.

"How is that possible?" Ariste asked.

"It's not," Rory said. "Even when the door is closed to hide the entrance, this cave is designed to drain any water that might seep in."

They stood in silence for a moment.

"Let's try again," Kira suggested. She made the connections more quickly this time, though she felt like it still took a long time. Then she focused on building energy inside her. She focused on the storm as her father had done. A storm had come with all its wind, lightning, and fury, and Kira just drew it into herself. She visualized the lightning flashing in her eyes as she had seen with her father. Then she pushed it into the sphere. Again, it flew out.

Opening her eyes, she watched the tiny sphere flash into existence, flash away, and release a tiny drop of water that fell to the center of the gate.

"Under water," she said, almost to herself. She suddenly felt exhausted and sat down again on the floor.

They looked around at each other, all sitting down around the circle like it was a campfire.

"What now?" Patala asked.

"We move the gate somewhere above the canyon," Matusu said. "How heavy is it?"

"Funny thing about that," Rory said. "Time has a way of hanging onto connections. It could have been in another place had we moved it before testing it, but now that we've created the connection, moving it in our time would break the laws of cause and effect."

Kira remembered learning about cause and effect in her temporal physics class. Changing a cause in the past to change an effect in the future makes the effect the cause for the change, resulting in a paradox. And the universe has a way of correcting paradoxes.

"So that's it then?" Patala asked. "We have to swim out?"

"Do you think all our people can swim through the gate out the tunnel and then up who knows how far to the surface?" Te'Roan asked.

"I'm not certain the back pressure of the water would even allow someone to enter," Rory said.

"What about moving the gate at the other end?" Kira asked.

Rory nodded. "If someone were to move the gate at the other end at a time after our tests, we would be able to open the connection and pass through. We could try again in the future and as soon as we get a positive test, we can start the gathering."

"So, we just need to leave a message for someone in the future to come here on or close after a specific date to dive under water, retrieve the gate, and bring it to the surface so we can open it. Does that about sum things up?" Ariste asked.

"Exactly," Kira said. "How do we leave a message to get someone's attention at exactly the right time?"

"Assuming anyone is anywhere near here," Te'Roan said, "we could leave a beacon to relay the problem to our rescuers and hope they can move the gate after the time of our tests."

Rory tapped on his devise and muttered to it. After looking at some figures on his display, he said, "The time to build and setup such a beacon exceeds the window of our rescue. Remember, we've already started the clock."

"What if we could find someone and tell them in a dream?" Kira asked.

Rory shook his head, "If one of our people is here on the date to initiate the dream with the rescuers, then we have the obvious paradox that we failed to open the gate."

"No," Kira said. "Some humans – they call themselves Oanit – have the ability to dream into the future. My friend Iactah can do this. He is a teacher or spiritual leader among his people."

"First explain to me how you have a friend who is a human," Rory said.

"Just wait," Patala said. "It gets better."

"It does get better," Kira said. "I am able to communicate with him through the dream."

"You entered the dream of a human?" Ariste asked.

"An Oanit – it means the People. His name is Iactah. And yes I entered the dream with the help of his spirit guide. What if Iactah could make connections through his dream to his people in the future?"

"You mean humans in the future," Rory said.

Patala looked at Te'Roan. "You don't seem as surprised as these other two."

"I knew a human helped her. He's likely the same one who helped us by distracting the warriors away from the path so we could get to Thresdenal. I think it might be interesting to investigate. Rory can stay here and think on other alternatives."

"Then it's settled," Kira said. "We are going to Iactah's village."

"We're going where?" Matusu asked.

"You'll love it. It's built like one of our villages."

"If you talk to him in the dream," Te'Roan said, "why do we need to go to his village?"

Kira looked to Ariste.

"We have to go somewhere," Ariste said. "Te'Marile has by now sent guards here to keep Kira away from the gate."

They all arrived back at the Sonal at sundown. Kira had insisted on taking a side trip to find those spires and note other landmarks that would lead to the spires. Trassa had food waiting.

"Where's Orr?" Ariste asked.

"Where Orr always is," Trassa answered. "Out on the desert scouting, hunting, guarding – whatever it is he does out there. We always knew he would become a guard. By the time he was ten, he could move across the desert leaving less of a trail than a bird. He would do his chores and help with the garden, but as soon as he had finished, he was off into the rocks and the sand."

Patala glanced at Kira, "Sounds just like someone I know. Except for the chore part."

"Chores got done," Kira said.

Trassa handed out water, fresh and cold. "Once, Orr came home carrying the biggest snake I'd ever seen. I still haven't seen one as big. He asked mother to cook it for dinner. She had already made dinner and told him he would have to cook it himself, which he did. He put it on a stick to rotate over the fire, but it wasn't balanced or fastened to the stick to keep it from slipping around as he turned it. After too long over the coals, half of it was burnt and the other half nearly raw."

"His snake cooking has improved," Matusu said.

"No, it hasn't," Ariste said. "I cooked that snake. In the guard, we never let Orr cook."

"That is true, and I'm glad of it." Orr's voice spoke from the darkness.

Everyone gave a start.

"But his stealth is second to none," Ariste added.

"I wish we could sit here all night and tell stories from my childhood. I've got some great ones about Trassa. But I've spotted an encampment of guards that could be here shortly after first light, assuming they wait until then to travel."

"Is everyone up to some night travel?" Kira asked.

After gathering their bags, Kira and Patala followed behind Orr on a rocky path to the southwest – opposite the direction the guards were coming from. They travelled for half the morning before stopping to determine their actual destination. Te'Roan and the others had followed at a distance watching to be sure the guards didn't see them or follow. "Well, Gatherer," Orr said, "do we have a destination beyond away?"

"I'm not sure. I guess we find a place to set up camp while I try to figure out the best route to Iactah's village. Getting to him in the dream isn't always direct. He says he follows the dream more than directs it."

"Maybe he can show you how to dream into the future. Have you asked him?" Patala asked.

"I did ask. He said I needed to follow my spirit guide."

"Who is your spirit guide?" Patala asked.

"Like I said before, we don't use spirit guides in the dream. Humans, or at least Iactah's people, are led by spirit guides to see things in the future. It sent him to find me by the river days before I even fell in."

"Have you ever seen anything in your dreams that would be a spirit guide?"

"I've only seen Iactah's spirit guide. It's a coyote. It led me to him in the dream."

"So, your plan is based on something you don't know how to do?" Orr asked. "And it hinges on something your friend Iactah may know how to do but hasn't been able to show you?"

"I don't think it stacks up that easily," Matusu said from behind Kira. "Kira's still our best chance of following wisdom to the end."

Ariste stepped up to the group. "I think we should focus on helping her figure out this spirit guide strategy. Maybe we can go and talk to this human. Did he tell you where his village is?"

"No," Kira said. "But when he left me near Thresdenal, he headed northeast. I'm sure over the next few days I can reach him in the dream and get directions."

"It would give us a place to stay for a while that has food and shelter," Patala said.

"Well, we need to put distance between us and the gate," Te'Roan said. "I propose we head more south than east for a few days to stay clear of Thresdenal and see what Kira comes up with in her dreams."

Orr stopped and looked at the stars for a moment, then led on into the darkness. "I know where there's a good water hole, we'll reach it by morning."

Kira's feet gave a little protest, but Orr and the others were risking their lives to help her. The least she could do was keep her complaints to herself, and she hoped Patala would do the same. She did notice that Patala was less likely to complain when Te'Roan was around.

Orr actually got them to the spring well before dawn, thanks to a nearly full moon that had come out. Matusu made sure everyone had food and water before sitting to eat. Kira wondered if this was part of his training – if the younger guards were in charge of food and menial tasks. No, she thought, he's always been helpful.

After a short rest, Orr led them to another spring in the morning light. He said this hillside offered a number of springs, and they should take advantage of them. The second spring had some trees that offered them cover from the afternoon sun. As the sun reached the western horizon, they started on again.

The journey across the desert went in spurts – trudging long distances, then resting at each water hole. Orr and Ariste didn't seem to mind, but Kira could see it was taking a toll on Patala and wondered if they should have found another way. Was everyone really necessary to this journey? She knew that Patala and Matusu could not stay behind in Thresdenal or they would be used as hostages against Kira. The last thing she wanted was to put them in greater danger. Though she couldn't help wondering if this journey was putting them in more danger. Perhaps they could split up, leave Patala and some others at a good water source somewhere. Though Orr was probably not the only guard who knew his way to each of the water sources.

As they reached yet another water hole on their fifth day from the gate, Kira sat down beside Te'Roan and voiced her concern. "Not everyone needs to make this trip," she said.

"Are you concerned that some of them aren't up to it? Are you up to it?"

"I'm up to it because I have to go. Not everyone does."

"You are the youngest of us – some might say the weakest. Who would stand down if you are willing to keep going? Do you really think Patala or Matusu would let you go on without them? I had to hold them back from jumping in that river after they realized you had been swept away."

"That was the right thing to do. Maybe you need to hold Patala back now."

"If the danger were that great, I would."

"Do you promise?"

"Promise what?"

"Do you promise that when the danger gets that great and I have to go on ahead, that you will hold Patala back?"

Te'Roan did not answer.

That night, Kira contacted Iactah, or at least she found the coyote who then led her to Iactah.

"My friends and I need a place of refuge for a time, may we come to your village?"

"You would honor me by visiting my village."

"You were pretty insistent I go to Thresdenal before."

"Yes. That is what the spirit guide showed. Now you have gone. I have not seen more of your path."

"How do we get to your village?"

Iactah described how he would travel from the area they were in. He mentioned some mountains and rivers as landmarks that would be hard to miss.

Kira told him of her need to guide people in the future through the dream and asked him how it was done.

He did not seem to understand her questions.

"I do not choose to dream into the future," Iactah said. "My spirit guide takes me there and shows me what I need to see for the People."

"Yes, but your dreams aren't bound by time. There must be a way I can do this."

"When the need is great, your spirit guide can show you."

"But I don't have a spirit guide," Kira said.

Iactah laughed. "I will think on this."

Though the village lay in a valley guarded by low ridges to the south and the north, it really wasn't hidden in any way like Kira's people would have hidden it. The village consisted of scattered stick and grass huts and a low stone building at what was more or less the center of the village. A stream meandered through the valley, and from their overlook on the southern ridge, Kira could see how the people were using it to irrigate their fields in Threden patterns. From what she had been told, this was not the way humans of this area lived. Iactah had been telling the truth. A teacher had shared what he should not have. But who's to say they would not have started doing it eventually. Kira knew from the planetary survey the Thresden made prior to being marooned that much older civilizations had invented various forms of irrigation.

They stayed concealed on the ridge while Orr and Ariste scouted the area. If the people weren't welcoming, as Kira said they would be, the guards wanted a clear path to retreat. Kira trusted that Iactah would speak for them or at least for her. After all, he had been led to her by a dream. He was a big believer in dreams and his guide.

It was just past sunset when Ariste and Orr returned.

"They don't seem to be planning or expecting any hostility," Ariste said. "A few men guard the fields, seeming most interested in keeping deer or other animals away from their crops. They will likely have a guard through the night in the village. They don't seem interested in sending out guards on patrol. Maybe they will later."

Ariste looked to Te'Roan. "We should stay here tonight and watch," he said. "If we do need to retreat quickly, I would rather we do it in the daylight."

"So, no fire?" Patala asked.

The morning brought rain just before dawn, and Kira really wished they had gone down to the village the previous evening. She understood that the others didn't trust Iactah like she did.

By sunrise, everyone was up and sitting low among the rocks waiting to travel.

Ariste kept watch on the village. "We will wait until they are up and moving about before we go down. No need to make them more nervous by being in their village when they wake up."

They waited as the drizzle ended.

"Someone is coming," Ariste said. "He came out of a hut and is walking straight for us."

Kira pushed past Matusu and looked over the rocks. "It's Iactah."

The man stopped halfway up the hill and motioned for them to come down.

"He's known for days that we were coming," Kira said.

Patala shook her head. "It would have been nice to spare us a night in the rain."

Kira grabbed her bag and started down the hill.

Matusu quickly caught up with her. "Is this wise?"

"If he had wanted to harm me, he had plenty of chances. Stop worrying Matusu. I trust him nearly as much as I trust you."

Iactah stood patiently until Kira and Matusu were a few steps away, then just turned and started walking toward the village.

"He's not much for greetings," Kira said. Looking back, Kira saw that Orr had stayed behind.

"He wants to watch our back trail," Te'Roan said. "Or rescue us if we are walking into a trap."

A fire circle sat in the middle of the village. Some things were universal. Stacked flat stones and logs served as seats in various places around the pit.

Iactah called out and several people came out from other houses. They stayed close to their doors perhaps not trusting these strangers. The first child Kira saw was a boy maybe five or six years old. He ran up to Iactah and took hold of his hand. Iactah said something to him and pointed to Kira. Letting go of Iactah's hand he ran up and held a hand out to Kira. She took it, and he led her to a seat near the fire, motioning her to sit. He said some things Kira didn't understand.

"Honor seat," Iactah said. Apparently he was the only one who spoke Kira's language or at least a little of it.

The others came and sat near her. More villagers came near. An older boy with a stick started pushing charred wood and ash from the center of the fire until he revealed hot coals near the bottom. He added small twigs and blew until a flame arose. Little by little he added wood until he had brought the fire back to life. Kira imagined this was a daily ritual.

Two women with food came to the fire circle. They began setting small cakes on stones nearest the fire to warm them. It all reminded Kira of the way people were welcomed with fire and food in Hochonal.

Now that they had arrived, Kira wasn't sure how to proceed. She needed Iactah's help, though she wasn't sure that he could even do what she needed. Remembering words they had shared out on the desert, she knew that language outside the dream was still a barrier. He knew only a few words of her language, and she knew none of his. And if they were going to do something, they needed to do it in time for the gathering.

Te'Roan, who hadn't yet found a seat by the fire, approached Iactah.

"I am Te'Roan," he said, gesturing to himself.

"Te'Roan," Iactah repeated. "Teacher. I am Iactah."

"Have you met other teachers?" Te'Roan asked.

"One teacher long ago teach people move water, grow food. Teacher save people."

Kira had spent so much more time lately in the dream with Iactah, that it seemed strange to hear him speak in such broken language again. It was going to be a long day waiting for time to meet in the dream.

"Now we need your help," Te'Roan said.

Apparently, Te'Roan had other plans. Did the man think he could speed the sun across the sky?

Kira hadn't really slept in days, she wondered if she needed a day and a night of rest before they started in on the plan. Like Te'Roan, Kira knew they were in a hurry, but she also knew how much dreaming took out of her, especially being in the dream with Iactah. It took more effort with him. The reality of things in his dreams were… slippery. Things just seemed to want to slip away.

Iactah sat silent for a long time, then he looked to Te'Roan. "You need vision."

"Yes," Te'Roan said. "We need you and Kira to have a vision and contact someone in the future."

"Kira save teachers. Save people."

"Yes," Kira said. "I need your help to save my people."

"Yes. Save teachers."

Te'Roan moved up close to Kira. "When he says teachers, he means us, right? When he talks about the people, he means his people? Somehow he thinks you're here to save his people."

"Save them how?" Kira asked. "They seem to be at peace here."

"You said he sees the future, maybe your act of helping us, will also help him and his people."

"Maybe I can clarify things in the dream. Right now, they seem content to feed us."

After they had eaten, most of the people left to work the fields.

Iactah invited Kira and the others to follow him. He led them to a low mud hut. Iactah crouched down as he went in. Matusu went ahead of Kira. He had to crouch even more. Patala and Te'Roan followed Kira inside. Ariste chose to stay outside to keep watch. She could tell that he still didn't fully trust how easily things were going. As Kira entered the building, she found that steps led down into the middle, so that once inside, the ceiling wasn't as low as it seemed. The room was lit by a small fire in a pit at the center of the room. The room smelled of smoke and burnt herbs. An angled beam of light came through the cone shaped ceiling from a small hole above the fire. The wood and reeds around the hole looked black from smoke.

Iactah pulled mats from a stack by the door and set them around the room. When he finished placing mats, he invited others to sit.

He pulled a large skin over the door and joined them around the fire. He added a few dry sticks from a nearby stack, and the flames grew. He then added pieces of dried brush to the fire. They burned with the scent Kira had recognized coming in. Her mother sometimes had them gather that herb to add to her cakes. Kira closed her eyes and pictured her mother's face. She had tried and failed to reach her mother's dream. In her heart, she knew, like her father, her mother was gone.

As she breathed in the sweet scent, she felt the peacefulness of the dream coming on. Quickly she opened her eyes. "Patala, this could take a while. Don't feel you have to stay – any of you."

"I can stay if you can?" Patala said, and Matusu agreed.

They didn't know what they were talking about, of course. They hadn't been through the training she had been through. The teachers would sometimes keep students practicing in the dream for a full day.

"If you need to go out to eat or for other things, even just to get fresh air, I'll understand."

Kira closed her eyes and entered the dream. As she surrendered more and more to the dream, the world around her became clear. She wasn't in Hochonal, where she usually started her dreams. Instead, she was standing in Iactah's village, only it was dusk, the perpetual dusk she had come to know as normal in the dream. The colors had faded with the setting of the sun, but the night didn't come. The sky wasn't right either, not quite red or pink, but somewhere in between.

She walked over to the fire ring and sat. No fire burned. The coyote walked up and sat across the fire ring, looking at her. It seemed to be expecting something of her. If the coyote just watched, Kira was certain that Iactah would soon arrive. A grass mat door swung open from one of the huts and Iactah emerged. The coyote didn't seem to notice him. It was more intent on watching Kira.

"Iactah, you are very good at this. I was worried we would have to wait until you were asleep."

"In the dream, we find what we need when we need it. You may have been here for days and only felt it as a moment, or days in the dream could be a moment outside of the dream."

Kira noticed that he didn't make the distinction of dream and real world as her people did. To him, the dream was another real world. She knew that he had more to do than spend time with her in the dream, so she got to what they needed to do.

"When you found me by the river, you said that your spirit guide had shown you where I would be and when I would be there. You were able to see the future in the dream."

"I remember. The guide often shows me things in the future. They are for me to guide and protect the People. You were shown to me because the guide knew we needed you to come and save the People."

"Save you from what? Are other tribes threatening you?"

"Other tribes do not harm us. Others will come, and you save us from them."

"I don't understand how I will help your people, but I hope I can. I came here because I need you to show me how a spirit guide can take a message to an Oanit or other human hundreds of years in the future to perform a task like the one you performed for me."

"I cannot show you this. A spirit guide needs to show you." Iactah gestured toward the coyote.

"Your spirit guide can show me?"

"Coyote is not my spirit guide. I am guided by Owl." Iactah looked around. As if on cue, an owl flew over the fire circle and lit on a tree, which Kira was fairly certain wasn't there a moment ago. The dream provides. "Coyote has only come to my dreams with you. Coyote is your spirit guide."

"I have a spirit guide?" Kira felt surprised and a little excited, like someone had just given her the perfect gift she hadn't known she wanted. "How do I tell him or her what I need?"

Iactah laughed and kept laughing. Just when he seemed to get control of himself, he would start laughing again.

"What?" Kira asked.

"Coyote knows what you need. You don't know what you need. I didn't ask Owl to show me a half-drown girl who needed my help. He came to my dream, and I followed him."

"How did you know how far in the future I would be there?"

"The guide showed me the days passing and the turn of the moon on the night I would find you."

"So, you're saying the coyote knows what I need? Apparently, I need to be stared at."

The coyote shook it's head like it was trying to get a fly away from its face.

"Remember, your spirit guide isn't really a coyote. This is just a form taken so you can see her."

"How do you know the guide is female?"

"Doesn't she seem female to you?" Iactah laughed. "Your guide is matched to you in many ways. You are female, so she is female. If she were a deer, it would be more obvious."

Kira starred into the coyote's eyes. They held more light and understanding than Kira was used to seeing in an animal. "Do you have a name?" She asked the coyote.

"My grandfather told me he learned the name of his spirit guide," Iactah said. "He was very old and had followed him for many years. There have been tales of other wise and old men and women who have learned the names of their spirit guides. It is a long journey. I have not travelled enough steps and may never travel enough steps. I call my guide Owl, though that is not his name."

Kira was starting to wonder if the spirit guide was a manifestation of the dreamer's consciousness, familiar yet separate. "Coyote, can you help me?"

Iactah laughed again. "Get up and follow her."

Kira stood, and Coyote stood. Kira walked toward her, and Coyote turned and trotted away.

Kira looked back at Iactah who sat by the fire ring. "Are you coming?" She asked.

"This is your journey, Kira. If I need to come help you, Owl will guide me."

Kira followed Coyote out of the village and up a slope into a thick grove of fire trees. Light passed overhead like days coming and going in moments – like the sun passing over on a cloudy day, then night would come and pass as quickly. If this was the spirit guide showing Kira that days were passing, they passed too quickly for Kira to count them. Soon they moved by in a flutter of dark and light. Then the flutter stopped, and they emerged from the trees overlooking the village in the same odd twilight. A young man stood by the fire ring. He looked up as they came to toward him. A smile crossed his face, and he walked toward them.

"You really came. You said you would, and you did."

He seemed to know Kira, but she didn't recognize him. He walked up and took hold of her hand, and she suddenly realized who he was. He was the small boy from the village who had been holding Iactah's hand.

"Are you Iactah's son?"

"Yes, we met when I was very young, every time you saw me, you told me that we would see each other when I was grown and here you are."

"So, it worked. I dreamed into the future, and I can talk to you."

"Yes. It's very strange. You are the first person that has ever talked to me in the dream. My father said it was the same for him. Very strange. We are usually alone in our visions and dreams. I mean, we see other people, but they do not see us. The spirit guide is the only one who seems aware of us. How do you do it?"

"I don't know. It's just something that my people can do."

"Do all your people share the dream?"

"Some of us are dreamers and can share the dream with other dreamers and non-dreamers. A non-dreamer can only share the dream when a dreamer comes to them or brings them into a dream."

"This is amazing. Father said we should be able to talk to each other. He taught me some of your language, but not this much. Or have you learned my language?"

"Since I met you this morning, I haven't had much time to learn your language."

"Is it still that same day in the waking world? Amazing."

"Do you have dreams of the future like your father?"

"I do. I have just seen my son being born. His mother is pregnant, about a month from giving birth."

"How is your father?" Kira asked.

"He is well. He will be excited that I saw you. He has been asking me about this meeting."

"Why did his guide not bring him here?"

"Who can guess why spirit guides do what they do?"

"You sound like your father."

Coyote turned and trotted away.

"I guess we have to go," Kira said. "What is your name?"

"Nintah. I am Nintah."

Kira turned and followed Coyote as she trotted back toward the trees. As they moved into the trees, the days began sliding past again. If we're going forward again, this will be the test, she thought. Can I connect with someone in the dream who knows someone I know?

Kira thought about her appearance. Nintah had known her in the real world and had his father with him when they met. Others she might meet had never seen a Thresden. She concentrated on changing her appearance to look more like a human, like one of the women in Iactah's village. She changed the color of her hair and skin. She made herself shorter and changed the clothes and robe into a white deerskin dress.

They emerged from the trees into the village again. A young man, not yet fully grown, sat by the fire. There was actually a fire this time. Kira concentrated on it, and it grew. She could influence the dream here. When the fire leapt up, the young man looked around to see who was there. When he saw Kira and Coyote, he looked puzzled. "Are you my spirit guides?" He asked.

"I don't think so," Kira said.

"If you aren't my spirit guides, how are you talking to me?"

"I am Kira. And this is Coyote, my spirit guide. Are you Nintah's son?"

"Yes, I am. I am Matah."

Kira let out a laugh. It's working, she thought.

"He told me about you – my grandfather also. They said I would meet you when I was older. I just thought they meant older like them."

"How is your grandfather?" Kira asked.

"He passed on last winter."

"I'm sorry to here that. He was my friend."

"It was his time," Matah said.

"Do you know, Matah, if he ever learned his spirit guide's name?"

Matah smiled. "He did. He was very old, but he told me he did."

Coyote turned and trotted away.

"That's my signal to go," Kira said. "Tell your father I said hello."

Kira followed Coyote into the trees again, but the light didn't waver as before. Kira felt a sudden chill and the trees swept past her and Coyote. The ground flew by under her feet. Coyote started to fade away, like sand being blown by the wind. Kira had a momentary feeling of being swept away.

Laying by the fire in the pit hut. She could feel a mat under her and a blanket over her. A hand touched her shoulder. Looking up, she saw Patala sitting beside her. Looking beyond her to the hole in the ceiling, she saw the night sky. A few stars twinkled.

"How long was I in the dream?" She asked. Feeling a dryness in her throat. "Did I dream all day?"

"You dreamed a day and a night and a day. It's early evening. We came in here yesterday."

Kira closed her eyes to let things sink in. It hadn't seemed that long in the dream. Though she had traveled years into the future. "That explains why I'm so hungry," she said, "and thirsty."

"Te'Roan, Matusu, and I have been taking turns watching over you and giving you sips of water. You drink while dreaming if we give you just a little, but it's not nearly enough."

Kira sat up, waited for the room to stop spinning then stood up. "Let's get something to eat. I have a lot to tell you." She started walking toward the door. "I got my own spirit guide. Well, she's a coyote. I always thought she was Iactah's guide, but it turns out his guide is Owl."

Patala followed Kira out of the hut toward the smell of food being cooked.

Chapter 12

Kira hadn't realized how hungry she was. Was this what Iactah went through when he followed his spirit guide? Maybe moving forward was more tiring, or maybe it was like climbing, the more you practiced, the more you could do. Kira took no more than a day of rest before going back to the dream.

She emerged in the dream near the trees. Coyote was there waiting for her. No greeting. Coyote just trotted into the trees. Kira followed. They walked on for a while, longer than they had travelled before. The trees seemed to grow and fall away around Kira and Coyote. Eventually they emerged from the trees down into the village. The village had grown. A proper sitting wall now ringed the center fire.

A young woman knelt by the fire, trying to light it with a bow drill. She didn't seem to notice Kira. Kira focused on the fire being lit, and a small flame rose from the center. The young woman fell back and looked around spotting Kira.

"Are you real?"

"That depends. Are you the daughter of Mattah?"

"Mattah was my grandfather. I am called Lenmana. You must be Kira."

"Wow, what about your father or your mother? I never met them."

"My father died soon after I was born. My grandfather told me about you, that you always came to visit our family. I have been going to the lodge every day since I was eight. I am nearly sixteen now."

"Every day? You must have really wanted to meet me."

"My grandfather said you visit our dreams to help save the People."

"I am following my spirit guide and hoping to save my people."

"Grandfather said you would help us. All the people know the coyote woman will help us."

"Help you with what?"

"The northern tribes killed my father and many of the men. Now they return each season to steal food. We need your help."

"I don't know what I can do. I only move through the dream," Kira said. "Men attacked my village when I was young. All I did was run. My father held them off while my sister and I escaped with a teacher and my friend."

"How did your father stand up to them? Can you show us?"

"Maybe I can help you, but not like that. The problem is this valley, and the bounty of your fields. Small villages like yours need to be better hidden. My home village was kept secret for nearly a hundred years."

"Where can we hide? How can we leave our fields? What will we eat?"

Kira didn't know the area well enough to answer. She was in the dream. She couldn't show up like Te'Roan and lead them to safety. Maybe they would be better if that teacher long ago never taught them to farm and to be so successful. Their stability and plentiful food supply made them an easy target. They needed to be like Hochonal, hidden, with fields along water but hidden.

"Lenmana, I can't show you exactly where to go, but I think I can show you what to look for." Kira wasn't sure how much she could control in this dream, but she had started the fire.

"Hold my hand," Kira said, reaching out to Lenmana.

Kira focused her attention on the fire, then started to shift the world around them. The cliffs of Hochonal rose up. The canyon where the stream ran that fed the fields dropped away. Houses rose up, not brick by brick, but like sand flowing up and together. In a moment they stood in Hochonal.

"This is Hochonal. The village I grew up in."

Lenmana looked around, her eyes wide. "You are a spirit guide."

Coyote looked up. Kira smiled. "A spirit guide with a spirit guide. No. I'm just a dreamer. I can only show you what I've seen or can imagine, not what will be. Come with me."

Kira started up the path that led above the village. From the top of the rocks, they could see the layout of the village. "Do you see how the village stays hidden? It kept my people safe because the hunters wouldn't come through here. They followed more obvious trails along larger waterways."

"I know a place like this, not just like this, but hidden like this. It's three or four days walk from the village. It might take more time to get the elderly there."

"Getting there hidden is more important than getting there fast. Can you travel across rock or through runoff areas – leaving little to no trail?"

"I think I know a way. We'll need to take our hidden grain stores, those we kept from the thieves."

Coyote stood and started down the trail out of Hochonal.

"It's time for me to go." As she followed Coyote, she looked back to see Hochonal shifting back to Lenmana's village.

Coyote led Kira into a grove of trees she didn't remember being near Hochonal. Soon they were passing through the familiar blur of trees and shifting light. They emerged on the edge of a canyon, where a trail led down a narrow ledge. Tucked into the wall of the canyon was a village, not unlike Hochonal. Brick and stone houses filled the broad ledge. If this was the new village, it had been many years since she had met Lenmana. A woman sat in a low, dug out circle in the middle of the village. She watched silently as Kira approached – a look of amazement on her face. She was just a little older than Kira, maybe Patala's age.

"You're here," she said, with a look of awe on her face. "My grandmother told me you would come. My uncles never believed her, but my mother also knew it was true and here you are. I wish she were here to see you."

"You must be Lenmana's granddaughter."

"I am Lena." She nodded. "My people owe you a debt, spirit guide. Our hidden village is safe because of the things you showed my grandmother. I pray that I am worthy to see whatever you have in store to help my people."

"I am not a spirit guide, but a humble traveler being guided myself."

"Just name what you need me to do, and I will do it, wise one," Lena said. "You have lived for many generations. What wisdom do you wish to share?"

How could Kira explain to this woman that she really hadn't lived for generations, that she didn't have any wisdom to impart? She knew Iactah had been told that he needed to save Kira so that she could one day save his people. He had probably passed that down to his children and grandchildren. With each new generation she visited, the story continued to be embellished.

This woman seemed so sincere in her desire to receive help like her grandmother, that Kira realized she may have started something she wouldn't be able to maintain. How many generations of Iactah's descendants would require this of her? For that matter, how many generations would she need to visit.

"How many years has it been since I visited your village in person – since I visited Iactah?" She asked the woman.

"I am the seventh generation from Iactah. Many seasons."

"How many seasons, exactly?"

"That is hard to say. Maybe a hundred or more."

Kira suddenly saw a flaw in her plan.

"Is that the path you would give me? Would you have me discover the number of seasons?"

Kira had not setup a method for keeping track of time. She knew how far into the future she needed to go but hadn't realized that this people would have no record of it. Could she wake up and instruct Iactah to keep a record? Could she go back and tell them to keep such a record. If that were possible, then wouldn't Lena now have that record and be able to answer Kira's question with exactness. Even if Iactah's people did start keeping a record, what's to say they continue it? No. The time she was looking for was 570 years in the future from her time. If she had started out with a calendar, that might work, but she had not. And how could she even keep such a thing from being lost in the future. She needed something fixed and constant – like the stars.

"Lena, I do have something you need to do – something very important."

"Anything, wise one."

Enough with the titles, she thought. "I need you to study the stars. I need you and your descendants to study the stars so well that when I visit them in the dream, they can show me the night sky."

"To what end?" Lena asked.

"With my help, they will learn how the stars change with the years." Kira looked upward and directed Lena's attention to the sky.

"This is the sky in my time." Kira made key stars appear along with the band of stars that blended like a trail of light across the sky.

"Do you see those three bright stars there and that forth one set off to the north?" Kira drew lines in the sky between the stars. "That is Rulan's Wave. It is part of a story I learned as a child. The stories help us remember the groups of stars."

Kira invited Lena to lay back on the bench and began to tell her the stories of the stars as she had learned them from her mother and father. She and Lena talked about the stars for what seemed like all night, until she had taught her all that she could remember. If her plan was going to work, she herself would need a more exact way to measure the stars, to know exactly what she would be looking for at the time she sought. She had an idea about that. Something she could teach to Lena's descendants.

Eventually, she felt the dream ending for Lena, it was time for her to go. She stood, and Coyote trotted up next to her.

"Teach the stars to your children. They will be more important than you know."

"I will, wise one."

"Please call me Kira."

Kira woke lying in the hut, Matusu and Patala sat across the fire from her. She was lying on a low cot someone had fashioned. "How long was I in the dream?" Kira asked.

"A night and a day and most of a night. Are you ready to eat?"

"First I need to talk to Te'Roan."

As Kira ate cakes and some fresh-cooked rabbit, Te'Roan – roused from sleep earlier than usual – answered her questions about constellations. He admitted right off that he was no great expert, but his knowledge did seem to exceed Kira's.

"What about your map devise? Can it show us what the stars will look like five centuries from now?"

"It's not equipped for that. It's for teachers to find their way here and now. The way finder, however, is what we use to program the maps. That can keep a history and project movements of the stars. I think our ancestors used it to navigate here."

"Where is that? How do we get a look at it?" Kira asked. She was starting to feel better as the food reached her stomach, but she was realizing that she was also tired. The answers to her own questions slowly hit her even before Te'Roan answered them.

"It's in Thresdenal."

"We should've grabbed that on our way out," Matusu said.

"It's not exactly something you slip into your pack. I think it was originally part of a much bigger system."

"Let's say we could get to it," Kira said. "Can you operate it?"

"It's not something I was trained to use," Te'Roan said.

"Of course, we need to talk to the teacher who keeps the way finder, Te'Juna," Kira said.

"Or Te'Marile. They are both trained to use the way finder."

"Probably calling herself Ka'Te'Marile by now. Do you think Te'Juna would help us? I never got a sense of whether she was with us or not."

"I'm not sure either," Te'Roan said. "You could reach out to her in the dream and see what she says."

"I'd have to find a way to ask her without telling her what we're doing. I think if they knew what we are attempting, it would throw more people over to Te'Marile's side. If she is with us, she's likely to see me as an authority she's obliged to help."

Kira didn't know if she could jump right back into the dream. She needed to eat and then really sleep and then probably eat again before she was ready to face a master teacher in the dream. Some of the teachers had been just on the edge of her dream trying to reach her, but she blocked them just as they had taught her. She needed to focus on dreaming into the future. Since she was dreaming into the future, it shouldn't matter when she got back to it. Yet, she felt an urgency about it.

"Te'Roan, maybe you should approach Te'Juna and let her know you're with me. See how she responds. Let her know that I need to see the stars as they will be when we arrive at the other end of the bridge." Kira picked up a stick and wrote the star date she remembered from testing the gate.

Te'Roan stood in a dream by the gate to Thresdenal. A woman approached from the shadows. It was Te'Juna. He knew she was experienced enough to show herself at any age she chose, and she chose to reveal herself as she was.

Te'Juna spoke. "Te'Roan, is Ka'Te'Kira safe?"

Te'Roan was surprised and relieved to hear her use the honorific title. Many in Thresdenal still looked on Kira as a child from the outer villages. "She is well. I have come on her behalf. We need to access the master map on the way finder."

"Did you lose your map or are you concerned something has changed? I assure you the world is as it has been since your device was last connected."

"We need to forecast."

"I see. Are you concerned that landmarks may erode? That is difficult to model far into the future."

"We are more concerned with the movement of stars."

"Ah, better, more predictable. How far a forecast are you talking about?"

"We need to see this date." He wrote the star date in the sand.

"So precise."

"We need to know the measurements between easily identifiable stars when we emerge at the other end of the bridge."

"If you know that's where the gate takes you then why do you need to know the star measurements?"

"We need to confirm the date."

"Does she know that if the date is wrong, it won't matter?"

"It's more complicated than that."

"What will she take with her to confirm the position of the stars? All the instruments are still locked away in Thresdenal."

"We can construct tools. Those principles are simple."

"Like riding a wind over the waves – a simple principle until a slight error sends you hopelessly off course."

"Will you help us?"

"I will need to teach her these things you call simple principles. Give me two days to create the forecast data and commit it to memory."

"Thank you. Your efforts will not be wasted."

"I wish I could say the same for yours. Te'Marile has sent senior teachers from Thresdenal to personally aid in the search for you."

With those words, Te'Juna faded from view. Te'Roan turned his mind toward consciousness.

When Te'Roan returned, Kira was sleeping. He let her sleep. Nothing he had learned was urgent. In two days, she would need to spend considerable time in the dream with Te'Juna. Te'Roan could go with her, though she was the only one who could really put the knowledge to use.

Patala offered him one of the cakes she had been cooking at the center fire. He wondered how long they would be here – how long it would take for Kira to find the person she sought. Just before dawn, Kira joined him by the fire.

"Did she meet you?" She asked. "Did she agree to help?"

"She needs two days to prepare," Te'Roan said.

"I feel like I still have a long way to go before I reach the descendants who need to measure the stars. Perhaps I can get through a few more generations before I meet with Te'Juna."

Patala handed Kira another cake encouraging her to eat. "What happens if Iactah's line dies out? Do we have another plan?"

"You mean like Te'Marile's plan?" Kira asked.

"Her plan is destined to add greater danger to this world," Te'Roan said. "We need to ensure that your plan works."

"Iactah's children have been good at avoiding the other humans so far," Kira said. "It's easy for a child, though, to want adventure instead of safety. I have to keep them on track, so the line does not die out."

"Expecting humans to just hide and farm for over five hundred years seems contrary to their nature," Patala said. "They are nomads who wander the land. They are destined to make more of themselves."

"We have hidden, and we were explorers before we came here," Kira said.

"But we have focused on a single purpose," Te'Roan said. "And besides, we live much longer than humans. We all know some of the elders from the first landing. We are merely the third generation to continue the work here. How many generations of humans will pass in the next five centuries?"

"Too many, I've already been skipping generations and feel like we've barely started."

Patala added wood to the fire, "You need to give them purpose or they will find one of their own."

"Right now, I have them watching the stars – which doesn't seem like much of a purpose."

"They need to know why they are watching the stars," Te'Roan said.

"Should I tell them it's to save an alien people who will be coming through a doorway in time to hop on a starship and fly home? We're talking about people who don't know the Earth is round, who think the only other intelligent life in the universe are a pantheon of gods who control the weather and carry the sun across the sky."

Te'Roan leaned forward. "Some of the founders believed that our mission here would actually save this world. Before being marooned, we cataloged budding civilizations across this world that grew and spread. Some fell into chaos, others were supplanted, but each was a step forward. Our knowledge of these things will protect this world from those who would exploit it. If we can show progress toward a higher civilization, we can give this world standing to be protected."

Kira sat silent for a moment. "And we force another group of people to hide like we have hidden. It seems like interference."

"Interference of one family line to save an entire world," Te'Roan said.

"Then that's the purpose," Kira said. "They need to stay safe and watch the stars for the signs that will save the world. How many generations do you think that will get us?"

"That all depends on how well you teach them Te'Kira." Te'Roan smiled.

"Ka'Te'Kira," Patala said.

After her forth sessiowith Te'Juna, Kira laid outside the shelter away from the fire looking up at the stars. She reviewed their positions, used her outstretched hands to set relative distances in her mind, and retold herself the stories of the constellations.

Kira returned to the dream not fully rested but having a clearer purpose of what to do. When she and Coyote arrived in the village, she found the village very different than when she had left. The village was no longer tucked up in the cliffs. It had fewer dwellings than before, and she could see a larger brick building at the edge of the village. Not the sort of dwelling the people had been building when she was last there. Kira wondered at how the dream could change like this. She had thought the worlds in the dream were a projection from the dreamer. Something more was obviously at play in the dream world of the Oanit.

A young woman, swollen with child, appeared on a bench outside the dwelling nearest Kira. She seemed startled to see Kira then smiled.

"Do you know who I am?" Kira asked.

"I think so," she said. "Are you Kira who travels the dream world with the coyote?"

Coyote shifted and sat, seeming pleased at having been recognized for her part in all of this.

"My grandmother told me of you. Some said you were not real, but I believed my grandmother. I am Chosovi, though the priest says I am now called Martha. So in the waking world I am Martha, but in this world I am still Chosovi."

"I am pleased to meet you Chosovi. What did your grandmother tell you about me?"

"She said you taught our people many things about crops and where to build villages. And she said you taught her the names of the stars and their stories. The priest and his guards made us take down the tower that showed the planting time and where we counted the passing of years."

"The counting helps understand the movement of the stars."

"All the people know. We continue to count the seasons on a small stone. Some villages have been made to move, if we must move, we will take the stone with us."

"I see that you are caring for the people. You must know that what you do is not just for your people, but for the world. I will teach you another way to know the passing of time."

Kira focused on making the night sky as brilliant as she could and began to point out constellations to Chosovi. Kira explained how gradually over many years the stars moved and that her children's children many generations from now would be able to know the passage of years by how the stars had moved. Kira told her stories of the constellations just as she had Chosovi's grandmother. The stories would help her remember the stars.

"That one there," Kira said, pointing into the night sky, "is Tala the Brave. This row of stars form his ship, and these over here form the wave that pushed him across the sea."

"What is a ship?" Chosovi asked.

Kira realized that having lived in the desert her entire life, Chosovi had no way of relating to some of these stories. This could be more difficult than she thought.

"A ship is like a hut with a tightly thatched roof turned upside down that can float on water."

"Like the reed boats used by the people who live where the river is flat?"

"Yes, like that – only larger, to hold many people."

"Like the priest tells about – how he travelled from his home."

"He traveled in a ship?"

"He said it took many days across the sea and many days across land to reach our village. Was Tala the Brave a priest?"

"He was an adventurer. He wanted to see what was beyond the sea. He believed the wave led him to a place to make a new home for his people."

"Was his old home invaded?"

"His old home was ruled by others who took what Tala and his family made and the food they grew. He wanted a place where he could keep what he made and eat the food that he grew."

"The priest tells us that we must share our food with him and his soldiers. Though he helps in the field and helped build the church, what we do not like is that he sent many of our strongest people to go build another church somewhere else."

"Did they choose to go, or did he make them?"

"He told them that his god would make our crops grow better and send us rain if those people went to build the other church."

"Are those people free to return?"

"I do not know. I do know that our crops grow and the rain comes as they always have."

"I cannot do anything about the priest and his men. I can only tell you that watching the stars and teaching your children of the stars will be vital to your whole world."

Kira turned their attention back to the constellations, and this time chose one that might make more sense to Chosovi. "You see there, low in the sky, that is Crian the Great Bird." Kira raised her hand and drew lines in the air to show how they connected to form the wings, head, and eye of a bird. "Crian carries messages between the heavens and the land sharing the knowledge of the gods with people."

"Which gods?"

Kira thought about conversations she had had with Iactah. The last thing she wanted to do was introduce a new theology to these people. "Like the Great Spirit. He is a messenger bird from the Great Spirit."

"Are you also a messenger from the Great Spirit?" Chosovi asked.

"No," Kira said, wondering how she could expound on that. She had gone into this with little thought about how Iactah's descendants would perceive her visits.

"Are you a god?"

"I am not a god." Kira knew that leaving it there would not help. Chosovi and her children would start to believe all sorts of things that just weren't so. "I am a friend of your ancestor Iactah, who lived long ago. He saved my life. Now I wander the dream world helping his children." True, yet vague – like so many of the non-answers Kira used to get from her father and the teachers.

"But how do you possess so much knowledge, and how can you wander the dream world after you are passed?"

Good questions, Kira thought. None of the others had been so inquisitive. Perhaps it was the coming of the priest and the clash of cultures that opened Chosovi's mind to start questioning the world around her.

"I am not of your people or of the priest's people. My people came here to visit your world and now have gone. My spirit guide helps me to reach across time in the dream and connect to the children of Iactah."

"Do you visit the children of other people?"

"No. I have only been led to the children of Iactah." Kira dreaded the thought of going through all this again in another line of succession, though now that she thought about it, that was a possibility, should this line end. How would she even do that though? Picking another line from this same village would likely also end. Most humans would not welcome her and allow her to make that first connection. The spirit guide also seemed to take an interest only after she visited Iactah in the dream. Certainly not all humans were as gifted at entering the dream or seeing the future as Iactah was.

"So, we are chosen," Chosovi said.

That phrase snapped Kira back from her musing. She paused for a moment. Maybe the girl had stumbled onto a purpose. Like Te'Roan had said. She needed to give them a purpose.

"Yes Chosovi. You and your ancestors and your children are chosen."

Chapter 13

Kira joined Te'Roan by the fire.

"Who is the best fighter among you and the guards?" She asked.

Without even pausing to think, Te'Roan said, "Ariste, without a doubt. He taught all of us."

"The guards fight different than the teachers," Kira said. "Wouldn't it be better to know the teacher fighting?"

Te'Roan looked at her for a moment, like he was deciding how vague to be in his answer. "You mean the way your father and I fought at Hochonal. You think that it is a different, secret form of fighting that the teachers keep to themselves?"

"Isn't it?"

"The teachers are taught the same fighting style as the guards. So your sessions with Matusu have already started you on learning to fight like a teacher."

Kira didn't think he knew about those.

"What looks to you to be a different style of fighting is a mindset born out of disciplined meditation."

"Can you teach that to me?"

"I can teach you to meditate, and I can even teach you the discipline of feeling and directing your energy when you fight. Though from the way you popped open the gate, I think you've figured out how to direct your energy. But without mastering the fighting techniques, you would have no means to engage your intention or power."

"Are you saying I need to learn to fight like a guard before I can fight like a teacher?"

"I'm saying that no one has greater fighting skill and precision than Ariste."

"I need him to teach me."

"Is there a battle coming I don't know about?" Te'Roan asked.

"No. But I'm afraid for the people in the dream. If they can't hide, they need to be prepared to fight."

"I'm sure they can take care of themselves. Our way has been to not share our way of fighting with humans. It's our advantage over their greater numbers."

"That's exactly why I need to learn it. I need to give Iactah's descendants an advantage when they face greater numbers."

"Maybe you haven't noticed, Kira, but we don't really go to war. We stay away from our enemies and only use our fighting as a last resort."

"That's what this is," Kira said. "Iactah's descendants need to know how to defend themselves to preserve their family line."

"How do you know that they don't just need to get up and leave. You may be better off teaching them to hide and survive, like we have done."

"But that isn't all we have done. We have also trained guards to defend the people. We have built a stronghold that can withstand our enemies."

"If you mean Thresdenal, it was always a temporary solution. It is built the way it is so it can be abandoned and buried by the desert. Everything about our existence here is designed to help us disappear."

"What about Te'Marile's people who went south? Will they also disappear?"

"Who can know?"

"Well, Iactah's people are not meant to disappear. We need to help them ensure that they don't."

Te'Roan seemed deep in thought. "Since they cannot hide forever, the best they can do is choose a place that no one else really wants. Once they have done that, I suppose it does come down to either peacefully enduring an enemy or fighting an enemy."

"Why can't they do both?" Kira asked.

When Ariste returned from patrol, Kira approached him. "Ariste," she said, "I need you to teach me to fight. Matusu has taught me some, but I need a master to teach me more."

He looked at her in silence for an uncomfortably long time. "I think that is good. We may not be able to always protect you. When do you want to start?"

"Now," Kira said.

Ariste's hand shot out slamming hard against her left shoulder, and in one fluid motion, he spun, lowering himself and sweeping Kira's legs from beneath her. She fell hard on her back, knocking the wind out of her.

"First lesson – how to fall," Ariste said. He reached out a hand and pulled her from the ground.

Kira immediately regretted not asking him when they were sitting down. Luckily, Ariste didn't continue to just knock her down. The need for his lessons was immediately apparent. He spent the whole lesson teaching Kira how to fall in any direction without getting hurt. By the time they finished, she was filthy and tired.

"Tomorrow I will show you how to fall while running and how to recover from a high fall."

"Let's do it now. I need to know how to teach it when I go back into the dream."

"You eat and rest, and then I will teach you more."

They moved to the fire where Matusu was pulling cakes out.

"Your form is improving," he said. "Do you understand now why a master teacher makes a difference?"

"You are a good teacher, too. He has just had more practice at teaching."

"Maybe Patala should learn as well, in case we are attacked," Matusu said.

"I'm not learning in case we are attacked," Kira said, "though that is a good point. I'm learning for the dream."

"Why do you need to fight in the dream? No permanent damage is done there. I don't understand."

Kira explained about the invaders who were threatening Iactah's people. Matusu made the same argument as Te'Roan. Kira pointed out that if those descendants were destroyed, any chance of opening the gate may also be lost.

Ariste and Orr sat down with them. "So you don't need to learn defensive fighting," Ariste said. "You need to learn the last fight."

"The last fight?" Matusu asked.

"They do not teach this to the apprentice guards – only to the captains and probably teachers. It is the fighting we do when the fighting must end. It has two effects. It puts a lethal end to the opponent in front of you, and it sends a message that creates fear in other opponents, so they lose their will to fight."

Kira didn't speak.

"I saw Te'Roan do that at the river crossing. It is brutal. Is that really necessary?" Matusu asked.

The others looked at Te'Roan.

"'Lethal end' doesn't really sound like our style," Patala said.

"It is a measure of last resort," Te'Roan said. "Wouldn't it be better to start with…"

"That's what I need," Kira said. "That's what they need. People are being enslaved. If we let Iactah's line end, we may never get another chance to save our people."

"Unlike defensive fighting, there is nothing kind or gentle about it," Ariste said.

"So knocking me down earlier was gentle?"

Ariste looked at Orr for a moment, and they both nodded. Then Orr laughed.

After eating some food, the training resumed. Learning to fall was actually the easiest part. Every strike, block, and counterstrike added bruises. Kira seemed to be receiving more than she was giving. She realized this was more intense than training in the dream with Matusu. In the real world, getting a landing wrong had consequences. But this forced Kira to get it right. Ariste was a patient teacher and nowhere near as cruel as he could have been. Every new lesson started with a demonstration with Orr. And Orr also helped Kira at each step by adjusting her stance and shifting her balance.

On day three, they started working through kill moves. Ariste would stop these moves short and say something like, "twist to the shoulder to break the neck" or "drive the blade upward to kill."

Kira knew that doing this herself would take much more training than she had time for. She had the form, but not the reflexes or the strength. When it came down to it, she was glad she wouldn't be actually fighting. She wasn't sure she could hurt or kill someone in the moment. She also knew it may be the only chance for Iactah's descendants and for Kira's people.

When Kira arrived with Coyote, she saw that a new structure had replaced the fire ring in the center of the village. Looking down into the stacked circle of stones, Kira saw water – a well. And the center of the village was now down the slope from the large brick building.

A boy faded into view. He looked closely at Kira, then looked around like he was checking to see who else might be there. He looked back at Kira and smiled.

"I'm Kira," she said.

"I know," he said. "My mother knows you. She tells me about the stars, like you taught her. She tells me and my brother. Are you really here to help us."

"I hope I can – you and your children."

The boy laughed. "I don't have any children."

"You will someday. Strong, smart children like you, I hope. What's your name?"

"I'm Peter, like the apostle."

Kira wasn't sure what an apostle was, but it sounded like something probably introduced by the new people.

"Peter, can you name the stars?" Kira concentrated on brightening the stars.

Peter looked at them and started pointing out constellations to Kira.

"Can you measure the stars?"

"My mom showed me, but I don't have my stick with me."

"Your stick?"

"It tells the distance between the stars. My mother said it is sacred. She said the stars will change and when I grow up, I will add marks of my own to it."

"That's smart. Can you measure here – without the stick?"

He held his hands up the way Kira had shown his mother.

"I've been showing my brother, but he's not as good at it yet."

Kira had been about to start teaching Peter the basics of fighting techniques Ariste taught her. Te'Roan's words kept echoing in her mind – hiding and retreating were the path to safety. Chosovi made it clear that they could not hide, but maybe Kira could improve their odds. Maybe she could teach one brother to retreat and the other to fight.

Kira continued her lesson on the stars and on retreating into the desert, left the dream.

Patala was beside Kira when she opened her eyes.

"Are you ready to eat something?"

Kira smelled some of Patala's cakes.

"I have to go back," she said. "I have to find Peter's brother."

Patala held out a cake.

Kira took a bite of the cake, closed her eyes, and returned to the dream.

Kira focused on Chosovi's sons as she followed Coyote through the trees. Not Peter, she said to herself. She entered the same village and saw a boy standing by the well. It was not Peter.

"Hello," she said.

The boy looked startled. "Are you Kira?" he asked. He looked older than Peter had. Kira wondered how much time had passed.

"I am Kira. Are you Peter's brother?"

"Yes. I'm Isaac. Are you real?"

"I'm real, and I can prove it. I can teach you something you don't know."

"Like you taught Peter?"

"Some things that I taught Peter and some things I did not."

"What things?"

"I will teach you some things you can use when you are grown up – things that you can teach your children. You and your children will be the protectors, while Peter and his children will watch and preserve."

"So I don't need to measure the stars?"

"I will teach you to name the stars and how to measure them, just like Peter."

"Mama made sure that both of us can measure the stars."

"That's good. Keep practicing. Now, are you ready to learn how to be a protector?" Kira shifted her clothing to a shirt and trousers like Isaac wore.

Kira woke from the dream as exhausted as if she had performed the training in the real world. She had conducted at least ten training sessions with Isaac. After each one, she would wake and review with Ariste and Orr before eating and resting. What had been only a few days for her were years for Isaac. Each time they met, she could tell that he was practicing and growing stronger. Even as she taught him, she wondered if she was undoing the work she had done with previous generations or the work her own people had done. They had stayed hidden to keep from influencing the people of this world. Now she was going directly against that.

Of course, a teacher had helped Iactah's people by teaching them her people's farming methods. He had saved them from starving. But Kira was teaching them secrets that would give them advantages over their human enemies. She was picking sides in human affairs. And she was going directly against what her people saw as the best way to survive in the face of a growing threat. What would her father say?

"Isaac, you can teach others to fight with you, but you must always respect the choice of others to retreat. You and those who follow you are protectors. Some would use this power you have to prey on weaker people. If you do this, I will give even greater knowledge to others who can take this power from you."

"Peter said he will not fight. He said you told him not to fight. Is it fair that me and my children fight battles while others hide and refuse to fight?"

"I will not lie to you and tell you it is fair or even right. I will just tell you it is necessary."

"Have you seen the future and know it is necessary?"

"I have seen a trend based on what my people have seen others do in your world," Kira said. "I see what your mother faced and what you are facing. I am preparing you for a possible future that I expect but do not know."

"My papa used to say thatch the roof tight on the sunny day because you don't know when the rain will come."

"Your father and my father would get along well," Kira said.

"I haven't seen him since I was little. He went away to work with the priests."

"I hope he will return, but even if he does not, you and those you teach can protect the People."

"I have thought about this, and we must separate from them," Isaac said. "When we stand up to the priests, they will send men to hunt us. I don't want them to blame my brothers and sisters who do not choose to fight."

"That is your choice," Kira said. "It sounds like a wise thing to do."

"Some think the priests are good. Some are kind."

"Are they all kind?"

"The soldiers who follow them are not kind."

"Then protect the people from the soldiers." Kira knew from her conversations with Chosovi, that the soldiers did the priests' bidding. A person could appear to be kind while commanding their underlings to commit cruelty. She had seen this among her own people, among the factions of teachers. When she first left Hochonal, she hadn't thought people could be both kind and cruel. She had grown up in a world of certainties in her little village. The maneuvering and duplicity among the council had cured her of such simplistic thinking.

Kira could think of nothing else to teach him. He was by now several years older than her. It was time to move on.

Kira had not imagined the events she would set in motion. Coyote led her first to Jose, Peter's grandson. He was a slave, living in a pueblo. Under the watch of cruel masters, he and others were marched to the mountains to harvest timber and bring it back to build large buildings for the foreigners. The foreigners kept coming. They kept telling his people they had to work to be cleansed of their pagan ways. Jose knew his family had left their pagan ways at the time of his great-grandmother. He did as the soldiers and the task masters said, yet still they told him he was not one of them. The priests gave him communion each Sunday, yet each Monday the task masters told him he was unclean and must work harder.

When Kira had first found him in the dream, he was inside a large building sitting on a bench looking at a wall decorated with images of people Kira didn't even begin to recognize. In the center, high on the wall hung a depiction of some sort of torture of a human man. She turned away and focused on the boy sitting on a bench, who had closed his eyes and was mumbling to himself. His mumblings kept repeating, like a chant.

The third time she asked what he was doing, he said, "Praying to make the demon go away."

"What is a demon?"

"Demons are evil monsters sent to torment believers."

"Who told you I was a demon?"

"The priest said that grandfather's dreams were of a demon sent from the devil. Why did you torment him?"

"Did he say I tormented him?"

"No."

"I've only ever tried to help your family."

"You didn't help us not be slaves."

"Are all the people slaves?"

"Grandpa's brother Isaac left with some who would not be slaves. But grandpa said we must submit."

"Have you met Isaac? Does he have children?"

"No, I haven't met him. I hear about them, but I don't know if he has children. Why didn't you tell him to submit?"

"It's complicated. I'm not a demon or a god…"

"Are you an angel?"

"What's an angel?"

"God's messenger. Angels visit people like saints and virgins."

"I am not a messenger from a god. I live in the time of your ancestors. My people are in danger like you and your people, but we think one of your descendants can help us. Someone who will be born far in the future. I teach your family to read the stars so they will know when the time is right."

"What do you need us to do?"

"For now, I need you to learn to read the stars and to live."

"So what you're doing is to help your people, not my people?"

"We help each other. My people know things about farming and living with the land, things we have shared. When the time comes for your descendant to help us, I will teach your people amazing things that no one has ever seen before."

"Will you free us?"

"I'm working on that. Now, show me what you know about the stars." Kira made the roof of the building disappear.

Kira came out of the dream perspiring from the heat in the hut. She saw that the coals of the fire still glowed, but no one was tending them. She stepped out of the hut into early dawn. The sweat on her skin suddenly chilled her as it met the cool morning air. Patala was by the cooking fire with Matusu and Te'Roan.

"Hungry?" Patala asked.

"Starving," Kira said. "Where are Ariste and Orr?"

"Scouting," Te'Roan said. "Last night, Orr saw a fire in the distance. They went to see who it is. They may be gone most of the day."

"I need them to continue my training. Isaac has left the tribe and formed a resistance against the slavers. I need to reinforce the training with his children if he has any."

"I can train with you," Matusu offered. "I may not be the master that Ariste and Orr are, but I think I can help you find some weaknesses you missed."

"Weaknesses?"

"You know what I mean."

"Let me eat something and then you can show me what you mean."

"Maybe you should eat and then actually sleep," Te'Roan said. "The dream isn't the same as sleeping. Your body may be at rest, but your mind is active."

"When we get through this, I will sleep." Oh, how I will sleep, she thought.

As she ate, Kira explained to the others what she had learned about Jose and how Isaac had split off. She was anxious to see if she could find a descendant of Isaac. She hoped he knew his son or grandson so she could stay in a forward moving timeline. Te'Roan continued to remind her of the laws of cause and effect that created immutable destinies to avoid temporal paradoxes. She had always pushed back against those seemingly useless lessons in mathematics and philosophy that had nothing to do with her life in Hochonal. Her father was right after all. She did need to expand her mind to more than what she saw in her small village.

After eating their morning meal, Kira and Matusu began their training session with Kira letting Matusu throw her so she could practice her landings. She had perfected the moves Ariste had taught her that allowed her to be thrown and almost instantly maneuver back into a fighting stance.

"You're going easy on me," she said. Kira knew Matusu's strength and could tell he was holding back.

"Injuries won't help you learn faster," Te'Roan interjected.

"They might," Kira said. "But we'll never know if Matusu keeps fighting like a little girl."

This time when Kira came at Matusu, he took the opening she left in her attack to throw her like he was taught.

Kira took a bit longer to roll out and back into fighting stance. She then took a step backward to give herself time to draw air back into her lungs. "That's what I'm looking for. These moves are just a dance if I don't have to recover from hitting the ground." She launched another attack at him, this time not giving him an opening to throw her. Kira landed three good blows that staggered him before she swept a leg from under him dropping him to the ground.

"Way to change things up," Matusu said as he rolled back onto his feet.

"Be ready for anything," Kira said, repeating Ariste's counsel.

Te'Roan stood up. "Are you ready for anything?" He asked.

"What do you mean?" Kira asked, still circling Matusu in her fighting stance.

"You are training these humans to fight aggressors with aggression. What happens when they face defenders, like our teachers?"

"You fought aggressively in Hochonal," Kira said.

"I was fighting to defend others and deter an overwhelming force. At the river, I fought the last fight to eliminate the enemy and rescue you and Patala. Had I been caught alone by a smaller group, I would have employed a defensive style designed to wear out opponents that I might escape them."

"Show me," Kira said.

Matusu moved away as Te'Roan took his place before Kira.

"Attack me," Te'Roan said.

Kira used the same attack sequence she had just used against Matusu. Te'Roan barely moved as he blocked each attack by redirecting the force of Kira's attacks off to the left or right. Kira stepped back for a brief moment and launched another attack, one designed to force the enemy off balance, then take advantage of their recovery to throw them to the ground. This time Te'Roan stepped slightly to one side and directed the energy of her attack downward. Kira landed hard, as if she had been thrown, though it felt as though she had thrown herself. She rolled out and back to her feet then stepped back, stood up straight, and bowed her head to Te'Roan.

"Why have you not been teaching me?" She asked.

"As I said before, this is an extension of what you are learning. The power to redirect an attack is built on the techniques Ariste is teaching you, but its real power comes from intention and a disciplined mind. Those come by meditation."

"This would keep Jose's people safe, if they could defend themselves at moments of crisis."

"It would take too long to teach you, let alone to teach them. The style can only be taught after extensive meditation training. It can only be properly wielded by one capable of letting go of all fear and aggression. Any fear or aggression disrupts the fighting style."

"Are you saying you have no fear?"

"I'm saying that through meditation and training, I can put fear aside to properly execute the defensive style."

"Do you mean you only have fear when you want to?"

"Emotion is like flowing water, we can dam it and redirect it, but left with no release, it will overflow our attempts to contain it."

"What am I supposed to do with that?"

"Meditate on it." Te'Roan stepped away and returned to his meal.

Kira did meditate on it as she entered the dream again. She was back in the open grove of fire trees where paths moved off in many directions.

Kira considered how she felt when the human warriors had come to her village, when she was swept away by the river, or even during fighting training. Her fear led to a release of energy that kept her alive.

Coyote stood beside her. Kira turned her thoughts to Isaac and Isaac's connections. Coyote started down a well-worn path through the trees, Kira was starting to realize that they followed a similar path at the start of each trip, then followed some new branch to someone she had not yet met. There were no signs of markers on the paths that meandered through the grove, but Coyote seemed to know which one to take. Sometimes the guide would stop at a fork in the path and then as if catching some scent, choose a path to follow.

She also noticed that each time she returned to the dream, her journey to the next person took longer. From what she learned about star positions from Jose, more than two hundred years had passed since the time of Iactah. The stars had shifted just over a third of the distance they needed to go before Kira would find the one who could help her. If she continued from the same starting point each time she entered the dream, she would spend half a night just getting to each new person. She didn't know how long she could stay in the dream.

They arrived at a desert clearing by a cooking fire. No huts or buildings could be seen. Standing by the fire was a young man dressed very differently from Peter, Isaac, and Jose who had been wearing shirts and trousers of woven cloth. This young man wore some items of woven cloth and some items made of skins like Iactah and his children and grandchildren had worn. The cloth items he wore were not like the ones Jose had worn. They were rougher and of colors that would blend into the sand and the rocks. He didn't wear the low shoe that Iactah's people wore. He wore soft boots, that rose more than halfway to his knee. If tightly sewn, Kira thought they would be good for keeping out the sand during desert travel. She may have to try making a pair.

"Hello," Kira said.

The young man looked up from the fire at Kira. His mouth moved as if he would smile but stopped before getting there. It reminded Kira of the stoic look she saw in Ariste and Orr when she first met them. The young man had a hardness about his face, and she noted a scar on his cheek and another below his chin. He didn't seem to be much older than Kira, yet he seemed more serious and weathered.

"You are the star watcher," he said. "My grandfather said you would come, when you hadn't come to my father."

"Is Isaac your grandfather?"

"That was the name the priests gave him. He gave it back and took instead the name Iactah that he learned from you."

"Did he tell you my name?"

"You are Kira. I am Niyol, son of Niachta."

"Niyol, has your grandfather taught you to read the stars?"

An ornate stick appeared leaning on a stone next to Niyol. Niyol seemed surprised as though he had conjured it by mistake. "I have learned it and made my mark. I will make more if I live so long."

"I hope you live long and have many children," Kira said. "What else did your grandfather teach you?"

"He taught me to fight like the star watchers. He taught me that we keep our children free by driving back the soldiers and the priests who have enslaved his brother's children."

"Are you able to drive them back?"

"They fear us and come in greater numbers. But we make sure the same ones do not come twice."

Kira began to sense the hostility she had enabled. This young man had been fighting his whole life and his father before him.

"Will you show me how you fight? Perhaps I can add to what I taught your grandfather."

"I would like that."

Niyol stepped around the fire to face Kira. She shifted her dress to clothes more like Niyol's and moved into a fighting stance. He also moved into a fighting stance, but different than what she had taught Isaac, lower. As she moved to attack, Niyol deftly stepped in even lower and grabbed her ankle. She had to abort her attack and fall backward to avoid being thrown. She continued her fall into a roll and back up to her fighting stance. She had never taught such an attack to Isaac.

"You have surprises," she said.

"I have fought since I was little. Grandfather taught us that every boy and girl in the tribe is a warrior."

As they sparred, Niyol continued to surprise her. During one counterattack, he suddenly had his knife in his hand. Kira knew the knife would have no real effect on her in the dream but realized the hostility she had unleashed among Isaac's people. In just two generations, they had become a warrior people. They had built on what she had taught them. Niyol's fighting style was efficient and effective. At the end of every successful attack or counterattack, he would stop short of what she could tell was a killing move. She could imagine him in battle moving from one combatant to the next, leaving a trail of bodies.

"Do you always end your attacks with a kill?"

"Mostly," Niyol said. "If we have one or two injured who have not died, we will sometimes leave them tied in the desert where they will be found as a warning to others."

"Does that work?"

"For a while, but they eventually return with more men. My brother thinks they are different men who come – who didn't see the warnings."

"Do you farm or hunt? How do you eat?"

"We have small farms in hidden places, though we don't tend to them like those in the pueblos. And we go to the mountains for deer, elk, and buffalo. The deer up there are fatter than in the desert. When the big herds of buffalo come, we take some and carry the meat back to our hidden places. We do not make a show of our farms and our hunting like the people of the priests."

Kira wondered at the thing she had done. In her time, Iactah's people had survived by being passive and hiding. This group of descendants were the furthest thing from passive. Which would survive? All Kira could do at this point was follow the connections, skipping generations where she could, but following the generations to where she hoped to find someone who could help her.

Chapter 14

At first light, Kira heard Ariste and Orr arrive back in the village.

"We need to leave," Ariste said. "A large group of guards and teachers are coming."

"How did they find us?" Patala asked.

"We trained them well," Orr said.

"I recognized some of the guards. They are loyal to Te'Marile, and Te'Srin is with them," Ariste said.

Patala turned to Kira who had just come out of the hut at the commotion. "Will you still be able to continue the dream from someplace else?"

"I should be able to. Regular dreaming doesn't seem to be tied to location, and Iactah found me because of a dream he had when he was days away from where we met."

"Gather your things and do your best to get rid of any evidence we were here," Ariste said.

Matusu began taking apart a shade awning he had made. "I suppose you mean things like this. Humans wouldn't have tied knots this way."

"Exactly," Ariste said. "We leave as soon as possible."

"I made woven shoes for some of the children," Patala said.

"I will explain it to Iactah," Kira said. "Where should we go?" She asked Te'Roan.

"I've noticed that your dreams take longer each time, which means we could be out here for months. We are going to need to go where we can find food and shelter. Any outlying villages will be watched."

"Could we hunt deer?" Kira asked.

"I can hunt," Orr said.

"We could go to the mountains before the cold comes," Kira said. "Isaac's grandson...well, he's not Isaac anymore, since he changed his name to Iactah...anyway, his grandson Niyol said that they go to the mountains to hunt deer because they are fatter than in the desert."

Kira thought she was the last one to have her things ready to go, when she realized everyone was waiting for Patala. She was sure that Patala was the first one packed, since she kept everything mostly ready to go in case this very thing happened. Patala was going about the village saying goodbye to all the children. She was taking shoes and giving them to Iactah. Iactah said they would hide the shoes until they were sure the guards were gone. Ariste and Orr were pretty sure the guards would not come into direct contact with Iactah's people. Even though the rebel faction wanted to change how things were done, getting the guards to interact with humans was a long way off.

As soon as Patala finished saying her goodbyes, they headed east toward an outcropping of rock. Like their first escape from Hochonal, the hard surfaces would hold fewer traces of their passing. They couldn't stay on rocks the whole way, especially after they turned toward the mountains, but the gaps in their trail would slow their pursuers.

They kept moving that first day until well after dark. They had stopped once before the sun set to make a small fire of dry sticks and cook some food. Then they had continued on. The place they found to sleep had good lookout positions and a little grass to sleep on. It had been weeks since Kira had walked so far in a single day.

"Patala," Kira said. "Will you make sure my blanket stays on me while I'm in the dream? I won't notice it, and I don't have the warmth of the hut."

Patala sat down beside her. "I'll be here until you wake," she said.

As Kira started to enter the dream, she was interrupted by her own yawn and snapped back to the real world. She closed her eyes and started again. She focused on being in the dream. The quiet dark village of Hochonal came into view. Wrong village, she thought and closed her eyes in the dream. Focusing on being in the fire trees near Iactah's village, she willed herself there. When she opened her eye's she was where she wanted to be, looking down the divided trails among the trees. Coyote was beside her. Then everything blurred and faded. She blinked and opened her eyes to predawn light on grass. It was morning in the real world. She had fallen asleep and lost a whole night of dreaming. She felt both angry and rested.

Kira sat up, and Patala stirred on the grass next to her.

"Sleep well?" Patala asked.

"Too well," Kira said, then took a deep breath and let out a sigh.

"I thought you were supposed to be watching me while I was in the dream."

"I did for about a bit until you fell asleep."

"How did you know I was asleep?"

"Your breathing changes. I was glad to see you get some rest. I was starting to worry about how little you've been sleeping."

"Now that I'm rested, maybe I can drop into the dream for a while before everyone's ready to go again."

Ariste stepped into view coming down from his perch on the rocks above them. "I'm glad you're up," he said. "Orr snared a rabbit last night, and he's cooking it a short walk from here. I know it's a risk, but he started before I could stop him."

"Is he in a spot the fire will be seen?" Patala asked.

"No," Ariste said. "The risk is Orr's cooking."

Kira's feet throbbed at the thought of walking. She looked over to where Matusu and Te'Roan had been last night, and they were gone. "Let me roll up this blanket, and I guess I'm ready to go."

The rabbit turned out to be one of the long, lanky desert rabbits that was as tough as tree bark. It took so long to chew a piece into something that could be swallowed, that they just took the cooked meat with them and chewed on it while they walked.

This became their pattern over the next four days – walk, sleep, eat rabbit while walking. Each night, Kira tried to enter the dream. Sometimes she fell out of the dream and into sleep right at the beginning and other times somewhere along the trail to find the next descendant. She was starting to worry that time passing for her was somehow affecting when she would reenter the dream. She reassured herself that she was connecting people, not years. She would meet the next person who had a personal connection with their parent or grandparent.

On the fifth day, conditions changed. Not only did they start climbing up out of the desert, squalls started appearing on the horizon. That evening they watched as lighting lit up some distant cliffs through most of the night. In the darkness before dawn, a light rain woke them and got them off to an early start. The travel went slower as they often changed course trying to find their way up the mountain. By afternoon, the light rain had shared enough water to create trickling streams in most of the canyons. As they moved up the mountain, vegetation around them increased. Leafier trees replaced the dry desert trees below. Water collected into constantly flowing streams. Eventually, large pine trees dotted the landscape and gave shade for grass to grow.

On the sixth day, Ariste snared and cooked two rabbits that were the plump, furry variety.

"Orr thinks around here will be a good place to set up a camp for a while," Ariste said. "Kira can get back to her dreams, and we can hunt for some game that will feed us for a couple of weeks. The storm likely cleared our tracks away. It will take some searching for the guards to figure out where we've gone."

Before long the rain started again, and they had found a place to set up a more permanent camp not far from a stream and a small lake. Kira and Patala set up a small hut to keep the rain off them, though everything was already wet in and out of the hut.

"Do you recognize any of the herbs around here?" Patala asked. "We may have meat up here, but it's going to taste dull."

"I'll take dull venison over seasoned desert rabbit. My jaw is still sore from chewing," Kira said.

"I suppose we better put together some version of a kitchen," Patala said.

"Here's a start." It was Matusu walking up through the trees carrying a large squarish stone. "Where would you like it?"

Patala picked a spot a little way out from under the trees.

Matusu set the stone down and headed out for another.

"Can we help?" Patala asked.

"Just help Kira get dry and dreaming. I'd hate to be here when winter arrives."

Patala and Kira finished stacking bows on the roof of the little hut, then Kira got out of the rain, wrapped in a blanket, and focused on entering the dream.

The walk from path to path seemed longer. Though at least in the dream, Kira's feet never hurt. When the coyote finally led Kira to an opening, a girl sat by a cooking fire just outside a brick building. Other brick buildings surrounded the area, some stacked two stories high. She wore a dress of skins, adorned with strips of colored cloth. Kira thought this odd. Though as the dream continued to reflect the reality of the time, she realized that people would continue to appear as they were, not as she might imagine them.

The girl saw Kira and smiled. So apparently Kira was no longer being called a demon.

"Are you the star woman?" The girl asked.

"My name is Kira."

"I'm Sihu. My father is Jose. He said you visited him when he was young. He said you might visit me or my children. No one knows who you will choose to visit, but we all learned the stars – me and my brothers and my sister."

"I'm glad you study the stars. What can you tell me about your family? Is your father well?"

"He stayed out of the fighting like you told him. He is a healer and teaches our traditions, now that the priests and soldiers are gone."

"The priests are gone?"

"And the soldiers. The priests kept sending away our food, and our people were hungry. They took young men to work their mines. When some of our chiefs resisted, they were beaten and some even killed. The people of many pueblos all rebelled at the same time and drove out the soldiers and priests. We now eat the food we grow. We trade with other pueblos. Father brought me a doll." A small doll appeared in her hands. She laughed.

"Things sound much better. Can you show me what you know about the stars?"

With each generation that passed, Kira saw a slight drift in their understanding of what she taught them. Even though to them her lessons were a generation or more apart, to her, she was teaching the same lessons over and over every few days. The girl was bright and eager. She would carry on the tradition.

"We still have the stick and father built a special stone near our pueblo to keep the marks. He was worried that if more soldiers and priests ever came, they would destroy the stick, like they tried to destroy our traditions."

"That is wise," Kira said.

When Kira and Sihu finished their lesson about the stars, rather than waking from the dream, Kira walked out of the clearing the way she had come. The coyote went with her, she focused on another connection, a connection to Niyol. The coyote looked down the path expectantly.

"Do we have to go back to the start every time?"

The coyote cocked its head like it was trying to understand then trotted forward through the trees. Kira followed. They went back the way they had come, then turned onto a new path.

As they entered another clearing, a young man sat by a campfire in a narrow canyon. From the way he was dressed, Kira could tell he was from Niyol's band of warriors. He had the same stern look and a few scars even though he was barely tall enough to be considered a man. He stood when he saw Kira.

"Are you the one who visits dreams? The one who taught Iactah to be a warrior?"

"I am. My name is Kira. What should I call you?"

"I am Gaagii, son of Niyol."

"Are your people at peace now that the soldiers have left the pueblos?"

"It is good that they are leaving the pueblos alone, but they have built other settlements and hunt us wherever they see us. I don't believe it will end until we are dead or they are driven out."

"Perhaps you should focus more on hiding and less on fighting."

"They will spread until there is nowhere to hide."

"I know how you feel, but this is about surviving. In all your fighting, have you paid attention to the stars?"

"I have. Many nights in the desert I spend looking up at the stars and reciting the stories my father taught me."

"Will you tell them to me?" The stars above them brightened a little, and Kira listened as Gaagii identified each constellation and the distances between them. His attention to detail amazed her. She added points in a few places.

When the lesson was done, Kira walked out of the clearing and back to the trails. This time, the coyote didn't hesitate. It led her to Gaagii's son Shin, whose people now lived as nomads in the desert, surviving by moving with the seasons and the game animals. Even with all their moving, they still passed on how to read and measure the stars.

Next she followed the trails to Sihu's granddaughter Takala. She was growing up much as her mother had in the safety of the pueblo. They recorded the changes in the constellations, marking them on the stick and on the stone Jose had raised.

Kira didn't know how long she had spent in each time, but she knew that the walk from the start to here must be quite long by now. Only by pressing on would she make up for all the time she had lost crossing the desert. She left the pueblo to find the next connection.

Matusu wiped the sweat away from Kira's forehead. She was burning up with fever. She must have become ill from going into the dream before she was thoroughly dry and warm. Patala was sleeping on the other side of the hut having been up all night watching over her sister. They were in a larger hut now, that Matusu and the others had erected around the cooking fire Matusu had built. Kira had been in the dream now for three days. They called to her to wake her, but Te'Roan warned them that trying to wake her in a more forceful way could harm her mind as it was pulled unwillingly from the dream.

Patala had been dripping water into Kira's mouth to keep her from getting dehydrated but was unable to give her any food. Kira had told them that the passage of time in the dream was hard to measure. All of them took turns hunting and tending to the fire to keep the bigger hut warm. Rain dripped from different places, and Matusu thought that one good day of gathering reeds from the nearby lake would be enough to put a proper roof on top.

Kira continued to move through connections in the dream, she focused her intention on alternating between warrior and pueblo dwelling families. Several generations went by with very little change, fighting among the warriors and farming in harsh conditions at the pueblo. Then a boy named Pimne, Takala's descendant six generations down, told Kira of a big change in their world. The soldiers from the south were all gone, and the pueblos were now part of another country called the United States. They had sometimes met these people from the United States. Some spoke another language, but many also spoke Spanish like the soldiers from the south. Pimne seemed to think it was better.

Shin's descendant, Delshay, who was several years younger than Pimne, told Kira of a great war that the people of the United States fought and how his people were not part of it, but the fighting was about whether there could be slaves. Now there would be no slaves, but the men who had fought in the wars were now being sent to hunt Delshay's people.

After Delshay, Coyote led Kira to Vincent Honanie. He was dressed differently. He wore long pants and a shirt with long sleeves and buttons up the front. He wore boots with a pointed toe and tall heel. After him, Kira met Lewis Honanie, Vincent's grandson.

Delshay had been the last of the warriors Kira met. He was the last one to dress like his people had dressed since Isaac broke away with his warriors. After teaching Lewis and hearing how the world had changed with machines that traveled across the land and in the air, Kira realized that Isaac's line was lost from the world. The path she had set them on led to their being hunted and killed as more people had settled the land. Lewis told her it had been more than sixty years since the last of the warriors were either killed or captured and taken away by the government.

Hearing that, she didn't continue in the dream. She simply closed her eyes and faded back to the real world.

Kira awoke in a hut she didn't recognize. Patala was sitting next to her with a hand on her head. She felt weak, like she did after dragging herself out of the river, like a great exertion had drained her of all her energy. She tried to speak, but no words came out.

Patala leaned close to her face and smiled. "You're back. We were very worried."

Kira tried to speak again but still couldn't.

"Don't try to talk until you've had something to drink. I have some venison broth warmed and ready for you. Let me help you sit up." Patala helped her into a sitting position then sat behind her to hold her up. "Matusu," Patala called.

Matusu must have been just outside because he came right in.

"Will you bring us a bowl of that broth there by the fire?" Patala said.

Matusu poured out some broth from Patella's little cooking pot into a small wooden bowl and brought it over.

"You were gone a while this time," Matusu said to Kira. "You must have lots to tell us."

When Kira thought about what she wanted to tell them, she felt more choked up, and she felt a tear welling up. She was too weak to stop it from running down her cheek.

Patala helped Kira drink the broth a little at a time. "Just a little for now," Patala said. "You've been in the dream for six days. Your body needs to learn what to do with food again. You also need to drink water."

Kira drank some water. She knew she needed water, but she just felt exhausted, like she could go to sleep for days. "Thank you," she whispered to Patala. "Six days is a long time to watch me lay here." She looked around the hut. "Where are we?"

"Matusu and the other men built a larger hut, and we moved you into it. Here we can have fire to stay warm," Patala said.

"Thank them for me," Kira said. "I think I need to sleep now."

Patala laid Kira back down and cover her with blankets.

When Kira woke again, she could see bits of sunlight streaming in through the doorway and the smoke hole in the ceiling. Patala had cakes cooking by the fire.

"Can I have one of those?" Kira asked. "Or am I still on a broth only diet?"

"You can try one, after you drink some more water."

Patala seemed especially motherly when Kira was sick or injured. Kira noticed that Patala's hair was tied back. What happened to that flighty girl who only thought about looking good for boys?

Kira drank some water and took a bite from one of the cakes. The cake tasted very different from the ones Patala usually made.

Patala smiled at the look on Kira's face. "Nothing is wrong with it. I just had to use different seeds and herbs than we have down lower."

"Are you sure it's safe?"

"The rest of us have been eating them for days and no one has gotten sick yet. Later you can have some venison. I'll start cooking some here soon."

Kira was grateful to hear that they had found deer. They had come up here to this cold wet place because she told them they could find fat deer. "Are the deer as fat as promised?"

"The one Orr brought in was bigger than any I ever saw in the desert."

Almost as if he had heard them talking, Te'Roan entered the hut carrying thick strips of meat to be cooked. "Venison neck strips as ordered. Orr says these have fat in the meat. Perhaps you and Kira should go outside while the sun is shining. I will start cooking the meat."

"Let's see if you can walk," Patala said as she helped Kira to her feet.

Kira could barely hold herself up. "Maybe later," she said as she sat back down on her blanket.

"You stay here and rest while I go see what kinds of berries I can find for us. Don't eat all the cakes Te'Roan. The others will want some when they get back from scouting."

Kira stayed sitting for a while listening to the meat sizzle as it came in contact with the hot stone.

"She barely left your side," he said. "How was your journey in the dream?"

"I think I messed up," she said. "I mean, our goal is progressing ok, but I really messed up their lives by encouraging Isaac and his children to fight." She told him about the generations she met, all that they went through, and how Isaac's line had ended.

"Do you think they would have fought anyway? From what I've learned, humans tend to lean toward fighting one another."

"I showed them how. I taught them to be more violent, and they got really good at it. One boy I met, Kuruk, was still too young to be a warrior. He seemed so innocent. His son, Taklishim told me that his father became a great fighter and bragged of his battles and the men he had killed. All I could see was the face of the innocent little boy. It's not what we have been taught. We aren't supposed to interfere like that."

"What about the other humans – the ones you told to submit?"

"They suffered too. For a long time, they suffered at the hands of one invader or another. The last one I talked to said they are not treated well. They have trouble providing. Though some in the country they are part of now try to help, it's often not enough."

"Yet they survived. Perhaps they survived the hardest times because the ones who fought took away attention from the ones who did not. Perhaps the ones who did not fight were left alone because the invaders were too busy with the ones who were fighting. You have seen the same strategy among our people."

"What do you mean? We do not fight."

"We are not fighting now, but if Thresdenal is threatened, the guards like Orr and Ariste are trained to go out onto the desert and harass the enemy, drawing them away from the city. This strategy has been employed from time to time with great effect."

"I see what you mean. The difference is that we are choosing the strategy."

"How do you know that Isaac wasn't choosing to protect Peter?"

"But so many generations died not knowing why they were fighting."

"How many of our people have died in this desert rather traveling the stars like we were destined to do?"

"I can't help but think how much damage we might do if we fully interact with them."

"Speaking of interacting with them, did you see any evidence of our people among them?"

"No, but I was limited to brief discussions with just a few isolated people."

"Who's isolated?" Orr asked, as he entered the shelter. "I have all the friends a man could want. I smell meat cooking. Are you ready to get fattened up, Kira? I saved these pieces for you to help you get your strength back."

"Where are Ariste and Matusu?" Kira asked.

"They went north, looking for game. I was scouting our back trail to the south. No signs of anyone following. I did pick up the trail of a group of humans, probably a hunting party. They passed by south of here a couple of days ago. They're probably heading to the part of the mountain with more streams and trees. It looks like a good place to gather some game before winter comes."

"It sounds like everyone is staying busy except me."

"From what I can tell, you've been the busiest of all – busy trying to save everybody. You spent six days in the dream, while the rest of us ate our fill of venison and slept each night between watches. The only one who even came close to being as busy as you was your sister. That girl never stopped checking on you. She reminded me of a mother with a new baby."

Te'Roan put some of the meat in a bowl and handed it to Kira. Orr used his knife to pick a piece of meat off the hot stone, and they ate in silence. The rabbit they'd eaten in the desert didn't even compare to this. She didn't care if they had Patala's spices. As she ate, she started to feel drowsy. It took some concentrated effort to finish the meat while pushing away the urge to lay down. When she finally finished, she gave the bowl to Te'Roan and laid down to let her body absorb the nutrition she had given it.

Kira woke in darkness. She could just make out forms in the hut by the red glow of coals in the cooking fire. Someone was moving near the fire. They added sticks and soon, yellow flames from the fire illuminated Ariste. Kira sat up to better see who else was there. She could only make out the sleeping form of Patala near her.

"Where is everyone? She whispered to Ariste.

"Orr and Matusu are sleeping in the small hut, and Te'Roan is on outside watch."

"Does that mean you are inside watch?"

"I'm on watch to make sure the fire doesn't go out and to stay close to the hut. Are you feeling better rested?"

"Apparently, since my body thinks it's morning."

"It's almost morning. This is last watch."

"Ariste, have you ever had to harass humans to lead them away from Thresdenal?"

"Where did that question come from?"

"Te'Roan told me it's part of the defensive plan for the city."

"I have. It is difficult to do without letting them know we are actually from Thresdenal. The city is supposed to be a great secret, but I think humans know about it or at least know something is there. We do what we call ghost attacks. We make attacks on their encampments without being seen – in and out like ghosts. If they do not leave, we escalate to physical attacks on their watchmen or scouts. We strike and disappear. After that, they usually leave."

"Why don't the villages do ghost attacks?"

"The villages are meant to be outposts. Some watch for groups approaching the borders of Thresdenal. Until just the past century, outer villages didn't even exist. They only became part of the plan after the first time skip. They also help distribute the population."

"They were also points of resource gathering for the new gate. Being so far out makes them poor advanced warning points. It took us many days to get from Hochonal to Thresdenal," Kira said.

"Te'Roan told me about the route you took, and it wasn't exactly direct. The typical path from Hochonal to Thresdenal is much quicker. But villages don't usually get approached. They are not on pathways humans travel between hunting grounds or to trade with other villages. Unless a village is surprised by a large group, as yours was, the people will usually just leave or hide until the danger passes."

Kira thought of the fate of the pueblos. "What is our defensive plan for an all-out invasion?"

"I believe that is what you are working on. The gate is our last fall back."

Kira felt again the urgency of finding a solution for the gate. She had to continue in the dream. If this line failed to reach the time in the future as Isaac's had, she wasn't sure how to she would get to that point. She drank some water, then laid down and entered into the dream.

When she first arrived at the grove of trees, she felt tired, like she had in the real world, but as she and Coyote started walking, her fatigue faded away. The walk was long this time, longer than the total time she spent on those early single connection visits. She wondered at the other connections they passed. There had to be hundreds of paths they did not take. What made the guide choose this path? And if this path were lost, could they try one of the others?

They arrived at a clearing where grass surrounded a dirt area. A fire ring made from a single stone circle sat in the middle. A young woman about Kira's age paced back and forth. The woman was wearing blue pants and a loose fitting button up shirt in a colorful striped pattern. She wore the most interesting shoes Kira had seen yet. They had a hard sole and a higher heel than Lewis's boots and then a sandal top with straps around her foot and ankle. Kira thought they looked very uncomfortable to walk in.

"Where am I," the young woman asked.

"You are in a dream," Kira said.

"No, my dreams aren't like this. Did you take me somewhere?" She looked at the fire and the benches, green boards on a smooth silver frame and a back rest of the same material. "Are we at a campground?" The woman asked.

"My name is Kira, I'm a friend of Lewis Honanie. Do you know him?"

"Yeah, I know him. He's my grandpa. Why's he hanging around with some young chick like you? Is this the park by the highway?"

"Has Lewis ever told you about the dream where he learned about watching the stars?"

"Oh my gosh, is this about that, and his stick he uses to measure stars? I thought he made all that up. How do I know I'm not just making all this up in my head from those stories he told me?"

"That is a question no one has asked me before. I can tell you of things you wouldn't know of yourself, but they are true."

"If I wouldn't know of them, how will I know they are true?"

"You could check on them and then return to the dream."

"Ok, what's Lewis's birthday?"

"How would I know that? I said I know him. I didn't give birth to him. Ask me something about stars?" Kira made the stars above them grow brighter.

"And then what, run to the library and see if you're right? Maybe you could do something you could only do in a dream."

Kira stepped forward and punched her in the shoulder. "Did you feel that?"

"I felt it, but it didn't hurt. Maybe I'm on some drug that blocks pain."

"I've been visiting members of your family for hundreds of years. None of them have ever doubted they were dreaming or that I am a real person visiting them. What is different with you?"

"You mean like what's wrong with me? Where do I start? How come you picked my family?"

This woman seemed very direct, so Kira thought she would be equally direct. "You have an ancestor who lives in my time named Iactah. He and I met and then connected through the dream. I can visit people's dreams, and he has dreams of the future. My spirit guide has been leading me through time to teach his descendants to read the stars."

"Wait. That's your spirit guide?" She gestured toward Coyote.

"She is."

"Woah, heavy. You should be careful. Coyote is a trickster."

"I haven't seen any trickery in where she has led me."

"My mother always said Coyote could lead you to great wisdom. Having Coyote as your guide says a lot about you. You must be cunning and tenacious. It also means you might be a trickster."

"I think we've drifted off the path. What is your name?"

"I'm Rosie, Rosie Naha. But shouldn't you know that? Shouldn't your spirit guide have told you?"

"My spirit guide doesn't talk to me. It simply guides me to descendants of Iactah."

"Oh yes, the one you said is my ancestor. I don't know about that. The furthest back anyone has told me about is my grandfather's grandfather."

"Vincent Honanie."

"Of course, you would know, because you know all my ancestors."

"I don't know all of them. Sometimes I skip a generation – as long as there is a connection. If you had never met your grandfather, I might have visited your mother and then you."

"Right, you can only meet somebody who knows somebody you know. Why not just jump over and meet my friend Linda. She'd love this."

"I don't know," Kira said. "I don't control it like that. Maybe it has to do with your family's ability to see the future in dreams."

"If I could see the future, I'd be doing a lot better. I'm not sure anybody in my family or on the res ever saw the future. That would've been helpful about, oh say, a hundred years ago."

"Your grandfather told me the year I met him was 1931 according to your counting of years. What year is it now?"

"I'm starting to think you're for real."

"Rosie, I am real. What year is it?"

"It's 1970."

"I understand science has advanced a great deal. How accurately can scientists measure the stars?"

"I guess they can see things accurately. They described the exact spot they landed on the moon."

"People have already gone to the moon?"

"Wait, why do you say already? Were you expecting it?"

"Eventually most sentient species discover space flight. How good are they at scanning space?"

"You're asking the wrong person."

"I think the time has come to teach you to read the stars beyond anything I taught your ancestors. How much do you know about astronomy?"

"I know I'm a Virgo."

"I don't know what that means, but when we are done, you will be able to map the stars more accurately than anyone in your history."

"There it is again, you talk about my history, you mention my people. I thought you meant native people, but now I'm thinking you mean humans. Who are you?"

"I'm Kira."

"I know your name, but who are you? Are you from outer space?"

"I was born on this planet. My people came from outer space more than twelve hundred years before your time. We are trying to get home and need your help."

"You should have led with that. Wow! What do I need to know?"

Kira began by explaining the structure of the universe and the celestial bodies that make up the universe. She was sure that whatever Rosie had learned about cosmology in school was overly simplistic and sometimes just wrong. She knew nothing about how gravity worked, other than it makes things fall and the further they fall the faster they go. Kira was glad they were in the dream because she could change the setting to show her diagrams and demonstrations to help explain these concepts.

When Kira showed her a diagram of the planets of her system moving not in an ellipse, but an elongated spiral around a star that was itself moving, she said, "Wow, you really are from out of this world."

Because of Rosie's limited mathematics skills, Kira stayed away from some of the more technical calculations. After all, it would likely be Rosie's child or grandchild who would need to know all the details. Kira just needed to set a foundation for Rosie, so she could set a foundation for her children. Kira continued to what seemed a reasonable stopping point. She knew that staying in the dream too long had bad effects on her body in the real world, and she had promised Patala she would be careful. Also, she didn't want to keep Rosie so long that it affected her normal life.

"I know this is a lot to take in," Kira said. "I've been learning about this since I was old enough to talk. Let's stop for now so you can sleep, and we can visit again later."

"I'm afraid I haven't paid as much attention in school as I should have. I feel like I've been trying to make sense of things without all the information. But this…this is far out."

Chapter 15

Outside the hut, Kira found Patala and Matusu sitting in the sun by a small fire. Apparently they had an outside kitchen as well. Strips of meat hung over the fire.

"Are any of those ready to eat?" Kira asked.

Patala, who had her back to the hut, jumped a bit at Kira's question. "Matusu seems to think they're all ready to eat. I don't think he's stopped eating since he got up this morning."

Kira picked a few pieces that looked more done than others and sat down to eat them.

"I'm famished," Kira said. "I just made the most bazaar connection. I met a girl who didn't believe she was in a dream. She's from a more advanced time. People in her time have travelled to the moon."

"Are they going to be too advanced for our plan to work?" Patala asked.

"How far in the future does she live?" Matusu asked.

"About 510 years – plus or minus a decade."

"Impressive," Matusu said.

"That's what I thought," Kira said. "I was surprised that they were already traveling to space, which kind of gave me away. Rosie, that's the girl's name, clued in when I used the word 'already' – showing that I had expected them to go to space at some time."

"What did you tell her?" Patala asked.

"I told her the truth. I figured she was going to have to prepare her children or grandchildren. We are close to finding the one who can help us. She talks like she's dumb, but that seems to be an act. I don't know why she does it."

"Maybe it's the times. Maybe she's just more popular if she comes off as not too smart," Patala said.

"Are you confessing something?" Kira asked.

Patala scowled at her.

Kira knew that if she were in better health, Patala would have likely punched her.

"It's likely that she just wants to fit in at school."

"She said her grandfather had told her about me and about measuring the stars, but she hadn't believed it. It took some work for me to convince her that I was real. I started her on the cosmology lessons we had when we were younger. Even though her people had gone to space, she was amazed at even the foundational things I showed her."

"You showed her."

"Yes, I replicated the presentations on planetary and stellar motion."

"Why does she need to know that?" Matusu asked.

"She won't directly need it, but I hope she can prepare her children to calculate stellar shift more exactly than measuring on a stick. Those measurements only get us to a quarter century or so, but we will need refined measurements. We may have to teach them to build more advanced technology – or at least tweak their technology. They can spot detailed topography on the moon, so I'm hoping we can build on that."

"I don't suppose we can hope for telescopes in orbit?" Matusu said.

"Look at us talking like we've ever done any of this before," Patala said. "We know about things and rely on technology brought here over seven hundred years ago. I wonder how advanced our own people are who didn't take a millennium off to live on a primitive world."

"It's like the teachers always told us, 'Don't limit your thoughts to just what is around you,'" Kira said.

"I like the one, 'You are vastly more than what you do every day,'" Matusu added. "Why were our teachers insistent on teaching us mathematics, natural sciences, language skills, and even cosmology at an early age?"

"Would our minds close if they waited too long?" Kira asked.

"Somebody wasn't listening in childhood development class," Patala said. "They were building a foundation before our interests diverged. Think of the teachers that work with technology in Thresdenal verses mother's expertise in plant hybridization and pathology. Those specialties take years of study even after our childhood studies."

"Doesn't it sometimes seem like a waste of education?" Matusu said. "My father knows all the math and engineering to build starships – actual starships – but he was the village builder. His time was all spent selecting and cutting stones."

"After my discussion with Rosie, I wish I had learned more. I guess not so much learned more but spent more time learning how to teach it."

"If you are going to be Te'Kira, you should learn how to teach," Patala said.

"Ka'Te'Kira," Matusu said.

"Stop it. I know I will always be just Kira with you two."

Patala handed Kira another strip of meat. "Have you thought about asking Te'Roan for help on how to teach?"

"Up until now, I haven't needed to. What I really need is one of those display devices like Rory had. Do you remember how he used it to display the target date for the gate? All I can do is simulate it and hope my imagination is correct. I'll be fine with the things I'm teaching Rosie, but when I get to the details with her children, I will really need to relearn some things. Also, I'm a little worried about language issues. The dream lets us understand each other, but when I get to teaching deeper math and physics concepts, the written language will be a problem. I'm certain we don't share a common character set."

"Do you remember when mother taught us to read? Well, when she taught you to read. She had already taught me. She taught us the characters and then the words. Pretty soon, it seemed as natural as walking or eating."

"What are you saying?" Matusu asked.

"She's saying that I need to teach them to read our language," Kira said.

"Then you can teach them the mathematics they'll need," Patala said.

"I may need a teacher to give me a refresher on the mathematics."

Kira returned to the dream just before sunset. The path through the trees was a long journey. When she arrived at the place she had previously met Rosie, she found a slightly older Rosie sitting, looking down the trail.

"Were you expecting me?" Kira said.

"When I woke up here or dreamed here or whatever, I thought I would see you and Coyote. I never come here in my regular dreams."

"Did your dream start here or did you come here from another dream?"

"If I do come here from another dream, I don't remember it. Do you come here from other dreams?" Rosie asked.

"I don't exactly come here during regular sleep. I enter the dream by meditating."

"Can you teach me to do that?"

"To dream without sleeping? I don't know. I don't think many of your people dream like Iactah. I can ask him next time I visit him."

"This is so weird that you live at the same time as my ancient ancestor. Does he visit his descendants?"

"I think his future dreaming is guided more by his spirit guide. He doesn't direct the dream consciously the way dreamers among my people do."

"Who is his spirit guide?"

"Owl. And I'm told he learned his spirit guides name before he died or dies. It's confusing to me."

"So, I'll bet gramps was a wise old wanderer."

"I guess he is. He found me in the desert far from his village. He said his spirit guide showed him where to go and that I would be there."

"Do your ancestors visit you in dreams?"

"Prior to entering the dream of Iactah, I only entered the dreams of people in my present. I believe the ability to dream across time is a combination of my ability and your family's ability. There's also some involvement from these spirit guides though I may never figure that out."

"It's this world. They are the spirits of this world. This is heavy stuff. I'm still amazed at the things you've taught me. I've had some conversations with teachers and professors who don't know about this stuff. I quickly learned to keep a lot of it to myself. They think I've read too much Arthur C. Clarke."

"What is that?"

"Science fiction. They think I've read too many science fiction stories about space travel. Truth is, I think I'm in the middle of a science fiction story."

"I can assure you that the science I'm sharing with you is not fiction. If I had time to teach you the math, I could prove it."

"I'll take your word for it. Thanks to your tutoring, I'm one of only three girls in my college calculus class. Most of my friends don't even know why they might want to calculate integrals."

"Do you think you will be a scientist?"

"A girl from the res doesn't get a lot of support for that sort of goal. I only know of one woman doctor from the res. The only physicist I know about from around here is a man."

Kira knew from their conversations that the res was short for the reservation – land that the country of the United States had set aside for native people. From what Kira could gather, it wasn't the best land. Though interestingly, it was exactly the kind of land that Kira's people had chosen to settle in to avoid contact with other people.

"I hope the things I've taught you help you see that we are part of a big and complex universe." Kira felt like she was quoting her own childhood teachers. "If you are able to work as a scientist, I think that will help prepare your children or grandchildren to understand the things I will teach them."

Kira moved the discussion to an in-depth look at the principles for measuring stellar movement or what Rosie called stellar parallax. Kira wasn't surprised at how readily Rosie understood the concept and how she asked additional questions. She seemed very interested in using some of the math she had learned to measure the distance to stars. Kira had chosen set dates and times to measure specific constellations where the parallax would be the greatest and easiest to measure. Rosie's understanding of why Kira chose those variables led her to offer solutions for measuring and mathematically adjusting for measuring from different dates and times.

As she said goodbye to Rosie and walked out of the clearing, Kira felt like she had gone as far as she needed to in teaching Rosie. She would miss her, maybe more than she missed many of the others. But Kira knew she was close to finishing her dream quest and finding the one who would be able to help them.

After returning to the fork in the trail, Kira looked at Coyote and said, "Who's next?"

Coyote started up the trail to another fork, which led to another opening with a metal bench next to a brick fire pit. Near the bench stood a boy, maybe seven or eight years old.

"Are you Kira?" He asked.

"I am," Kira said. "Who are you?"

"I'm Danny. Danny Loloma. My Grandma Rosie said I might meet you."

"I'm glad to meet you Danny. Did your grandmother tell you why you would meet me?"

"She said you would teach me to be a scientist like her. And that you would teach me more than she even knows."

"Did your grandmother teach you about the stars?"

He nodded. "She has a big telescope, and we look at the stars. But we haven't measured them yet."

"What if I told you I'm going to teach you a new language – one that will help you understand how the stars move and how galaxies work?"

"I can read. Mrs. Gorman says I'm one of the best readers in my class."

"I bet you are very smart, like your grandmother." Kira sat down on the bench next to Danny and imagined a white wall into existence across from the stacked bricks of the fire pit. A display of characters appeared above the wall. "These are the letters of my language," Kira said. Another row showed up below the letters. "And these are the numbers."

"They look funny," Danny said. "What sounds do the letters make?"

"What do you mean?" Kira asked.

"You know, like A is for apple. B is for boy. C is for cat. What sounds do your letters make?"

Kira highlighted one letter at a time and hoped that her explanation was making sense. Because the sounds had no direct meaning, they came out as just sounds. She could see that they might have a problem with words from the letters being understood in the dream because they didn't speak the same language. She also knew that she didn't need to understand every word being shared in the dream. Many new words had been introduced in the dream that related to ideas that Kira had no reference for. She just heard those in the native language of the speaker. Like the words demon and angel.

When Kira finished teaching Danny the letters, she moved on to numbers. He quickly grasped the numbers. From the time she spent with Rosie, Kira knew that their main number system, the one a child would know, was base ten. She had learned to do math in multiple bases, so she decided starting with base ten would be the best way to go. Learning the symbols for zero through nine was easy for Danny, though a couple of questions quickly revealed his knowledge of mathematics was still very limited. And Kira decided to start at the beginning.

After the numbers, Kira showed him how letters formed simple words in her language. This is where he visibly struggled to understand. Kira realized he was trying to read a word in a language he didn't understand. He wouldn't have the recognition that Kira had had when she learned to read her first word, because he didn't already know the word.

Kira ended her presentation on language and moved to constellations and telling him the stories of the constellations. He seemed more interested in that. Unlike many of his ancestors, Danny knew all about ships and had even been to the ocean on a vacation. He understood the story of Tala the Brave. He asked if he was something called a Viking. When he explained to Kira what Vikings were, that seemed about right. Danny seemed to know more about the world as a small child than most of his ancestors learned in their entire lives.

After their star lessons, Kira thought the boy should get some real sleep. She said goodbye to him and left the clearing.

Kira looked up the trail thinking that she could handle another visit or two, looked at Coyote and thought better of it. "I'm going to need to work out this language thing before we move on," Kira said.

Kira sat outside across from Te'Roan who had his map device propped on a stack of rocks displaying a very complicated lesson on language heuristics.

"How come you just call that thing a map device if it can show other things?"

"It's mostly used as a map," he said. "That's really its most complex function. This other information is just stored in the data crystal. It comes in handy when we're traveling and need to brush up on lessons."

Kira started to wonder if she shouldn't just learn Danny's language, which seemed a lot easier than trying to teach him to read her language.

"He's not going to need the whole language," Te'Roan said. "Think of it like Bonstat, the scholar's language and also a dead language. We use that all the time to label ideas and scientific concepts even though we don't use it day to day. You don't speak it. I don't speak it."

"Orr speaks it," Ariste said.

"Really?" Kira asked.

"Of yeah," Orr said from across the fire circle. "Mother was a linguist. Wouldn't feed you if you didn't ask in Bonstat."

"But all of us know some terms from Bonstat to describe academic concepts and scientific names. You just need to identify that set of words and help him learn those words. You'll also want him to be familiar with some of those Bonstat characters to use in mathematical formulas."

"That's something we need to brush up on," Kira said. "I'm really good a remembering and explaining the concepts, but the details of the math aren't something I remember as well."

"Let's start with the teaching of language." Te'Roan brought up what seemed to be a lesson plan for teaching languages. He grabbed a hold of various items and tossed them away. "Here are the essentials," he said. "I'll leave you to go through them."

"Why do you use your hands to move things around when your thoughts control the device?" Kira asked.

"I find the gestures help me focus."

Kira took control of the map device. She expanded one of the topics and began going through it.

Kira entered the dream with a fresh review of language and mathematics lessons running through her mind. When she reached the clearing, Danny was waiting. He was a little older. She found him with a stick in his hand drawing in the sand at his feet. As she got closer, she saw that he was drawing the characters she had shown him.

"Have you been practicing?" She asked.

"You're back," he said. "Yes. I practice them every day. My friends think I made up my own language, like Tolkien did."

"Who is Tolkien?"

"He wrote fantasy books and created a whole Elvish language. Grandma read me The Hobbit, but not Lord of the Rings."

Kira surmised that these were stories. She was glad to hear they were writing down their stories – a key to sustaining a culture. Her history of Earth lessons said this is why some cultures outlived the time of their dominance. Unfortunately, her people's knowledge of the history of earth ended 700 years before her time – more than 1200 years before Danny's time. Her knowledge of earth history was the rise and fall of nations at constant war with their neighbors. Some groups of people in isolated areas and others in more populated areas, continuously fought over territory and religious beliefs. Occasionally, groups would remain stable long enough to produce a few centuries of culture and art. Those pieces of art or stories that were preserved would carry on through the fall of the nation and influence subsequent cultures. Most of the people never developed to such a state but spent their lives struggling to survive.

She was also glad she didn't have to convince him that the earth was round and that it moved around the sun, not the other way around. Where her history of earth had ended, that was a big deal, as was the usefulness of the number zero being used by only a few cultures. The only problem she saw with all this advancement was that bringing her people into this time and then meeting up with a spaceship might be difficult to hide.

"Do you remember the sounds of the characters I showed you?"

Danny pointed to each character and made the sound for that character, drawing another character below each of the characters.

"What have you drawn below the letters?" Kira asked.

"Those are the letters of my alphabet that make those sounds. Some sounds like this one are made from two characters together."

These sort of resembled letters Kira had seen in her history lessons, and she could see how Danny's language was one that relied on letters that formed phonemes rather than pictographs, which should help them find common ground for learning words.

"I have ten words that I need you to learn," Kira said. "They will help us label and talk about math and physics. Are you ready to learn them?" Kira imagined the white wall that showed the first word she needed him to learn.

Kira left their lesson feeling that they had made some progress. So much so that she turned up the trail and concentrated on meeting with Danny again. This time when she entered the clearing, Danny sat in a metal and cloth chair by a campfire ringed by rocks, no longer a small boy. He wasn't a full grown man, but he was getting close.

"You've grown," Kira said with surprise.

"Time has that effect on people. How long has it been for you since we last met?"

Kira was surprised by the question. Danny was thinking in abstract ways she hadn't seen from most of his ancestors, other than from Rosie. "It's only been a few moments for me – like leaving a room and walking into the one next to it."

"I'm fifteen now, by the way. Not quite grown up."

"Among your ancestors, you would be a man now, but you are right, you have some growing to do as humans go."

"How old are you?"

"Somewhere around 570 years old. I'm hoping you can help me get to a more exact number."

"You're funny. How old are you in your time?"

"I'm only twenty-two. In my culture, where people live longer than in yours, that is very young. Most of the other teachers call me a child."

"You are a teacher?"

"Barely."

"I think you're doing ok."

"Wait until we get to advanced mathematics."

"I'm already in calculus, with the help of my grandma, so I think I'll be a quick study."

"Kira asked him about calculous – what was taught, what applications they covered."

Danny gave a basic definition of calculus and explained some of its uses. Kira realized he was just at the beginning edge of what mathematics could do.

"Well, this is a good place to start this lesson." Kira brought up a function that he would call an integral. "This is one of the functions you just mentioned written in the symbols I taught you. Now let's build on this to see how we can use it in stellar cartography."

Kira was pretty sure she had his attention at stellar cartography. Like his grandmother, he was a natural learner. She was thankful to teachers that had taught him the abstract math required to get to this point. He was quick to see applications in the mathematics she was teaching him.

"You seem to enjoy learning this," Kira said. "Do you want to be a scientist?"

"It could be interesting. I know my grandma enjoys it. She feels like her work helps lift our people. I think if I can help our people, that would be a good thing. I want to go to university, though from what you're saying, I may know more than they are teaching when I get there."

"Don't think for a moment that I'm teaching you all there is to learn. Your universities can teach you about what it is to be human. They can teach you about your history, about cultures from all over your world, about art, and all that your people have achieved. Even in science, you can study many more areas than I am qualified to teach you. Let's stop here. You have plenty to think on and incorporate into what you already know about mathematics."

The next visit went very much like the previous. At the end of the lesson, Danny seemed hesitant to ask a question.

"You can ask me anything you like," Kira said. "I know we've covered more than before. It can be overwhelming."

"It's not that," Danny said. "It's just that … how do I explain any of this?"

"Who do you need to explain it to?"

"Well, in my high school physics class, I used some of the math you've taught me to solve problems faster, but my teacher complains that I don't show my work. She thinks my work is just doodles. And sometimes, when my answers are more exact, I get low marks because they don't match the textbook answers."

"I don't think you'll be able to convince anyone of how you know what you know."

"It's frustrating, because their understanding of gravity and motion are simplistic, they don't take any quantum variations or galactic fluctuations into account. If they really tried to travel outside our solar system, they'd be hopelessly lost within a few lightyears. All the models act as though the sun and the other stars are fixed points, not points in motion."

"I'm not sure you'll find many to agree with you in your world, perhaps only the most brilliant have observed the longer range forces at work. You may want to talk to your grandmother about how she got through her education, knowing as much as she did."

"She told me that she went along to get along," Danny said. "That just doesn't seem like me."

"Me either," Kira said.

"She told me graduating and getting through college would be better for the tribe than proving that she was right to a bunch of people who didn't matter."

"You are destined for great things. The knowledge you are gaining means everything to me and my people."

"I just wish it could mean as much to my people."

Kira didn't have an answer to that. She knew all that his people had suffered just to survive. They certainly deserved to benefit from all their sacrifice.

"Get some sleep," she said.

Danny faded from the dream, and she and Coyote returned to the path.

When Kira next entered the clearing, Danny sat on the ground. The bench was gone. The fire pit was gone. Dark gray walls encircled him. One formed behind her as she entered. He just sat looking up at the stars. He wore tan and brown pants in various shades of no apparent pattern. He wore a thin light brown shirt stained and even torn in a few spots. His hair was cut short, his face was bruised, and he looked much older.

"Danny?"

"Somehow I keep finding a way to see the stars."

"What's going on Danny? Where are the bench and the fire? What happened to you?"

"I wondered if you would come."

"Where are you Danny?"

"I'm a prisoner of war. I'm in Afghanistan. Do you know where that is?"

"I don't. Are your people at war? Has someone invaded the pueblos again?"

"No. Well, we are at war, but not at our home. It's another country. It's high in the mountains on the other side of the world. They have me at a place just outside Armal, a small village."

"How? Did someone kidnap you? Why are you a soldier?"

"Do you remember that talk we had about going along to get along?"

"Those were your grandmother's words, not mine."

"Of course, you would remember, it was just a few minutes ago for you. I didn't remember those words so well at college and ended up leaving and joining the army instead."

"You're a soldier?"

"Right now, I'm a prisoner alone in a dark room."

"You're not alone."

"That's right. I've got a 570-year-old alien visiting my dreams."

"I'm only twenty-two."

Danny laughed. "We're the same age – just half a millennium apart."

"Danny, I'm going to stay with you through this. I'm going to help you."

"I appreciate the sentiment, but how are you going to help? Are you going to tell my younger self not to join the army? Wait, can you do that? Can you go back to a time you already visited?"

"I can go back," Kira said. "But I can't do anything in your past to change this outcome."

"Why not? It's in all the time travel movies."

"I can't break the law of cause and effect. If I go back to change an event because I know about the event, cause and effect always corrects the course."

"So H.G. Wells was right."

"I don't know who H.G. Wells is, but if he told you that, he is correct."

Danny chuckled. "He's an author from a long time ago. A long time ago for me. You should visit him, he would love meeting you."

"I can't just visit anyone. I thought your grandmother would have explained that to you." Kira rehearsed how she travels through time.

"I always thought that spirit guide thing was more of a metaphor or a religious tradition. So, do you think there's something about my genetics?"

"I know a teacher who would love to find out. Maybe you two can meet someday, and we can unravel this whole mystery."

"I'm afraid I won't be much help at reading the stars from here, and even if I had a window, without a good telescope I can't get the readings you need."

"You need to focus on staying alive."

"I can't stay in the dream with you either. They come in and beat me and ask me questions multiple times a day, usually just before giving me food."

"At least they're feeding you."

"Just enough to keep me alive. They want to know things about my unit and our orders. They think if they make me afraid enough I'll talk, but I know if I talk, they won't need me anymore and will probably kill me."

"Do you think you can escape?" Kira asked.

"I don't see how."

"I think I can help you," Kira said and left the dream.

Kira woke with a start in the hut. It was night. She could see Patala sleeping on the other side of the small fire.

"Patala, wake up."

Patala lifted her head and looked at Kira, then sat up.

"You said you wouldn't do that anymore," Patala said.

"Wake you up?"

"No. Stay in the dream. You've been in there for two days, everyone's been worried."

"Sorry, I've been teaching Danny. He's amazing, but now we might lose him before he can help us. Where's Te'Roan?"

"Maybe sleeping or maybe on watch. They don't always tell me."

"I need to find him."

"Now."

"This can't wait." Kira slipped on her shoes and stepped outside. The night air was cold. She wondered how much longer they could stay up in the mountains.

She looked around the empty camp, then just made out Ariste sitting under a tree looking out into the night. He had said that sitting by a fire was no way to keep watch. Looking at a fire dulled one's ability to see in the dark.

"Ariste, where is Te'Roan? Ariste gestured toward the small hut."

Kira walked over to it and shook the door that lay across the opening. "Te'Roan, I need your help."

The door swung away, and Te'Roan climbed out of the hut. "What is it?"

"Danny, the one we've been looking for is in trouble. I need to teach him that teacher meditation, where you eliminate fear. Then I need to teach him the teacher fighting style so he can escape."

"I already explained that it could take months just to teach you to meditate, and you know the fighting techniques."

"Then we need to start now. You've never had a student as motivated as me. Let's focus on the essentials."

"The essentials?"

"Yes, you know the main meditation and the three or four most useful fighting moves."

"This isn't like any fighting you have learned. It isn't like a teacher lesson you can just memorize and recite. This is a change to the way your brain thinks and the way your muscles are conditioned to respond."

"Right. I need all that in a short version."

"You have been in the dream for two days. Eat, sleep, and in the morning…"

"We can start in the morning?"

"In the morning, we can discuss how we might proceed."

"I'm counting on you," Kira said. Then turned and went back to her warm hut.

Chapter 16

Kira wasn't sure how long she had slept, but when she woke, light was cutting low through the door of the hut. Patala wasn't in the hut but had left a full water skin and some cakes for Kira. Kira hadn't realized last night how thirsty she was, but it hit her with her first drink from the bag. She nearly drained it and then ate the two cakes.

Kira went out of the hut into the morning light. Only Orr sat by the fire adding some fuel beneath a freshly loaded rack of meat strips.

"Orr, I thought cooking was off limits for you."

"When they leave me unsupervised, they can't complain."

"Where is everyone?"

"Scouting, gathering, hunting – you know – stuff to stay alive. Ariste said you were up in the night excited about something."

"Worried about something would be more accurate."

"We thought you might slip off into dehydration and starvation again. I was ready to wake you up, but Te'Roan said not to."

"He knows how important it is that we get someone to free the gate. It doesn't matter what happens to me."

"What happens to you matters to all of us, especially Patala and Matusu. And I think you're going to be needed back in Thresdenal more than you know."

"Right now, I need to make sure nothing happens to Danny. He's alone in prison trying to survive. I think the teacher meditation can help him, but Te'Roan thinks it will take too long to teach it to me and have me teach it to Danny."

"Seems to me that people you meet in the dream learn things pretty fast."

"They do. In our training at Thresdenal, the teachers sometimes taught advanced lessons in the dream. They said neural pathways formed faster without the conscious part of the brain getting in the way."

"I work very hard not to let the conscious part of my brain get in my way."

"You're brilliant Orr. Which way did Te'Roan go?"

"The way he went may not be the way he returns. The best way to find him would be to sit here with me and tend to this meat."

Kira didn't have to wait long. Te'Roan returned with Patala and several water bags.

"Are you ready to teach me?" She asked.

"It will be the dead of winter before you're even competent at meditation."

"Orr had a good idea."

"I did?"

"You can teach me in the dream. You and I both know that some lessons are better learned in the dream, especially ones that involve a new way of thinking."

Te'Roan looked at Orr, who shrugged. "If you are to be taught in the dream, maybe you should be taught by a master."

"Do you think Te'Juna would do this?" Kira asked.

"I do. I also know that her abilities in the dream far surpass my own."

Though Kira knew that her guide could drop her into the dream with Danny right where she had left, she still felt a sense of urgency to get back to him.

Her first session in the dream with Te'Juna required almost painful focus to calm her mind. It seemed odd to meditate in the dream since the dream itself required meditation. Te'Juna made sure that Kira was in the master teacher's dream, not the other way around. Te'Juna didn't recite meditation platitudes the way Kira thought she would. Instead, she reminded Kira of situations that caused her fear and then talked her through removing the fear from the situation.

Kira thought about fleeing Hochonal, being carried away by the river, and being locked in the room in Thresdenal. She thought how her greatest fears centered around situations that were out of her control. She didn't seem to have the same fear about climbing difficult rocks or traversing the desert in darkness. She felt less fear about things she did when she was taking action. Being acted upon was perhaps what bothered her most.

Was that normal? She asked herself.

She knew that some people feared to act because of all the ways they might fail, but that wasn't her. She never feared failing. It seemed a natural, occasional consequence of trying. Failing to try was worse. In the river, she had felt almost overwhelming fear until she got herself oriented and made conscious choices about how to maneuver to get out of the river.

When Kira felt she was getting a grasp on what created fear and how she controlled it, she heard a growling noise. She opened her eyes to see a mountain lion crouched right in front of her, lip curled back, ready to pounce. Kira immediately lost all sense of calm. Her whole philosophy of acting rather than being acted upon went flew of her mind. She was frozen with fear. Before she knew it, she had broken both her layers of meditation and left the dream.

Realizing she wasn't done, she returned to the dream.

"That was lesson one," Te'Juna said. "We will resume tomorrow." The woman faded from the dream.

The next morning, Kira found Te'Roan. "If you learned this out of the dream, what did your teachers use to scare you."

"Snakes, falling from cliffs, drowning – in our final tests, guards violently attacked us. I think this dream thing may offer some early advantages, but you told your mind if it gets scared it can leave the dream. Eventually, you may have to perform lessons in real life."

"I can't believe I have to wait until tomorrow."

"You have no need of another lesson right now. First you need to practice. You can practice in the real world or in the dream. You need to train your mind to stay focused no matter what happens."

Kira grabbed hold on those last words, what happens. Fear, at least for her was about what happens or even what might happen after things had started happening. The mountain lion hadn't pounced, but she feared the eminent pounce. Kira began meditating again. This time rather than slipping into the dream, she focused on clearing her thoughts and listening to her internal voice. Being present with what was happening rather than projecting and allowing fear to guide her would take practice. She kept this up for what she thought was a long time, then remembered her promise to Patala and stopped for a meal.

After eating, Kira entered the dream and practiced meditating there for what she considered the same amount of time as she had in the real world. She came out of the dream as the last of the day faded to darkness.

That night's session with Te'Juna reviewed the lesson from the day before, then Te'Juna started asking about Kira's persistent fears.

"The first lesson focused on immediate fear of harm," Te'Juna said. "This second lesson is more about the fears that keep a person's mind busy in the night when they can't sleep or during mundane chores when the mind is free to wander. Persistent fears are about things like drought in coming years, being found by enemies even when no enemies are about, or the loss of a loved one who isn't even sick. These are fears that help us plan for the future, but they can also cloud the mind in the present."

As Kira meditated in the dream with Te'Juna, the teacher would whisper out these fears. She must have had dozens of them. Kira found herself trying to dismiss worries she had never considered before. The more novel the worry, the more her mind wanted to hang on to it and consider it.

Kira and Te'Juna's lessons continued for the next eight days. Every time Kira thought she had mastered it, Te'Juna would change things up, forcing Kira to adjust her tactics for clearing her mind. She found that meditating in the dream created more progress than doing it out of the dream. In the dream, she was more adept at clearing her mind of even the most worrisome things Te'Juna came up with. Even Kira's very real worry about how Danny was doing and how much time would pass in his time could be set aside. In theory, Kira could pick up right where they left off, but she didn't completely control that part of dreaming.

When she woke on the ninth day, she had real-world questions for Te'Roan, but he wasn't around. Matusu told her he had gone hunting with Ariste and Orr. She saw this as an opportunity to dismiss worry. She returned to her hut and dropped into meditation. As her mind passed by the idea of acting rather than being acted upon, she realized what she needed to do next. This was not a decision based on fear or worry, but on acting.

Kira shifted her focus to entering the time dream.

Coyote waited for her, and they made the long journey up the trail to Danny. Kira concentrated hard on getting to a time near to when she left.

Danny sat on the ground in the empty cell. "That was quick," he said. "You were gone less than two days."

"I was hoping to get back sooner than that, but it's not an exact science," Kira said.

"They've only interrogated me once since you left. Apparently, this group of terrorists considers interrogation inappropriate on holy days."

"I'm sorry I had to leave before, but I needed to consult with one of my teachers on a form of meditation that might help you." Kira explained the meditation to Danny just as Te'Juna had explained it to her.

"Do you think I can master it?" He asked.

"The dream helps. Remember the mathematics we went over in the dream? They would have taken months or years to teach you in the real world."

"As I recall, they did take years."

"Ok, the total time was years, but outside the dream they would have taken daily lessons over a period of months or years. Let's get started."

"Is there a tone or a chant with this meditation? Because I'm thinking my captors will shut this down if I start chanting. They are already sick of me talking about everything except what they want to know. I mean, if they would just stop and listen, I've been sharing some great stuff with them. Yesterday, I explained how to tear down and rebuild a carburetor on a dirt bike."

"I'm not sure what a carburetor or a dirt bike are, but I'm guessing it has nothing to do with what they want to know."

Danny looked away from Kira and seemed to concentrate for a moment. A machine appeared. It had two wheels and a complex array of metal machine parts. It was leaning a little, propped up on a peg. Danny got up and went over to it. He grabbed onto grips attached to a bar that appeared to control the direction one of the wheels pointed. Swinging his leg over it, he sat on top of the machine on a pad that served as a seat. It looked to have foot and hand levers – a complicated machine.

"This is a dirt bike."

"You're getting good at imagining things into the dream."

"Thanks. And this," he said pointing down into the machine, "is the carburetor. It mixes gasoline and air in the right proportions for the internal combustion engine. Do they have internal combustion engines where you're from?"

"I know what they are, but we don't use them. The industry needed to harvest all the raw materials and create such fuel would leave too many signs we were there."

"I wonder if I could start this up. He lifted a cap from the part of the machine in front of him. "Nope. I forgot to imagine fuel." Danny stepped off the machine, and it disappeared. "Back to the meditation training I guess."

"The meditation won't require any chanting. It's a way to train your brain. The actual ability you're honing, the ability to clear your mind of fear and worry, is something you use while you are awake and active. The teachers who have used it combine it with a form of self-defense fighting."

"Can you teach me that?"

"Not yet. I want to though. It's amazing. They hardly move, but redirect an attack away from themselves."

"Sounds like some martial arts from Asia."

"You are in Asia now, right? The continent on the other side of the western ocean."

"I'm in a different part of Asia than the part famous for martial arts. Here they are more into shooting and blowing things up. Don't get me wrong, they are into fighting, but hand-to-hand combat is less likely. So if you've got a fighting style for avoiding a bullet or catching a bullet out of the air, sign me up for that one."

"Perhaps we should worry less about fighting and more about clearing away fear." Kira instructed Danny on his meditations, then began working on some basic fears. Since Danny had grown up in the desert as Kira had, she started with something that would get an immediate response – first a rattle snake, then scorpions. He did better than Kira had on immediate physical fears. Of course, he was a soldier. He had likely been conditioned by his training to deal with immediate fear. She hoped this would help him learn quickly.

As they finished the lesson, Kira suggested he get some sleep, and she walked out of the cell.

Coyote trotted ahead of her.

"I don't think we can take months and years like we did with our other lessons. We need to come up with ways to keep him alive."

Back on the trail, Coyote circled on a spot next to a tree and laid down.

"You spend the whole visit laying down or sitting at the edge of the clearing and now you want to lay here at a critical time. Do you know something I don't? I would wager you know a lot of things I don't."

Coyote yawned and put her head on her front paws.

"Whenever you're ready," Kira said. She walked about a bit, feeling a little anxious. Coyote didn't seem anxious about anything. Kira took the hint and sat down to clear her own mind. Just as she felt she had sufficiently dismissed her fears, she heard Coyote quietly yip. She opened her eyes to see Coyote standing, ready to go.

Coyote led Kira back into the cell to find Danny practicing his meditation.

"How long were we gone this time?" Kira asked.

"Less than a day as far as I can tell. I think I'm getting the hang of this."

"Time to move ahead to worry."

"Worry?"

"All the nagging things you worry about. Will the rain come? Will too much rain come? Is the night watch awake or will something slip by them? These are the things that keep you up at night."

"I understand. Things like, 'Did I leave the dome light on or is my alarm set so I don't oversleep?'"

"Whatever works for you? Since the things that worry you are very different from the things that worry people in my time, I don't think I can suggest things the way my teacher did. As you consider your worries, say them out loud."

Danny went through the exercises many more times than Kira had. She thought back to when she had been locked away. After a while, you gain greater patience than you had ever thought possible. When they finished the lesson, Kira could tell from his demeanor that he was tired. Leaving the cell, she was tempted to leave the dream and get some rest herself, but she didn't want to risk losing this window of time to help Danny.

This time when they reached the trail, Coyote didn't wait, but led Kira up a nearly identical trail back up to a clearing. Only this time the clearing was different, across the clearing on a wooden porch attached to a building was Rosie. She sat in a chair with armrests and motioned for Kira to come sit in another chair next to her. She was much older than anyone Kira had visited before.

Kira was confused. A fear hit her mind, and her training kicked in to dismiss it. At least she dismissed the emotions of the fear. The thought remained. Had Danny died, and the guide was trying to build an alternate connection?

Rosie smiled when she saw Kira. "I never thought you would visit my dreams again," Rosie said. "Not after you started visiting Danny. He's learned many amazing things with you. He comes and shares them with me. You know, I have a doctorate degree and have trouble keeping up with his math. It's a shame he had so much trouble in college. Do you know he's joined the military? They've sent him to Afghanistan. But maybe you know that. Have you talked to him since he went over there?"

Kira wondered how many people Rosie got a chance to talk to. "I have talked to him. Are you aware of his situation?"

"What situation?"

"He's been taken prisoner. He's in a dark cell when he's not being interrogated. He said he's near a village called Armal."

"But he's alive?"

"He was alive the last time I talked to him. But I have no way of telling how long ago that was in your time."

"Well, we can't leave him there. Thank you for coming and telling me."

"I wish I could take credit for it. I thought I was going to visit Danny again when Coyote led me here."

"That trickster will take you where you never expected, but I'm told that Coyote is a wise teacher."

"Is there something you can do for Danny?"

"The thing about being a native woman with an advanced science degree is that I've met a few people who can do things. Thank you Kira."

Rosie faded from the dream. And Kira sat down on the chair wondering what she should do next.

The coyote came over and rather than doing its regular circle and settle routine, it just flopped onto the ground.

Kira felt it too. They were both tired. Kira allowed herself to fade from the dream.

Kira knew she was in trouble when she woke to find Patala sitting next to her. Their hut was lit only by the small fire. No light shown through the door or the small gaps in the walls. Something was different. She felt the warmth of the fire and a definite chill coming from the wall behind her.

"What time is it?" Kira asked.

"Perhaps the better question would be, 'What day is it?'"

Kira sat up, then immediately laid back down as her head pounded in protest. "How many days was I out? I'm famished."

"Three days Kira. You can't keep doing this to yourself."

"If you saw what they have been doing to Danny, you wouldn't want to leave him. The dream is his only relief from the isolation and torture."

"I know he's important to the plan, but so are you."

"I'm not doing it because he's important to the plan. I'm doing it because he's important."

"And you're important to us and to me." Patala didn't say anything for a few moments, then said, "I have some broth for you."

"How long have you been keeping it ready?"

"I made it tonight. I've been making it for you the last two nights. Don't worry though, Matusu and Orr have both volunteered to take care of any extra food I prepare."

"Is everyone getting enough food?" Kira asked.

"Oh yeah, Ariste brought in another deer just before the snow came."

"Snow?"

Kira didn't expect that her long journey into the dream would leave her sister and friends in this kind of trouble. As the sun came up, she stepped out into new snow well above her ankles. They would need those deer skins to wrap their feet against the cold. Would they have enough for everyone?

When she stepped back into the hut, Patala handed her some cakes.

"How soon can we leave?" Kira asked.

"We have some preparations to make. Ariste and Matusu spent most of yesterday smoking meat and tanning the new hide. Orr has been making the hide we have into boots that will keep the snow off our feet. He said they won't be as sturdy as the guard and teacher boots they wear, but better than woven shoes."

"That's what Isaac's people did. I thought they were better for the sand, but maybe they made them for all conditions."

Patala worked around the hut packing away bedding into one spot. "Te'Roan suggested we gather in here to discuss where to go. He has talked through the dream with some of our allies in Thresdenal. He's hoping that since we are so close to the goal, they will be able to rally support in your favor."

"My favor? I'm not looking for anyone to follow me. I'm simply advocating that we stay as close to the protocol as we can. Wisdom has carried us this far. It will see us through to our eventual rescue."

"What if we can't open the gate? How can we expect to hide for another 550 years?"

"We can't. I've seen glimpses of how nations have flowed into this land and treated their own indigenous people. I can only imagine how they would treat our people."

"Te'Marile's plan of a dominant settlement somewhere with more resources may be looking like a better option," Patala said.

"It's only a better option if Danny can't move the gate. He's very bright. We just need to guide him through it at the right time."

"What's to keep the people of his time from coming against Danny just to get at us?"

"I think he's come to realize that no one in his time would believe him if he told them about us. His knowledge of the cosmos is so far ahead of their own science that they think he's just coming up with fanciful ideas from his imagination."

Kira heard footsteps at the door.

"May we come in," Te'Roan said from outside.

"Yes, come in," Patala said.

Kira had a brief flashback of singers coming to visit Patala back in Hochonal. Looking at her sister's dingy clothes and uncombed hair tied back behind her head, Kira almost laughed at the thought.

Te'Roan entered, followed by Matusu, Ariste, and Orr. Orr handed a pair of deerskin boots to Kira and another to Patala. Kira noted the high upper part and straps for tying above the ankle like the warrior tribe's footwear she had described.

"Thank you," Kira and Patala said almost in unison.

When everyone had settled around the low fire, Te'Roan said, "I have some news from Thresdenal, and we have some choices. I have been in touch with three other teachers who were loyal to Ka'Te'Losa. They have been quietly working to understand who is with us and who is with the Faction, that's what they are calling those who have broken from protocol and taken control. They do this at great peril, as the Faction control not only the bureaucracy, meaning they have control of food distribution and teacher assignments, as well as control of the majority of the guards. Those loyal to wisdom seem to be less united as they are also those more in favor of open debate about daily matters, which often seem to get in the way of presenting a unified voice."

"Can we keep them focused on this one thing?" Kira asked. "Certainly, if we made the choice as simple as follow the protocol or not, we would see unity."

"Do you really think the Faction will allow us to keep things that simple in an open debate? Besides, they have sent most of the loyal traveling teachers away on assignment. If we convene a council now, the vote will go strongly toward the Faction."

"They are traitors to the plan," Matusu said. "Can't we have them arrested for treason and then call a council?"

"Who would arrest them?" Ariste asked. "Many older guards side with us, but this Faction has done a good job of placing their supporters in key leadership positions among the guards. When we call for arrests, we may likely find the tables turned and be arrested ourselves."

"Isn't that where we already are? Or at least where Kira and Te'Roan are? The rest of us haven't actually been accused of anything yet."

"We might be able to use that to our advantage," Patala said. "We could slip back into the city and work among the people to garner support for Kira, while she and Te'Roan work on solving the council problem."

"Ariste and I should be able to gain support among some of the older guards that are left."

"And what? Stage a coup?" Te'Roan shifted his body leaning forward a bit more. "We can find a way to bring the majority over to our side without bloodshed. I would wager that many of the guards that seem loyal to the Faction are only acting loyal out of fear. If we can overwhelmingly convince the people that the founders' plan will succeed and that it is their best chance to save their families, those guards will side with us."

"I know we expect that the people will want to follow wisdom as it was meant to be followed, but Te'Marile will have considered all of this," Kira said.

"Dreaming into the future?" Te'Roan said. "I guarantee she hasn't considered that."

"How do you know one of the teachers you talked to didn't let that slip, and she already knows? All she has to do is call me a liar while promising people all the plenty they have gone without."

Ariste cleared his throat as if to speak, and then waited for silence to sink in. "In battle, one must always consider what his opponent wants. Does he want to kill me, or does he want to get past me? Does he simply want to subdue me that he may rule over me? We must ask ourselves what the Faction wants. More specifically, if Te'Marile is leading the Faction, what does she want?"

"She wants power," Kira said. "She thinks she knows what is best for everyone else, and she wants them to do things her way."

"One battle tactic, when faced with a force of equal or greater strength, is to appear to give them what they want. Offer them a glimpse of victory. In hand-to-hand, you would offer them an opening to gain an advantage. When they move to take that advantage, you close the trap."

"But what trap can be sprung after acquiescing to Te'Marile's separation plan?" Kira asked.

"I don't think this is something we will be able to settle right now, but we need to have a plan of where we go next," Te'Roan said.

"For starters," Patala said, "we need to get off this mountain. Another storm like the last one might make travel impossible."

Ariste reached out to warm his hands. "Patala's right. Orr and I have found better routes down the mountain than what we took coming up. We should avoid scrambling down rocky areas with the added weight of the meat we'll be carrying."

They were all looking at Kira. "Let's pack and move," she said. "We'll figure the rest out on the way."

As Kira walked into their first camp with Patala, she was delighted to see firewood gathered in a pile and a sleeping area flattened out between a fire pit and a wall of rock. Ariste had been here a few days earlier and thought it would make a good first camp on their way off the mountain. They had dropped below the snow level, which was mostly melted away at this point. Orr had said the ground needed to cool for a few more weeks before winter snow started to stay for the season.

Even though Kira was hungry and tired, she moved away from the group to enter the dream and find out what was happening with Danny.

Coyote led on the now familiar, long journey up the trail. She arrived to find the bench and fire pit and Danny. He no longer wore his military clothing but wore his typical blue pants and a simple tan button up shirt.

"From the look of things, you seem to be out of your prison."

"Over a year now."

"What happened?"

"Thanks to the training we did, I was able to hold out until a rescue arrived. They said they had thought I was dead until they received a call from someone at the Pentagon saying I was alive and local command launched a rescue. Apparently, my grandmother convinced someone that I was alive, and if they doubted her, it would be an insult to our sacred beliefs." Danny laughed. "When she told them what village I was near, they started to believe her."

"You should thank Coyote. I hadn't thought of going to your grandmother."

"I thought you had rules about going backward in your journey."

"Technically, I didn't go backward since every visit was a forward progression in time. No backtracking means no paradoxes."

"What are you doing now that you're not soldiering?"

"I'm still soldiering for a couple months. They've got me riding a desk in Georgia until I'm officially discharged."

"I will try and decode all that later, except for that part about Georgia. Where is Georgia?"

"It's in the United States, so even though I'm not all the way home, I'm at least safe in my own country now. I've applied to get back into college in Arizona, so I'll be close to home."

"I don't have time to share a lesson today. We are traveling, and I wanted to check on you. Review what I've taught you and look at those stars. You and I still have much work to do."

As Kira exited the dream, she found that Patala was still awake by the fire.

"Just in time," she said. "I was about to pack away the food and lay down for the night."

Kira noticed three sleeping forms not far from Patala and her. "Who's on watch?"

"Matusu took the first watch. Ariste just returned and went to sleep after scouting the area one more time."

Kira told Patala the good news about Danny and wondered at how all of it had come about.

"So the dream actually did save Iactah's descendants," Patala said.

"I suppose it did. Though I'm not sure it offset the loss."

"You can't keep blaming yourself for the fate of Iactah's various descendants. From what you've told me, all the indigenous people in this region will suffer, not just one family."

"I know. I just feel responsible for that one family. Long ago one of them asked me if I was an angel or a demon – a protector or a tormenter. I really don't know."

"You need to stop dwelling on the past and look at the work we have left to do. We need to stop Te'Marile from leading people away and irrevocably hurting all the humans. How long do you think it will take before she or those that come after her start industrializing their resource-rich settlements? What chance would early humans have against our technology."

"At their current state, not much, but by Danny's time, human's are fighting global wars. The place he was being held prisoner was literally on the other side of the planet. What they call the Asian continent. They are smart and determined. They've even achieved space flight."

One of the sleeping masses shifted and sat up. It was Te'Roan. "They've already achieved space flight?"

"They land on the moon in around five hundred years."

"That's no possible. Our models say it should be closer to seven hundred years from now. How long have you known about this?"

"Rosie told me about it, so I've known for a while. Why?"

"Our model is based on the development of many worlds. A deviation that far indicates they were influenced."

"It wasn't by me. I didn't even start talking about actual cosmology until after Rosie had told me about the space flight."

"Can they manipulate gravity?" Te'Roan asked.

"I don't think so," Kira said. "Danny didn't seem to know anything about gravity beyond observable effects. Nothing in their mathematics and physics indicates they've been able to achieve planetary escape by anything other than brute force. I'm pretty sure we haven't manipulated them."

"Just because we haven't doesn't mean we won't. I'm more worried about the motives of the influencers."

"Do you think they might interrupt our plans?"

"They might not interrupt what we are doing here, but they might notice what Danny is doing in the future. They might see him as a threat to what they are doing there."

Patala handed Kira a dish with some cakes and dried meat. "This is getting a little more conspiratorial than the facts warrant. Perhaps, like Kira said initially, they are smarter than we gave them credit for."

Kira woke early on the third morning after leaving their mountain camp. No frost covered their camp as it had at the previous two. They were back in the desert and had reached the edge of the area Ariste and Orr had scouted. Kira pulled the map device from Te'Roan's bag and brought up a terrain view with their location at the center. An outcropping of sandstone curved to the south and then west toward Thresdenal. It would be a good path to follow with few places to leave tracks.

Kira zoomed in and studied the area for canyons and cuts that might interrupt their travel. Moving on the tops of rocky areas was often difficult because of the gaps you might have to go around.

When they were about two days away from Thresdenal, Orr located a secluded spot to hold up while they figured out what to do. Nearby rock outcroppings provided a good vantage point to watch for anyone approaching.

As the sun set, Te'Roan dropped into the dream to find out what was happening in the city.

Kira decided it was a good time to check in with Danny and assess what to teach him next.

When Kira arrived, Danny had the fire going.

"Was that going when you got here?" Kira asked.

"No, I imagined it too life. Neat trick. I wish we could do that in the waking world."

"Just will things into being? That would be nice. How is your star measuring going?"

"I think I've got enough data to be about as accurate as we're going to be. I'm surprised my grandmother didn't mention it."

"Mention what?"

"She has been getting regular snapshots from the Hubble Space Telescope every six months for the last nine years. She makes a point of staying friends with the director, who always has some discretionary time. She's been able to avoid what is a very lengthy and iffy request process."

"Have you been to this telescope? How large is it?"

"No. Neither has my grandmother. It's in orbit."

"You have a telescope in orbit?"

"Yeah, we have more than one. You know that little spot in the sky you've had us measuring with a stick?"

"I believe one of your ancestors set up a stone, but yes."

"I have deep-space, high-resolution images. Using parallax equations and some of your fancy gravitational stellar shift calculations based on Rosie's twice-a-year images, I've got an exact measurement for you – at least as exact as humanly possible." Danny willed the wall and some kind of projector into being and made the number appear on it. "There it is in all its glory. It took me a while to get this into my head. I felt like one of those nerdy people who memorize pi to way too many decimal places."

"Pi?"

"What we call the constant factor in determining circumference and area of a circle."

"I had a teacher who made us memorize it to sixty-four decimal places. It was extremely tedious."

"Almost no one would graduate high school if we made teenagers do that."

"I was six."

"That is some serious accelerated learning. When did you learn calculus?"

"We didn't really break our math into discrete subjects the way you do. What you call calculus was just sort of integrated into the subject of mathematics from the beginning."

"What does this stellar distance tell you?"

"It tells me that our window of opportunity will open and close within a few years. And you and I have to move to the next phase of our project. Opening the gate."

"We're opening a gate? Where is this gate? Do I have to open it?"

"The gate is an anchor point for a bridge that traverses from my time space to your time space."

"Explain to me again, why a super-smart alien race couldn't just put a timer switch on this end. You can't possibly rely on meeting a time-dreaming native everywhere you go."

"We don't really need you to open it, as much as, get it out of the water it's submerged in."

"Wait a minute. You said we're only about five and a half centuries apart. I can't think of anywhere that's had that kind of geological shift in the American Southwest. Did you setup your door in a dry lakebed?"

"It's in a remote canyon where we thought it would remain hidden."

"What canyon? Of course, you wouldn't know names. Can you show me on a map?"

Kira brought up a three dimensional map display above Danny's projector thing.

Danny laughed. "If only."

Kira didn't see the humor but put a red dot at the location of the gate in the canyon.

"Now slowly zoom out," Danny said.

"I'm reconstructing what I can remember," Kira said. "It already looks like a child's drawing compared to the real thing."

"Ok, how do you suggest we find it? Can you find out coordinates? Never mind. Our longitudinal lines are arbitrary. Do you know where Greenwich, England is?"

"Where?"

"Forget it. Maybe you can find a direction and distance based on some landmark that wouldn't have changed."

"Are the pyramids in Egypt still standing?" Kira asked.

"You mean the Great Pyramid of Giza? Yes. I was thinking of something closer."

"If I got you coordinates using that as zero longitude and the rotational equator as zero latitude, could you figure out the longitude and latitude in your global units."

"Would you use degrees? There are 360 degrees in a circle. Why an Egyptian pyramid instead of one on this continent?"

"Are the ones on this continent still around? They seemed like the jungle might consume them."

"It did. They were restored."

"The Egyptian pyramids in the middle of a desert had already lasted more than three thousand years when my people surveyed them. I can get you the gate coordinates next time I visit."

"Wait a minute. Doesn't opening a bridge take a lot of energy?"

"I suppose it does."

"Our scientists figure that opening a bridge through time space, what we call a wormhole or Einstein–Rosen bridge, even an atom-sized hole would take the energy of a nuclear bomb the size of a planet."

"What is a nuclear bomb?"

"It's an explosive device where we split the atoms in plutonium and uranium. Though the biggest bombs use that reaction to set off a fusion reaction that combines hydrogen atoms into helium."

"Please tell me this is all theoretical, and you are not splitting or fusing atoms on-world."

"Just a few times, but we've never released enough energy to make a hole through space."

"Do you have any idea how dangerous that is?"

"Yeah, we kind of figured it out. It was all before my time."

"Our bridge takes less energy. It works on an understanding of quantum entanglement that I barely understand."

"You're not going to teach me about quantum physics are you?" Danny asked.

"No, I'm not. Maybe someday, after I see how humans are getting along with their nuclear bombs, I may reconsider."

Kira faded from the dream.

Chapter 17

Kira woke, wrapped herself in her cloak, and moved to build up the fire. Te'Roan was on watch, sitting above on some rocks and looking out over the desert.

When Kira had coaxed the fire back to life, she added more wood and pulled some dried meat from her bag. Their next step weighed on her mind. Te'Roan said that members of Te'Marile's faction had left the city, but they didn't say where they had gone.

"With some of Te'Marile's supporters gone, maybe we can tip the vote in our favor," Kira said.

Te'Roan said he had thought the same thing, but his contacts said it wasn't enough. "I'm sure Te'Marile is counting numbers very carefully," Te'Roan said.

Kira stared into the fire. She knew they had a chance of opening the bridge now, and she knew that many of Te'Marile's supporters would switch sides if they knew that. Te'Marile played on people's fear that if they didn't do something that broke from the plan, the time they suffered in exile would be wasted. They would have no progenitors. Even though protecting a developing civilization was essential, protecting one's progeny was paramount.

"Look who's up before the sun," Patala said as she moved to sit beside Kira.

"I'm trying to think of a way to shift support away from Te'Marile."

"Are you saying you want to gather people to your side?"

"Of course," Kira said.

"Isn't someone who can dream through other people's connections called a gatherer?"

"It isn't that simple. I don't have any proof of the things I've seen. To anyone else it's going to sound like a made up story, like I'm pushing my agenda."

"Isn't that exactly what Te'Marile has done? She's made up a story to gather more power to herself," Te'Roan said. "She wants to make this a place where we rule over humans. She's not the first one to push for that. We've had such rebellions before."

"But not where the rebels have carried the majority," Kira said. Kira pulled a warmed piece of meat from next to the fire and handed it to Patala.

"The only difference this time is the gate," Te'Roan said. "Everyone knows we are close to the time to pass through the bridge, and since it isn't happening, she's able to tell a stronger story than others have done."

Kira picked up a piece of meat for herself. "So how do I prove to people what I have seen?"

"Just tell your story," Patala said.

"Do you mean just show up in their dreams and start talking?"

"I've never known you to be shy, and I'm pretty sure you spend more time in the dream than you do in the real world."

"I definitely feel safer there," Kira said.

"A dangerous notion," Te'Roan said as he walked up to the fire.

"What do you mean?" Patala asked.

"Safety in the dream is an illusion that has led people to lose themselves there."

Patala looked concerned. "You mean like when Kira nearly starved to death by staying in the dream too long?"

"Kira was there with a purpose, and I'm pretty sure she woke up because her body was warning her that all was not well. There are other dangers in the dream. A person can get so fascinated by the creations of their own imagination, that they can start to think it is real and prefer it to the real world. That usually happens to the elderly who lack a community of dreamers. Another danger is dream predators. I don't think they were a part of Kira's time dreaming, but in our dreams, some prey on others in the dream, doing psychological damage."

"I read about that in my teacher studies," Kira said. "It is generally not a problem unless you know such a predator, but for someone who can move through connections in the dream, like me, I may meet someone like that without knowing it."

"What kind of psychological damage can someone do in the dream?"

"A talented dreamer can make a world around the person that seems as though they have woken up, but they are still in the dream. Because the dream can defy reality, because it's all based on imagination, the attacker can make subtle changes to the world around the person making them doubt their hold on reality."

"That doesn't sound like something that happens by accident," Patala said. "Do you think Te'Marile would try and use something like that on Kira?"

"From all accounts," Te'Roan said, "a prodigy like Kira has nothing to worry about. She would be the dominant dreamer in any situation. And Te'Marile doesn't come close to matching Kira's talent. So she wouldn't be able to hold onto a dream sufficiently real enough."

"I worry that if they figured out about entering human dreams," Kira said, "they might use that against them."

"Don't think they haven't tried a hundred times," Te'Roan said. "Every time one of these rebel factions has risen up, they have tried to coerce humans into helping them. I'm sure dreaming has been a part of it. Luckily, any past dreamers with your ability to connect were also committed to following the protocol. They generally left humans alone."

"I wonder every day if I should have left humans alone."

Kira spent most of the day reviewing topography and planetary navigation. It was like she was in school again. In school, she learned this stuff for tests and then promptly forgot most of it. Now she had to actually memorize it – not just memorize it – but know it well enough to explain it to someone from a different species and culture.

Late in the afternoon, she had studied all she could study. Since she was unlikely to reach any of her people in the dream until later at night, she decided to visit Danny.

Just before entering the dream, she used Te'Roan's map device to once again look up the location for the large pyramid in Egypt – what Danny had called the Great Pyramid at Giza. Using that as a prime meridian she adapted it to the human 360 degree model.

Why had humans hung onto the Babylonian model? Why had the Babylonians hung onto the Sumerian numbers model? Granted, she was impressed when she found the Babylonian astronomical record spanning 800 years of observation, but their whole reasoning behind the 360 degree model was based on simplicity over accuracy. Though, they built a close enough calendar.

Doing a little math, Kira was able to set longitude and latitude for the location of the gate with the pyramid as a longitudinal origin. Danny would have to do the math to shift to the meridian his Global Positioning System used. This Greenwich place didn't even show up a footnote in the histories Kira had access to. Maybe it didn't even exist as a named place when Kira's people's history cut off. With her longitude and latitude coordinates firmly memorized, Kira entered the dream.

Danny waited on the bench by the fire pit.

"How long has it been," Kira asked.

"Long enough that I worked through the equations you taught me and also wrote a conversion app to convert any set of pyramid-based coordinates to Greenwich-based coordinates."

"Tell me again why you use this place Greenwich, England. It wasn't even mentioned in my histories as late as your eighth century."

"Look at you talking the human timeline lingo. Greenwich is the meridian because to the victor go the spoils. The English or British, as the empire is known, invented the first maritime clock, a clock that would remain accurate while sailing. This clock set to a specific time allowed them to compare it to the time of day based on the sun from any point on Earth to get an accurate longitude. Twenty-four hours in a day means that each hour of difference is equal to fifteen degrees of longitudinal difference. Since they invented the clock, they set the prime meridian in their own home at Greenwich, England. If you're going to set an arbitrary location, there's no place like home."

"Your science is full of inherited and borrowed random choices."

"Don't get me started on the imperial system."

"Do I dare ask?"

"No. Whenever I need to measure based on anything you've taught me, I use metric measurements. They at least have some observable basis."

Kira could tell that this subject could quickly lead them off track, as fascinated as she was by their mixing of customs and science. She visualized into existence what Danny had called an overhead projector and made numbers appear in the three-dimensional space above it.

Danny laughed. Her use of the projector seemed to amuse him.

"All I need to memorize that number, convert the coordinates, and go hiking?" Danny asked.

"The entrance to the cave is along a canyon wall, so depending on how rockslides and erosion have changed the topography, you may need to do some climbing."

"Hiking, climbing, and spelunking, a triple adventure. How secret is this whole thing? I mean, climbing and spelunking might go better if I bring some friends along."

"I would rather our passing from the bridge to our rescue ship make as little commotion as possible."

"Oh, I'm not going to tell anyone I'm getting directions from an alien. I have friends who would go with me based on something as simple as, 'I heard about a cool cave and want to check it out.'"

"I have more to teach you about what to do with what you find there, but I think I should save that. For now, focus on finding it."

"Roger that," Danny said.

Kira took that as an affirmative. "I hope you know how much this means to me and to my people. You may yet be our salvation."

"Just returning the favor," Danny said and faded from the dream.

Kira woke leaning on a rock face near Patala, who was eating what Kira assumed was an evening meal as light faded in the west.

"Do you have any more of those cakes?" Kira asked. "I'm starving, and I think today's dreaming is just getting started."

Matusu and Orr climbed up from the stream area below. "Is our little dreamer back with the living?" Orr asked.

"Not for long," Kira said. "We've hatched a new plan." Kira glanced at Patala. "When we go to sleep tonight, I'm going to do what gatherers do and start moving through connections to present my case to as many people as I can find through the dream."

"And what will you say?" Matusu asked.

"I'll just tell them who I am, and that wisdom is working. I'll tell them my story and let them make up their minds."

Orr smiled. "Our dreamer's all grown up and becoming a politician."

"She's taking a position of hope over fear," Patala said.

"Fear is a powerful motivator," Te'Roan said from a little ways above them on the rocks.

Kira hadn't even noticed him there. "Perhaps the last hundred years has reinforced hope over fear as a guiding light of our people."

"I applaud your optimism. Where will you start?" Te'Roan asked.

Patala set down the cake she was eating. "I suggest that she start with the people we are connected to that we know want to help us. They will be receptive and should be the first to hear what's going on."

That night as Orr and Matusu made their way out into the desert and the others settled down to sleep, Kira slipped into the dream.

She didn't go to the time dream where she was certain Coyote would be waiting. She went to Hochonal, to her dream place. As she looked around, she saw the familiar glimmers at various places indicating her connections. She instinctively knew each connection as if their personality were somehow embodied in the glimmer. She knew from the glimmer near their house that Patala was sleeping, and Kira slipped into her sister's dream.

"So I guess now I'm not going to get any sleep either," Patala said. She was sitting by the fire in their house in Hochonal.

Only it was different. Things we smoother and cleaner. Kira noticed a comb on the table next to Patala. It was a fine bone comb. Kira hadn't seen one like it until she visited Thresdenal.

"You'll sleep just fine. Only a dreamer in meditation doesn't reach a full state of sleep. Even then, it's not the same as being fully awake. I'm not as tired after one night of dreaming as I am from a night of travel."

"So where do we go from here? Are you going to tell me your story?"

Kira laughed. "I think it's best that I look for connections from your dream. That's a lovely comb by the way."

"I saw one like it in Thresdenal. I guess I liked it and brought it here."

"I think you have some dreamer talent of your own," Kira said.

Patala shrugged.

Kira looked at several places that might be likely connections.

"Can you tell who it is before you go through?"

"I can if I already know them. Like Te'Roan's connection is just outside the door there."

"I don't see anything. What does it look like?"

"It's kind of a shimmer of light. The first time I saw one, I only saw it out of the corner of my eye – like when you see movement in your peripheral vision. With practice, I was able to focus and see how the light bent and glimmered."

"How did you know it was Te'Roan?"

"It's just a feeling, like recognizing a familiar face or hearing a familiar voice. I perceive the personality."

"Do you see other glimmers? Do you see Matusu?"

"Yes, but Matusu isn't sleeping right now."

"What's it like in a dream of someone like Te'Roan or Ka'Te'Losa who know lots of people?"

"With Te'Roan, I see doors all around, I also see bright doors – more obvious – those are dreamers actively forming their dreams. When I shared the dream with Ka'Te'Losa, I suppose there were passages all around me, but I didn't really know what to look for then. My visit to Rory from Ka'Te'Losa's dream was more of a test. Things are much clearer to me now." Kira gestured to Patala to follow her. "Let's go see what other connections you have."

They left the house and were greeted by a blazing sunset of pinks and oranges. Kira had almost forgotten that sunset from their little village. "Is it always like this?" She asked.

"I think it's the thing I liked the most."

Kira looked about and saw several shimmers. A few she recognized, others she didn't. I think I see a connection to that woman who helped sell your blankets in Thresdenal."

"Terrice? Go visit her. She would love to hear we're alright."

Kira moved into the passage and left Patala's dream. She was standing in the market in Thresdenal, next to the table where Terrice sold blankets.

The woman, Terrice, sat behind the table and looked closely at Kira. "Do I know you?" She asked.

"I'm Kira, Patala's sister, you sold some of her blankets."

"Of course, you're a dreamer aren't you?"

"I am. Patala wanted me to tell you that we are alright and to tell you some of what we have been doing." Kira explained to her about the gate and the time dreaming with the humans and how they were very close to opening the gate and being rescued. Kira couldn't tell if Terrice believed her, but she listened amiably.

"Are you the gatherer?"

"I am."

"My grandmother told me that for the plan to work, really work for everybody, we would need another gatherer when the time came. She was a big believer in providence. She used to say that the universe supplied what you needed when you needed it. I felt that way when your sister showed up and made her beautiful blankets. She is really an artist you know."

"Thank you," Kira said. "I have to go now and visit some other people."

Kira looked about. The marketplace was full of shimmers. She chose one and walked through it. She met a man she vaguely remembered seeing in the marketplace. She told him much of the same things she had told Terrice and then moved on. By her fourth or fifth visit, she felt like she really had her story down and could move more quickly. She took on a more formal tone to cut down on any chatting that might go on. This was more common among marketplace people. As she began to meet people who worked at a craft or farmed, they seemed to be less inquisitive.

Kira originally thought that people would be startled by her showing up and maybe a little scared – not that she was a frightening figure. She found most people expectant and excited to see her. She wasn't sure why she thought someone appearing in their dreams would be odd as they had all had teachers visit them in dreams. The difference was that they usually knew the teacher who visited them. The gatherer, a stranger, was something different.

Kira woke in the dark with her cloak snugly tucked around her. She could see the low coals of the fire and hear Patala breathing next to her. She turned to look at her sister.

Patala opened her eyes as if coming out of a deep sleep. "I saw you," she said.

"And I you."

"How did it go? Did you see Terrice?"

"It went well. I saw her. She was happy to hear you are alright. I think she misses having your blankets to sell. She said you are an artist."

Patala smiled. "I just think things should look nice."

"I talked to twenty or more people. Most were very receptive. I ran into a few that seemed skeptical, though most were excited to know a gatherer had come. I guess my abilities were a closely guarded secret among the teachers."

"Maybe you are more of a threat to their authority than we thought."

"That sounds dangerous," Kira said. "So many visits in one night is bound to be talked about. I worry Te'Marile will come after us even more now."

"Do they know where we are?"

"I didn't tell anyone. For all they know, we could be anywhere."

"Anywhere sounds like a nice place to be," Patala said as she drifted back to sleep.

Kira pulled her cloak close around her in the cool morning air as they left their camp.

"Are you sure we have to move?" Patala asked. "This canyon is pretty cozy, and water is an easy walk away, mostly on stone."

"The guards hunting us have the same training as Ariste and Orr," Kira said. "Those two can track a leaf in a windstorm."

As their group climbed out of their little slot canyon, Kira looked back and couldn't even tell anyone had been there. Whatever impressions they left in the sand would be wiped away by the next big wind or rain.

They travelled away from Thresdenal and out into the desert. When they reached a point where rock and canyon cover ended, giving way to the open desert, they held up in the rocks until dark. With the coming of the first star, they moved slowly out onto the desert.

A wind rose up, and Kira had to pull up her hood and face covering to protect her from the sand. It was probably for the best as her cloak would keep her from being too noticeable at a distance. It wasn't as useful when moving, because even though it blended with the terrain, it couldn't hide movement. This was why the guards like Ariste and Orr moved as if they had no advantage from their uniforms, keeping distance from objects that might reveal their movements to anyone looking from above.

The further they went out on this desert plain, the less concern they had of being seen from above. Aside from the occasional shallow runoff cut, the land was wide open. Orr assured them they could cross it in a single night. He wanted to avoid spending the day in one of those cuts. He said they were natural trails for fox, coyotes, and badgers. As much as Kira trusted her spirit guide, she was aware that surprising a live coyote in close quarters could get dangerous.

A faint glow showed on the eastern horizon as they made their way off the desert plain and into another maze of rocks. Ariste told them they could rest here for a while, then make their way to where a stream sometimes ran. Orr would go ahead and scout the area.

All of them knew that the guards looking for them would be checking areas known to have water. Water was life in the desert, and only a few places had reliable sources. Luckily many of the streams ran for long distances through desert canyons, and it was impossible for the guards to watch the entire length of them. This also meant that Orr and Ariste liked to choose access points along streams that were difficult to reach.

Their camp that day was no different. It was a nook in a narrow canyon a scramble and a climb away from a small desert stream.

Kira entered the dream. Danny was standing by the fire pit and seemed agitated. "I know why your gate isn't working," he said.

"Did you find it? Were the cave drains blocked allowing water the accumulate?"

"Oh, I'm sure your drains would work if there were anyplace for the water to go. The government built a reservoir there. They built a dam and backed up the river right over your gate. Or at least over the coordinates you gave me. The coordinates are underwater."

"Can we drain it?"

"Even if they would open the dam and drain it, it may take a decade or more. And the dam is a power source for multiple cities.

Draining it won't be an option. Maybe you should have one of my ancestors start draining it or keep it from being built."

"Cause and effect."

"Right, cause and effect."

"The only choice is to move it," Kira said.

"You can move the end point for your bridge?"

"Theoretically, yes. Remember when I told you about how the gate uses quantum connections? The two ends of the bridge are already entangled. If you can remove it from the water, we can open it and pass through even though it's position has changed."

"How big is this portal?"

"You won't be able to just pick it up and carry it out by yourself. It's sitting in the floor of the cave and essentially makes up the bottom of a sphere big enough to walk through."

Kira shifted the dream, so they were in front of the gate. She left the bench since Danny was sitting on it.

"You'll have no trouble identifying it," she said, "as it's made of metal and different than the stone around it."

"What holds it down?" Danny stood and started walking around it.

"Gravity. It's likely to be heavy."

"How heavy?"

"I don't know exactly. But I assume that since your people are able to fly to space and dam up rivers, you might have some machines that can extract what will look to most people like a big chunk of decorated metal."

"The only way I'm going to extract anything from a state protected water way…wait a minute. I have an idea. I have to check with some people and let you know."

"What people? Have you told anyone about this?"

"Not directly, but there is an archeologist or anthropologist, I guess he's both, who is suspicious about a lot of what you left behind."

"Our plan is to not leave anything behind."

"Well, then I better keep the details to myself – cause and effect." Danny faded from the dream.

Kira woke when Te'Roan touched her on the shoulder.

"One of my contacts in the city told me that Te'Marile is planning an exodus from Thresdenal," Te'Roan said. The people who she sent away have returned with word of a colony site that will allow growth and prosperity, what Te'Marile is calling Assured Preservation."

"She is a politician. How will our going back to Thresdenal help?"

"With the gatherer with us, not in exile, we should be able to draw enough people to our side to disrupt a full exodus."

"What will keep her from arresting us the minute we arrive?"

"I've had some people looking through legal statutes, and now that you've started gathering, you have a basis for claiming an offense due to the interruption of your gathering. We can arrest Te'Marile before she arrests any of us."

"Won't this just create a legal standoff?" Ariste asked.

Everyone was awake and gathering now.

"Not if we arrest her vigorously enough," Orr said. "Along with a couple of those upstart guard captains."

"She will be well guarded. She has to know that not everyone in the city supports her," Matusu said.

Te'Roan smiled. "A few ways into the tower are little known and rarely used. If one of these can be unlocked, we should be able to get to Te'Marile without going through the main force of guards."

"Why do you think Te'Marile hasn't planned for such an event?" Patala asked.

"Because she has been sending guards out farther and farther to try to find us. She thinks we are hiding far from Thresdenal with no way to stand up to her," Ariste said.

"Ariste, who among the guards will support us? Could we get even a small number to hold an area while we get word out about the legal foundation for our actions?" Kira asked.

"Many of the captains who believe like us have dispersed into the desert to avoid being arrested themselves," Ariste said.

"I can get help from a teacher, but opening a passage takes quite a bit of strength. What about a guard that can help open the way?" Te'Roan asked.

"There must be plenty like this one." Orr gestured to Matusu. "I know a lot of the younger guards just want to do the right thing. We just need to convince one of them what that is."

"Before we left, I instructed a few mid-level guards to hold tight and wait for word," Ariste said.

"How do we reach them?" Kira asked. "I've been making more connections than I thought possible, but every new connection is a surprise. Reaching a specific person is difficult."

"I can do it," Matusu said.

Everyone looked at him. Kira was curious to hear this.

"I don't mean I can reach them in the dream, like Kira. I mean I can sneak in and move among the younger guards. The leaders in Thresdenal don't know me. No one will be looking for me. I can open the passage."

Ariste nodded. "He's right. They are certainly looking for me and Orr, but no one will be looking for a young guard. Matusu and I can go ahead to scout, and I can show him how to get into the outer areas where he can move among the guards. Orr can go between, advising on the best path for the rest of you to take."

"Are you worried we'll slow you down?" Patala asked.

"Not at all," Ariste said. "I'm concerned we will lead you into a trap, and of all of us, Kira must remain free for this to work."

Kira had hoped they would be able to spend more time resting in their little nook while she reached out to more people. She had started making connections in the outer villages and feared that she hadn't reached enough people there.

As they paused at midday in the shade of an overhanging rock, Patala sat down next to Kira. "Do you remember those first days of travel out of Hochonal? We were so new to it that we would simply collapse any time Te'Roan let us stop."

"Speak for yourself," Kira said, smiling.

"Ok. You would only lean against rocks or trees. I think you were trying to prove how tough you were."

"Now we travel the desert like veteran guards."

"I wonder when I'll get used to having sand everywhere."

"If things go as planned, you won't be worrying about that much longer. We'll be among the stars. Do you know that Ka'Te'Losa was part of the marooned? She wasn't very old when they landed. She said that she still had dreams of seeing stars and planets from space. I can only imagine," Kira said.

"Rory was part of that first generation too. His granddaughter bragged about him the whole time we were at their village. He built the first gate and came through in the first skip."

"What do you think it's like?" Kira asked.

"Like nothing we've ever experienced."

Matusu walked toward the tower with purpose. He knew his guard uniform was dustier than many of the others, but no dustier than it should have been coming in from the desert. The passage that Ariste had shown him wasn't completely unguarded, but a guard in uniform barely got a glance. His plan was to avoid the guards he had trained with. So far he only saw a lot of new faces on the younger guards, and the few older guards he saw weren't ones he knew. He wondered how far Te'Marile had gone in replacing the guards with her loyal followers. Matusu finally walked up to one of the guards stationed near the tower.

"Not very many people out today," he said.

"It's been like this since the defection." The guard looked over Matusu's clothes. "Just in from the desert?"

"Yes, went with a group scouting passes on the north." Ariste's words rang in Matusu's head. If questioned, keep it simple. Some version of the truth is best. You'll be less likely to trip yourself up.

Matusu quickly realized that for his plan to work, he was going to have to get a clean uniform. No one assigned to duty in the tower would look the way he looked. Guard uniforms, however, were not something he could get at a marketplace shop. He made his way toward the barracks, hopefully some guard had left a uniform while off duty. He entered the second barracks. Three young guards were there. He was certain they knew he wasn't in the right place. Guards knew their barracks.

"Have any of you seen Taxon Windsight?" He asked the men, thinking of the first name that came to mind – a boy from Hochonal.

"Not in this barracks," one of the young men said. He looked at the other two who both shook their heads. "Never heard of him. Maybe one of the south barracks."

The south barracks were the last place Matusu wanted to go. Half the guards there would know him and know that he had disappeared the same time as many of the senior captains. "Thanks," he said and left the barracks, trying not to look like he was hurrying. He skipped the next barracks over, not wanting to look like he was methodically searching for something. When he reached the fourth barracks, he stopped at the door and listened – no sound. He stepped inside. The place was empty.

He could tell from the missing personal bags usually stored by the head of the mats on the floor that the group were probably on leave. He notice lumps under the blankets on three of the beds. This is where you would store a clean, carefully folded uniform if you went away. The first one was obviously too small. He carefully folded it as every trainee was taught and moved to the second one. It looked like it would fit. He thought about swapping it for his own and thought how furious he would be if someone put a dirty uniform under the blanket on his bed.

He checked the door to see if anyone was coming and then quickly changed into the clean uniform, folding his own and stuffing it into his pack. If time allowed, he would return the clean one. Though if things went as planned, the guard's missing uniform would be the last thing he worried about.

Matusu made his way across Thresdenal toward the tower. He stopped briefly at a water tank to wash his face and hands. The hood covered his hair which was no doubt matted with dust. Reaching the tower, he headed into the market section. The guards there didn't really look at who was coming and going, they were mainly there to answer calls for help. Anyone could get into the marketplace. Getting into the teachers' halls was something else.

His plan was to bluff his way through. At least that was his plan until he saw who was guarding the teacher halls. Kyril had been a trainee with him. Matusu was surprised to see him already guarding a post. The departure of so many senior guards must have left them short of experienced guards. With Kyril at the entrance, Matusu had no way of maintaining anonymity.

He would need a distraction big enough to draw the guard away for a moment, but not so big that it brought the whole security force into the area.

As he was walking away looking around for something he could use, a voice called out from behind him. "Matusu."

Matusu turned to see an elderly woman in a teacher's robe, who didn't even come up to his shoulder. "Te'Natha," he said, bowing slightly.

"I thought that was you," she said. Didn't you leave the city with Kira?" Then a look of awareness crossed her face, and she looked side to side. Moving closer and speaking in a lower voice, she said, "Has she returned?"

Matusu didn't answer. He was surprised she remembered his name. Though why should he be surprised. Once you met a teacher, they seemed to always remember you. That aside, he didn't know whose side she was on or if she might be part of Te'Marile's faction.

"I've heard rumors," she said. "People have been seeing Kira in their dreams. Some say the gathering has started."

"I wouldn't know about that," Matusu said.

"Of course, you would," she said. "You are the girl's best friend. If she is back, she is in danger. Te'Marile has heard the rumors too and is working on a plan of her own to leave Thresdenal for a new colony. It's ugly business departing from wisdom."

Matusu wasn't sure if the woman was saying this as an ally or if she was bating a trap to get him to reveal himself. "What do you think should be done?" He asked.

"We should give the girl a chance. We should let her do what she was born to do and gather the people. If the bridge isn't opened in time, at least we will have all the people together to debate and decide."

"Have you said as much to Te'Marile?"

"Not so directly. It's hard to know who to trust." Te'Natha smiled knowingly. "You're probably feeling that right now. You're wondering if you can trust me." She looked over her shoulder at the entrance to the teachers' hall where Matusu had just come from. "If I were to guess, I'd say that you are in this part of the tower because you want to get into the teachers' hall." She paused a moment studying his face

— the way teachers did, leading children to believe that teachers could read minds. "Let me put your mind at ease by helping you get to where you are going. Is that guard someone who will recognize you?"

Matusu nodded.

"Put your sand guard up and follow me."

Chapter 18

Matusu raised his sand guard over his nose and mouth and followed the woman toward the guard station. His muscles tensed. If she was going to betray him, his best chance to escape was to violently disable the guard and flee. He knew better than to try to physically defeat a teacher. He had no doubt this small woman had the skills to use his own strength to put him on the ground.

As they approached the guard station, Te'Natha cleared her throat, getting the guards attention. "Did you see any teachers go that way just now?" She asked pointing away to the left. With her other hand held low, she motioned for Matusu to go past her into the teacher hall. As the guard looked where Te'Natha had pointed, Matusu slipped by.

"No, Teacher," the guard said.

"Hmm. They must still be in the halls," she said and followed Matusu into the teacher halls.

Te'Natha quickly caught up with Matusu. "Where do we go from here? Don't tell me you are here to commit violence? You don't have the skills to go up against teachers or the senior guards."

"Believe me that is the last thing I would try. I've seen firsthand what guard captains and teachers can do."

"So, Ariste and Te'Roan were with you?"

"I haven't said anything about Ariste or Te'Roan."

"You just did. What about Kira? Is she alright?"

"She is well," Matusu said.

"Still a man of few words. What is your plan now? If you're hoping to get to Te'Marile, I'm afraid she's better guarded than you're ready to handle."

"You would be surprised what I'm ready for. But I simply need to find a hidden passage."

"Those are guarded as well."

"Hopefully not all of them." Matusu was counting corridors as they walked. He turned left down one, then right down another. It seemed that Te'Natha was going to stay with him the whole way.

"Are you going to Ka'Te'Losa's quarters?"

"I hope no one has moved into them yet," Matusu said.

"No. Things are still too unsettled for that. Are you telling me there is a secret passage in her quarters?"

"If there isn't, I'm going to be in trouble."

"Where are you getting this information?"

Matusu didn't answer.

"I suppose if Ariste had come here himself, he wouldn't have made it past the front gate without being recognized. That man's walk gives him away at a hundred paces."

"What's so special about his walk?" Matusu asked.

"Have you seen a mountain lion walk? It just looks dangerous."

"We could have used him at Hochonal."

"Jornatha was there, wasn't he?"

"Yes."

"Equally dangerous. Maybe more."

"You knew Jornatha?"

"He could have led the teacher's council if he hadn't chosen to go to Hochonal."

"He's probably the reason Kira, Patala, and I are still alive – him and Te'Roan."

They entered Ka'Te'Losa's chambers – a series of three rooms. They moved through the first two rooms to Ka'Te'Losa's personal chamber. Matusu went to a wall built from a series of interlocking stones. Counting the stones along the wall, he came to one that was about waist high and just as wide. He pushed the stone to no effect at first. When he put his weight into it, it slid away. A thin gap opened up on the right, so he could slide it to the left. As soon as Matusu had slid the stone as far as he could, Ariste and then Te'Roan emerged from the opening.

"It's about time," Ariste said. "Te'Roan was coming up with very elaborate alternative plans, but I insisted that we could count on you."

"I had some help," Matusu said and motioned to Te'Natha.

"Well, if you're going to enlist help," Te'Roan said, "you won't do much better than my aunt." Te'Roan hugged the small woman.

"You will be happy to know that your young protege was very good at keeping secrets."

"You didn't tell him I'd asked you to watch for him?" Te'Roan asked.

"Maybe you could have let me know to look for her," Matusu said.

"Couldn't risk you asking about her," Te'Roan said. "And I didn't think she could open this passage alone. But look, it all worked out. Now, let's gather our allies and make our move."

"What about the gatherer?" Te'Natha asked. "She should be here."

"She will be. Once we have a foothold and a place to keep her safe, Orr will bring her in."

"I guess that's my cue," Te'Natha said as she turned and left the room.

"Where's she going?" Matusu asked.

"She is making contact with other teachers who can help us," Te'Roan said.

"We have one more errand for you," Ariste said to Matusu. "Two guards from the south barracks are waiting to hear from me. They are senior guards I asked to stay and wait."

As Matusu approached the south barracks, he kept his hood and sand shield up. He had already passed at least five guards that he recognized. He went up to the first barracks, this was usually where senior guards resided. From the outside it looked the same as the other buildings, but inside, it was divided into private spaces and a common area. Matusu entered and saw a group of guards sitting at a table. He didn't recognize any of them.

"It's customary to drop your shield when entering a barracks," one guard said.

"Unless you're here to rob us," another said.

Several men laughed.

Matusu lowered the shield covering his nose and mouth.

"I can tell by the mother's milk still on your chin that you're not a senior guard, so what's your business here?" The first guard said. He seemed to be in charge or at least the most senior of the group.

"I've been sent with a message for Arnin."

The same senior guard turned away and called out, "Arnin, you have a message – maybe from that girl in the marketplace."

Matusu heard movement from one of the rooms and a tall man walked out. He wasn't just tall. His shoulders and chest were so broad that even with his uniform untied, it looked too small for him.

Arnin looked at Matusu for a moment like a curiosity, then finally said. "Wait for me outside."

Matusu turned and stepped outside, remembering at the last moment to raise his sand shield. He stood there thinking, wondering if he had misheard Arnin. The big man finally came out and motioned for Matusu to follow him.

When they were several dozen paces from the barracks, Arnin turned to Matusu and asked, "So what is the message?"

"Ariste says, 'It's time.'"

"Have you talked to Creet yet?"

"No, not yet."

"He's supervising the watch at the south gate. Go tell him. I will gather our group who are loyal to Ariste."

Matusu headed for the south gate, which wasn't far from the barracks. As he approached the guard house where the supervisor would be, a guard at the gate called out to him, "Matusu, is that you?"

It was Renning Tore, another guard Matusu had trained with. They had become good friends. It seemed that even covered up Matusu had a recognizable look. "Hi Renning," Matusu said. "Have you seen Creet?"

"He's in the guard house. Where have you been?"

"I'd really like to catch up and tell you about it, but I'm on assignment." Matusu continued walking toward the guard house.

"One of the captains from up in the tower came looking for you a while back. He didn't say what it was about."

"Huh," Matusu shrugged. "I can't imagine." Then he stepped into the guard house and lowered his face shield. Only one man was in there, sitting at a table. "Are you Creet?" Matusu asked.

"The one and only. What can I do for you?"

"Ariste says, 'It's time.'"

Creet stood, and at the same moment, Renning walked in behind Matusu.

"Hey," Renning said, talking to Creet. "This is Matusu, my friend that the captains from the tower were asking about. Permission to go and report that we've found him."

Matusu's heart raced. He looked to Creet.

Creet smiled. "That won't be necessary. I was just about to escort Matusu there myself. I'm putting you in charge here until I return." With that, Creet moved out from behind the table, and put a hand on Matusu's shoulder. "Let's go," he said.

When they were away from the guardhouse, Creet said, "How is Ariste?"

"He's as strong as ever," Matusu said.

"Have you been with him this whole time?"

"Yes."

"His serious, few words manner has rubbed off on you."

"Should we worry about Renning telling others about me?"

"Do you think he means you harm?"

"No. I think he's just…well…Renning."

"I know what you mean. Can't help but like the kid. Hopefully he aligns himself with the right side when things heat up."

Matusu noticed the direction they were walking. "Are you really escorting me to the tower?"

"That's where Ariste is, right? Our job is to secure the teacher's hall. A captain there is waiting with a squad of men. The others think he is loyal to Te'Marile, but his allegiance lies with the gatherer, should she ever return."

"She will return."

"I've heard the rumors. What do you know?"

"I know she has already started reaching out to people."

"Why did she leave?"

"She needed to stay clear of Te'Marile so she could work on opening the gate."

"And has she opened the gate?"

"Not fully. But she's close, and when it opens, Te'Marile will have to concede to wisdom."

"I wouldn't be so sure. It isn't that Te'Marile doesn't want to preserve the people, she fears the bridge."

"She has always said she wanted to move to a different protocol because the bridge won't work."

"I know what she says, but you need to know why she says it. Te'Marile came through the first time skip as a child. She lost her father during the skip and essentially lost her mother."

"How does someone essentially lose someone?"

"How much do you know about time skip syndrome?"

"Nothing," Matusu said.

"It's a rare condition people can experience from a time jump. It causes mental disorders like schizophrenia and psychosis, followed by premature death. There have been so few cases that we don't know if it's caused by environment or genetics. Anyway, Te'Marile's mother suffered from time skip syndrome. She first suffered a mental breakdown, which led to abuse of both Te'Marile and her sister, and then she died."

"So Te'Marile is trying to stop everyone from making the next time skip because she is still traumatized about what happened to her mother? That was a hundred years ago."

"I refer you back to what I said about the causes. We don't know if it's genetic. What if Te'Marile believes it is?"

"Then she is going to do everything she can to not time skip again."

"And then there's her father, the gatherer," Creet said.

"Her father was a gatherer?"

"He opened the gate, but never came through himself. And so what Te'Marile wants is to avoid the gate, and because she is Te'Marile, she assumes that what she wants must be what is good for everybody."

"You sound like you know her."

"I should. I married her daughter."

They walked in silence the rest of the way to the tower. Matusu followed Creet into the tower and into the teacher halls. Not far from the entrance to the halls, Creet greeted another guard who joined them as they walked. Other guards fell in behind them. Soon, they had a group of more than a dozen guards. Matusu wasn't familiar enough with the teacher halls to know exactly where they were. Turning down a hall, Matusu saw Ariste and Arnin standing over two guards who sat tied and gagged on the ground.

"You've gathered a good group here," Ariste said.

"Is she inside?" Creet asked.

"These guards wouldn't confirm it," Ariste said. "Let's see."

Ariste opened the door to Te'Marile's chambers. No one was in the first room. Ariste motioned for Matusu and Creet to follow him. They continued into a second chamber and then a third. She wasn't there. Ariste and Creet searched the chambers until they found a trap door in the floor. Not unlike Ka'Te'Losa's chamber, Te'Marile's had a hidden escape route.

"Perhaps we can catch her," Matusu said. "How far do you think the tunnel goes?"

"Far enough," Ariste said. "She must have heard us mustering outside or had some sort of warning network setup."

Creet dropped the trap door and started walking out of the chamber. "If she knew we were coming, then we have to move fast to secure the tower." He exited the chamber and barked orders to the guards standing there. "Arnin, take six men and secure the main gate. The rest of you come with me to secure the teacher halls in case we have to fall back here."

"Matusu and I will secure the way for Kira," Ariste said.

All the guards headed out in various directions. They seemed to know their jobs, having planned for this contingency. Matusu followed Ariste to Ka'Te'Losa's chambers and the secret passage there, now closed.

Kira waited in silence. She had been inside underground passages like this before and looked forward to being free of this one. Patala held her hand, which made all the difference compared to last time. Orr sat a little way back, watching for anyone who might have followed them in.

A crack of light at the end of the tunnel showed an opening they could crawl through.

"Wait," Orr whispered. He moved past them in the narrow corridor. "Let me make sure it's safe." He crawled through the opening.

If enemies waited for Kira on the other side, Orr would be the best one to clear the way.

"It's ok," Orr said. "It seems things are going our way."

Kira and Patala crawled through the opening into the sleeping chamber. They both hugged Matusu. "You did it," Kira said. "We're all here."

"Hopefully, we didn't all just crawl into a trap," Te'Roan said. "Te'Marile fled her chamber, and we've sent guards to secure the tower and the teacher's hall. There's no telling what Te'Marile and her group are up to."

"So things aren't all going our way," Orr said. "Show me where she fled from, and I'll track her."

"I wish it were that easy," Ariste said. "By the time we followed her trail out of the tower, she could have dozens of guards waiting for whoever follows. We need to consolidate in the tower and then find out if she has fled the city or intends to start an open conflict."

Ariste motioned for the others to follow and led them out of Ka'Te'Losa's chambers and through the halls.

Matusu moved up next to Kira. "I need to tell you something," he whispered.

"Now?" Kira asked.

"It's about opening the gate. It's something one of the senior guards told me."

They entered the council chamber. Te'Natha and a few other teachers were seated near a corner of the council chamber talking. They stood when Kira and her party arrived.

"Do you have Te'Marile?" Te'Natha asked.

"No, she has slipped away," Te'Roan said.

"No matter," Te'Natha said. "We have identified precedent and have enough testimony to have her authority, temporary as it was, put aside in favor of Kira." Turning to Kira, Te'Natha said, "Your dreams have reached many among the teachers and people we know. You have enough support to be named a gatherer. And since you are the only one we've got, you are the gatherer and can lead in both the teacher and municipal councils."

"Unfortunately, Te'Marile is not without resources to fight this," said one of the other teachers, Te'Mornoon, a tall man with receding golden hair, who leaned on an ornate staff. "As a senior member of the council, Te'Marile can make an appeal directly to the people. She has already created a great deal of loyalty among the guard captains and will use the fact that the gate is still not open to sway people to her cause."

Creet entered the chamber. "Ariste, we've secured the main entrance to the tower, as well as the side marketplace and residential entrances. The city guard supporting Te'Marile have formed up outside the main entrance in force."

"Have they made any move to attack?"

"Not yet. I think they just mean to keep us in here. Reports from our lookout in the residential side of the tower say that guards are moving on that side of the tower as well."

"Come with me to the overlook of the main entrance," Ariste said. "Orr, will you see to the residential side and send me a report? And take Matusu with you."

Kira turned to Te'Roan. "What should we do?" She asked.

Te'Roan walked to one of the council benches and sat down. "I guess we wait."

"Or we go to the marketplace and get some food for a meal," Patala said as she turned to Te'Natha. "Where can I prepare some food?"

Te'Natha smiled. "I like you. I can see your mother in you. Let me show you our kitchen."

Before she left, Patala turned to Kira. "You never told me they had a kitchen," she said.

"You never asked," Kira said. "You didn't think they starved me during training did you?"

"Hmm." Patala shrugged and followed Te'Natha.

When Patala had left, Kira turned to Te'Roan. "You don't think Te'Marile means to cut off our food supplies and starve us out do you?"

"The tower was built as a refuge. We've always maintained food stores here in case of storms or large-scale threats from humans."

"We can't have stored enough to last forever."

"Maybe now is a good time for you to focus on helping your friend in the future get that gate open."

"I thought about it while I was in that tunnel, but if I enter the dream, I might be in there a long time. What if things aren't going so well, and we need to run? Waking me from that dream isn't really an option."

"This time, we have dozens of guards with us. If we have to take turns carrying you, I think we can do it."

"Let's at least wait for Ariste to let us know where we stand. In fact, I'm going to find Ariste." She headed toward the doorway.

"Wait," Te'Roan said, standing up. "I can't have you getting carried off again. I'll go with you."

As Kira moved through the teacher halls, they somehow seemed different. Perhaps she was different. As a student, just learning about her abilities, these halls seemed bigger – or maybe she felt smaller. Over the past few months, she seemed to have grown into them.

At the entrance to the teacher's hall, guards held positions inside and outside the entrance. They moved barricades to let Kira and Te'Roan pass. The marketplace was unusually quiet as they passed, though most of the merchants seemed to have stayed with their goods. At the main entrance, several dozen of Ariste's guards held positions behind barricades set out in front of the main gates, which still stood open.

Beyond the gates, at a distance, stood what looked to Kira to be the entire remainder of the guard force. Seeing them all together like that surprised her. She had not realized so many guards existed. Dozens and dozens of them formed an arc that gave them space to react to a bow shot, but no gaps for those in the tower to slip through. The fading light of dusk made them look almost numberless.

Ariste stood by the door where many of the guards outside could clearly see him. "It's a siege," Ariste said.

"Are you sure they won't attack?"

"They have no reason to. They can simply wait us out."

"How long will our food last?"

"Usually we could last for months, but Te'Marile seems to have anticipated this. She moved the bulk of food reserves out of the tower. We have half a month at most."

"Where is the food? Maybe she just hid it somewhere else in the tower."

"I have guards searching for it, but the rumors from the marketplace are that Te'Srin led people moving loads of something out of the city."

"So, it's gone?" Kira asked. "I'd like to give that man a scar on the other side of his face."

"It would seem that the Faction has begun their journey to establish a hidden colony in the south and may have taken the bulk of our stores with them."

"I've had confirmation of that," Te'Roan said, as he walked up behind Kira and Ariste. "According to some teachers and guards I spoke with, Te'Marile has prepared for an exodus from the city, quietly inviting anyone that she believed she could trust."

"What's in the south?" Kira asked.

"Jungles and mountains," Te'Roan said. "It might be possible to hide a civilization there for the next half century."

"Only if she enlists humans to help," Ariste said.

"We've already built everything needed to hide a civilization here," Kira said.

"The jungle hides places far richer in resources, not to mention water and rich soil. She could build a hidden city at the level of our home world."

"That's going to leave a deep footprint."

"Especially if she has convinced the majority of the population to go with her," Te'Roan said.

Ariste stepped forward toward the guards. "Close the gates and prepare the night guard," he ordered.

Chapter 19

Back in the room she and Patala shared, Kira dropped into the dream and focused on the path in the trees and Coyote. It felt different arriving in the wilderness, while in the real world being in the stone structure of the tower. Coyote waited for her at the edge of the trees and led her through the winding pathway. At the now familiar clearing with a fire ring and bench, Danny sat with his arms stretched out across the back of the bench, watching her as she emerged from the trees.

"We found it," he said. "About forty feet below the surface of the reservoir. The door in the cave opened like you said."

"Did you get it out?"

"We're working on it. It's on public land, so there is a lot of red tape to go through."

"Red tape?"

"Paperwork. Bureaucratic approvals."

"You mean you have to involve your government – the same government that failed to protect your ancestors?"

"In this case, we've just said we're bringing up stone artifacts."

"Rosie told me plenty about government."

"Yes, Grandma had her disagreements with the government. But she and others kind of paved the way for things to get better for our people."

"How many people are involved now?"

"We have Sam, the archeologist. He's been working the historical find angle to allow us access with equipment. I think he knows something about this is more than just an archeological find. Then there is the main diver, a guy named Cory, who gave me a crash course in SCUBA so I could go down with him. Then two of Sam's students who had worked on the other discoveries."

"Please tell them as little as possible. If the more militant side of your government gets involved, things could go very badly."

"On a more technical note, does this gate need to be completely stationary for you to come through?"

"It weighs a great deal. I can't imagine anyone would want to be carrying it while it's in use."

"We wouldn't be carrying it exactly. We're bringing in a barge with a crane to lift it out of the water, so when it finally comes up, it will be on the barge."

"A barge?"

"A large flat boat. I'm wondering if it will simply open when it's clear of the water. Or will we have time to get it to solid ground before it opens? Maybe you could wait until you've confirmed with me in the dream."

"Our dreams are not synchronized in time in that way," Kira said. "The portal in our time and in your time are synchronized. It started when we first tested the connection. We could start running periodic tests and when the test shows the portal in open air, we could wait a specified amount of time before fully opening it."

"It's still going to take us time to get the permits and the barge in place. Once it's out of the water, we should be able to get it somewhere secure in twenty-four hours, one day. How often can you run the tests?"

"I believe if we run them intermittently, we can do them pretty regularly. They take very little power compared to the fully open gate. Perhaps we could run them once a day. When the test comes back clear, we will wait one more day and open it. So, it could be anywhere from one to two days after it's clear."

"Ok. Start testing, and I'll press forward on hauling this thing up."

"Danny, there's one other thing you should know about me and my people."

"Something weirder than that you are from outer space?"

"In the dream, I have altered my appearance to look human. When you see my people, you will know that we are distinctively not human."

"How not human? Do you have gray skin and big heads or are you lizard people with sharp teeth?"

"Let me show you." Kira shifted from the facade she had worn for so many months in the dream. She felt her height increase a little. Looking down at her hands, she saw her own slender fingers and pale skin with just a hint of blue. She reached up and lifted her hair from her shoulder so she could see it. Its blue and lavender strands shimmered slightly. She also noted that her clothing had changed from the skin dress like Iactah's people wore to her own clothes and teacher cloak.

"Wow," Danny said. "You changed, but somehow, you're still you."

"Do you think people will be frightened?"

"You actually look very kind – not threatening at all. You should see some of the monsters people have come up with in movies about aliens."

"I thought you have not met any alien species."

"We haven't, but science fiction writers and filmmakers have vivid imaginations about what they think might be out there."

"The universe does have its monsters, just like some of the predators on your world. But they don't reach a point of civilization required for space travel."

"I suppose that makes sense. What about world-conquering, resource-stealing aliens?"

"They do exist, which is one of the reasons my people make periodic checks on worlds like yours."

"I really didn't need to know that."

"Perhaps I've said too much. I will turn my attention to running tests on the gate."

"And I'll get your steel saucer out of the reservoir."

"Thank you Danny."

When Kira awoke from the dream, she immediately left her chamber to find Te'Roan. As she moved into the halls, she saw the mid-day light shining down through the skylights and narrow clefts in the stone walls. Te'Roan was eating in the teacher common area with Patala, a few guards, and two of the teachers.

Kira sat down across the table from Te'Roan and Patala. "Danny found it," she said in a hushed voice. "It's deep under water, but he says they can get the equipment to bring it up."

"There is no way he can lift it out by himself. How many people are involved in this now?"

"More than we would like, but it's going to work. We need to get people to the gate right away. We need to start running tests each day, so we know when the gate is out of the water."

"What if Te'Marile has sent people to stop the gate from being opened," Patala said. "She might have people in place in Sonal waiting for just such an opportunity."

"We need to protect the gate until we can get there," Te'Roan said. "We should send someone there as soon as possible."

"I will go with them," Kira said.

"If you go now, I fear we will never unite the people back to following wisdom. You need to unite them and lead them there."

Matusu wasn't sure why he was included in a meeting of senior guards, but Ariste had insisted. With all his assignments, he hadn't found time to get back and talk to Kira.

"We've been able to determine that Te'Marile has had to pull away a portion of her forces to transport the food stores away from the city. I've looked at the guard patterns from up on the tower and seen some opportunities to get a few men through."

"Do you intend to send men after the food?" Orr asked.

"That would be the prudent thing to do, and I want it to look like that's what we've done. We actually have something more important to do. I need you and Matusu along with two guards of your choosing to escape the tower and set a pursuit course after the food but break off and head to Sonal. We are very close to opening the gate, and we need you there to stop any of Te'Marile's followers from interfering."

"No one seemed to interfere with us last time we were there, but if you want me to take a little trip home, I'm ready."

"Good, you and your group take up a position at the south residential entrance and wait for an opening."

"What kind of opening?"

"When the guards pull back, you go. I'm not sure how long we can divert them from their post. I'm counting on the fact that they've only been trained to defend the city from people coming in, not from people going out."

After grabbing his bag, Matusu followed Orr to just inside the south residential entrance. He watched out a slit in the door, while

Orr watched through the other slit. A guard named Nolor, Orr's nephew, and a guard named Pantu, stood behind them. Both men were older than Matusu by more than a couple years, and both knew the way to Sonal, should they have to split up.

As the sun dropped to the horizon, Matusu heard a commotion starting from both inside and outside the tower. Whatever Ariste was up to, it had begun.

Of the six guards watching outside the south entrance, five left their posts and ran toward the sound.

Without a word of warning, Orr pushed open the door and charged at the guard who was looking in the direction of the commotion. The guard never even heard Orr until he was a step away, and by the time he turned around, it was too late. Orr lowered his shoulder into the guard's chest and knocked him to the ground.

The guard lay there for a moment, gasping for air.

Orr kicked the man's spear away and stood over him. "Stay down boy!" Orr said.

The guard started to sit up, and Orr put him back on the ground with a fist across his face. The guard lay still.

"Is he dead?" Matusu asked, running up behind Orr with the guard captain's bag.

"Oh, I hope not. I know his mother." Orr took his bag from Matusu and started off.

Nolor and Pantu followed behind, keeping an eye on their back trail.

Te'Roan watched the mayhem athe front gate from a window high above. Ariste had started the breech by having his guards at the gate swing it open quickly and throw about a dozen large bags of cooking oil out into the open space between the door and the opposing guards. The bags burst on impact spreading oil across the stones in front of the gate. Then, from just above the gate, Ariste and another man lit smaller containers on fire and threw them onto the oil. The whole area in front of the gate turned to low flames and black smoke.

From behind the barricade just inside the gate, Ariste's guards began rapid firing blunted arrows through the smoke into the line of guards. The first volley hit the opposing guards, and men began crying out and scrambling to get shields up, several guards within the gate and at openings above the gate blew horns, like the ones used at the main city gates. The horns bellowed above every other sound.

As the smoke started to clear, Te'Roan could see several opposing guards on the ground, others limping, trying to get into some sort of formation. Ariste's men had been aiming at the enemies' legs. They were trained to hold their shields to protect their torso and face. Ariste hadn't wanted anyone killed, just less maneuverable.

With the smoke clearing, a group of twenty or so guards charged out of the tower toward what looked to be a weak point in the line. The charging guards didn't carry spears, but instead had training staves. The opposing guards that hadn't fallen were quickly knocked off their feet.

The charging group looked as though they would punch a hole in the line. When the second wave of opposing guards surged up from behind to reinforce the weak point, Ariste's men withdrew in unison, retreating back toward the gates. When they were safely inside, they pulled the gates closed behind them.

Ariste joined Te'Roan at the upper window. "Did you see any casualties?" The guard captain asked.

"I think it went exactly as you said it would. All our guards are accounted for, and the others only suffered bruises to their bodies and pride."

"That won't work again. They will take precautions next time and may even prepare a counterattack. I would have had a counterattack ready for the moment the gates opened."

As the commotion at the tower gates ended and darkness fell over Thresdenal, Kira dropped into the dream to continue making connections and introducing herself as the gatherer. She began finding more and more interconnected links, people who knew others she had already visited. This was a good sign. She also found herself talking to more and more people from the outer villages. They seemed more receptive of a gatherer and less skeptical. Their opinions of wisdom and the gathering weren't tainted by the politics of the city.

She was startled when passing through the dream of a person from an outer village to find a connection to Te'Marile. She had come across that connection many times among the other teachers and even had her own connection to the woman, but she was suddenly reminded that her absent adversary was just a thought away. When traveling through the desert, Kira had blocked the teacher from reaching out to her in the dream. She had sensed her trying and was certain she only thought to trick Kira into giving away their location. Now things were different. Now Te'Marile knew exactly where Kira was.

Kira stepped through the connection into Te'Marile's dream.

Te'Marile wasn't in the tower or even in Thresdenal in her dream. She stood by a waterfall in a small desert canyon. Mists of water rose around them and watered the green moss and delicate vines that clung to the rock walls near the waterfall. It reminded Kira of the spot she and the others had found on their flight from Hochonol, though it was not the same place.

Te'Marile stood ankle deep in the pool of water at the base of the waterfall. She turned her head and looked at Kira, apparently sensing her arrival.

"So now, after all this time, you visit me in the dream?" Te'Marile said.

"I couldn't risk it before."

"You are at less risk from me than you are from those you ran away with. Those who would use you without considering the cost."

"We've been to the gate. I can open it. Your plan is no longer necessary."

"You may find it more necessary than you think."

Kira thought the woman looked too comfortable. She shifted the dream so that Te'Marile stood on a boulder, a river roaring past her on both sides falling off into churning rapids below.

"The protocol is working!" Kira shouted over the noise of the falls. "You don't need to put humans or your followers at risk by breaking from wisdom!"

Te'Marile seemed to concentrate for a moment and the sound of the falls dimmed. Everything else stayed as Kira had made it. "How much did Rory or any of the master teachers tell you about the first time skip? Or even Ka'Te'Losa? They were all there."

"Rory explained how to open it by connecting with the gate, like connecting with the map device, a lesson you conveniently left out of my training and then used against me in front of the teacher council."

"I know you think I'm standing against you, but I think you will find that I am the only one standing for you."

"By chasing me and my friends across the desert?"

"By giving you an alternative to dying as a martyr for people who only care about what you can do for them."

"No one has asked me to die."

"They asked you to die when they bestowed on you the honor of forming the bridge."

"What are you talking about?"

"What do you know about the gatherer who opened the gate for the first time skip?"

"I only know that he was part of the first marooned and one of two gatherers. They were both older and so another gatherer was needed for the second time skip."

"His name was Ka'Te'Rensool. He was my father."

"I didn't know."

"Of course, you didn't know. That might have brought up questions like, 'How long did he live?' or 'Why didn't he leave any directions on how he did it?' Questions that would be difficult for Ka'Te'Losa to answer."

"I guess you are going to tell me the answers to those questions."

"We don't really know how long he lived because he didn't come through the bridge. He would have been the last one through. There was plenty of time before the gate would close. We waited and watched on the other side until the bridge just blinked out of existence, and he was gone."

"I'm sorry."

"I don't tell you this to gain your sympathy, but as a warning. Whether he died within the bridge or died alone centuries away from us, we don't know. That doesn't need to be your fate, Kira."

"Thank you for telling me. Now let me tell you something." Kira lowered the stone under Te'Marile so the river tugged at her feet. I am going to honor your father by finishing what he started. I am going to open that gate and whether I cross the bridge or not, I am going to send the people I love, those I have left, across to safety."

Te'Marile just looked at Kira as if trying to understand her at some deeper level.

"I wish you the best Kira Waterborn. Should you find yourself standing alone beside a burnt out gate in our time, reach out to me in the dream, and I will guide you to our colony."

Te'Marile faded from the dream, and the dream shifted, leaving Kira standing alone in her own dream in Hochonal.

Kira woke to the noise of Patala bustling about their room.

"Oh good," Patala said. "You're awake. We need to pack and be ready to move."

"Has the siege been broken?" Kira asked.

"I think the guards outside changed their minds about waiting us out. They started forming ranks this morning. And Te'Roan said he thinks they intend to breach the tower."

"When did you talk to Te'Roan?"

"At our morning meal, we've all been up since dawn."

"How many guards are forming outside?"

"All of them from the looks of it. Which is three times more than we have. So pack what you need in case we have to leave quickly and keep it with you."

Kira heard a loud boom echo through the tower. She jumped up and started packing her bag, which was mostly ready as she hadn't really taken time to unpack. Three more booms and Kira and Patala were on their way down to the council hall. The hall was empty, so they proceeded toward the sound. Teachers and guards lined the halls leading to the main entrance. They worked their way through until they reached Ariste.

After another boom, obviously coming from the tower gate, Kira asked, "What's happening?"

"The guards outside have decided to assault the tower and take it by force," Ariste said.

"Why the change?"

"We don't know, except that they seem to think they should be in control of the tower."

Te'Roan walked up from the market area. "I know why they suddenly want to control the tower," he said. "Ariste and Kira come with me."

They followed Te'Roan across the market area to stairs that led to the upper floors and then up more stairs and eventually to a ladder that went up into a hole in the ceiling. Kira had never been on top of the mesa. They followed a well-beaten path to the edge where they could look out over the whole valley. Kira could see the entire city, the wall and gates, the outer city, and the farms and groves planted to the edges of the valley.

"There," Te'Roan said, pointing into the distance.

At the western edge of the valley, Kira could just make out movement, what looked like a group of people.

"Humans?" She asked.

"Look closer," Te'Roan said.

"Our people from the outer villages," Ariste said.

"And guards," Te'Roan said, "our guards coming back from the desert."

Just then Kira noticed more people to the north coming down through the groves there. As they watched, people emerged from the passes on the east and the south. The outer villages were gathering back to Thresdenal.

"They heard you Kira. They heard your plea and came to the gatherer," Te'Roan said.

Kira couldn't believe it. Some of them must have been already traveling here while she was interrupting their sleep in the dream.

"The guards outside are trying to take the tower to use as a stronghold before the people from the outer villages and the exiled guards get here," Ariste said.

"We have to hold the tower," Kira said. "What can I do?"

Te'Roan looked out over the city. Kira looked the same direction. People in the farms were coming out of their fields and homes. Some were starting to walk with the newly arriving villagers.

"They are shaking off their complacency," Te'Roan said. "How many of those guards down there do you think are just following orders?"

Kira understood what he was getting at. "Let's go see," she said and started toward the ladder.

When they arrived back at the main gate, which was showing some cracks from the beating it was taking, she climbed up to the overlook above the gate. For the first time, she got a look at the battering ram they had constructed and the roof they had put over it to protect them from attacks from above.

"Guards of Thresdenal!" Kira called out over the booming and the shuffling, which just continued.

"Guards of Thresdenal!" Kira yelled louder.

Kira took a step back from the window and closed her eyes. She reached out for the storm. She thought of the battle that would ensue if she didn't bring this to an end. She saw the lives that would be wasted over nothing. She saw the storm grow and lightning flash and drew it into herself. She opened her eyes and stepped up to the window.

She called out again. "Guards of Thresdenal!" She pushed forward the energy inside her. It burst out across the courtyard like a wave. Men and women fell back. The guards holding the ram suddenly let go. Kira could see people across the city stepping back and turning to look up at her. "Stars that is exhausting," she muttered to herself as she put a hand on the window ledge in front of her.

"Guards of Thresdenal! People of Thresdenal!" Kira called out again. "Do you hear me?"

A few nodded.

"I am Kira Waterborn of Hochonal. I am the gatherer. Many of you have seen me in your dreams and know this is true."

A few more nodded.

"The gate to our rescue has been opened. The time has been set. Join me in crossing the bridge and returning home to the stars."

A few guards set their hands again to the battering ram, but more did not. People of the city who had been mere spectators or been going about their day now walked toward the tower. Kira felt a bit lightheaded and almost fell backwards. Te'Roan caught her and held her up.

"That energy burst really drains you doesn't it?" She said.

"I wouldn't know. You are only the second dreamer I've ever seen do it," Te'Roan said.

Kira realized that the other one was her father. Perhaps he had been close to being a gatherer himself.

Kira looked out over the people coming in among the guards and the guard formations breaking up. Then everything went dark.

Kira woke in her room with Patala sitting by her. "What's going on," she asked. "Why am I here? I was at the…"

"At the window above the gate. Yes, I know. Te'Roan brought you down after you passed out."

"I what? That's not what…" Kira tried sitting up but laid back down. "How long?"

"How long what?"

"How long have I been out?" Kira asked.

"Just a few hours. You haven't even missed the mid-day meal. Would you like me to bring you something?"

"No. I need to go to the council room. We need to organize the departure." Kira forced herself to sit up.

Kira arrived in the council room to a group of teachers and guard captains discussing among themselves. She recognized guards from both sides, but no teachers who had been aligned with Te'Marile. All three of the master teachers who had tested Kira were there. She walked up to Te'Juna and asked to have a word.

When they had stepped away from the others, Kira asked, "Was Te'Marile's father the gatherer who opened the gate at the first time skip?"

"Yes," Te'Juna said.

"Did he fail to pass through the gate with everyone else?"

"Yes," she said. "He was either lost in the bridge or never entered."

"Is that the fate of all who open time skip gates?"

"Certainly not. Gatherers have been opening and passing through bridges for tens of thousands of years."

"Either way," Kira said. "I am committed to opening the gate."

"I assure you that no one has asked you to sacrifice yourself. The gatherer can cross the bridge just like everyone else. The loss of Ka'Te'Rensool is both a tragedy and a mystery."

"What other important details don't I know about the first time skip?"

"Kira, you must realize I was not a senior member of the teacher council and had little to do with it other than walking through. I have spent time with Te'Marile, who has also asked about this subject. I told her the same thing I just told you. The difference is that she never believed me. People who make a habit of lying like to believe that others are lying too."

"I believe you, Te'Juna. You have been helpful to our cause even when we could not share everything with you."

"Child, we have been faithful to our cause together."

Chapter 20

Kira looked about the main entrance and felt as empty as the tower she stood in. The merchants had taken their wares. Every bed and chair that could be moved had been taken from the tower. The regeneration device had been removed to be carried with them, as had the way finder and its data core. In three days, the tower and the city were packed up and abandoned. Wisdom taught not to gather many possessions. This was the reason. The people were always just visitors who must pack up and leave.

Kira raised her hood and stepped out through where the main gates had hung. Those too had been removed, broken, and scattered. Many of the people from the outlying villages has setup a camp to the west of the city. They were ready to go when the people of Thresdenal had sufficiently packed up provisions. People from Thresdenal shared what they could not carry. Food would be their most essential item.

Te'Roan walked up beside Kira. He was packed and, along with the other teachers, waited only for Kira to lead them out among the people.

"Was it all so temporary that we could abandon it in days?" Kira asked.

"I think they have known this was coming and had already prepared," Te'Roan said.

"Is everyone gathered?" Kira asked.

"All who are coming with us," Te'Roan said.

Some of those still loyal to Te'Marile had slipped out of the city over the past three days. She and the teachers who followed her must be guiding them through the dream to their secret colony.

"How many left with Te'Marile?" Kira asked.

"Less than a tenth of the people, about four hundred."

"Not much of an uprising when you only get a tenth of the people."

"I think she had a lot more on her side before your display from the window. She had convinced them you were an unskilled child without the power to be the gatherer."

"I hope they won't be looking for another demonstration. I'm just starting to feel like I can travel again."

"We won't be traveling like before, weaving through canyons and trying to leave no prints," Te'Roan said. "This time we are a migration following the most direct path. With over four thousand people together, humans will not attack."

"They may choose to harass stragglers, though," Kira said. "We need to have guards front and rear keeping everyone together." She looked up at the tower one last time. "May the desert take you," she said and started walking west.

As the shadows along the trail stretched out toward the east, Kira walked into their first camp. Ariste had taken some guards and gone ahead. He had chosen the spot and got a few cooking fires going. Kira purveyed the small valley.

"No hidden ledge near a water hole?" She asked.

He laughed – or at least gave what passed as a laugh for Ariste. "Hiding is no longer possible. In fact, I prefer everyone camp here in the lower valley and leave the surrounding hills for the guards to watch."

Kira saw that Ariste already had guards directing people to not stop at the rise but continue down to camp together.

"A small stream runs off to the west there. People should go in groups to get water," he said.

Kira passed the word to other teachers as they arrived, and they spread it among the people. Most of the people seemed to be traveling in groups according to their villages or what part of Thresdenal they had lived in.

Patala had been traveling with Terrice and the other merchants. She had explained her plan to Kira before they left, "I don't want to give the impression I'm some sort of leader like you," she had said. "I think if I stay with the merchants, I can help Terrice and still be close enough to check on you."

The merchants and artisans moved to a spot close to the center of camp and set out some wares they had brought with them. Though commerce wouldn't be a part of their short journey, they were willing to share if people needed anything.

Patala walked up to Kira carrying a stack of blankets. "Kira, I know you're busy, but do you know any families that need extra blankets? The nights are cold this time of year."

"The other teachers have been working directly with families from the villages and communities," Kira said. "Perhaps they know how they can best be shared."

Te'Roan was sitting nearby and stepped up to relieve Patala of the blankets. "If you'd like," he said to Patala. "I can help you find homes for these."

They walked off together toward camps of people who continued to arrive.

Kira turned back to the fire where Ariste was warming them some cakes. "It hardly seemed like traveling today, compared to the long treks we've taken across the desert."

"A well-trodden path can make all the difference, not to mention a safe camp at day's end."

"I was going to say we are making slow progress."

"Families do tend to travel slower than fugitives. Would you like to push ahead?"

"I don't see the benefit. The gate can't be opened until the people are there and ready to pass through."

"I sent a small group of guards ahead to check on the village and bring a report from Orr."

"I can get a report from Orr and Matusu tonight if you'd like. I've finally recovered enough to dream again – at least for a short time."

"I would rather you save your strength for opening the gate," Ariste said.

"Fine. I can ask one of the other teachers to do it. It would hardly be an effort for Te'Natha to reach out to Matusu."

"If that is what you want, I see no harm in it. Just know that the guards I sent will bring back a report either way."

Kira decided to wander through the camps. She saw that, as people arrived, they camped close to where Ariste had setup the main camp. People seemed to circle it, until the camps became a series of circles with Ariste's original camp at the center. She invited all who had not yet started fires to come and cook at her fire. Wood was scarce, so not all would be able to have a fire.

Kira wandered until she met the last group to arrive. "How was the journey?" She asked an elderly woman.

"Well, Teacher, I haven't walked so much since I was a child. I helped my father survey the ground where the wall of Thresdenal was built."

Kira was startled that the elderly woman gave her the deference of calling her Teacher. Then she realized that she was wearing a teacher's robe, so why wouldn't she call Kira by that title. Most of the elderly women Kira knew were themselves teachers and seemed to enjoy calling her child. "You came through the first time skip?" Kira asked.

"Oh, yes. That didn't require much walking."

"What was it like?"

"It was like being nowhere and then coming back. I have to tell you that I am not looking forward to doing it again. But it will be worth it to travel among the stars."

"Do you remember being in space on a starship?"

"Oh, those are the best memories of my life. Being on a starship, seeing new worlds – exhilarating. One moment, you're gazing out on a star system, and the next, you're traveling across the system at near light speed. Yes, it's worth the walk to the gate. I'm Erlini, by the way."

"Pleased to meet you. I'm Kira."

"Oh, Gatherer, I didn't recognize you."

"I hardly recognize myself these days," Kira said. "I'm just a girl from a remote village. Nothing special to see."

"You don't know how grateful we are. Not just me, but my children and grandchildren. We get to go home."

What had been a nice conversation had quickly shifted. All the doubts Kira still felt flooded up, making it difficult for her to speak.

When she did find her voice, she just said, "I hope we meet again soon at the gate."

"At the gate," Erlini said.

The second day and evening went pretty much like the first. The only difference being that the encampment was near a large grove of fire trees, which provided enough wood for everyone's fires.

A guard jogged into camp and up to Ariste. Kira hurried over, thinking that it might be word from Sonal.

"Captain," the guard said. "We spotted a group of eleven humans following us today. They stayed far off. We think it's a hunting party that came across our trail."

"We do leave quite a trail," Ariste said. "If I found a trail like ours while out hunting, I'd go have a look at it too."

"Would you like us to drive them away?" The guard asked.

"Send a squad of four to shadow them for the night. If the humans become a threat, the guards can report it, and we'll take action then."

"No word from Orr and Matusu?" Kira asked Ariste when the guard had gone.

"Nothing yet, I expect a report at any time. I will let you know if I hear anything."

Patala arrived next to the fire by Kira. She had her bag and her blanket.

"Have you had enough of the merchants?" Kira asked.

"If you mean have I heard enough about weaving and carving and artisan pottery, then the answer is no. I find every bit of it interesting. But last night, as I was looking up at the stars telling myself the stories of the constellations, I realized something. After you open that gate, we don't know where we'll be."

"Wherever we go, we'll be together," Kira said.

"I know we'll make sure we go to the same places, but I mean we won't be together like we have been. You'll probably be made the head dreamer of a fleet or learn how to pilot starships, while I'll be cleaning kitchens or sewing uniforms."

"I rather picture you doing something with children. Starships are filled with families, and while many go about the work of running the ship and exploring space, someone has to make sure the children are taught. Someone has to make sure they all have shoes."

Patala shook her head. "You weave a beautiful tapestry Gatherer. Wherever we end up, I thought I'd rather watch the stars next to you tonight."

"I would like that."

A group of guards jogged into the light of the fire. "Captain," one said, approaching Ariste.

Kira walked over the hear their report.

"You have a report from Orr?" Ariste asked.

"He said that a squad of Faction guards had set up a camp between the village and the gate. Orr said they watched him and his guards arrive in Sonal, and when he went up to confront them, they had left. He hasn't seen any sign of them since."

"Thank you," Ariste said to the guard. "Get some food and rest." He then turned to Kira. "Now we know. All is well, and we'll arrive there ourselves tomorrow."

The third day started like the two before it, but not long after midday, Kira reached the well-worn stones that meant they were near Sonal. As she walked down the path into the little village, Patala jogged up next to her.

"Have you figured out where to put all the people in this tiny village?" Patala asked.

Kira had not. "Any suggestions?"

Ariste chimed in. "Your job is to lead them here and open the gate. Most of them have been alive much longer than you. Let them figure it out for themselves."

"Don't you think they will look to Kira for guidance?" Patala asked.

"Asking for guidance and getting guidance are two different things," Ariste said. "Every outlying village or community from Thresdenal has leaders, let them lead."

"We'll only be here a few days," Kira said. "I'm sure they can work things out."

"They seemed to all want to camp close to you on the way here. Perhaps we should set our camp outside the village, so we don't overwhelm the people of Sonal."

Arriving at the village, Kira was met by Orr, Matusu, and Orr's sister, Trassa.

After greeting everyone in turn, Kira asked, "Where is Rory?"

"When the advanced group of guards arrived, he went up to check on the gate and make sure it was ready for you," Trassa said.

"Perhaps after we rest a moment, I'll join him. In the meantime, would you mind directing us toward someplace to camp?" Kira said.

"I would be honored if you would use the same room you used last time," Trassa said.

"We have over four thousand people coming up behind us," Kira said.

"That is not a problem. Sonal was built for the gathering. Just below the village on the path toward the water, is a large plain that has been kept for this day. It has a large grove of trees and easy access to the water."

"I will send men to set up our camp at the center," Ariste said.

"Won't you be staying in the village?" Trassa asked.

"The people seem intent on gathering their camps around the gatherer, so I may be back and forth between both places depending on how long it takes us to open the gate."

"I thought you had already opened the gate," Trassa said.

"It's complicated. We have a few details to work out before we fully open it," Kira said. Rory had obviously not told her the details of the complications, and Kira thought it best not to start any kind of panic.

"Let's at least get you fed before you start working," Trassa said and headed toward the center of the village and the village fire ring.

Matusu sided up next to Kira and took hold of her arm. "I need to talk to you about something," he said.

Kira stepped away from the group with him to where they wouldn't be heard by others.

"Are you aware of what happened to the last gatherer to open the gate?"

"You mean Te'Marile's father," Kira said.

"So, you know her father was the gatherer?"

"Yes. And he never came through the gate."

"That doesn't bother you?"

"Yes, but it doesn't change anything. Besides, I talked to Te'Juna about it, and she said gates have been used many times before without losing the gatherer."

"And you just take her word for it?"

"Like I said, it doesn't change anything," Kira said.

"I think it does," Matusu said.

"Te'Marile obviously felt the same as you when she warned me." Kira turned to go, and Matusu pulled her back.

"Wait, please. Te'Marile told you?"

"Yes. She tried to make me think that she was the only person who cared about me and my safety. Such altruism seemed out of character for her."

"I would say, since it's almost certain she had a hand in chasing us across the desert. When I described that teacher who was with the humans to Orr, he knew who it was and said he was part of the Faction that wanted to break from the protocol, like Te'Marile."

Kira considered the lack of empathy that attack took compared with the concern Te'Marile attempted to show for Kira's life. "I just have to assume her concern for me was another manipulation."

"I think her real concern is not ending up like her mother," Matusu said.

"She didn't mention anything happening to her mother," Kira said.

"She wouldn't," Matusu said. "That would make her seem selfish." Matusu told Kira about how Te'Marile's mother suffered time skip syndrome and went mad.

"It seems she has good reason to be afraid of going through the gate again. But what kind of narcissist convinces all those other people to go astray just to allay her own fears?"

Matusu looked at Kira for a long moment, like he was trying to think of something else to tell her. She knew he feared for her. Despite Te'Marile's duplicity, the gate did seem to present some risks to the gatherer. Kira hugged him.

"Let's get something to eat," she said.

When Kira did finally make her way up to the gate, with Matusu and Ariste in tow, she found Rory standing next to it with his display device in hand, apparently running tests.

"Does it still work?" She asked.

"Hmm?" Rory looked up. "Oh, you're the only one who can tell us for sure. I do know the energy levels are good."

"Tell me, Rory, how many of these tests can we make and still have enough power to fully open the gate."

"How many? Well, it depends on how far apart they are."

"Let's say, once a day."

He looked down at the display rod and began muttering to it. "You could run a test once a day for sixty-six days without dropping below the necessary threshold for a full opening."

"Well, let's hope Coyote has us well synchronized," Kira said.

"Coyote?" Rory asked.

Kira wondered if she should tell him about Coyote and her dreams. He might think she was crazy. Of course, crazy or not, she was still the only one who could open the gate. "My connection with the person in the future who is moving the gate is directed by a spirit guide who happens to be a coyote."

"What a marvelous manifestation," Rory said with a look of awe on his face.

"Manifestation?"

"Yes. I'm no expert on dreams, mind you, but I do know about quantum connections. What you see as a coyote is the manifestation of your intentions on a quantum level. The indigenous people of this world must have capacity for quantum connections that are independent of time and space. Remarkable."

"I agree that it's remarkable. One of them told me the spirit guide is an extension of the life of the world helping its inhabitants. She believes I have been granted a spirit guide because I was born here."

"Yes," Rory said, nodding his head. "I can see how that explanation also works."

"Rory, you are trying to come up with a hypothesis to test aren't you?"

"Of course. Don't let my observations make you think I'm some idle theorist. I'm every bit as much a pragmatist and engineer." Rory backed away from the gate to stand by Kira. "Shall we run another test?"

Kira had been practicing her device control with Te'Roan's map device. Closing her eyes, she quickly connected with the gate and formed the sphere of dots that linked all the internal connections. She harnessed the energy inside her and pushed it into the connection, forcing the sphere to split and project away. She opened her eyes to see the tiny bridge open and then close. A drop of water fell onto the gate.

She heard an audible sigh from Matusu who stood behind her.

"It's just as well," she said. "We ought to show everyone how to get here so they are ready when it really opens."

Kira walked up the cliff trail and back to the village with Matusu and Ariste. She had half expected that the gateway would be ready to open. After all, in her last dream with Danny, it had seemed that her time and the time Danny came up with were very close. He said he was very close to getting the gate free from the water.

As soon as they arrived back at the village, Kira excused herself and went to the room Trassa had offered her.

She entered the dream and sought out Coyote at the base of the fire tree grove. She didn't have to wait long for Coyote to trot up to her. "Let's see if we can find out how Danny is doing," she said.

Coyote led her up the winding trail through the trees. When they arrived at a clearing, Danny sat on the bench looking about like he had last time Kira met with him.

"Hello Danny. How is the project coming along?"

"I wish I could say we were done, but you probably know we aren't. We got the barge into place. They keep one at the other end of the reservoir. However, now we are waiting on parts for the crane."

"Crane?"

"A crane is a hoist that swings a cable out over the boat. I guess it gets its name because it kind of looks like the bird."

"And this is the hoist you will use to remove the gate from the reservoir?"

"Yes. We were able to get some air bags strapped to it in the cave and can maneuver it pretty well. Cory wants to add more airbags and then also lift it with the crane. That way if the crane fails for some reason, the gate won't drop all the way to the bottom."

"So you trust Cory? He understands about keeping secrets?"

"Sam, that's Dr. Freeman, explained to Cory that it's an archeological artifact that can't be talked about until it's somewhere safe, or someone might try to steal it. He also had Cory sign a non-disclosure agreement."

"And signing an agreement is enough?"

"Usually."

"Has Sam seen it?"

"I had to take him along on the dive to sell the story to Cory. But like I said before, Sam's pretty sure that whoever made your villages and that mesa aren't from around here."

"He doesn't know we're from outer space does he?"

"I think he believes you were from a civilization that was much more advanced than you were trying to let on. Like Mesoamerican refugees or something."

"What kind of refugees?"

"The people who built the pyramids in the jungles in the southern part of this continent."

"We were going for a little less civilization than that, but if that's all he thinks, we may be in the clear."

"He's suspicious of me knowing things he doesn't think I should know. He's curious how he never heard of this artifact at the reservoir. Apparently, he's really into documenting the oral traditions of native people, and this never came up."

"I'm afraid he will just have to remain suspicious. Have you found a place to put the gate on dry land?"

"I'm working on getting it into a warehouse or barn. I thought it would be better if your people came through inside a building. How many people are we talking about?"

"At last count, 4,014. But a few women are with child, so that could change."

"Ok. I will need a big warehouse or barn – or maybe an airplane hangar."

"A what? Never mind. I will find a place."

"You will want a way to level it," Kira said.

"Does is need to be on stone like it is now, or could we make supports out of wood to cradle it?"

"Wood should be fine. It doesn't get hot, or we couldn't walk on it."

"Got it."

"How much longer until parts arrive?"

"They had them in Phoenix, so they should be here tomorrow or the next day. Then we have to make the repair, something that Cory and the barge operator said they could do."

Great, Kira thought, another person involved. She didn't have any choice she supposed. It could be worse. One of them could have reached out to their government.

"We will keep testing on our end. My people and I are ever grateful for your help," Kira said and left the dream.

On their eighth morning at Sonal, Kira's meal was interrupted by arguments and a crashing sound. She had chosen to sleep the previous night at the camp. She thought some of the people were getting restless and having the gatherer among them might calm them. She realized the sound was coming from the direction of the trail to the water. She got up and went toward the sound, which seemed to be drawing the attention of everyone within hearing distance. As she reached the trail that turned down toward the water, she saw two women shouting at each other. One was being held back by a man that seemed to know her, and the other by a guard that had just arrived.

Kira, not waiting for them to quit yelling, marched right up between them. They quit yelling immediately. It was only then that she pulled up her hood against the morning sun.

"What is happening?" She demanded.

"She took my family's pot to get her water," said the woman being held back by the man.

"You told me I could use it," the other woman said.

"After I had finished with it. Today, you didn't ask, and I needed to get water for my children."

Kira saw the shattered remains of the pot between them on the ground. "It seems you no longer have anything to fight over," she said.

"Gatherer," said the woman whose pot was taken. "You must instruct her to replace my pot, or I will have nothing to carry water in."

"Were she able to provide another, she would just have used that."

"You have to do something to make this right."

Kira thought on Ariste's words a few days earlier.

"What I have to do," she said, "is open the gate so we can all go home."

No one said anything, though Kira could feel the tension rising. She was surprised no one shouted out, "Get on with it then!" But they did not. Kira looked around the group and said, "I will form a council of three teachers to hear your disputes and help you work them out." Then she just turned and walked away without looking back.

Kira walked straight to Te'Juna. Kira gave a small bow of deference to the woman, which made Te'Juna smirk.

"Gatherer," she said, also bowing, as if reminding Kira of their roles and who should be bowing to whom.

"Te'Juna, the people need your wisdom. I would ask if you would sit at council with Te'Rochrael and Te'Unoalie to decide grievances among the people until we can open the gate and get them through."

"I have not been chosen by the voice of the people," Te'Juna said.

"Nor have I," Kira said. "Their own leaders can decide disputes within their various groups as they have always done. But right now, we need someone to decide disputes among the groups."

"So you've chosen three old teachers, intolerant of errors, to fill this role."

"I'm asking three master teachers who have counseled together for years to help keep the peace at this last step of a very long journey."

"Are you certain you never completed your oration studies?" Te'Juna asked. "I am willing, but you will have to recruit the others. If we are a council of equals, I can't have them thinking I'm in charge."

"Thank you Te'Juna. I will invite the others and leave organizing and announcing to the people to you." She turned to leave and then turned back. "I will also inform Ariste, should you need his assistance."

Kira made her way through the camps to Te'Rochrael and Te'Unoalie, who both questioned her like she were taking her exams before they agreed to sit on council.

Ariste seemed to think it was a good idea and assigned a squad of guards to be on hand whenever the master teachers held council among the people.

Kira hoped this whole thing would be over soon. She debated whether to reach out to Danny or to go test the portal. She decided to test the portal first. Checking with Trassa to see if Rory was at the gate, Kira found Matusu and Te'Roan to escort her. They had both insisted she not go out of the village alone, so she made sure they got to share the drudgery of climbing up and then back down along the canyon wall.

The whole journey to the gate was again anti-climactic as a drop of water hit the floor. Rather than immediately heading back to the village, she asked Rory if he would mind her sitting in his workroom while she reached out to Danny.

Kira and Coyote arrived to find a fire blazing high in the fire ring. Danny sat on the bench, hands out to the fire.

"I'm sorry it's taking so long," he said. "I know it's been more than a week, and the guys are really trying to get the crane running. Additional parts came in this afternoon, so the barge operator says we'll have it running tomorrow."

"Are you sure the gate is still safe? With the gate room open, anyone could go in."

"Sam has been sitting guard, camped out on the barge. People in boats keep coming over to see what we're doing. No government authorities. Though they are fine since we have our paperwork."

"Is Sam a soldier like you?"

"Better. He's an archeologist. He knows all the laws about protecting ancient sites and how to put the fear of being arrested into people."

"As much as I want to keep this secret, I would very much like to meet Sam."

"If Sam knew about who you are and the things your people know, he'd go crazy. You know, in a good way. Your people know things about Earth cultures that we're just piecing together from clues."

"Because of our time skip and long life, some of my people who will come to the gate were studying your world in your eighth century."

"You have no idea how many scholars would love to talk to them."

"I can imagine. You should know that official relations with a world are very delicate matters. I am not remotely qualified to make such an introduction."

"I understand."

"I imagine when our rescue arrives, they may be in a better position to advise on such a possibility."

"Then I look forward to the possibility," Danny said and faded from the dream.

Chapter 21

The next morning when Kira tried the gate, all she got was another drop of water.

"Rory," she said. "Do you think they could be ahead of us?"

"What do you mean?"

"Danny seemed to think that they would have the gate out of the water sometime today, but what if I'm talking to him a month from now based on the link between the gates."

"Kind of mixes up a person's brain to think about, doesn't it?"

"I hope it isn't a month from now," Kira said. "People in the camp have used up most of the food they brought with them. Trassa and Orr have been distributing food from the village caches, but those are dwindling fast. I was hoping everyone would have a little to take with them."

"The connections you've made with your friends in the future are unprecedented. I believe providence has had a hand in it. If so, will providence, in the form of a coyote, let everyone starve?"

"You said Coyote was a quantum projection of my intention."

"What is providence if not a projection of intention?"

Kira shook her head. "I suppose we can send out hunters."

The following morning, Kira ate half a cake by the fire, as she had decided to ration her food.

"Ariste, have you ever dealt with a food shortage?"

Ariste nodded. "They've happened from time to time at Thresdenal."

"What did you do?"

"We went through the communities and assigned all the biggest, strongest men to hunting parties."

"Hunting in the desert doesn't require much strength."

"No. However, having them out of the city meant they were eating less rationed grain, and they weren't standing up to guards if things got disorderly."

"I don't think we have the luxury of sending groups too far from Sonal. As soon as the gate opens, we want to bring everyone through."

"One day hunting trips might produce some small game, but not what you need to feed everyone."

"That's what I was afraid of," Kira said. "At least we have plenty of water." She took a drink from her water bag, slung it on her shoulder, and started up the trail toward the village and the gate.

"Would you like me to join you?" Ariste asked.

"No. Thank you though. I'd like you here in case of trouble. Te'Roan and Matusu will be waiting at the village."

Kira's feet felt heavy this morning. She considered how much food a person needed. This desert was no place to find food in abundance. Perhaps that was another reason people chose to leave with Te'Marile.

Matusu stood by the trail into the village, determined not to let her slip by without him.

"Te'Roan," he called. "She's here."

Te'Roan came out of one of the houses and joined them.

They didn't speak much. This was their tenth trip to the gate – the tenth trip to observe yet another time-traveling drop of water.

When they were about halfway, they spotted Rory on the trail ahead of them. Even he wasn't up at sunrise anymore.

They soon caught up with him.

"Is this the day?" Rory asked cheerfully.

"Could be," Kira said. His cheerfulness made her feel that maybe it was the day. Of course, what were these few days to a man who was nearly two hundred years old. He had travelled in space, been marooned, built a gate, time skipped, built another gate, and was ready to time skip again.

As they entered the gate chamber, Rory pulled his display device from his bag and began mumbling to it. It took just a moment and he stepped away from the gate. "Whenever you're ready," he said.

Kira connected and pushed. She opened her eyes to see the now-familiar tiny bright orb floating above the gate. It held for a moment then vanished. She didn't see anything drop. No water plopped onto the gate. All four of them, Rory, Matusu, Te'Roan, and Kira, stepped forward, bending low to spot the water droplet. Nothing.

Rory tapped his display device a few times. "The energy reading and test log say you opened the test bridge. The gate is free from the water. It worked. It worked!"

"It worked!" Matusu and Te'Roan shouted in unison.

Kira just looked at the dry floor of the gate. "He did it," she said. "Danny saved us. Iactah's children have saved us." Kira dropped to her knees and felt the dry center of the gate. They all mattered, she thought to herself.

"We'll be outside when you're ready," Te'Roan said. "It's time to gather the people."

"Tomorrow," she said. "I told Danny that when we found the gate clear of the water, we would wait a full day to get it somewhere safe before we opened it."

"A full day then," Matusu said and exited the cave.

After Te'Roan and Matusu had left, Kira turned to Rory who was smiling his old gentle smile.

Kira hugged him tightly and then stepped back. "How does the gatherer go through?"

"Just step through like anybody else," he said.

"How does the gate stay open?"

"The connection is held across the gate. It doesn't matter which end the gatherer is at."

"Are you sure?" She asked.

His demeanor changed to a more thoughtful look. "You are worried about what happened to the last gatherer," he said. "Ka'Te'Rensool was my friend you know. Oh, he was older than me, and I gave him the deference his station deserved. But he often talked with me as we built the gate and prepared for the time skip."

"What happened to him?"

"I guess no one knows more than I know. He had sent the captain of the guard through first with multiple squads and the senior engineers, followed by teachers intermixed with the general population. He insisted on going through last. As a junior engineer on the gate and a bit of a gate expert, I was the second to the last to go through. You know – in case we had a problem on that end."

"You were the last one to see Ka'Te'Rensool?"

"I was. Just as I was stepping into the bridge, I heard him say, 'What's that?' I turned to look, and he was looking away from me. And then I was in the bridge."

"What was it? What did he hear or see?"

"That question was debated in council for months. The truth is that we'll never know."

"So, something distracted him from going through the gate, and he never got back to it in time?"

"It would seem so," Rory said. "And you don't have to go last Kira. I would be honored if you let me go last."

That night, Kira sat around their fire in the camp with Patala, Matusu, Te'Roan, and Ariste. Trassa joined them with the people from Sonal. Rationing had ended and turned to a feast. Teachers were sent around to ask that people reserve a couple of days food for the other side of the gate.

After eating her fill of cakes, Kira left the fire and made her rounds to all the other village and community fires. Everyone seemed glad to see her, wishing her well. Thoughts of the uncertainty of tomorrow crept into Kira's mind, but she dismissed them. Now was the time to celebrate.

She found Te'Natha among her family and their community from Thresdenal. "Te'Natha, could I ask a favor," she said. "Each of the teachers know their communities and villages. Will you please gather an accounting? I want to make sure no one is away when we go to the gate."

"It would be an honor," the teacher said.

"The trail is narrow, and it will be a long day. We must have careful coordination so everyone makes it through."

When she returned to her own fire, she found that Patala had set out another batch of cakes to cook.

"It's not venison," Patala said. "But I want you to eat your fill so you will have plenty of energy tomorrow."

"Thank you," Kira said. "I think it will be a long day."

Ariste walked up to the fire. Kira hadn't noticed he was gone.

"Is everything alright?" She asked.

"I was just checking with the guards," he said. "All are accounted for except Orr and young guard named Nolor. They went off hunting today."

"I will reach out to them tonight. Hopefully Orr goes to sleep soon," Kira said.

"Thank you," Ariste said.

Eating all the cakes Patala kept handing her eventually started to weigh on Kira. She had trouble keeping her eyes open. Not wanting to fall asleep before reaching Orr, she excused herself from the fire and moved to her blankets, where she sat and entered the dream.

The familiar village and the half-light of the dream surrounded her. Where she used to see a few openings to others' dreams, now she saw thousands. She wandered through the village focusing on Orr. She couldn't remember visiting his dream before. She found her connection to him. It just felt like Orr. She approached a glimmer on a fold in the stone wall. He wasn't asleep, so she waited.

After a while, she felt the way to his dream open. As she approached, it closed again. He was drifting in and out of sleep. Probably not on watch, but ever the watchful hunter. She waited for the opening again, then as soon as she saw it, she stepped through. Orr sat on a rock by the fire circle in Sonal.

"Kira," he said. "Nice of you to join me. I guess we're dreaming now since Nolor and I are out..."

Orr started to fade away, and Kira felt herself being pulled back to her own dream.

She grabbed ahold of his translucent form. "Orr!" She shouted and pulled him into her dream in Hochonal.

He became more solid, more alert. "What did you do?" He asked.

"I pulled you into my dream," Kira said.

"You dream-napped me? Is that allowed?"

"It's probably not ethical, and it took a bit of effort. It's important that I tell you something and that you remember it."

"What is it?"

"You and Nolor need to get back to Sonal right away. We've opened the gate."

"That's great," he said. "Nolor and I found the trail of some deer and were…"

"Hurry back," Kira said and pushed him from her dream. She hated to be so brusk but pulling him from his dream and holding him in hers took some effort. She didn't think she had much mental energy to waste right now.

She woke from the dream and walked over to Ariste, who still sat with Te'Roan by the fire.

"I found Orr, and he knows to hurry back."

"Thank you Kira," Ariste said.

Kira returned to her blankets to sleep for real.

Dawn was just a dim glow in the east when Kira woke. Patala wasn't even up yet. Kira rarely rose before her sister. She quietly got up and gathered her things. All that time in the desert had made packing in the morning second nature to her. Patala woke just as Kira finished packing her bag.

"Are you going already?" Patala asked. "You really shouldn't open it until everyone is lined up and ready to go."

"I'm just going up to the cave to prepare."

"I'll come with you."

"You rest a little longer and then help people with their children. They are bound to get restless during the waiting, and you are better with them than anyone I know."

"You know I miss the children in Iactah's village. Once they got over how different we looked, they wanted to include us in everything. Whenever I wasn't watching you dream, I played with the children."

"And made them shoes. I will take Te'Roan with me to be safe."

She looked over to see Te'Roan throw his own bag on one shoulder and drape his blanket over the other.

They walked silently up the trail. When they had entered the cave, Kira sat by the gate to meditate.

She worked on building energy, starting with the storm. She imagined the storm growing. She recalled the fear at fleeing Hochonal, the rage of being attacked by the river, the torment of being locked in darkness. Bits of lightning sparked and added to the energy she was building. Each spark was not what it had been. It just lacked power. She considered the loss of her parents, the loss of an entire line of Iactah's descendants. She thought of the fear in Thresdenal as factions fought for control of the tower. More sparks came, she felt the wind or the fury building.

Rory was the first to arrive. "People have started coming up the trail. Give me a moment to set the gate to fully open," he said.

Kira stood and watched as Rory finished releasing the test restraints. She felt the surge of energy she had built up.

"It's ready to form the bridge," he said. "I recommend we stand much farther back than we did for the test."

Rory led Kira back several paces nearly to the entrance to the gate room. Te'Roan stood next to her.

Kira turned and faced the gate. Closing her eyes, she focused on connecting with the various points of light. The spear of dots formed with all its connecting lines. Something was different this time. She could almost see the surging energy between the connections. Focusing the energy she had built inside her, she pushed. The pulsing sphere didn't even quiver. She focused on building the storm and the raging wind and lightning again and pushed. Still, nothing happened.

Again, she tried and nothing. She repeated the process over and over until she felt tears on her cheeks. *I can't fail them,* she said to herself.

She turned and looked at Rory and then Te'Roan. "Nothing is happening. I'm making the connections. It's all there, but I don't seem to have the power to open it, to push it out to the other end."

"A fully open gate is many times more powerful than a test gate. Maybe you need time to build up your strength."

"Kira," Te'Roan said. "You have more strength than any dreamer I've ever known. Maybe you just aren't fully drawing on it. Let's take a break from it and get some fresh air."

As she and Te'Roan left the cave, the first rays of the sun peeked over the horizon. Kira took another look at the land around them.

She wiped away the tears from her cheeks. "In the still of the morning without wind or heat, it really is beautiful," Kira said. She turned so her hood blocked her face from direct sunlight and sat down on a stone ledge.

"Why can't I do it?"

"Think about all you have learned," Te'Roan said. "Apparently, there is more to opening the gate than just making a lot of connections, just like there is more to being the gatherer than reaching a lot of people."

"Every time I've opened it before, I focused on my fear and pain – what my father called the storm and let it push the connections out into infinity. I would let it rage and build inside me until it nearly burst forth."

"You have had a lot of that type of emotion to draw on. I don't think gatherers are meant to work by fear. What else do you feel?"

"I feel gratitude over what we've overcome – how close we are despite all we've been through."

Kira stood and walked up the trail to the rim of the canyon. She could see people coming up the trail. She focused on the warm rays of the sun touching her clothing. She focused on pulling that energy into her. She could hear the river flowing far below and pulled on the energy of the falling water – life of the desert. She moved her thoughts to the people on the trail below, all their hope, and pulled energy from that thought. She recalled the joy she felt in camp the night before. She captured the surges of gratitude she felt at every laugh and hug she had seen the night before.

Kira felt the energy building inside her. She held onto it.

She thought about her lessons with Te'Juna to dismiss her fear. She let go of the fear and the fury. A river of emotion flowed through.

She thought on the thousands of shimmers in her dream, each a connection to her people. The gatherer was more than the connections. She felt their hope and their unity.

It was more than the storm and more than her fear. She wanted to see it, visualize it, but avoided slipping into the dream, she didn't want to waste any of what she was building. She felt it like a glowing orb of warm light, like the sun.

Kira opened her eyes again. She felt a smile crease her face as she looked at Te'Roan.

"Well?" He asked.

"It's…it's beyond words. I've been doing it wrong this whole time."

"You've been working with what you had. Are you ready?" Te'Roan glanced down the trail.

Kira saw the long line of people coming up toward the gate. She nodded and started back down to the cave.

Rory waited in the gate room.

Kira smiled at him and closed her eyes. The tiny orbs of light appeared, connections flying between them faster than ever. The pulse of energy reverberated through her. It was her energy, the energy flowing to her and through her. She let it go, and on its own it burst out pushing the orb out into infinity.

She fell backward as if every bit of energy had flowed out of her body. Rory and Te'Roan caught her and held her up. When she opened her eyes, a brilliant ball of light filled the room. The shimmering orb was like an extension of the gate. Like Rory had said, the gate was a small slice of the base of the sphere. Colors shifted and moved. Kira could sense the energy of the bridge and her connection to it. Her own energy now felt like a spark compared to the roaring fire it had become.

Kira turned and looked at Rory, who was smiling, "Is that it? Is it ready?"

"It's ready," he said and gave a little laugh. He reminded her of a boy who got his new top to spin for the first time.

Kira turned to Te'Roan. "First you and Ariste and his chosen guards like we agreed. Danny should be waiting. Let him know I'll be along near the end."

Te'Roan left for a moment and returned with Ariste and his group of guards. He hugged Kira. "See you in the future," he said and walked through the gate. Ariste and three groups of guards followed.

Kira felt a connection with each one of them as they entered. She felt their presence as they traversed the bridge and sensed when they reached the other side.

Kira motioned for more to come through. Kira was surprised at how many faces she knew. People hugged her or put a hand on her shoulder in thanks. Two guards came through with the regenerator fastened on a palanquin suspended between them. She hoped they wouldn't be there long enough to need it. Even so, they couldn't leave it behind. She had a fleeting thought of the technology Te'Marile had been able to get away with. No, she thought, that woman gets none of my attention today.

When Rory's family came through, his children and grandchildren all gave him hugs. They each carried an oddly shaped bundle, which Kira gathered were filled with Rory's gadgets.

"Is all your technology packed up and going through?" Kira asked.

"Every last one, except, of course, the gate."

Patala and Matusu arrived together. Patala gave Kira a hug and said, "We've decided to wait here with you.

"How many more?" Kira asked.

"I'd say we're about half-way through," Matusu said.

"Most of the families with children have gone through," Patala said. "Everyone seemed to agree that they were a priority. And some of the mothers worried the gate might close before they got through."

"Patala made sure to hug every child and tell them the gatherer wouldn't let that happen," Matusu said.

"Every child?" Kira glanced at Patala and smiled.

Matusu nodded, also smiling.

The three of them stood together as the people continued to make their way through the gate. Kira noticed that many older people were now arriving. Many of the oldest, the ones who had done this before stopped in front of the bridge and just breathed in and out for a moment, as if reconsidering, then stepped in. That did not help comfort Kira about making the trip herself.

Te'Juna, being escorted by Te'Natha, stepped up to Kira and hugged her, "You did well child," she whispered. Te'Natha squeezed Kira's arm affectionately, and they both proceeded to the gate.

Finally, a group of guards arrived and lastly Orr.

"That's it," he said. "We swept the area and the village. Every leader said they had a full count."

"Well, all that's left is to close the door and leave," Kira said.

Rory led Orr and Matusu and the three remaining guards to the door.

Patala turned to Kira. "You aren't going last are you?"

"Someone told you about the last gatherer didn't they?"

"I just worry."

"Rory asked if he could go last. So watch for me right behind Orr."

When the others had returned from closing the door, Orr sent his three guards into the bridge.

Patala hugged her sister and stepped into the bridge.

"Matusu," Kira said, "I believe you're next."

"Orr and I talked about it and..."

"Since when are you and Orr in charge? I won't be the last one through anyway. That honor goes to the gate's builder, Rory."

Orr took Matusu by the arm. "Come on," he said as he led the younger man into the bridge.

Kira turned back and looked at Rory. "Well, I guess I'll see you on the other side." She hugged him, turned, and walked through.

As she stepped in, she first felt like she was falling, then like she seemed to stop accelerating and just floated with colors shifting all around her. She could sense all the connections. She tried to move, but realized her body didn't move. It was still poised to take another step. She felt like she was nowhere, yet because she could feel all the connections with both ends of the gate and with everyone who had gone through, she also felt like she was everywhere.

Then suddenly she could move and was stepping through light into a shadowy room. Te'Roan caught her and handed her off to Ariste. He led her down a wooden ramp and onto a flat dirt floor. Looking around, she saw Patala who immediately stepped up and hugged her. Matusu also stepped up and hugged them both.

"Welcome to the future," Matusu said.

Chapter 22

Kira looked around. The large building they were in was rectangular with high ceilings. It seemed to be made of all metal with a dirt floor. Light came from artificial light sources attached to the ceiling and of course, the glowing orb that was the bridge. The people were spread out through the building sitting on their blankets in groups of families and friends.

Kira sensed Rory entering the bridge and looked back to see him emerge. As Ariste helped him down the ramp, Kira took him by the hand and smiled, "You did it Rory. Your bridge brought us safely to the future."

"I guess it did," he said looking around.

"Where are we?" Kira asked Te'Roan.

"It's some kind of farm facility," Te'Roan said. "Judging from the adjacent corals and prints going in and out of the large doors, this building seems to be used for working with animals."

"That must be what I smell," Kira said.

"My guards and I checked the area on first arrival," Ariste said. "Though we were unseen, we did note that people passed by in vehicles on a road not far from here. Humans are dwelling in nearby buildings, but there are only a couple in the immediate area, who I believe assisted in bringing the gate here," Ariste said.

Kira thought one of those must be Danny, who she very much wished to see. At the moment, though, the large glowing sphere was her immediate concern.

"What now?" Kira asked Rory. "Do we turn it off or does it go off by itself?"

"Either way," he said. "If we're done, you can close it. Or if you like the look of it, it will go off by itself sometime in the morning – morning in the time we came from."

"I can still control it?" Kira asked.

"You have been controlling it this whole time," Rory said.

Kira closed her eyes and the sphere of lights appeared before her. Where she had focused before on pushing energy into the sphere, she focused on pulling it back. Kira felt a jolt of energy surge through her as the distant sphere hurtled into its twin. Kira opened her eyes, and the bridge was gone. Just the circle of the gate remained.

"Maybe we should have practiced that during our tests," she said to Rory. She breathed in heavily trying to calm herself.

Te'Roan approached Kira. "You need to meet someone," he said. "Follow me."

He led her across the building to a small door. He opened it, allowing Kira to see that it was nighttime where they had arrived. Te'Roan motioned to someone outside to come in.

It was Danny. Though Kira wanted to hug him, she instead bowed to honor him. He was shorter than her, but taller than the humans she knew in Iactah's village. "Thank you," she said.

He obviously didn't understand her language. She tried a few of the words she knew in Iactah's language. He didn't seem to recognize those either. He said something she didn't understand, but as they stood there looking at each other, the sentiment was clear.

Kira gestured for him to come with her to the middle of the room.

"Everyone," she said and waited until she had everyone's attention. "This is Danny. He is a descendent of my friend Iactah. He lifted the gate from the water and brought it here to allow us to arrive safely."

Around the room, people stood and bowed to him, expressing sentiments of gratitude.

Danny nodded graciously.

The way Kira saw it, they now had a few new problems to deal with — namely, communications with Danny, a way to contact the rescue ship, and how to feed people. She couldn't believe she hadn't worked out the plan better than this. Everything had been focused on getting here, like some ship would be waiting for them.

Kira asked Te'Roan, Te'Juna, Ariste, and Rory to join her for a moment and led them and Danny to the corner of the room by the door. Even though she knew Danny wouldn't understand their conversation, Kira didn't want to leave him standing awkwardly alone in the middle of the room.

"The way I see it," Kira said, "until one of us learns his language, we can't talk to Danny outside the dream. And we have no way to navigate this world beyond where he has brought us. First things first, how do we contact the ship?"

Rory spoke up. "We contacted the ship when we fully opened the gate. The ship would have detected the energy like a beacon. If they followed rescue protocol, they are on their way here — assuming they are listening somewhere in this star system."

"That's a big assumption," Te'Roan said.

"It's protocol," Te'Juna said. "If we are in the time window, they are listening."

"And how long until they respond or reach out to us?" Kira asked.

"They should be close enough that they could arrive anytime, two days at most," Rory said. "Starships are fast. Though given that the civilization now has space flight and, as you said, an orbiting telescope, they will approach with caution."

"I have noticed that most people brought a few cakes with them, but if we are here more than two days we will need food," Kira said. She turned to Danny and considered asking how they might obtain food. Even the entire village of Sonal did not have enough food for this many people. How would one person have that much food? No. They would ration and prioritize feeding the children until rescuers arrived.

She thought she could at least ask Danny for water. She grabbed the water bag that still hung by her side and held it up to him. She opened it and poured a little water into her hand.

Danny nodded and gestured for her to follow. He led her through the door. Te'Roan and Ariste followed close behind. He walked to a smaller building. Danny turned a nob that protruded from the wall building and water came out. He shut it off and stepped back.

"I will assign guards to fill water for people," Ariste said, "so that we don't risk too much exposure to other humans that might be around."

Kira looked around this place they had arrived at. Off in the distance, she could see the glow of lights from what she assumed was a city. She also saw lights moving along what must be a roadway. Looking up, she looked at the stars. This may be her last night observing the stars from this world. For a moment she wondered if she might see a starship coming. On returning to the stars, she would leave behind Danny, never to see him again. Even if she returned after only a few months on a starship, centuries could have passed on Earth.

"We should return," Te'Roan said, "and leave the water collection to guards."

Kira knew they were in no danger, for though she couldn't see them, guards watched from hidden spots all around them.

Back in the building, Danny sat on a bench near the door, while Kira and the other teachers walked among the people assessing how much food they had and explaining that the guards would be filling their water bags and pots as needed. Since the building had no openings in the roof, they would not have fires inside.

When Kira returned to where Danny sat, he stood and walked to the door. He opened it and pointed outside. A fog had set in that dimmed the light from the city and even the nearby road. Kira had seen that in the desert before, but it was unusual. She stepped outside and moved to the side of the door. Danny followed her. The fog continued to thicken, completely blocking out the stars and the moon.

The fog moved past her and swirled beneath a dim lamp on the building with the water. Kira closed her eyes and reached out like she did with the gate and the map device. She sensed the gate and several map devices in the building. She sensed possible connections to something else. Some device was nearby, off to her left. Something she wasn't quite able to connect with. It was getting stronger, perhaps closer. Pulling up her hood and face guard, she walked to the corner of the building and looked into the fog hoping to see through it to whatever was there.

A woman's voice from around the corner startled her, "Is there something I can help you with Teacher?" A guard squatted by the wall keeping watch in the darkness.

"I just sensed something in this direction," Kira said pointing off toward what looked to be an open field – at least the part she could see.

"That's just a large field, already harvested and lain fallow."

"You sound as though you are more than a guard."

"I spend my childhood on a farm," she said.

"What is your name?" Kira asked.

"Lorisel," she said.

"I am Kira."

"Gatherer, it is an honor. I did not realize it was you."

Just then a white glow appeared through the fog. Kira's heart leapt. She tried to stay calm. "I would say the field is no longer empty," she said.

"I will go and see what it is." The guard stood.

Kira put out a hand and held her back. "I already know what it is," Kira said. "Please go and inform Ariste that our rescuers have arrived."

Soon, people poured from the building. Te'Roan and Ariste stepped up next to Kira.

Kira began to walk forward toward the light. She looked back to see that Danny had taken a few steps back. He didn't appear to be afraid. He just seemed to be withdrawing. After all, he was not the one in need of rescue. As Kira walked into the field, she could see not just one dim light, but dozens of them.

The low light she had first seen became a beam of light that shone on her and those closest around her. A silhouette of a person walked toward her. As the person got closer, holding up a smaller light, Kira saw it was a young Threden woman, maybe a bit older than Patala.

"Greetings, Teacher," the woman said.

Kira lowered her face guard and hood. "Greetings," Kira said. "Welcome to Earth."

"Thank you. Do you know a woman named Juna Stormwatcher? Is she with you?"

Kira turned back to those behind her. "Where is Te'Juna," she asked. She heard the question quietly echo through the crowd.

"Here I am," said Te'Juna, making her way up next to Kira. The master teacher stood looking at the woman before them. "Jantere?" She asked.

"Yes," the woman said. "It's me."

Te'Juna stepped forward and embraced the woman. They held the embrace as two who had not seen each other in a long time. "I know it's only been a few months for you," Te'Juna said. "For me it has been a lifetime."

Te'Juna turned to face Kira. "May I introduce my older sister, Jantere Stormwatcher. Jantere, this is our gatherer, Ka'Te'Kira Waterborn."

Jantere bowed. "It is an honor."

"The honor is mine," Kira said, bowing in return.

"I apologize for the fog and the darkness. We saw that there are many indigenous people about. Their satellites indicate they aren't yet star travelers, so we wanted to be cautious."

"Most do not know we are here," Kira said, "though a few have helped us."

"We have lights we can set as a path from the building where your gate is to our landers," Jantere said.

"We appreciate that. And we would like to keep people in family groups as much as possible."

"Of course."

"Our guards can help set the lights and direct people," Ariste said.

"I would appreciate that. Are you the guard captain?"

"This is Ariste," Te'Juna said. "He has kept us safe and together on this journey."

Other people now emerged from the landers, as Jantere had called them. They carried small lights that they set on the ground along their path.

"I will go back to the building to help bring everyone out," Kira said.

"I will also send some people to help retrieve the gate," Jantere said.

On her way back to the building, Kira met up with Patala. She took her older sister by the hand and said, "Come with me. You and I need to stay together so we are on the same lander."

They went into the building which was almost empty at this point. Guards were picking up what few items had been left behind. The only sizable thing left was the gate. Rory stood next to it, still smiling.

"Are you ready to go back to the stars?" Kira asked. "We were greeted by Te'Juna's older sister."

Rory laughed. "I don't remember her name, but I remember she was pretty. By the stars, she probably looks like Te'Juna's granddaughter." He laughed again.

A large door slid open near the small door they had used. Two men entered, each carrying a small block with a handle. In the light of the building, Kira now saw the clean gray uniforms they wore. They had no hoods or face guards. They weren't dressed to fend off the sun or hide among the rocks. They walked up to opposite sides of the gate, lowered their blocks, and seemed to stick them to the gate.

Kira had always wanted to play with magnets, though she got the sense these were much more. They lifted the gate like they were lifting an empty basket between them. Then proceeded to guide it back toward the large door.

"It looks as though my contribution to this exodus has ended," Rory said. He squeezed Kira's shoulder, turned, and followed the men with the gate. Looking around, Kira saw that she and Patala were the last ones in the building.

As they approached the door to leave, Danny walked in.

Kira went up to him and embraced him. Then she stepped back and bowed. She hoped he understood the honor. Patala also bowed. Kira wished they had a common language, but maybe this was enough.

She and Patala turned and left. Behind her, she heard the large door slide shut and looking back saw the lights turn off. She stopped there and watched Danny walk from the building to a vehicle. White and red lights appeared, and he rolled away into the night.

Kira wondered if he worried they might take him with them or if he had hoped they would take him with them. She took Patala's hand, and they boarded the first lander together. Matusu and Te'Roan were there. Orr and Ariste were the last ones to join them.

"All counted?" Kira asked Ariste.

"All counted Gatherer."

Epilogue

Danny seemed to wake in the middle of an ancient village in the desert. He quickly realized he hadn't woken up, but had entered the dream, like when Kira used to visit him.

"Hello, Danny," Kira said. He turned to see her standing next to an ancient fire ring. She glanced at it, and a campfire rose from it.

"I didn't think I'd see you again."

"I thought I should at least visit you in the dream, where I can thank you properly."

"That was months ago. I thought you would be far away by now."

"I thought so too. But the Thresden leaders had a different plan, so I'm not that far away after all."

"Meaning you can come visit."

"Perhaps. For now, we've set up a base in your star system to watch how things develop."

"Where?"

"That's not important. I don't need you pointing your space telescopes at us."

"So this watching thing only goes one way?" Danny asked.

"I can visit in the dream."

"I can see that. Where are we?"

"This is my village – where I grew up."

"I know this place," he said. "Over here is the kiva." He walked over to the regeneration circle.

"You call that a kiva?"

"My people used them for various gatherings and ceremonies."

"We used it for something different. A regenerator would be set on the center pillar, and we would sit in the circle to be healed from radiation damage from the sun."

"That's what first gave you away to Sam. He said that low pillar in the kiva was too perfectly level and circular. No civilization around here had built anything that perfect. He started searching the area for more villages and found them."

"He's been uncovering our villages?"

"Not just your villages. He saw that they kind of formed a circle and at the center of that circle was a mesa that had been hollowed out. The desert had filled it in, but his students and other archeologists have been clearing out the sand."

"Any civilization of that time could have dug that out," Kira said.

"But none ever did – not on this continent and not to that extent."

"Nothing can be done about that now. The Thresden are not worried about what we left behind at Thresdenal, that's the name of the city. They are worried about what your people have been up to."

"Native Americans?"

"No. All humans. You are ahead of your expected development. The Thresden leaders suspect interference."

"Sounds like a conspiracy theory."

"I want to show you something," Kira said walking down the path toward the creek below Hochonal. She stood next to the reeds that grew at the bank. "This was one of my favorite places. I would stand here and wait for my father to come in from the fields."

"Is this where you mostly visit in your dreams?"

"This is where I always visit. I know my people are from the stars, but this is home."

"So, you get to stay close by."

"Yes. I get to stay close by and help protect it. And I want to know if you will help me should I need you."

"Of course, just ask."

"Oh, there's something else. Something about your planet and especially your family that I'm told we have never experienced on thousands of worlds."

"Our charm?"

Kira smiled. "Dreaming across time. It's a new mystery they want to figure out."

"I'm as bewildered by it as anybody. My ancestors may have taken any answers about that with them when they crossed to the next world."

"That's what I suspect as well. We'll see." Kira took another long look around Hochonal. "Good night Danny."

About the Author

Robert Shawgo Jr., born in Washington state, spent many of his formative years wandering the deserts of Southern California. Attending Brigham Young University and traversing the diverse wilderness of Utah, he not only learned to love writing, but to imagine all the stories yet to be told.

Made in the USA
Middletown, DE
25 May 2024